I0590407

Escala's Wish

A novel by

David James

Tales of Valla ™

Trash Panda Publishing
www.trashpandapublishing.com
We publish novels written by raccoons

First Edition - Published December 2025

ISBN Hardcover (case laminate):	979-8-9999799-0-2
ISBN Hardcover (with Dustjacket):	979-8-9999799-5-7
ISBN Paperback (6x9):	979-8-9999799-6-4
ISBN Paperback (4.5x7.5):	979-8-9999799-4-0
ISBN eBook:	979-8-9999799-2-6
ISBN Audiobook:	979-8-9999799-3-3
Library of Congress Control Number:	2025923019

Cover art, design, and custom sprayed-on edge design
by Mersades Bergmann
Original human-created artwork. No generative AI was used.
For more information, visit
www.thescriptoriumpublishing.com

The raccoon logo for Trash Panda Publishing is a registered trademark of David James.
www.trashpandapublishing.com

"Valla" is a registered trademark of David James. www.Vallaworld.com

Dedication

To my wife, Tonya—
Thank you for being the best thing
that ever happened to me

Valla Maps

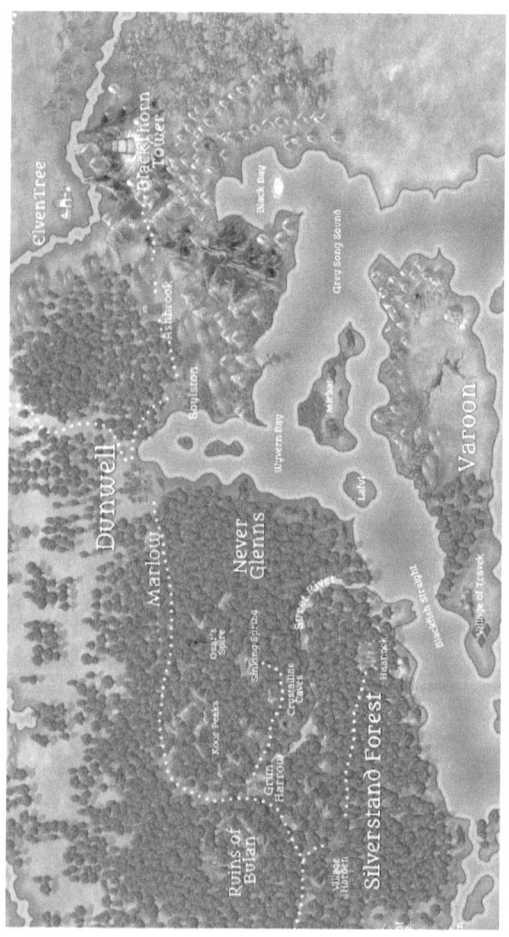

Please visit www.vallaworld.com **for more maps.**

took. Teryn's soft heart would never let him ignore a child in trouble.

The court believed they were upholding the sanctity of the True Cycle; a law forged almost twenty years ago when Lord Rowan Winter foolishly brought a human woman into their realm, into the court itself, the audacity of that! And today, they judged a fey who had broken that law.

But the court had been mere pawns in Morvena Winter's game. And now, with the court's guilty ruling, the Wane had come for him, a slow, sorrowful unraveling. His magic, once woven into the life of the fey realm, slipped away thread by thread.

Teryn's vision blurred, and his wings crumbled.

The gathered fey watched in silence. This wasn't exile or imprisonment. This was erasure, and soon, not even memory would hold him.

"A lesson," she whispered, studying his half-faded form, "for anyone else who might think to mock me."

Teryn's lips parted, but the words dissolved before they formed. His fingers vanished, his skin flickered, light breaking through places where nothing remained.

"I was here," he wanted to say. "I mattered."

But no one heard him, not even himself. And then, only silence because he was gone.

Morvena turned from the vacant air where the pixie had hovered only moments before. His name, what was it? Already it slipped through her mind like mist, impossible to grasp. She steadied herself and fixed her gaze on Lord Rowan Winter, the unyielding ruler of the Court of Dreams. The silver streaks in his wings caught the light, but not a flicker touched his face. He was motionless, stoic; as impassive as a mountain boulder. He stared straight ahead, unreadable.

She savored the moment, then turned and flew toward the palace, leaving the Court of Dreams to mourn what they could no longer remember, nor could she.

Chapter 1

4853 After Purge, Present Day
Material Plane, World of Valla, the City of Dunwell

It's five bells after the noon meal, and I'm outside The Stag and Hound on Tavern Lane in Dunwell's Alehouse Quarter.

I'm three feet tall and weigh 35 pounds, but I carry myself with confidence. My reddish-brown skin resembles polished cherry wood, and my vibrant green hair sticks up in wild directions, like I touched a lightning bug while standing in a bucket of water. My eyes are a striking amethyst, and like all gnomes, I have pointed ears. I also sport a rather large nose, and people will tell you I'm generally happy, so there's often a smile on my face.

As late afternoon settles over Dunwell, a modest city of 50,000 souls west of the capital in Eronvale, on the continent of Tor'vaen, townsfolk begin their daily promenade down Tavern Lane. Folks are already weighing their evening options, scouting which tavern has the best roast, strongest ale, or most interesting bards.

The street hums with chatter, laughter, and gossip. Nestled in the cobbled bustle is The Stag, one of Dunwell's finest taverns. Larger than most, it boasts a timber-framed facade lit by wrought-iron lanterns that flicker to life after dusk.

The Stag's common room is where I earn my keep; it's a space both grand and worn, with a massive hearth at one end and a small wooden stage at the other.

Presiding over this establishment is Robbie Pints, the tavern's esteemed owner, known to regulars simply as Pints. No one knows his age, but judging by his wrinkles and graying hair, I'd wager he's seen at least sixty winters. Stout and broad-shouldered from years behind the bar, he carries the solid strength of a man shaped by hard work and hearty meals, with a slight paunch betraying his fondness for his own fare. Thick gray hair frames his face, and his beard is full and neatly trimmed.

And I'll add Pints is smart. How do I know? Well, he hired me. I'm a bard extraordinaire, and my job is to fill the drinking room of The Stag, as most folks call the place.

To do this, I plant myself outside The Stag, pitching the unforgettable night waiting just beyond its doors. Along Tavern Lane, every bard and entertainer does the same, each hired by a rival tavern, each trying to outcharm the rest.

Our job is to draw them in, make them laugh, cry, and most importantly, loosen their purse strings. It's all flash and charm, a contest of charisma. But truth be told, I'm only competing with myself. Everyone else is just fighting for second place.

I am Wigfrith Foreverbloom, Bard Medic of Misty Springs, and I was born for this.

As evening shadows form in the cobblestone street, soot-stained laborers who finished their shifts at five bells head up the Tavern Lane.

Across the way, two female bards in laced bodices flaunt legs and cleavage outside the Golden Goose Tavern, their flirtatious smiles offering little more than trouble.

Their songs have slurred refrains, more chant than melody, and their voices sound like alley cats drowning in sour wine. Stories? None to tell. They offer only bawdy ballads and crude jests, enough to fill their tavern with laughter, shouting, and drunken buffoonery.

That's fine by me, that's not the crowd I'm after.

Their kind will drink the cheapest ale, fall into a stupor, and likely end the night breaking a chair over someone's head.

No, I seek a different kind of guest, those who settle in for the long tale. The ones who leave with their hearts a little fuller… and their purses a little lighter, too.

Around six bells, the merchants begin to drift down Tavern Lane, their shops shuttered and their coin purses jingling with the weight of a day's earnings. They come seeking food, drink, and a bit of amusement. Many are easily swayed by revealing outfits and the batting of eyes offered by the bards at the Golden Goose, but a few, the more discerning ones, are drawn to something else. Something with flair, with finesse…something with me.

Then, at seven bells sharp, the real opportunity arrives: the pickier patrons, the nobler class. Notice: I didn't say *noble* class. These are the ones who think themselves above the common rabble, flush with coin and ambition, those who already control parts of this city or desperately want to.

They aren't here for slurred limericks or lewd jests. No, they crave wit and wisdom, sharp intrigue and intelligence, the kind of performance that flatters their own cleverness.

7

And that's precisely why Pints hired me, to bring them into The Stag. For they order the finest wines, oldest whiskeys, and choicest meats and cheeses, served on polished boards, not slopped in bowls.

This is my audience.

Ah, and here they are now, just as I foretold, a small cluster of elegantly dressed noblers making their way toward The Stag.

With a practiced flick, I adjust my forest-green cape, so it drapes neatly over my gray-green leather tunic, the one with the sunflower embroidered proudly over the left breast, laced up with rawhide and flair. My fingers brush the silver rose at my throat, fixed to a black leather choker, a mark of subtle elegance, naturally. I clear my throat. Then, with all the power and presence a gnome bard can muster, I raise my voice to meet the moment.

"Friends and folks! You've heard bards spin tales of dungeons and dragons, devils and demons, knights and maidens, vampires and wizards! Tavern tales meant to amuse the common folk, desperate to escape their dreary lives for an evening!"

I gesture up Tavern Lane with theatrical disdain, singling out a portly dwarf hawking stories outside the Lion's Mane Inn, his chainmail clinking and a gravy stain glistening in the setting sun.

"Take, for instance, that windbag." I lower my voice just enough to be scandalous but loud enough to be heard.

"He once told me he wears that chainmail to convince passersby that he's an adventurer. His act? Bravado and borrowed glory. He'll sing in the first person, weaving

8

exploits so daring you'll swear he faced them himself. But I happen to know he hasn't left Dunwell in twelve years."

I half whisper, as though letting them in on a great secret: "And should any of you own a certain volume entitled *The Chronicles of Sir Roderick Bellamy the Explorer*, you'll find his 'original' tales suspiciously familiar. Just saying."

A few passersby chuckle, clearly appreciating my wit.

The dwarf bard scowls at me. He's annoyed, of course, but let's be fair, most of us bards have been trading barbs as long as we've been trading ballads. The streets of Tavern Lane are thick with bards who've long since grown accustomed to a little public mockery.

"Most bards in the city tonight will fill your ears with secondhand tales," I proclaim. "They'll sing of someone else's adventures or worse, spin yarns passed off as truth."

I place a hand on my chest and offer a mock-noble bow. "But I am not most bards and tonight, at The Stag, you won't find a tune to sing along to between mugs of ale. If that's what you seek, you're in the wrong place. What I offer is something rarer. A true story, a tale filled with love, betrayal, revenge, and redemption.

"It's called 'Escala's Wish,' and it's a tale of twists and intrigue for those clever enough to keep up. This isn't a straight path, mind you; it winds and doubles back, layer upon layer. And if you took one too many knocks to the head in your youth, best move along—you'll lose the thread before the first verse is through."

There's a ripple of laughter from the crowd outside The Stag, and I catch a man in his twenties elbowing his rotund friend.

"Tonight, dear friends, you'll hear a tale I have never told before. This is the story of Escala Winter, a mischievous pixie from the Court of Dreams, whose single kiss nearly unmade the fey realm and set our world teetering on the edge of total destruction.

"For those who ask, 'Who is Escala Winter? What is the Court of Dreams? And how could a single kiss doom us all?' I say step inside. Hear it with your own ears."

I gesture to the open doors of The Stag.

"I offer more than a tale for those willing to part with a few coins. I offer secrets—secrets that nearly shattered the True Cycle and all of Valla along with it."

A skeptical voice cuts through the hush. "And what makes your tale any different from his?" The speaker points toward a dwarf bard tuning a battered lute down the lane.

"I tell many kinds of tales, ancient lore, old fables, stories of wars, and travelers' rumors. I've spun them all. And when I do, I tell you what they are. I never stitch a lie to my own name," I said.

"But when I say a story is true, when I place my reputation upon it, you may be sure it is truth as surely as the breath in my chest. I knew Escala Winter. I met her after she was cast out of the fey realm—yes, I said the fey realm. She was banished from the Court of Dreams for violating fey law. I stood with her and a band of brave adventurers as we tried to help her.

"She was told to remove boulders from the True Cycle." I grinned. "A fool's errand, perhaps, but I'll let you decide that for yourself. I saw what she did. And I walked beside her when our dear world of Valla nearly ended. I was there when Blackthorn Tower fell," I said. "You remember that night, just a year ago, when it was destroyed?"

A few heads nod.

"I saw the sky burn green." I say.

A ripple of chatter moves through the crowd—they remember. Just over a year ago, Blackthorn Tower, high in the Shadowspire Mountains, erupted in green flame visible even from Dunwell.

"But I won't give the story away for free, so step into The Stag and be the first in Dunwell to hear what truly happened."

More enter the Stag.

"If you're after the same old crude songs and tired tales about greedy mayors or kissing mermaids, keep walking— plenty of that down the lane. But if you crave something different, something original, something magical… step inside before the room is full."

More noblers enter The Stag, intrigued by my promise of a story unlike any they've heard. And why shouldn't they be? In all my years of barding, I've learned most performers carry a repertoire; a safe stable of songs and tales trotted out night after night until even the drunks can recite them. Familiarity might fill a few seats, but it eventually breeds boredom. Crowds crave something new, something fresh, something they haven't heard before.

And a tavern fills quickly when word spreads that tonight's story is being told for the first time—original, unborrowed, and unrehearsed. Of course, that comes with pressure. If you promise something new, it had better be good.

And mine is.

I'm a bard extraordinaire and I know a good story when I see one. And the moment I met Escala and heard her plight, I knew I had to help her, if only to share her tale with all of Valla, starting with the crowd at The Stag tonight. Sure, folks know faerie tales: lullabies, tavern songs, half-mocking ballads. But few believe faeries are real, and fewer still dare claim they've seen one.

So, when I step into the street and promise not merely a tale, but a true story—about a faerie I knew, and secrets of the fey realm—that's not just another evening's diversion.

That's uncommon and irresistible. And trust me, people will pay dearly for something that rare.

The Stag's common room is filling fast, and Pints collects coins, ushering all the guests inside. With my work outside done, I push through the packed common room toward the stage. The room hums with chatter and anticipation.

I pass Pints, who gives me a playful punch on the arm. "You drew a huge crowd," he says. "Make it a long story— I've got a lot of wine to sell!"

I flash him a grin. "Oh, it'll be long," I promise. "And unforgettable."

I look at the huge crowd in The Stag and whisper to myself, "By the gods, you crazy little pixie... even gone, you still know how to draw attention to yourself."

Chapter 2

On stage, a small table holds a mug of ale to wet my whistle, and a stool rests nearby for when my legs grow tired.

The place is full tonight, and I scan the room, quietly taking stock. It takes a moment for the crowd to notice—the din softens—but the hush always comes, and then all eyes turn to me.

"Good evening, friends, I am Wigfrith Foreverbloom, bard of Misty Springs, and welcome to The Stag and Hound," I declare, voice lifting just enough to ripple through the clatter of mugs and laughter. "This fine establishment is owned by none other than Mr. Robbie Pints. The fare Mr. Pints has prepared tonight is as fine as any I've seen, warm bread fresh from the oven, hearty stews full of flavor, and platters of meat and cheese that'd make a noble jealous. Need a drink? Lift a hand, and one of Pints' sharp-eyed serving girls will be there before your thirst settles.

"Now, I could stand here all night talking about refreshments, or, if you'll indulge me, my own dashing good looks." That gets a proper laugh. "But you came here for the story I promised. 'Escala's Wish' is the tale of a curious pixie from the Court of Dreams who, with a single kiss, nearly destroyed the fey realm, and the material plane as well."

I rub my hands together. "Let's begin."

Chapter 3

My tale begins just over a year ago, in the forests outside Dunwell, where a young man of about twenty dozed beneath a broad oak after a morning spent gathering herbs. His eyes were closed, head bowed, chestnut hair tumbling in soft, careless waves across his brow. He wore a loose green tunic with rolled sleeves and an open leather vest. His sturdy trousers were tucked into worn boots, and a short sword hung at his hip.

Beside him, a satchel lay open, revealing the morning's harvest: moonshade petals, ember-edged firebloom leaves, silverthorn sprigs, bundled whisperwind grass, and sealed buds of dragon's breath.

A dainty pixie emerged quietly from a nearby bush, her nearly transparent wings fluttering as she hovered above the moss. Barely a foot tall, she had long golden hair and wore a fitted royal-blue gown adorned with crystals. Her skin was a light copper hue, and her youthful, heart-shaped face lifted in a bright, playful smile that hinted at mischief. She moved with graceful ease, slender, strong, and poised like a miniature ballerina.

Then there were her eyes, brilliant blue, and impossible to ignore. They held you fast, demanding a second glance, then a third, until you no longer knew if you even wanted to look away. And even when you managed to break free from her gaze, the memory of it lingered, like a dream you never wished to end.

This was Escala Winter.

Escala hovered over the sleeping man, her head tilted in curiosity. Behind her, perhaps twenty yards away, was a door-sized portal of swirling light; floating two feet above the ground was a hidden crossing between the fey realm and the mortal world.

A second female pixie peeked through the foliage of the same bush, her translucent wings barely fluttering. Her jet-black hair was tied back in a simple ponytail, and she wore a gown of deep emerald silk threaded with silver. Her skin gave off a gentle, pale glow, and her dark eyes were wide and alert.

"Escala, stop!" the second pixie whispered, concern evident in her voice. "You'll break the Oath!"

Escala rolled her eyes, a playful smirk tugging at her lips. "He's adorable, Rihanna!"

Rihanna, hands knotted at her chest, whispered, "But the Oath!"

Escala flipped her golden hair over her shoulder. "It's just a kiss, and no one has to know."

She turned her gaze back to the young man, mischief dancing in her eyes. Her delicate wings lifted her gently into the air as she floated toward him, drawn by irresistible curiosity.

Escala heard a faint sound near the crossing as she flew closer. She glanced back, a slight frown creasing her brow, but saw only Rihanna peeking from behind the ferns, her eyes wide with apprehension.

"Escala, please," Rihanna whispered. "We should go back; the crossing is closing soon."

Escala flicked her hand dismissively. "You worry too much." Then, looking down at herself, she sighed, this small size wouldn't work for what she had in mind.

She muttered an incantation, raised her arms, and scattered a cloud of glowing faerie dust. In a flash, she was a beautiful elf. She turned once, inspecting her new form. "I look fabulous," she said, preening.

Suddenly, there was a sharp crack from the dense brush. Rihanna flinched, her eyes darting to the edge of the crossing.

"Did you hear that?"

"It's just the crossing," Escala whispered. "I've got time for one kiss."

She bent down and kissed the sleeping man with surprising finesse. Magic flared as their lips met, and the young man's eyes flew open.

"Who... who are you?" he stammered, voice thick with confusion.

Escala cupped one of his cheeks and stood over him, dreamy-eyed. Then she gently stroked his face, speaking words laced with subtle magic, and he suddenly calmed.

"I am Escala Winter from the Court of Dreams." Her voice was silky. "I've just changed your life forever," she whispered. "You'll never know a kiss as good as a faerie's."

She batted her eyes, scattering faerie dust across his face as her voice dripped with magic.

"You'll search all of Valla, but no woman's kiss will ever satisfy you again. You'll always think of me and want to please me whenever I call."

She placed a finger under the young man's chin, lifting his gaze to meet hers.

"You'll never forget this kiss," she said seductively as she stared into his glossy eyes, her voice like velvet.

With a flick of her finger, she pushed his chin away like she was dismissing a child. He slowly reached for her, trying to caress her face, eager for another kiss.

She recoiled instantly, slapping his hand aside. "Don't touch the faerie," she snapped. "No one touches the faerie."

Suddenly, Rihanna screamed.

A blur of fur and fangs burst from the underbrush. A massive wolf charged into the clearing, crashing into the young man and knocking him flat just as he was trying to stand. Before Escala could react, the wolf lunged at her, driving its paws into her chest, jaws snapping inches from her face.

The impact threw her to the ground, and the beast was on her, its teeth sinking deep into her arm. Pain flared white-hot, and her spell shattered, shrinking her instantly back to pixie form.

The wolf's massive paw ground her wings into the earth. Its jaws snapped, tearing through the delicate membrane, ripping one wing nearly clean from her back in a single brutal motion.

Escala shrieked in pain.

The creature reared back, claws slashing down again. Escala rolled just in time to avoid the worst, but one claw caught the chain around her neck, a gold necklace with a glowing gem that pulsed like trapped moonlight. The chain snapped and vanished into the grass.

Escala twisted to avoid the wolf's jaws as they lunged at her face, hot saliva splattering her skin. Pain throbbed in her torn arm, and her half-shredded right wing dragged uselessly behind.

She knew she was going to die.

Rihanna burst from cover in a blur of green silk, flying straight at the wolf. Her black ponytail streamed behind her. She stopped midair, tiny wings thrumming, just inches from the snarling muzzle.

"Leave my friend alone!" she cried, thrusting both hands toward the wolf's eyes. A burst of searing light erupted from her palms, hitting the beast's face in a blinding flash.

The wolf recoiled with a sharp yelp, clawing at its eyes as sparks danced in the air.

Rihanna dropped to Escala's side, slipping an arm beneath her shoulders. "Get up," she cried. "The crossing's almost closed!"

Rihanna struggled to lift Escala. "You're heavier than you look."

The wolf continued to paw at its eyes and shook its head, its vision clearing.

The young man had regained his feet near the pixies, hand near his sheathed sword, but not drawing it. His eyes were glassy and fixed on Escala, still under her spell. He ignored the chaos around him and took a hesitant step toward her, voice trembling with confusion.

"Why?" he asked in a distant voice, still under the effects of Escala's magic.

But those were the last words Escala heard him speak.

Enraged and wounded, the wolf turned on him with a feral snarl and leapt, jaws gnashing. The man was too dazed to raise his arms, and the beast tore open his throat with ease, spraying blood across both pixies and the vibrant grass.

"Stop!" Escala screamed, trying to fly toward him, but her torn wing wouldn't carry her.

Rihanna quickly supported Escala, wrapping an arm around her waist. "We can't save him! We have to go, hold on to me!"

With a jolt of pain through her ruined wings, Escala wrapped her arms around Rihanna's waist, and Rihanna hugged her back. Nearby, the wolf tore into the young man's throat, blood soaking the grass.

Rihanna strained under the weight, wings thrumming as she lifted them into the air. Twenty yards away, the crossing flickered—unstable and shrinking fast.

Escala looked back, face drawn in terror. Rihanna clutched her tightly, wings pulsing in frantic bursts as they climbed, ragged, uneven, just clearing the brush. With a final push, she gained a few feet—three, maybe—veering toward the fey crossing now hidden ten yards ahead in thick fern.

The wolf kept tearing, blood and flesh spattering wide as the faeries fought toward the crossing.

Then—suddenly—it stopped.

The wolf raised its head, blood dripping from its muzzle as it locked eyes on the fleeing faeries.

Escala's heart lurched.

The wolf crouched and leapt.

"Faster!" she cried, her voice cracking with fear.

They weren't going to make it.

Rihanna was just feet from the crossing, wings trembling with strain and terror, when the wolf vaulted through the air. Her scream tore through the night as its teeth closed around her waist. Her body jolted mid-flight, wings faltering. One arm clutched Escala; the other flailed, fingers digging at bristled fur and crushing jaws, blood everywhere.

"Rihanna!" Escala shrieked, their fingers slipping.

Then—crack—the wolf's teeth broke through bone, splintering Rihanna's ribs as it held her fast.

Rihanna screamed in agony, and her grip gave way. Escala tumbled back toward the ferns below, the world spinning as blood rained down. She tried to fly, but her wings hung shredded and useless. She dropped like a stone.

Above, Rihanna writhed in the wolf's jaws. As Escala was falling, their eyes met one last time, sorrow etched deep in Rihanna's gaze as her life slipped away.

Then the wolf's jaws clamped down on Rihanna's small frame with a sickening crack as it reached the apex of its leap.

A spray of green-blue magic burst from Rihanna's chest, then silence.

"No!" Escala screamed. "Don't touch the faerie!"

Her shattered wings dragged behind her as she plunged into the ferns. Above, the wolf followed as gravity took over, Rihanna's broken body clenched in its jaws, fey blood raining like falling stars.

Escala slammed into a thick fern; its coiled stems bent, then snapped back with sudden force. Pain shot through her ruined wings as she was hurled upward—blood misting, the world spinning—just as she was flung through the flickering crossing.

The wolf landed a second later, staring up through the vanishing crossing, its eyes filled with rage.

It still held Rihanna's lifeless form tightly in its jaws.

That was the last thing Escala saw as the crossing collapsed in a flash of silver light. And then darkness claimed her.

Chapter 4

───────────

"Well, how's that for an action start?" I ask, glancing around The Stag. A sea of mugs rises in salute, accompanied by cheers, hoots, and scattered clapping. I grin and nod, satisfied. No boos, no taunts, no demands for refunds—always a possibility if a tale trips over its own feet. Not that I'd know from personal experience, of course, only from what I've witnessed happen to others. Smiling, relieved to have survived the most perilous part of the evening, I press on with the tale.

When Escala awoke, she lay in an all-white feather bed in a room that felt oddly familiar. Lifting her head sent sharp pain through her temples. Recognition crept in; this was her childhood room, the bed where she once dreamed of starlight and harmless mischief.

As Escala stirred beneath the silk sheets, another pixie hovered in the doorway, arms crossed, wings flicking with impatience. She wore a fitted forest-green dress with a short, flared skirt and regal tails that shifted as she moved. Moonstones caught the light at her throat, and her cold, smoldering eyes held nothing but contempt.

Escala groaned and turned away, burying her face in the pillow. It was her stepsister, Audrey.

"Well, look who's finally decided to rejoin the living," Audrey said, her voice sweet but barbed. She gave a dismissive huff. "Though I doubt it'll be for long. The Court of Dreams has summoned you, the Dream Weaver himself has called for a trial. In a few days, you'll be judged for violating the True Cycle. And you know what happens to the guilty, don't you? The Wane awaits." Her voice was singsong and cruel.

To receive the Wane was to be erased and forgotten; it was the worst possible punishment for violating fey law.

Escala's fingers gripped the sheets. "No," she whispered. "I didn't mean to…"

Audrey's expression was all polished cruelty. "Intent doesn't matter; consequences do. You've shamed the court, you've embarrassed mother, and our house. And worst of all, you've made our father choose between his blood and the law."

That word—father—struck deeper than any insult. Escala turned her face to the wall, trembling.

Audrey flicked an invisible speck from her sleeve. "In case you're wondering," she said, "I saved you. If I hadn't dragged your pitiful little wings back from the crossing, you'd be nothing but a smear on a fern just like your precious Rihanna. Did you even get to say goodbye to her?"

Audrey tilted her head with a mocking smile.

"I should've left you there, but I cared. I searched and found you half dead by the crossing and brought you back." She let out a bitter laugh. "Not that it matters. You'll be tried, convicted… and erased."

False sympathy flickered in her eyes. "And none of us will even remember you. It'll be like you never existed at all. But at least you get to say goodbye to the court. See how generous I am? A proper stepsister to the end." She lifted her chin smugly.

Escala forced her head up to meet Audrey's icy stare.

I scratch my nose and run a hand through my hair. "Now, some of you might be wondering what in the name of a trickster spirit is a Dream Weaver, and why would such a summons carry the weight of doom? Ah, my friends, the Dream Weaver is no king, queen, or god, yet he is just as powerful. Once mortal, he stepped outside the True Cycle, shedding his shell to become timeless, pure magic—able to take any form. His power is beyond measure; that's really the only way to describe it.

"The Dream Weaver did not create the fey realm, no, the gods did that, but he created the fey creatures that inhabit it by weaving them into existence. Every thread of magic was his work, so when a fey is summoned to trial under his name, it means a sacred fey law may have been broken, and that's serious business.

"To put it in terms we might understand, imagine our king hauling you into his court for treason… or your mother accusing you of putting a frog in your sister's bed when you were seven." The crowd laughs.

"It's about the same thing and should the court convict a fey of violating those laws—especially the True Cycle—the sentence is not simple punishment. The convicted fey is sent to the Wane.

"We don't have anything like the Wane in our justice system. Here, you can be fined, flogged, imprisoned or even hanged. In the fey realm, there are only two punishments: exile or the Wane.

"Exile is self-explanatory: you are cast out, forced to live outside fey society. For a fey, that's a death sentence. Fey are deeply social, bound together like a hive of bees—always near one another, always buzzing with noise. They do everything together. A lone bee can't survive; neither can an exiled fey. In time, they die of loneliness.

"Could you join another court? Oh, in theory, maybe, but in reality, no. Fey are notoriously petty, insular, and suspicious of outsiders. Each court holds its own view of the True Cycle and does not readily welcome strangers. It's about as likely as walking into the Silverstand Forest, strolling into an orc camp, and announcing, 'Hey guys, I'm moving in!'" The crowd laughs.

"Now, the Wane, it isn't like hanging, though the result is the same. You're not just killed; you're unmade. Your magic returns to the fey realm itself, and you are erased… and forgotten.

"That is what Escala Winter now faces if the Court of Dreams finds she interfered with the True Cycle.

"We all know the True Cycle—birth, life, death… even the quiet moments between. Every fey in the Court of Dreams is taught never to interfere in mortal lives.

"But when Escala kissed that young man just to see if she could fall in love, it disrupted the Cycle. She never meant to hurt anyone; she just wanted to understand love. But that's the thing about the True Cycle, it doesn't care about intent, only about consequences."

After Audrey left, Escala curled deeper into the bed. Audrey's words echoed through her head: *Rihanna is dead because of you.* Her mind whispered the truth: she had broken the law. She had kissed a mortal, and two people had died. Now she would likely face the Wane.

She tried to sleep, but nightmares seized her—Rihanna's hand reaching, eyes wide with terror, the wolf's jaws crashing shut. She awoke in a cold sweat, trembling with fear and grief, then buried her face in the pillow and wept.

Chapter 5

I lift my lute from its velvet-lined case, settle onto the stool, and let slow, mournful chords fill the common room of The Stag.

"That night, Escala lay wounded in her childhood bed. She knew her trial awaited, and likely, the Wane."

My fingers drift gently across the strings.

"Her best friend, Rihanna, was gone because of her recklessness. Rihanna had warned her, pleaded with her, even, but she hadn't listened. As she replayed the moment for the thousandth time, she remembered hearing something strange, a sound she'd dismissed as the crossing. Now, in hindsight, she knew it had been the wolf. What a fool she had been.

"Escala's tears streamed relentlessly as memories overwhelmed her, bringing with them the heartbreaking truth: she would never see Rihanna again.

"She looked up at the full moon above the garden in the center of the palace. Her eyes welled up as she began to sing:

> *Beneath that weeping willow's shade*
>
> *Our friendship and trust I did betray*
>
> *Now echoes of your laughter fade*
>
> *My heart lies broken, alone, afraid*
>
> *I wish that fate would let me mend*
>
> *My mistake that cost you, my friend*
>
> *I would trade my wings, embrace my fall*

To bring you back—I'd give my all.

I keep playing my mournful tune as the melody, and my tale works its way into the hearts and minds of the folks gathered. As I play on, many drift into memories of their own failures, perhaps feeling Escala's pain, I can see it in the distant gazes and solemn expressions.

Music has a way of doing that—it drifts past the mind's defenses, stirs what's been buried, and wakes emotions thought long gone. It doesn't ask permission; it simply moves in and pulls forgotten feelings to the surface.

So do my stories.

I stop playing, resting my hands on the lute, and continue with the tale.

As Escala sang, her voice spilled into the corridor in a soft, aching melody, where her father, Lord Rowan Winter, stood just beyond her door, listening in silence. When she finished singing, he knocked. "Escala?" he said gently. "Daughter... are you awake?"

He waited a moment, then opened the door. Moonlight streamed through the latticed windows, casting pale patterns across the chamber. Escala sat on the edge of her bed, arms wrapped tightly around herself, face turned toward the stars. One of her wings was mangled and broken.

Lord Rowan flew in, his wings soundless. He was just over a foot tall, but nothing about him felt small. His fine features were etched with age and control, high cheekbones, sharp jaw, and dark hazel eyes. Silver hair fell just past his shoulders in soft waves, tied back with a circlet of star-metal.

He wore a navy velvet tunic stitched with silver constellations. At his waist: a braided silver belt, a rune-marked pouch, and a lapis-handled dagger.

Realizing I need to liven things up, I say, "I've got an idea. Every time I say, 'Court of Dreams,' you all take a drink, deal?"

The crowd cheers.

I twirl a finger in the air, signaling to the serving wenches, then shout, "Court of Dreams! Court of Dreams! Court of Dreams!" Laughter erupts as the crowd downs their drinks.

I spot Pints across the room. He grins and gives me a thumbs-up. Good, I'm doing my job: keeping spirits high and coins flowing.

"Okay, with our new game in place, let's continue with the tale. Now remember: Escala is a princess in the Court of Dreams."

I pause—sure enough, a few folks raise their glasses, remembering the rules.

"Yes, a princess of the Court of Dreams, visited by her father, Lord Rowan, sovereign of the court itself, above the six royals who rule beneath him, and together they are about to convene a trial in the Court of Dreams."

The slower ones finally catch on and start to laugh.

"Anyway," I say, "Escala turned to him, her face streaked with tears. He studied her, unsure how to bridge the distance between grief and duty. His heart longed to pull her into his arms, to comfort the daughter of his one true love, Teresa, and whisper that everything would be all right, that he would protect her."

I look at my audience again, "You might be thinking, 'For the love of the gods, Wigfrith, there are a lot of characters in this story—who is Teresa?'"

There is a bit of polite laughter but far more applause than I feel necessary.

I raise my hands in mock surrender. "Guilty as charged! Yes, this story has quite the cast, and I promise I'll explain it all. Teresa—Escala's real mother—is at the heart of a beautiful, tragic love story I'll share soon.

"But for now, just remember: Teresa is Escala's true mother. But let's return to this tense moment between a daughter who's broken fey law and a father who must judge her fate."

Seeing her father in his stately robes, Escala blurted out, "Daddy, I'm sorry." She limped over to him, wrapping her arms around him and burying her face in his chest.

Lord Rowan, unsure how to respond and careful not to jostle her injured wing, awkwardly placed a cautious hand on her shoulders.

"Escala… please, tell me what happened," he said.

She couldn't contain herself and it spilled out in one breath: "I didn't mean to break the law, I wasn't trying to be reckless. I just… I just wanted to understand what love feels like—like you and Mom."

Lord Rowan placed his hands on her shoulders and gently eased her back, meeting her eyes.

His voice was firm. "Escala, Morvena is your mother."

Escala was stunned. "She is not," she said, her voice quivering.

"Escala, under the court's law, when I married Morvena nineteen years ago, when you were just a baby, she became your mother."

Tears welled in Escala's eyes. The law, he was always talking about the law. But what about love? Hadn't he once loved Teresa? What happened to that?

"She'll never be my mother," she said defiantly. "Morvena is my stepmother."

Rowan's tone hardened. "Morvena loved you and raised you as her own from your first birthday. You will treat her with respect. Do you understand?"

The words weren't new, but they still hurt.

Nineteen years ago, Morvena had indeed married Rowan, becoming queen consort. She brought her daughter, Audrey, into the union as well.

For Rowan, it was a political marriage—a strategic alliance to steady the court and present a picture of family—or so Escala had been told by others.

But what passed between them behind closed doors? She was never told, and Escala had long since stopped asking. So, this conversation was well-worn ground, and she didn't push it further now.

Rowan's voice softened, but the question came again: "What happened?" There was duty in his tone. "They say you broke the Oath and that you tampered with the True Cycle."

He studied her, searching for denial, hope, anything.

"I only kissed him to find out what love felt like," Escala said quietly. "Like you and Mom."

Rowan held her gaze for a long time.

At last, he spoke. "What I did in my youth doesn't matter. Fey law was different then. But now, interference with the True Cycle is strictly forbidden—for you, for all fey. I don't understand why you and Rihanna would knowingly defy both my order and the court's law."

She said nothing.

"But why didn't the boy fight the wolf?" he asked. "They say he had a sword."

Escala kept her eyes on the floor and said, "I kissed him… and I charmed him."

Rowan covered his face with a hand.

Escala added, "When the wolf came, he just stood there because I didn't command him."

Escala limped over to her bed and sat down.

"It tore him apart. I tried to help, but the wolf turned on me. I would've died, but Rihanna… she saved me."

Rowan hovered, watching her.

"She warned me not to kiss him, but I didn't listen."

"And the mortal boy?" he asked.

"I didn't mean for him to die," she said.

"But he did." His voice tightened. "And so did Rihanna."

"I didn't mean to—"

"No," he said, louder now. "But you did violate the Oath, and the Oath was made to prevent exactly this."

His wings flicked, a sign she knew too well; his patience was failing.

"You crossed into the material plane, tampered with mortal will, led Rihanna into danger she never agreed to, and you even used fey magic to charm a human!" His voice trembled on the edge of fury. "And now!"

He lowered his voice. "And now, you've given the court every reason to condemn you to the Wane."

"I wanted to see if I could fall in love with a kiss like you did!" she pleaded.

He seemed to ignore her plea and said as if to himself, "I must weigh centuries of law and legacy… against my own daughter."

"You mean," she whispered, "you'll choose the court?"

"I mean, you've put me in a place where there is no right choice."

He moved closer, his cloak making a soft sound with each step. The calm he usually showed was slipping away, worn down by grief and anger.

"The Court of Dreams exists to protect the True Cycle at all costs. That's why the Oath exists. And I have never, never let personal feelings sway my judgment."

He paused, thinking carefully before he spoke. "And that responsibility has cost me dearly." There was pain in his voice, but he quickly regained his steady tone. "Still, duty to the Cycle demands it."

His face grew stern. "But if I give in now, if I change the law for you even a little, I risk everything. Not just my honor, but the trust of the court and the safety of the True Cycle. That rule is what keeps the Court of Dreams from falling into chaos, like the Court of Nightmares."

"I'm so sorry, Daddy…"

"I know," he said quietly. "But the law doesn't care that you meant no harm. It only sees the harm you caused."

He stood still for a moment, caught between his duty and his love for her. He looked into her eyes, and something inside him gave way.

Then he rushed to her and held her tightly. "I love you, daughter," he whispered. "You have to know that. More than any crown or rule. You're the best thing I've ever made, the best thing I have left."

She clung to him, pleading through tears. "Help me, Daddy."

But he didn't answer.

He drew back, barely, just enough to see her face. "The trial will be in a few days. The court needs time to gather."

Escala's lip trembled. "What do I do?"

He hesitated, then reached up and gently tucked a strand of hair behind her ear. He lingered, just long enough for her to hope he might say the words that would declare her innocent.

But when he finally spoke, his voice was cold and detached—the voice of a judge, not a father.

"At the trial, I must appear impartial. It doesn't mean that I don't love you."

He turned to leave and said, "Rest, Escala."

And with that, he was gone.

Escala sat back on the bed, reeling. He hadn't promised to protect her or even said a word about saving her life—only rest. She wrapped her arms around her ribs, feeling more alone than ever.

Chapter 6

"Friends, this is a good time to explain fey life and society; you know, the birds and the bees. The hussy bards at the Golden Goose aren't the only ones who can make proper folks blush." A ripple of laughter follows.

"You've heard stories about faeries, but what I'm about to tell you isn't in any bard's song or notebook. Here's the truth: the most important thing to understand about the fey is that they don't belong to the True Cycle at all."

There are puzzled looks, and I realize I need to slow down. "Anyone here not alive?" I pause and sweep my gaze around The Stag, lifting a hand to my brow to mimic a sea captain scanning the horizon. After a slow, dramatic turn across the room, I declare, "Nice to see the living for once. Last night, I had a bunch of undead here—they loved the show but didn't pay. Said they were all dead broke!"

Laughter fills the room.

"Alright, since you're still breathing, let's talk about the cycle of life. We're born, we live, we die… and then comes the afterlife. Those who never served a god drift to the Fugue Plane of existence, left to await judgment—or worse. But the horrors of that place are too grim for tonight, so let's move quickly on. For those who did serve a god, who kept their god well pleased, the reward is far brighter: their souls are carried to the deity's realm for eternal revelry.

"And knowing stories about what happens on the Fugue Plane, I can tell you this; I wish more people knew what their gods actually wanted, because it isn't pretty for those who don't keep the gods happy."

The crowd chuckles.

"No offense to priests," I add, raising my mug, "but if sermons had more story and less scroll, folks might remember what the gods value and have a better chance of actually keeping them happy. Just saying."

That gets laughs and a few raised mugs.

"Ancient verses are sacred, sure, but a tale with a moral? That's what sticks." I raise my mug as if to salute myself, and the laughter builds.

"I'm kidding," I say. "But if you fail to please your god, there's no paradise for you, just a ride down the River Styx and eventually a horned roommate."

More laughter. "Or maybe reincarnation… into a mug." I peer into mine. "Mr. Snookers? The cobbler who died three winters ago, is that you?" The crowd roars with laughter. I look back up from the mug. "Take my advice, listen to the priests. Except you, Mr. Snookers, there's nothing we can do for you now."

The room gives me a round of applause, and I take a mock bow.

"Well, you get the idea about the True Cycle, we're all bound to it… all, that is, except the fey. Escala said that all fey—sprites, dryads, pixies, hags, nymphs, quicklings, brownies, even the bogeyman—yes, he's real—exist outside the True Cycle. So, when fey die, they don't pass on to the afterlife; like we do. They instead return to raw magic and are absorbed back into the fey realm itself. And that's why Escala was so shattered about Rihanna.

"Now, maybe you're wondering, 'Alright, Wigfrith—if the fey live outside the True Cycle, then where do they come from?' Well, I've got the answer, first from Escala herself and later confirmed by other fey. There are five known ways a fey can be brought into being: three are common, one is rare, and one, at least according to Escala, has never happened at all.

"Why should you care how the fey are made? Motive, my friends, motive. Every great story turns on it. And in this tale, the way a certain pixie came into being sparked a jealousy so fierce it birthed a very dark design. But I'm getting ahead of myself... so let me start with the three common methods of creation.

"The first and most common way is the classic fey romance. Boy fey meets girl fey, is struck by her beauty, and puts on the confident, mysterious act. Hoping to spark her curiosity, he leans in with a sly smile and says, 'I'm full of surprises.' She shoots back, 'Yeah? Like thinking you've actually got a chance?'" Laughter breaks across the room.

I laugh too and say, "And you thought this was going to be a serious story; something different from the Golden Goose."

More chuckles.

"Alright, the real first method of creation is as follows: two fey go out drinking, one thing leads to another, and by morning, they find each other just tolerable enough to make a child."

I spot a round-bellied man beside a rosy-cheeked woman, and I raise my mug and say, "Sound familiar, sir?"

They look at each other and burst into laughter. The man slaps the table, beaming, and the crowd joins in. Bit of a risk, I know, but I've got a decent nose for who can take a joke and who'd rather take a swing.

"Alright, seriously, the first method is exactly what you'd expect: mating, just like us mortals. Two fey come together, and if they're different types, say, a sprite and a pixie, the child always takes the form of the mother. So, if the mother is a sprite, and the father is a pixie, the baby will be a sprite. This is the most common method, called 'fey breed.'

"The second common creation method is also mating, but this time between a fey and a mortal, such as a human, elf, or dwarf; take your pick. Before you ask how that's possible, I should explain that most fey can shapeshift, also known as polymorph, that is, transform into humanoid forms."

I squint playfully at the crowd, scanning suspiciously, and I say, "I'm not entirely convinced there aren't a few polymorphed fey in here right now."

More laughter, as couples exchange glances and grins.

"Now listen closely, unlike when two fey mate, when a fey and a humanoid have a child, the baby will take the father's race. Thus, if the father's a brownie and the mother's human, the child will be a brownie. The fey refer to this second method as 'fey touched.'

"The third method of creation is, well... This one's darker."

I begin pacing the stage.

"You've heard the faerie tales of hags stealing babies, witches lurking in cradles, that sort of thing. Those stories are meant to scare children into staying in bed.

"They aren't true, well, not exactly. Fey don't steal living children, that part's pure invention. But legends often wrap lies around a seed of truth. Let me explain.

"When a woman becomes pregnant, something ancient stirs. For a time, her womb is touched by raw, primordial magic—the magic of life, drawn from beyond the material plane. And when the child is born, that spark settles into the soul, and it enters the True Cycle."

I can feel the room hanging on my words, every eye fixed squarely on me.

"But in the case of a miscarriage… the child's soul never enters a body, it lingers—unborn, untethered. It is a spark with no body; it has not entered the True Cycle.

"If a female fey longs for a child but does not want to mate normally with another fey or mortal, she may seek out such a wandering spirit, and she may ask if it would become fey.

"If the spirit agrees, it enters her womb and is born—a fey child, just like in the first method. If it refuses, it drifts on.

"And that," I say, "is where the tale of fey 'stealing children' was born, a twisted truth wrapped in fear and the sadness of stillborn children. This method is known as 'fey called.'

"Now, if you're remarkably sharp, you'll realize something's missing. None of these three methods explains the origin of the first fey. So, allow me to present the fourth and fifth methods.

"The fourth method is known as the Dream Weaver. This path is open only to powerful mortals who, through sheer arcane mastery, transform themselves into beings of pure magic. Think of it as the opposite of necromancers becoming liches, the same idea of forsaking mortality, but with much better skin care. By severing their ties to the material world and shedding their mortal shell, such wizards step outside the True Cycle and reshape themselves into pure magical energy. In doing so, they became the first of the fey.

"The power and dark magic required for such a transformation are both outrageous and nearly impossible to attain. In fact, it has only ever been achieved once when Volpe Inferna, eons ago, severed his mortal shell and became the first Dream Weaver. Without his act, and the fey he shaped thereafter, there would be no fey at all. Yet Volpe is no god. He built no temples, demanded no prayers, and sought no worship. Instead, he drew directly from the fey realm itself, crafting beings of pure magic, lesser than him, yes, but bound to that realm. And, like mortals in their kingdoms, these fey formed cliques, communities, and eventually courts, each ruled by the ideals and desires they held most dear.

"Any fey created directly by the Dream Weaver are considered royalty. Rowan Winter is one such example. Morvena, however, was not born of the Dream Weaver's direct hand, and so she holds no royal birthright. Yet, much like mortal thrones, lines of succession exist within the Court of Dreams, and you'll learn more about them as my tale unfolds.

"Now, let me tell you about the fifth method of creation—dream-woven—the rarest of them all. Though it has never been known to occur, it would mean the Dream Weaver shaped an empty vessel from the realm's raw magic and breathed life into it with something far older: a drifting spark, a soul that has perhaps forgotten its own name. As far as anyone knows, it remains only a legend."

I glance around again. "It's heavy stuff, I know."

"Let's talk about the fey realm itself," I say, swirling my drink. "It's not all moonlight and petals. The fey have hearts and hungers and, like us, they feud, fight, and fall in love. And as I've said, the fey are profoundly social beings. Like us, they gather into kingdoms and communities, and so it was only natural that they divided themselves into Courts—Dreams, Nightmares, and Twilight.

"The Court of Dreams is made up of those fey that value beauty, balance, and belonging. They are a deeply communal court, where everything is infused with passion—wrapped in music, dance, and artistry.

"The fey of the Court of Dreams seek only joy and harmony as they walk beside the True Cycle. They see themselves as its guardians—sworn to protect, yet never to interfere. For any fey who dares to meddle with the Cycle, the punishment is swift, and the consequences severe.

"The Court of Nightmares?" I shake my head. "They are nothing like the other courts. The fey in that court are twisted by hatred—especially toward mortals. To them, the material world is a stain—fragile, foolish, unworthy. They don't merely despise humanity; they loathe the entire True Cycle of life itself. They see the Cycle as something to be shattered. Their goal is simple: unravel everything. Tear down the natural order, remake existence in their own image, and replace life with unending terror. They don't want balance— they want domination. And they will do anything—corrupt, torture, devour—just to see the last light of the world snuffed out. You've probably heard the bedtime stories meant to keep you in bed? Escala says they're all true.

"The Court of Twilight wants to remain hidden, and they rarely cross into Valla. They couldn't care less about the material plane—which, given the Court of Nightmares' thoughts on us here, is perfectly fine by me."

There is weak laughter. I don't think the crowd knows what to make of all this.

"Tonight, you'll see what happens to a pixie who breaks fey law, and I'll let you decide whether their justice is fair. Just remember, even the kindest faeries can be cruel."

Chapter 7

P ints gives me the signal—a fresh batch of something hot and wonderful has just come out of the oven, scarce and pricey as ever. I make the announcement, let the crowd buzz for a moment, then dive right back into the story.

"Some of you might be wondering; what became of the young man the wolf killed?" I glance around, noting the few nods in the crowd. For the rest, I arch a brow. "Does it even matter to the story?"

Resting my hands on my belt, I rock back on my heels. "Indeed, it does, good folks." I pull one hand free, raise a single finger toward the rafters, and repeat with a grin, "Indeed, it does!"

"He had a name. Not the wolf, the young man."

"The young man had a name," I repeat.

Then, with the hint of a smirk, I add, "Though the wolf probably did too."

The crowd laughs.

"It's a name some of you may recognize," I add. "That young man was Jonathan Graves, the son of Victor Graves."

Murmurs move through the crowd.

"Yes." I nod slowly. "*That* Victor Graves—the wizard whose tower blazed green against the sky last year. He lived in Blackthorn Tower, perched high in the eastern Shadowspire Mountains. Truth be told, most knew little about it beyond its ominous name and the fact that Victor resided there with his son, Jonathan. They brewed and sold potions here in Dunwell, and many knew Jonathan—a quiet, polite boy often seen gathering rare herbs in the Silverstand Forest for his father's work. But we later learned Victor's craft went far beyond simple potions. I gave you a hint earlier when I described the herbs Jonathan had collected before the wolf killed him. Did anyone catch it?" I ask.

A hand rises, partly obscured behind two well-dressed guests, one wearing an absurdly elaborate hat with an oversized feather jutting from the brim.

"Pardon me, ma'am," I say, "but could you kindly remove your hat so I might see the genius behind it?"

The audience chuckles as the rotund woman blushes and removes her hat. Behind her sits a tiny, elderly gnome with wild snow-white hair jutting in every direction. Perched on his shoulder is a mangy owl, gray, soot-smudged, and frayed, like it lost a fight with a fireplace. One eye looks straight ahead while the other blinks off to the side. Its wings move stiffly, and its hoot carries a strained note.

The gnome pats the owl and says, "There, there, Cybill. I'm sure he thinks you're lovely."

Then, to me, he adds, "Anyone with magical schooling knows that moonshade petals enhance dreams, firebloom stabilizes conjurations, silverthorn clears illusions, and whisperwind grass eases pain. But most importantly, dragon's breath. In the hands of an archmage? That's soul-separation stuff. Likely used for the Spirit Split spell."

I'm surprised the gnome knows those components. His tone suggests it's common knowledge.

"And your name, good sir?"

He grins. "Gnomes have many, and if I told you all of mine, we'd be here till sunrise."

The crowd laughs, but I don't mind. I like a sharp mind in the audience; it keeps me nimble.

"I am Tully Vesper Skincat Watercan," he says. "Just a humble gnome, here to enjoy the magic of Valla and your excellent tale. This beautiful creature is Cybill."

Cybill lets out a raspy "Kreeek!" as he scratches her head.

"Well now, Mr. Watercan you're spot on. Are you a wizard?"

Tully adjusts his vest. "Not anymore, I gave it up when I realized that sorting bones in the attic of a certain manor named after a skull wasn't all that thrilling. Plus, I had too many potions explode in my face, and I happen to like my eyebrows just where they are, thank you very much."

Laughter ripples through the tavern.

"Well, nevertheless, you know your craft, so tell us, what's the Spirit Split spell?"

Tully's eyes glint with delight. "Ah, Spirit Split," he says. "It's the art of removing your soul from your body, carefully, mind you, and placing it in someone else's skin." He pauses. "Your old body just kind of... stands there. So maybe don't try it in the middle of the street."

The crowd laughs again.

"And when you're done traipsing around in the other body, you can return to your original body... usually. But it's more than possession," Tully continues. "With this spell, the new body doesn't just hold your soul—it holds your memories, desires, and your intent. As I think about it, Spirit Split has a lot in common with other old magics, like bones—bones have magic, you know. Bones, and healing apples, and—ow!"

Cybill nips him sharply on the ear.

"Fine, fine," he mutters, holding his ear and turning to the bedraggled owl. "I won't talk about healing apples. I know it's still too soon… I'm sorry, Argos," he seems to whisper to no one.

He comes out of his odd daze, turns his attention back to me, and says, "Where was I? Ah, right, the Spirit Split spell. When it is used properly, the caster can animate constructs and even simulate life. But when darker magic is layered on top of the spell, well, then you're not just borrowing a body; you're rewriting what it means to live. That kind of magic is about control, about shaping the world into something that won't forget you."

I give him a deep, exaggerated bow and sweep my arm toward the crowd. "Ladies and gentlemen, the one and only Mr. Tully Watercan! Let's give him a proper Stag thank you!" And they do—stomping, clapping, whistling.

Tully stands, he's older than he first seemed, and bows. Cybill flutters up, shedding a few ragged feathers before settling with a huff.

I pick up where Tully left off. "Using Spirit Split, Victor Graves learned to craft wooden totems of bears, snakes, and wolves that, when thrown, became living creatures. They only lasted for a fleeting period of time, but they were the real thing when they were animated, and they were terrifying."

I glance at Tully. "And Jonathan," I say, "had been out gathering herbs for Spirit Split for his father. When he didn't return, Victor went searching, checking the places Jonathan usually foraged. Eventually, he found him, dead. The bushes were torn apart; the grass was soaked in blood. Jonathan's throat had been ripped out, and his sword remained sheathed."

Victor dropped to his knees and cradled his son to his chest, ignoring the wounds, the blood. His boy was gone but Victor knew magic that might reveal the truth.

He whispered arcane words, and as they left his lips, his glowing hands cupped the boy's face. White energy poured into the dead body, and the corpse's eyes opened.

Victor continued to hold him. "Son, who killed you?" he asked.

The corpse answered from beyond, voice hollow: "Wolf."

Victor asked, "Why didn't you fight it?"

"Charmed."

Surprise flickered across Victor's face.

"Who charmed you?" he asked.

"Escala Winter," responded Jonathan's corpse.

"Who is Escala?" Victor asked, concerned she might be after his son for reasons tied to his secret work.

"Elf."

An elf? That was odd. Victor knew elves could charm, but why charm his son?

Knowing he had only one question left before the magic expired, Victor focused on what mattered most.

"Jonathan," he asked, tension in his voice, "did you tell Escala anything about my magic?"

"No," the corpse replied.

A thin smile crept across Victor's face as the glow faded, and his son's eyes slid shut. "Good boy," he said, gently patting the pale cheek as death reclaimed its hold.

He knelt, placed a hand on Jonathan's chest, and whispered, "We're going home now, son, you still have work to do." With a quiet flick, a second spell slipped from his fingertips, and the corpse stirred, limbs twitching as unnatural life took hold.

Victor rose slowly, surveying the glen. The air was thick with blood, crushed herbs, and damp soil. Sunlight pierced the canopy in narrow beams, catching on grass still wet with red. His dark robes whispered as he moved.

Broad wolf tracks marked the soft earth, leading from the brush to the body. Victor crouched, studying the claw marks and scattered blood. A faint glint caught his eye—something metallic nestled in the moss.

It was a fine gold chain, delicate as silk, with a pendant no larger than a fingernail at its end, swirling with midnight blue, silver threads, and tiny points of starlight.

Victor slipped it onto his pinkie, its weight featherlight. This was not mortal work; this was fey, without question.

He moved on, following the bloody tracks and signs of a struggle. Then another shiny item caught his eye in the bloody dirt; it looked like a small piece of transparent lace.

Frowning, he lifted it with a twig and studied it. Holding it up to the light, he turned it over, realizing the fragment was nearly translucent, laced with fine veins; this was no scrap of lace. When he tilted it again, a subtle hint of pearl and lavender gleamed in the light. It was a faerie wing.

Carefully, he tucked it into a linen pouch, his mind racing.

A faerie had been here, not just an elf.

With a small fey necklace and a faerie wing already in hand, he now searched the area with renewed intensity. Beneath the gnarled roots, he saw it, a duskwood totem, carved in the likeness of a wolf mid-howl, muzzle stretched in an eternal cry, jaws agape and fangs bared. While carved wood, it felt disturbingly alive.

Victor reached for it slowly, gloved fingers brushing away bits of earth and leaf. When he turned it over, he saw the mark on its base.

He stared for a moment, then closed his hand around the totem.

A soft rustle of wings stirred the trees behind him. Probably just an owl.

Victor didn't look up.

He slipped the totem into his cloak and stood.

What he had found just changed everything.

Chapter 8

_____

I t was late, and Escala lay on her bed, sobbing; her small frame trembling.

There was another knock on her door, this one firmer than her father's. Escala pulled the covers over her head, hoping the visitor would go away.

The door burst open, and Morvena swept in.

"Escala!" Morvena barked. "What in the nine hells is wrong with you?"

"What do you want?" Escala said weakly, without looking up.

Morvena narrowed her eyes. "Look at me when I'm speaking, you disgraceful ingrate," she snapped.

Escala rolled onto her back, gasping as her broken wing caught in the blanket. She forced herself to meet Morvena's glare, defiance burning in her eyes.

Morvena descended lightly into the room, her wings folding behind her as her feet touched down. She crossed toward the bed, circling it with measured steps until she stood at its foot. Her eyes narrowed further, and she pointed a long, ornate finger.

"You've embarrassed me for the last time. For years, I poured everything into shaping you into something worthy, and this is how you repay me? Breaking laws, shaming the court, dragging my name through the mud with your reckless games? I've defended you, and still, you defy me. Well, I'm done. Whatever judgment comes next... you've earned it!" Morvena yelled.

"You didn't raise me!" Escala shouted back. "You tolerated me!"

Morvena's eyes flashed.

"Tolerated you? I saved you! You were a wild, broken little spark. I gave you a name and a place. And what did you give me in return? A scandal!"

"You never loved me," Escala shot back, "not for one single day. You fawned over Audrey, your precious little star, while I was always the mistake you swept behind the throne!"

Morvena's hands clenched into trembling fists.

"Audrey is everything you're not—disciplined, graceful, obedient. She earned my favor, while you squandered every chance."

"I never had a chance!" Escala spat. "Not with you breathing down my neck, waiting for me to fail. You wanted this to happen—you like that I'm in this mess!"

Morvena stepped closer, her next words coming out in a venomous hiss: "Don't you dare twist this into martyrdom. You broke our sacred laws and meddled in the True Cycle. Your games got a fey and a human killed, all because of a kiss—because you were trying to fall in love?"

"Dad did," Escala said smugly.

"SILENCE!"

Morvena's voice dropped dangerously low. "There is no such thing as love, Escala. Not real love, not the kind that lasts. Love is a myth—it's an invention of poets and fools who can't stomach the truth. Love is just another hunger, dressed in prettier words. Love is a weakness for most, a tool for others. The mortals use it like a weapon—dangling it like bait."

Morvena clasped her hands and pressed them beside her cheek, tilting her head and fluttering her lashes in an exaggerated display.

"Love me, and I'll stay."

"Love me, and I'll change."

"Love me, and I'll make you happy," she mocked.

Her hands dropped to her hips, her expression hardening into a scowl. "Pathetic."

"And your father?" Morvena continued. "He was the worst of them—dreamers always are. You want to know what lasts and matters? Power and legacy. The things you throw away every time you flap your little wings and run off to play rebel princess."

Escala just stared at her.

"I carried this court when others would've let it fall. I've done what needed doing—quietly, thanklessly—while you danced through moonbeams, pretending the rules don't apply to you." Morvena glared at her. "But they do, and they always have, and now, finally, you'll learn that."

She rose into the air, wings casting long, sharp shadows across the chamber as she hovered above Escala's bed.

Her voice rang out, cold and thunderous. "You've disgraced your father!" She descended slightly, pointing a trembling, furious finger downward. "The lord of the Court of Dreams—you've made him a laughingstock! Do you have any idea what you've done? How can he hold his place among the fey elite when his own daughter tramples our laws like petals? When her childish games end in blood?"

The words landed like stones in Escala's heart. The memory of her father's proud countenance, the trust in his eyes, flashed through her mind.

"You killed one of our own! A fey life lost because you couldn't control your whims. Do you think the court will forget that? Forgive that? No! And they won't forget who raised you either, because everything you've done reflects on him."

What had she done? She could not look at Morvena.

Morvena paused, steepling her fingers as she studied the ruined princess.

"And you've embarrassed me! I spent years raising you, teaching you right from wrong, loving you like I loved Audrey. I married your father when your mother abandoned you. I understand why you push back against me, but your father? Why have you disrespected him? You're a princess of the Court of Dreams! How is it you behave like a draxie from the Court of Nightmares?"

Escala tried to hold back a sob. Her wings, still too fragile to lift her from the bed, trembled.

Morvena turned her back. "Before you get the Wane, you need to apologize to the court and to your father," she said, her voice dripping with disdain. Morvena shook her head and flew to the door. She turned, eyes blazing.

"Once the Wane erases you, Audrey will take your place and finally make Lord Rowan proud. We won't miss you, and your father won't either. He's tired of being ashamed of you. And soon, no one will even remember you."

She slammed the door.

Chapter 9

The eastern wing of the Court of Dreams lay quiet that night. Lord Rowan Winter sat alone in a carved teak chair, his wings drooping with weariness.

A silver-braided fey woman stepped inside—it was Junel, Escala's nanny and governess. Rowan appointed Junel at Escala's birth to assist Teresa, and Junel had never left Escala's side. Through childhood, she had soothed Escala to sleep when she was no bigger than a teacup, taught her letters, manners, and the winding ways of the fey. In many ways, Junel was Escala's mother in everything but name.

As Junel entered, Rowan rose. Her wings, veined and translucent like autumn leaves, carried her gently to the floor, her frail frame still moving with a grace untouched by all she had endured.

"Thank you for coming, Junel."

She bowed her head. "Of course, my lord."

"Please," he said, waving a hand. "No titles tonight."

She looked up at him, her eyes softening. She could see the worry etched in his face as she settled onto a cushioned bench near the fire. "I knew you before the throne, boy. No need to pretend with me."

He gave a weary chuckle, but it carried no mirth. Sitting across from her, he clasped his hands so tightly his knuckles went white. "It's Escala," he admitted, voice low. "I fear for her fate more than I dare show the others."

"She's going to be sentenced, isn't she?" Junel said.

"I think so," Rowan said. "The council members have made up their minds; they're just dressing it up with procedures. They are going to give her the Wane."

Junel reached out, resting one of her hands gently on his.

"Morvena has made this political, and she's poisoning the Court one whisper at a time," he added.

"She's afraid of Escala," Junel said. "She's worried that Escala will disrupt the order she so desperately wants for the court."

He stood, suddenly full of restless energy, and walked toward the tall window at the chamber's far end, looking out at the garden below.

"Escala reminds me of her mother," Junel said softly.

"Don't."

Junel was quiet for a few minutes, then said, "Do you remember when she was five, and she got lost in the Lantern Garden? Everyone was panicking, guards tripping over themselves to find her. And where was she?" She smiled gently. "Curled up in a tulip blossom, singing to a cricket like it was her pet."

Rowan smiled, remembering. "I don't want to lose her, Junel."

"You haven't yet."

"They're going to vote," he said. "They'll try to make it look fair, but the verdict was sealed the moment she kissed that boy. Morvena has likely seen to that."

Junel nodded slowly. "Then you have to decide what kind of father you'll be."

"She reminds me of me when I was young," Rowan whispered. "She has such a fire for life, and she pushes boundaries just to see if they'll break." He laughed to himself. "That stubborn heart of hers—always leading before her head catches up. She only kissed a human, Junel. I did far worse—I loved one, and I still do. I even brought her into the court. I convinced myself I could have both— Teresa and the court—that I could bend the laws without truly breaking them, and that the others would understand. What a fool I was."

Junel rose and hovered near him. Her voice was soft. "You changed everything when you brought Teresa here."

"I know."

"No, Rowan, you don't." Junel's eyes flashed, a rare fire behind her weathered face. "Before you brought that mortal into our realm, the Oath wasn't law—it was tradition. Unspeakable, yes, but not punishable by the Wane. That didn't happen until she left. I remember the council chambers," Junel continued. "Morvena speaking of the 'danger to the Cycle,' and the way she said that your love of a mortal had interfered with the True Cycle and corrupted the balance."

"I thought..." Rowan said. "I thought she was just angry at me."

"She was, but she was also afraid your actions would inspire others to interfere with the Cycle, and she convinced the Dream Weaver to implement the Oath, to ensure no one else could do what you did," Junel said. "She made interference unforgivable."

"She made it fatal," Rowan corrected, "and now Escala is going to pay the price for a law—for an oath—written because of my folly."

"It wasn't folly," she said, "it was love."

Rowan closed his eyes.

"If they sentence her... if they give her the Wane..."

Junel didn't let him finish.

"They won't," she said firmly. "Not if you fight for her and show the judges what mercy looks like, and not if you tell them what you just told me."

"They won't listen to me," he said.

"They might if you speak as her father, not as a lord of the court, but as the one who broke the law for love and lived to regret it," Junel said.

"It's incredibly risky," he said, "to discuss court business privately."

"And you've never taken risks before?" Junel said.

Rowan turned and gave her a hard glare.

Realizing she may have overstepped, Junel turned to leave. At the door, she glanced back. "Fight for her, Rowan. Teresa would want you to."

Then she was gone.

Rowan remained still, gaze drifting back to the garden, lost in thought.

An hour passed.

Then, at last, he knew what he had to do, it was the only chance left to save her.

He flew to Escala's chambers, his wings barely a whisper against the polished stone.

The chamber door groaned as he opened it.

She sat on the bed, arms wrapped around her knees, face buried in folded limbs. Her wings hung limp, bandaged.

He hovered in the doorway. "Escala," he said.

She turned.

"If the trial goes how I fear," he said, voice tight, "you won't see me again."

"Then why?" she asked, eyes glistening. "Why did you come?"

"To remember you."

She opened her mouth, but no sound came.

"I love you," he said. "I loved you before you were born, when you were still in Teresa's womb. I loved you when you couldn't fly. I loved you when you smiled, when you danced, and when you shouted 'Ri-Ri!' every time Rihanna came to visit. I love hearing your voice and listening to you sing. I love your curiosity, your joy—and yes, I even love you when you've broken every rule I ever gave you. And I will love you still, even after they take your name from the stars."

She covered her mouth, a weeping sound escaping through her fingers.

"They may take everything from you, Escala. But before they do, you need to know—her name was Teresa Whitmore. She was your true mother. I loved her from our very first kiss, and I love her still. We were so young, so wild, so free. Neither of us had responsibilities yet. And she knew me for who I was—not the title, not the crown, not the court. She didn't even know about any of this," he said, gesturing to the air around them. "She fell in love with me, and loving her was the last choice I ever made for myself before duty claimed everything else."

Escala stared, stunned, questions tumbling through her mind, but Rowan had already turned to go.

He paused, wings beating once, and flew back to her. He gathered her into a gentle embrace, kissed the crown of her head, and pulled back just enough to memorize her face. His eyes filled with unshed tears.

With one final kiss to her cheek, he let her go.

Wings low and heavy, he crossed the room and slipped quietly through the door.

It closed behind him with a soft, final click.

Escala had no idea her father wasn't going to bed. He was going to gamble everything on a plan to save her life.

Chapter 10

———————

Before you can see what comes next, it helps to know what came before. Twenty years ago, Rowan Winter stepped into the mortal world. He wasn't the cold ruler people know now. Back then, Rowan was restless, reckless, and, most of all, curious. That was when he met the woman who changed his life.

She was eighteen and lived with her family in a small farmhouse on the edge of Marlow, a quiet village north of Dunwell. Their land bordered the forest, where a narrow creek wound through trees and wildflower gardens. Rowan found her there for the first time, among the wildflowers and running water she had loved since she was a child.

Her name was Teresa Whitmore.

Teresa was the kind of girl who read too many storybooks and never stopped loving them. She made wishes on rainbows, believed in dragons, and once claimed a willow tree winked at her under a full moon.

Her mother called her fanciful, and her brother teased her, but Teresa didn't mind; she held onto it as if it were part of her soul.

Evenings were her favorite. Fireflies lit up, and shadows stretched across the fields. As the sun went down, the woods turned golden, and for a while, the world felt like the stories she loved, full of hidden magic waiting to be found. She danced barefoot on the grass by the creek, spinning to music only she could hear, her happiness turning into song.

That was how Rowan found her.

One evening, he crossed into Marlow. Twilight had settled, and he moved quietly through the thick brush at the edge of the village. People were inside, their laughter and lantern light shining through the windows. He crept closer, curious about how mortals lived.

He moved quietly between hedges and through the groves when he heard a light, joyful voice singing through the trees. He turned, following the sound through the leaves until he saw her.

She danced among the wildflowers beside a small, bubbling creek, hidden behind thick bushes. It was a secret place only she knew.

She wore a simple dress that swayed with each step, bare feet tiptoeing on the damp grass. Her arms stretched wide, head tipped back, golden hair swirling as she twirled. Her face was tanned, slightly oval, with sky-blue eyes that shone with wonder.

He hid among the dense bushes, watching her dance and sing, her radiance spilling into the twilight like sunlight lingering past its hour. Her voice was pure and bright, weaving melody and hum into a duet with herself. Rowan's heart quickened, each beat drawn to her. He could not look away; her voice, her beauty, her unbridled freedom had captured him entirely.

He came back the next night, and the night after, and again the one after that, always hidden, always cloaked in fey magic. What he was doing was not forbidden by fey law... not yet.

One night, she stopped mid-dance and said aloud, "I know you're there. If you're going to keep watching me, at least have the decency to say hello."

So, Rowan stepped from his hiding place into the moonlight, letting her see him but not as he truly was.

He didn't lie, but he didn't show his full self either. Rowan was a pixie, and like all pixies, he could cast polymorph; and he did so.

What Teresa saw was a young man about her age, tall, maybe six feet, lean and trim. His brown hair curled at the edges, and his face held the softness of youth, with dimples when he smiled. But it was his eyes that caught her breath; they were warm, hazel, and kind, and his smile was gentle, almost shy.

As he stepped from behind the hedge, he clasped his hands in front of him and bowed his head.

"You're a dream," he said.

She blushed and asked his name, and that was how Teresa met Rowan.

He said he was a cartographer mapping the Silverstand Forest southwest of Dunwell. She believed him, and even if she hadn't, it wouldn't have mattered. From their first words, something sparked, and they were drawn to each other like stars caught in the same orbit.

They met again the next night. And the one after that, and the night after that. Soon, every spare moment of his visits belonged to her.

At first, he remained in the material plane for a day or two. However, over time, his visits gradually extended into weeks. He rented a room above a weaver's shop in Marlow, remaining in human form.

Weeks passed, and their friendship grew. But they weren't simply friends, they were pulled to each other by something much deeper.

In the evenings, they danced, and he taught her fey steps, never saying where they came from; she taught him the local ones. Their laughter joined the shadows, their feet moving in harmony, joy carrying them into the night… and the dreams that followed.

One night, by the creek where they first met, hidden behind sunflowers and hedges, she kissed him, soft and sudden.

And in that moment, something broke open in Rowan's heart.

He hadn't meant to fall in love, but he had.

He should have returned to the fey realm, for he knew he was meddling with the True Cycle, breaking traditions older than memory. A mortal's love for a fey was interference in its purest form. But after that kiss, he could not return to the court, not without her.

And her attraction to him had nothing to do with castles or wealth, she didn't even know he was a lord of a court. To her, he was just a kind-eyed cartographer who listened and who didn't attempt to charm her with games or empty promises.

In the evenings, he'd lie beside her in the grass, holding her hand, talking of castles in the sky and bard songs as if they were real. She fell in love with him just as deeply.

A month passed, then two, then five. And every day, they loved each other more.

By the third month, she started noticing things. Like how he never grew facial hair. How he'd slip into a strange language now and then. Or the day they startled a mother fox in the forest, Rowan knelt, whispered something glowing, and the fox rubbed against him like a cat while he stroked the creature.

When she asked about it, he just smiled and said, "I've always had a way with animals."

One night, beneath her favorite oak, she looked at him closely and asked, "You're not just a traveler, are you?"

Rowan didn't lie; he couldn't. He told her about the fey realm, the Court of Dreams, his title, and the Oath he was breaking just by loving her. But he did not reveal his true form.

Teresa stared at the stars for a long while. She had always believed in the magical things of Valla and beyond, and Rowan simply made them real. She took his hand and said, "Then I guess we'll just have to be careful."

That was the moment he knew he'd never leave her.

He stopped returning to the court, and they spent every waking moment together, sharing things only lovers do.

But the True Cycle always turns, and even young lovers find trouble.

Their troubles began when Teresa started getting dizzy on warm afternoons. Her appetite changed, and she grew nauseous in the mornings.

When the signs became clear when she missed her moon, when the sickness came, she tearfully told Rowan. She was terrified, not of having a baby, but of what it would mean because they were not married.

I look at the crowd in the Stag and see they are reflecting on their memories of young love. "We all like to call ourselves kind-hearted, don't we?" I say, "But let's not lie, not when it comes to an unmarried woman with child. We don't offer compassion; we sharpen our tongues. We trade whispers, heap shame, and brand her family with scandal. Teresa knew it, and she feared it. And who could blame her, when our own city can be so merciless?

"I'll remind you of what I said earlier about fey creation. Teresa's pregnancy fell under the second method—a mortal joined with a fey. She now carried a fey-touched child. And remember this: when a male fey mates with a mortal woman, the child always takes after the father's race. Which meant her baby would be born a pixie."

Rowan knew that if the thought of bearing a mortal child had shaken Teresa, the truth of carrying a pixie child might break her. Yet he could not hide it from her. In the stillness of his small room above the weaver's shop, he let the polymorph spell dissolve, revealing his true form, a pixie prince scarcely a foot tall, his delicate, iridescent wings catching the lamplight.

Teresa had read of moonlit realms and winged folk, and though wonder lit her eyes, fear did not. Rowan told her their child would be born a pixie, and he swore, with the full weight of his crown and his heart, that he would protect them both.

Her hands trembled as she reached for him. "We'll figure it out together."

She had not yet begun to show when she told her parents. As you might expect, fury followed. Her father demanded that Rowan marry her at once.

Later that night, after her parents had gone to bed, her brother James brought a potion to end the pregnancy and tried to make her drink it. Teresa refused, fled in tears, and ran to Rowan's room.

That was the first time she truly felt afraid. Rowan held her close, whispering promises of marriage, but he knew it would never mend the deeper rift. Her parents did not yet know the child she carried would be a pixie, and even if they wed, there was no life for such a child in Marlow.

In Rowan's eyes, only one path remained: they would have to flee to the Court of Dreams and raise the child among the fey. But that path was fraught. For Teresa to enter, the court itself would have to accept her. And even as lord of the court, Rowan could not decree it. Fey society was too intricate, its laws and politics woven tighter than any crown upon his brow.

When he explained the plan, to his surprise, she said, "I love you. I trust you."

The night they left, Rowan, in his human form, stood at the meadow's edge, his cloak wrapped tight against the evening chill. She came with one bundle wrapped in a worn shawl, hand resting over her small belly. She stepped into his arms. He took her to a crossing, and holding hands, they passed through.

They arrived at twilight, when the sky glowed gold and violet, and the air hummed with quiet magic. Rowan led her down a secret path, trying to avoid questions and stares. But word spreads fast in the Court of Dreams, and by the time they reached the palace, Morvena was waiting. She stopped them from entering the Court. Rowan turned back into his pixie form. Once she recognized him, Morvena glared.

"You've brought a blight into the Court of Dreams," she said, blocking their way.

Teresa silently stood with one hand on her belly as Rowan flew forward to confront Morvena.

"She is my betrothed," Rowan said, voice steady. "And she is with child."

"She does not belong here."

Rowan, stubborn fool that he was, said nothing.

Weeks passed, and Rowan spoke of them getting married after the baby arrived, but he never proposed. Six months later, Teresa gave birth to a radiant pixie girl—blonde, blue-eyed, with a storm in her veins.

Rowan Winter, Lord of the Court of Dreams, had an heir.

And ready or not, the court had a princess.

They named her Escala Winter.

Teresa was the first human to live in the Court of Dreams. Now, remember what I said about how fey are born? Well, here's why that matters: motive, my friends, motive.

While the court toasted the new princess, Morvena smiled sweetly, but inside, she fumed. To her, it was all wrong. No fey-touched pixie should be a princess; it was scandalous. And watching the court bow to Escala made her blood boil. It was outrageous that she towered over them physically, although when alone, Rowan took his human form too, but to usurp her place was too much.

Why did this bother Morvena so much? It was because she was fey-born, which, if you will recall, is the third and darkest method of fey creation. Morvena was created from the spirit of a stillborn mortal child. So, while fey magic gave her form and place, it did not give her peace, and from her first breath, she hated the mortal world that denied her life.

And now, a mortal had claimed the heart of a fey lord, birthed his heir, and stood poised to marry into the highest circles of the court. This was an outrage!

Worse, this mortal's fey-touched child had something Morvena never would, legitimacy to the throne of the court.

To Morvena, every time someone spoke Escala's name with reverence, it felt like swallowing poison. And every soft smile for the little princess was like a blade beneath her ribs.

This wasn't envy, it was betrayal. The court had declared that Teresa Whitmore's blood, human blood, was more worthy than hers.

Morvena smiled, bowed, and curtsied as Teresa passed, her anger growing. She waited and, like all careful predators, smiled as she did.

Rowan had chosen a mortal for his mate, and if they wed, Teresa would be queen. And golden-haired, blue-eyed Escala, the princess, would be the future of the court.

Teresa hadn't just taken Rowan's heart; she had stolen the legacy Morvena once dared to believe was hers. Morvena would stop their marriage.

Her revenge would be slow, cold, and generational.

Chapter 11

People often think love can survive anything, but it cannot always protect you from cold, unwelcoming hearts.

When Teresa Whitmore crossed the veil for Rowan, she was carrying his child and held a silent hope, never spoken aloud, that she could learn their ways and eventually be accepted. She tried for a while. Junel told me that, and there was always something tired in her voice, as if effort had never been Teresa's problem.

She picked up the court's ways, put on a smile when murmurs wound around her, and dropped her eyes when stares clung too long. Better to look away than meet empty eyes.

Rowan brought Junel, an old, steady-handed pixie who had been his nanny, to guide Teresa through the court's rules and help with the baby. He believed time would help and that perhaps the court would see that the baby would benefit from Junel's touch.

But the court had never been known to change for anyone.

It moved in quietly as fog. No sharp insult, no single moment to mark the start. Just glances that lasted too long, talk that changed when Teresa stepped into a room, then carried on as if she'd never been there.

Rowan noticed it, though not as quickly as Teresa did. He tried to help. He took his human form more often, stood by her side where people would see, and held her hand at court events.

No one argued with him; that would have been simpler.

Instead, they shifted just enough to keep their hands clean. No one dared defy Rowan, but they left Teresa out of everything, treating her like a spirit haunting the halls.

It wore away at Teresa, day by day, until she started to fade. Her laughter ceased, and even her words with Rowan lost their old warmth.

And then, one day, she stopped singing.

That was what Rowan noticed.

She used to sing, always, little scraps of song and half-remembered tunes while folding linen or sweeping a room, humming to occupy the silence with something gentle and alive.

Rowan saw the court's poison working in her, saw how they wanted Teresa gone and would not rest until she left.

Some said it plainly, though even that was softened, wrapped in concern.

"Your guest must miss her home."

The council never named her consort; Morvena made sure of that, citing fey law that forbade mortals from holding titles.

Escala was only three weeks old when the court threw its Moonturn revel. Music and cheer spilled through the halls, lanterns casting silver over dancers and the fragrance of sweet wine wafting through the air. Rowan wore his ancient silver, radiating with ancient enchantment, and Teresa stood next to him in green.

Teresa hadn't wanted to go, and Junel saw it plain as day. She moved with stiffness, clutching Escala close, as if the baby alone could protect her from the court's eyes. So she went.

She remained at Rowan's side, their daughter in her arms, forcing the right smiles and meeting each gaze. But not a soul in that hall saw her as kin. Some looked straight through her, and in the Court of Dreams, that was the sharpest cruelty of all.

And the court's chill didn't stop at Teresa. Little Escala, swaddled in silk and wonder, gurgled in her mother's arms, blissfully blind to the tempest gathering around her.

"She's so small," one noble muttered. "Are we sure she's even fey?"

"A runt," said another. "Her wings don't even flutter properly."

"I heard her cry sounds like a mortal's," someone added.

"She'll never fly right. How can her mother teach her?"

Teresa caught every word, every single one.

When the music died, and the halls stood empty, Junel found Teresa by the moonwell, Escala sleeping in her lap.

"I don't belong here," Teresa whispered.

Junel said nothing as she knelt next to her, watching the water ripple.

"If I stay," Teresa said tearfully, "Escala will never be accepted; she'll always be the outsider's child. I won't let that be her life." Tears slid silently down her face.

Junel gently laid a hand over hers and didn't argue because Teresa was right. The court was cruel, and pretending otherwise would be a lie.

And the one behind it all? Feeding rumors and watching from the shadows?

Morvena.

She had always hated humans.

She hid that anger well until Rowan fell in love with Teresa and brought her to the Court of Dreams. And then she unraveled.

From the moment Teresa arrived, Morvena began to break her, not with curses, but with silence and small, strategic wounds, all untraceable and deliberate.

It wore Teresa down and hollowed Rowan as he watched the woman he loved lose her joy.

Morvena whispered to the elders about the risk of human frailty, madness, and death, spreading fear of humans interfering in fey matters, and the court listened. Because Morvena never shouted, she whispered and planted seeds.

The invitations to events stopped coming.

The servants "forgot" things.

Even Junel couldn't shield Teresa completely.

The court believed Morvena, as they always did because if a lie is whispered softly enough, for long enough, you forget who first spoke it. You just start believing.

Rowan tried to defend their relationship but the more he defended Teresa, the more isolated he became, and the whispers only grew louder, the court's disapproval sharpening.

In time, even Rowan began to change. Not in how he loved her, but in how he bore that love.

Every night, he arrived later, spoke less, and rarely smiled. And Teresa saw it—the quiet helplessness in his eyes.

One evening, he returned home, hollow and quiet. He wouldn't say what had happened.

The next morning, Teresa turned to Junel, who had become her closest confidante. "Why is Rowan so sad?" she asked. "He won't tell me. What happened at court yesterday?"

Junel hesitated, then shook her head. "It's nothing, dear. Nothing to worry about."

But the silence only deepened, and Rowan grew colder still. The whispers and the isolation pressed in on all sides.

Finally, one afternoon in the garden, as Junel and Teresa walked with baby Escala among the blooming dream blossoms, Teresa stopped. "Please," she said, her voice trembling. "What has the court done? Why is he pulling away from me?"

Junel reached for Teresa's hand and held it gently. "They've ruled against your marriage," she said. "If he proposes, he will lose his position and all of you will be exiled from the Court of Dreams."

"And Escala?"

"Her too."

This was hard for Junel. She dabbed at her eye but continued: "Unless Rowan marries a fey who agrees to adopt her, Escala will be deemed illegitimate. She'll never be recognized as a princess; she will never even belong to the Court of Dreams."

Tears welled in Teresa's eyes. "So the choice is exile… or giving Escala a real future by marrying someone else?"

Junel gave her hand a quiet squeeze. "I'm so sorry, my dear."

Teresa could only nod as tears filled her eyes. She turned away, clutching Escala tightly to her chest, and hurried back to their home.

That news broke her more than anything the court had ever whispered. That night, she made the hardest decision of her life.

To give her daughter a chance at a normal life, she would leave.

Chapter 12

There are names I don't speak lightly, and Victor Graves is one of them. To understand what happened to Escala, I need you to understand who he is because no one starts out a villain, not even him.

Victor Graves was born in Marlow, near Dunwell, and from the start, he was different. While other boys played, Victor sat alone, staring into puddles as if he saw another world beneath the surface. By nine, they called him a prodigy. At twelve, he crafted enchantments no one understood. At sixteen, he mastered the Spirit Split spell but instead of using it to cheat death, he channeled pieces of his spirit into wooden totems he had carved.

Totems became his obsession. Now, totem magic wasn't new; old witches had used it for centuries. But Victor refined it, recording every detail, material, command, and rune in journals brimming with sketches and calculations. He pushed what could be done with it beyond what any mage in Valla had ever accomplished.

From sixteen to eighteen, he perfected a wolf totem carved from duskwood. The figure, mid-howl, fangs bared, was both beautiful and deadly, infused with his own magic. Over time, he took pride in numerous creations, such as bears and panthers. However, the wolf, his initial creation, held a special place as his lifelong favorite.

But as unique and gifted as Victor was at this age, underneath it all, he was still a young man, one tempted by and drawn to young women, and the call of young love.

Victor's father sold potions in Dunwell, and Victor would often come with him to work the booth and see the wares of the big city, but really, it was to see a beautiful girl about his age from the same village of Marlow. Her family worked in their booth in Dunwell with them. She was happy and outgoing, and full of questions; he, on the other hand, was quiet, and full of secrets. But he noticed her. How could he not? She was beautiful.

Every market day, while she helped her father fold textiles or argued prices with the local weavers, Victor would linger nearby, arms full of unnecessary supplies, pretending to browse.

But he never said much; he just listened for her laugh. He watched her climb onto carts, sketch flowers in chalk across crates, and twirl when she thought no one was watching. To Victor, she was more wondrous than any spell he could conjure.

He gifted her his most treasured work, the wolf totem, as a testament to his devotion. His first true totem, hand-carved from duskwood, its howl caught forever in motion and infused with a touch of his soul through the Spirit Split spell. To him, it was as beautiful as she was.

Today, a boy might offer flowers or a necklace if he were wealthy. But Victor gave her the one thing he valued above all: his magic, his wolf, and his heart. It was, to him, the equivalent of an engagement ring, a pledge of himself. He expected she would feel the weight of the gift instantly; the rarity, the craftsmanship, the unthinkable intimacy of giving away a piece of his very soul.

But he never explained. And so, to her, it was simply a carved wolf.

She took it, smiled, and said, "Thank you."

Victor never once told her how he felt. Shy to the point of silence, he feared she would laugh, or worse, turn him away. And he was probably right. To Teresa, he was just the boy from the market, a friend at most, never more.

So when, months later, she told him that she was leaving, that she'd met someone, Rowan Winter, a lord from the Court of Dreams, and that she was in love, he said nothing. She never knew that, in that moment, her gentle words had shattered him and quietly broken his heart.

She left for the Court of Dreams carrying the only thing Victor had ever made with love, the wolf totem.

After that, Victor changed.

He stopped speaking to townsfolk, stopped attending festivals. Then one day, he simply vanished. Two years later, he returned and something was wrong. He never spoke of where he'd been. He only returned to his bench, carving totems with a restless fury, faster, sharper, each one stranger than the last.

He made a river run backward, simply to see if he could. He shaped a creature from candle smoke and shadow, then tried to pour half his soul into it, drifting through the world as a wraith for a week before stitching himself back together.

Yes, he'd always been odd, but now he was something else: distant and withdrawn.

He left Marlow behind and raised Blackthorn Tower through powerful sorcery, its jagged spire clawing at the mist high in the Shadowspire Mountains.

But like anyone facing rejection, Victor tried to move on. After Blackthorn Tower rose from stone and sorrow, he married a local girl from Marlow whose family had dyed cloth for generations—her name was Elira Tannswell.

Was it true love, or merely a passing distraction? Did Victor genuinely love her, or, as Morvena would one day whisper, was it nothing more than another mortal draping that word over something far less noble?

Elira gave him a son, Jonathan. But soon after the boy's birth, she vanished from daily life. She no longer came to the market, no longer walked the streets of town. And just like that… she was gone. No one in Dunwell or Marlow has seen her in years, which is entirely another story, but not for tonight.

"Now, friends," I say, pacing the stage, "I skimmed over Victor's heartbreak, but make no mistake, what passed between him and Teresa was no small thing. It's the stuff of ballads, the kind of sorrowful tune that begs for a quiet lute and a few too many drinks. Maybe one night, I'll tell it all from the beginning. But tonight, for time's sake, I ask you to draw from your own hearts the weight of rejection Victor carried."

I glance at the women in the crowd. "And ladies, I imagine some of you might sympathize with Teresa. She never meant to wound him. She viewed Victor as a friend; he was kind, maybe a little strange, yet harmless. She thought she could confide in him, share the spark of her new love for Rowan. She thought he'd be happy for her.

"But what she didn't know was that each word of her love for Rowan pressed the blade of rejection deeper into Victor's heart. Not because she was cruel, but because she was trusted, and sometimes, that hurts worse.

"If you've ever had your heart broken so deeply it left a scar," I say, "then raise a glass to Victor Graves."

A few mugs lift, slow and unsure, half toasting, half wincing at the name. After all, it's not every night you drink to the villain.

After the toast, I continue, "What I'm saying is, most of us know what it's like to love someone who never once looked back, and that, friends, is how monsters are often born."

76

Chapter 13

When Teresa arrived at the Court of Dreams, Morvena started plotting. She whispered to the right people, spread half-truths, and let her lies grow in the fertile ground of gossip.

"Teresa has grown tired of the fey realm," she murmured once to a pair of dusk dancers in the garden.

"It's difficult, I imagine… for a mortal being betrothed to the lord of a fey court. All that responsibility to raise a fey princess, I don't see how she can possibly do it," she said to a group of nixies.

"She longs for her old life, you know, simpler things for a simple person," she told a pair of sprites.

Morvena always spoke pleasantly, but her words cut deep. She never accused anyone or spoke badly of Teresa. Instead, she let questions hang in the air, and by the time the first rumor spread, she didn't have to say anything more.

"She's gone," said a black-winged elder near the Spring Gallery. "Teresa left him."

"They say she returned to the mortal world," whispered another. "She couldn't handle the responsibility."

The fey shared dozens of stories. None were the truth, but every version sounded believable.

Through it all, Morvena moved through the Court of Dreams with calm grace. She never announced her place beside Rowan. She simply stood there, and soon people assumed she belonged.

It's strange, isn't it? Sometimes lies don't need to be shouted. They just need to be whispered often enough by someone who looks the part.

Rowan mourned Teresa's leaving, and through it all, Morvena stayed by his side. She was steady and patient, giving him comfort and reassuring the court.

She never said the word "Queen." Not aloud.

But soon enough, others did.

Rowan knew the hard truth of what must be done to secure Escala's future: if she was ever to be recognized as heir to the Court of Dreams, he would have to wed a fey.

At first, the hints were subtle. Advisors gave quiet nods, and council members exchanged lingering glances. One name kept coming up: Morvena.

Morvena was not born into royalty, but she was deeply respected and stood for tradition and order. She already had a fey-born daughter, Audrey, who was just a little older than Escala. The courtiers whispered that if Rowan married Morvena, it would bring stability, and the two daughters would grow up together, both meant to rule in harmony one day.

Rowan saw the logic, and to him, it was the only way to protect Escala's future. For her, it made sense. Still, his heart was broken because he loved Teresa. But his duty as lord, his love for his daughter, and his wish for her to live as a true fey left him no choice but to let go of Teresa. Quietly, he decided to hide those feelings, no matter how much it hurt.

Teresa was gone, but Escala was still there, and Rowan promised himself that she would thrive. He would make sure she had the best life possible, one that honored the sacrifices he and Teresa had made. He wanted her to be accepted and celebrated among the fey, and one day crowned queen after he was gone.

So, just as Teresa had done before, Rowan made a choice. He did not choose for himself or his own wishes, but because he loved his daughter. In the end, he married Morvena.

After the wedding, Morvena acted the part of stepmother well. She fussed over Escala with sweet words, brushed her curls aside, and called her "my little star." She laughed softly when Rowan was near, showing just enough care to win his trust.

But her kindness was empty, and when Rowan was not looking, her true self showed. Her voice turned sharp, and Escala was scolded for speaking too loudly, too softly, and too often. She was told she was nothing like Audrey, Morvena's perfect daughter. Chores replaced play, and criticisms replaced praise.

Whenever Escala cried to Rowan, he would turn to Morvena and ask about her ways. Morvena always had an answer ready.

"You know how little ones are," she would say with a gentle, sad smile, carefully adjusting her sleeve. "When they feel ignored, they make up stories to get their father's attention. She wants to be the only light in your sky, Rowan. I'm trying my best, but sometimes I worry her mortal blood makes it harder than it should be."

Rowan's jaw tightened at those words. The warning in his eyes was clear. He didn't want anyone to mention Teresa.

But Morvena never said Teresa's name around Escala, at least not directly. Escala knew almost nothing about her real mother, only that she had left when Escala was a baby. Still, Morvena kept that absence fresh with quiet reminders.

Escala learned early that the palace ran on rules, spoken and unspoken, but after she met Rihanna, a black-haired pixie with a reckless streak, those rules began to matter less. The two became inseparable, slipping away into groves and

79

hidden glades, chasing shadows and laughing beneath the roots of the lunasyl trees. Escala stayed outside as often as she could, not only for the freedom of it, but to put distance between herself and Morvena and Audrey.

By her teenage years, Escala no longer questioned who Morvena was; she knew. What she couldn't understand was why her father, proud and stoic Lord Winter, loved someone so empty and hollow.

She tried once to ask about her real mother, but Rowan stopped her. "We're not discussing this," he said. "Not now, not ever."

She never brought it up again.

So there it is: the tangled family tree of Teresa, Rowan, Morvena, Escala, and Audrey.

Now, as Escala's trial approached and tension spread through the palace like ivy on stone, Morvena returned to her favorite pastime: whispering.

Whispering was her gift, and Morvena connected with everyone for the days leading up to the trial. By the time the court was assembled, rumors were circulating throughout the fey. Her goal was simple: to crown her daughter, Audrey, the next princess of the Court of Dreams.

You should know Audrey.

She was Morvena's daughter, fey-born and no less deliberate than her mother. There was something else in her, too, something older, quieter. She had come into being from the spirit of a mortal child who had never drawn breath, a life the True Cycle had turned away.

When Morvena decided to become a mother, she waited at the edge between worlds, looking for a spirit just separated from life, one that never touched the mortal world.

Then she found one and called out softly. "Come to me," she whispered. "I am like you."

One whisper was enough, and the spirit moved toward her.

"Would you be my daughter?" she asked. "Would you become fey, outside the Cycle that cast you aside?"

The spirit said nothing, but its answer was clear. Through magic that mortals can hardly imagine, Morvena drew the soul into her womb. Months later, she gave birth to a pixie girl with shadowy eyes and a smile that never quite reached her cheeks.

She named the girl Audrey.

From Audrey's first breath, Morvena began to whisper, "Mortals ruin everything. They are poison to Valla."

She filled Audrey's head with warnings about mortals, half-truths about Rowan's human lover, and stories about Escala, the fey-touched pixie who stood where Audrey thought she belonged.

Over the years, those words took root. She doesn't deserve to be a princess," Audrey once said.

"She won't be," Morvena replied, tucking a strand of hair behind her ear. "My plans aren't finished yet, and there's still much for you to learn."

And Audrey learned. She smiled when people watched, curtsied when she was supposed to, and laughed at all the right times.

At Morvena's urging, she turned her attention to Escala, studying her every move—the unguarded laughter, the awkward charm of her stumbles, the spark in her eyes whenever she spoke of the mortal world... or of boys. In each misstep, Audrey recognized the very traits she herself had been warned to suppress.

"That crown doesn't belong to her," Audrey said.

"Give me time," Morvena answered.

Then came the "accidents."

When Escala was twelve, her spellbook vanished the night before her Academy trials. Days later, it turned up at the bottom of the scrying well, soaked and unreadable. Audrey had been there, but no one could prove a thing.

At fifteen, Escala wandered alone into the Echoing Glade, where swollen streams coiled like serpents through a tangle of ferns. When her wings snagged on the branches, the current seized her and dragged her under. She nearly drowned that day—her river-warding charm, meant to keep her safe, had come mysteriously untied. There was no proof of foul play, yet whispers began to spread, for Audrey had been seen nearby. The timing, the place, the loosened charm—all of it together painted a picture too suspicious to ignore.

Later that same year, Escala fell ill after a midsummer feast. She had eaten only a handful of sugared berries before her lips turned pale, and her breaths came shallow. The healer called it a simple case of spoiled fruit, but others whispered the berries had been tainted. Once again, there was no proof, but Audrey had been the one seen offering them to her.

Behind closed doors, Morvena would hiss, "Audrey, you're too reckless. Let her bend the rules and get caught. The court will handle the rest and give her the Wane. You'll be princess, and we won't even remember her."

One warm night, Audrey and Morvena sat in the shadows of the Whispering Pavilion, a place where the wind carried no secrets and the walls remembered nothing.

"Escala and Rihanna have been crossing more often," Audrey reported. "They are using a crossing near the mortal city of Dunwell on Valla. They never stay long and are always back before dawn, but they're sloppy."

Morvena smiled, fingers tapping together.

"You have a plan?" Audrey asked.

"I do."

Morvena crossed the moss to a statue, brushed aside ivy, and whispered an arcane phrase. Three stones rose from the water. Beneath them, a small ivory box surfaced. She lifted it and opened it to reveal a velvet pouch.

She pressed it into Audrey's hands.

Inside lay a wolf totem, carved from duskwood, its surface dark and smooth, the lines of the beast etched with a craftsman's care.

Audrey frowned, "What is this?"

"Something I recovered from Teresa's things years ago. She left it in the court when she fled back to Valla," Morvena said. "It's a magical wolf totem."

Audrey ran her fingers over the carving, "What am I supposed to do with it?"

"It will attack whoever you say. Just drop it on the ground."

"You want me to use this?"

Morvena's voice dropped. "Not yet. But one day soon, Escala will stumble, drawn into some foolish pursuit of mortals and love. When she does, you'll follow, and when the moment is right—"

"Release the wolf," Audrey finished for her.

"You are learning." Morvena's smile curved slowly. "In the mortal realm, wolves raise no suspicion. And if a pixie strays too far from a crossing and happens upon a wolf... well..." She paused. "Nature is dangerous, and accidents happen."

Chapter 14

I take a slice of bread, trim a piece of cheese, and lay it on top.

"Some of you sharp listeners might've noticed things aren't unfolding in order as I share this story. That's intentional. I threw you in the fire first, so you'd feel the heat. Now I'm walking you through the ashes, through the backgrounds and histories, so you will understand the motives of the characters in this tale."

I take a bite, chew, and swallow.

"To recap so far: Escala's in her chambers, her wings healing, and her heart bruised. Her father has said goodbye, and she thinks it is because she will get the Wane and be erased and forgotten, but she doesn't know he is risking his rule to try to save her from the Wane. Meanwhile, Morvena's been doing what she always does, spinning whispers into ropes and dragging the court by the neck. She has poisoned the well, turning half the fey nobles against Escala. They're ready to convict her of breaking the Oath—a law her father passed after the human woman he loved vanished into the mortal world. leaving Escala behind.

"And while all that's happening, back in the material plane," I say, "Victor Graves searches for his son, Jonathan, who never came home from gathering herbs, and finds him dead in the woods.

"I think that catches us up. So now I can move the story along, so let's go back to the Court of Dreams, to the secret chamber where Morvena and Audrey often meet to plot."

The room was dark when Audrey arrived. Curtains smothered every crystal window. The enchanted lanterns hung dim in their rings. Even the star-glow fountains were dry. Only a few candles flickered in shallow bowls on the floor, casting nervous pools of light. Morvena stood at the center, hands folded against her chest.

Audrey hesitated, then cleared her throat. "I left it behind."

Morvena turned slowly. "You left what behind?"

"The wolf totem."

"You mean," she said, "the wolf totem I gave you."

Audrey nodded.

"The one you used to attack Escala?"

Audrey looked down and nodded again.

Morvena inhaled slowly. "And you left it where?"

"The glade near Dunwell Crossing, on the mortal side. I had no choice; the crossing was closing. The wolf was still attacking; if I'd called it off, they would've seen me."

Morvena said. "Do you understand what you've done?"

"No one saw me."

"That doesn't matter," Morvena snapped. "Do you think mortals are blind? Do you know how many sorcerers read

85

meaning in every burned leaf and snapped twig? How many hedge witches dream of proof we exist?"

"I was careful."

"You were careless!" Morvena yelled, her voice cracked like a whip. "You think it can't be traced? You commanded it so, it will carry your mark. If someone finds it and brings it back across the veil—"

She cut herself off. She'd let her voice rise too far, too loud for even this room.

Morvena turned her back again, breathing slowly. Audrey shook as she hovered in place.

"Do you remember what I told you about the True Cycle?"

Audrey nodded. "You said we must respect it in public and move around it in private."

"Yes," Morvena hissed. "You never break it outright and never leave a trail."

Outside the Hall of Whispers, the Court of Dreams was already preparing for Escala's trial.

The rumors, carefully seeded over seasons, were now moving like a wildfire through the court.

But now, one misplaced totem could leave a trail that threatened to undo it all, not just the past week's maneuvering, but years of careful, invisible work.

"We have to find it," she growled. "Now, today, before anyone else does, or everything we've built could be ruined."

Audrey asked. "How? The crossing won't open again until tomorrow."

"Then we'll open it ourselves."

Audrey hesitated. "That'll require blood."

Morvena turned slowly. "Then bleed."

"What exactly do you think will happen if someone finds the totem?"

"If it's found by a mortal, maybe nothing. The fey realm doesn't answer to their rules. Most mortals wouldn't even know what they'd found. But if a fey finds it, one who's crossed…"

She stopped, pressing a hand to her forehead.

Audrey kept her voice low. "What then?"

"Then they'll trace it back to me."

It wasn't just evidence; the totem was already linked to the very people Morvena had worked to erase.

And she'd handed it to her daughter like it meant nothing.

"If they connect it to you," she whispered, "they'll ask where it came from. And if it leads to me, they'll question the trial, the attack, everything, and we could both face the Wane."

Not waiting for a reply, Morvena flew from the room, streaking through the corridors with a speed that shattered her usual poise. Her pulse thundered as she dove into the eastern stairwell and vanished into the silent lower halls.

She didn't stop until she reached the Hall of Veils, a shadowed chamber buried deep beneath the Court of

Dreams. It was a dark chamber used for a dark and now forbidden form of crossing known as a blood crossing.

Since fey are pure magic, their death releases that magic back into the fey realm. When one dies, the realm opens to receive it, like a mouth taking a bite, then snapping shut. Clever fey exploit this instinct: a cut deep enough to spill blood convinces the realm they are dying. The veil parts, ready to receive the dying fey, a crossing forms, and the fey can slip through before it closes.

Because the practice was forbidden in the Court of Dreams, Morvena only dared practice it here, in this ancient, hidden chamber. With a blood crossing, she could fix her destination, a place etched in memory, unlike the wild, shifting points of a natural crossing.

Kneeling, she drew a thin shard of bone from her robe, its edge still dark with dried fox blood. She pressed it to her palm and cut. The air trembled, a tunnel appeared, and a forest emerged in the distance.

Behind her, Audrey appeared in the archway, breathless but composed. "You're opening it?"

"Of course I am," Morvena snapped.

"We don't even know if the totem's still there," Audrey said, calm but uncertain.

"I don't care," Morvena said, her voice low and edged with steel. "I will find it."

"And if someone's already picked it up?" Audrey asked.

Morvena looked up, her face hardened. "Then I'll take it from them."

Audrey didn't respond, she knew what that meant. Morvena would leave no witnesses. The crossing buzzed with energy and Morvena stepped through into the material plane.

Chapter 15

———————

It took just a second to cross through the unnatural crossing Morvena had created with her own blood, and she was now hovering above the ferns in the forest near a small clearing and pond. Morvena crouched low in the brush, wings folded as she surveyed the area.

Thirty yards away, an older man knelt with one knee sunk into the earth, his back to her. Sprawled beside him lay a younger man, his limbs twisted at unnatural angles. His throat was torn wide, a gaping ruin of flesh and sinew. Blood soaked his shirt and pooled beneath him, his skin drained to a ghastly, milk-white pallor.

This was the boy the wolf had killed, but who was the other man?

The older man knelt, one hand trembling as he touched the dead man's pale face, while in his other hand he held something small and metallic. The older man raised his hand toward her even though he was not looking at her.

Morvena instantly recognized it and managed to dart upward just in time, as the bolt struck a nearby oak, feet from where she had been hiding. The tree exploded in a shower of splinters and fire. How did he know she was there?

"You left your mark, Escala!" the man bellowed. "I have your necklace, and now you will die!"

A lance of fire erupted from his staff. Morvena twisted through the smoke as the blast tore a crater in the moss.

"I'm not Escala!" she screamed, hurling a bolt of fire. It slammed into the barrier of his shield and hissed away to nothing.

"Liar!" he roared, thrusting his staff toward her. From its tip burst a snarl of arcane webs, lashing through the air.

She moved aside, every ounce of speed and instinct needed to keep her from being ensnared.

"I want her dead too!" she snarled, slinging a blast of Void fire across his shield.

"Lies!"

Morvena raised both hands, catching the spell in a net of arcane threads; his web shattered into sparks.

"You think I'm trading spells to protect her? Please," she yelled.

She dashed behind a tree as he unleashed another attack—a cloud of poison gas that swallowed the ferns where she'd been.

"Who are you?" He hurled magic missiles at her.

She batted aside most of the attacks, but one strand clipped her wing. Agony ripped through her, and she staggered, her wing hissing as it was burned. Through clenched teeth, she cried out, "Why? Why do you want her dead?"

His magic surged again, and another spell burst from his staff, jagged and red. Morvena spun aside as the beam sliced past her ear, scorching bark.

He growled, "She killed my son," his gaze flicking to the boy's body sprawled in the blood-soaked grass. That single glance was all Morvena needed. As his eyes lingered on his son, a whip of shadow snapped from her fingers, coiling around his staff with a venomous hiss. One vicious tug and the weapon tore free, clattering onto the crimson-stained earth.

He stood empty-handed while she hovered ten feet away, wings thrumming, both of them breathless, eyes locked on each other.

"You're not the only one who wants her dead," Morvena said. "You want vengeance? So do I."

The man didn't move. Power still flickered in his hands, but he didn't cast.

Morvena glared at him, magic coiling in her palms. "We can keep trying to kill each other, or we can end her together—your choice."

He narrowed his eyes. "Who are you?"

Morvena's wings twitched, one red with a magic burn, as she bared her teeth in something like a smile. "Someone who hates her just as much as you do."

Neither lowered their guard, but for the first time, they weren't trading spells.

His smile was slow, bitter. "One of your kind stole a woman from me nearly twenty years ago. She said she was going somewhere… fanciful," he continued. "She called it the Court of Dreams." His lip curled. "Sounded like nonsense. But I've learned better than to dismiss nonsense."

Morvena hovered defensively, ready to strike.

"So, tell me, is there such a place?"

"Does it matter?" she asked carefully. "Sounds like it was years ago."

The older man extended his hand, and his staff flew from the ground to his outstretched hand. "She disappeared with a fey prince named Rowan Winter, and now, years later, my son is murdered by a pixie calling herself Escala Winter." His eyes narrowed. "And now you show up, naming the same girl. You're not just a coincidence, you're a thread I've been pulling at for twenty years."

"This woman... what was her name?" Morvena asked.

"You already know," he said.

Morvena smirked. "I know many things."

"You knew Teresa." It wasn't a question.

"She briefly passed through our court."

"Briefly?" His grip on the staff tightened again. There was surprise in his voice, or did she detect hope?

"She left," Morvena added. "Rather quickly."

"What do they call you?" he asked.

Morvena's brow arched. "Why would I tell you that? Names have power," she said. "And I'm not in the habit of giving mine to strangers. Especially ones who throw lightning at my head."

Victor's voice was gravelly. "Fair."

A long silence stretched between them.

Finally, Morvena said, "What was your son's name?"

He looked down again. "Jonathan. And yes, names are powerful, but so am I—you can call me Warlock Graves."

She nodded once, slowly.

Victor glanced up. "And you?"

Morvena gave him a cool look. "Let's just say I hold a position of some significance in the court you're so curious about."

Victor narrowed his eyes. "You're not just *any* pixie, then."

"No," she said. "And I doubt you're just *any* warlock."

They watched each other for a moment—two predators, each calculating the reach of the other's teeth.

Victor's eyes searched hers. "You said Teresa was there for a short while—how short?"

Morvena answered quickly, "She lived among us for less than a year, and that was almost twenty years ago. But she didn't belong there, so she returned to Valla."

"Did she leave alone?"

Morvena hesitated.

"She wasn't the same when she left," Morvena said at last. "She left things behind."

Victor looked puzzled.

"A child," Morvena said.

He didn't respond, but his eyes burned with fury. "You didn't answer my question. What is your name?"

Morvena lifted her chin, just slightly. "Lady Morvena. Of House Winter."

Victor's face hardened.

"Winter. So, it was true," he nearly spat.

"She didn't marry him," Morvena said coolly. "If that's what you're thinking."

Victor's eyes darkened. "Doesn't matter now. She went willingly enough. And this child, this Escala, she is not your child."

Morvena immediately shook her head.

He looked back at the boy, saying nothing for a long moment.

Morvena flew slow circles, adjusting her cloak in measured, elegant gestures, as if unfazed. But inside, her mind was racing.

"Did Escala kill my son?" he muttered, eyes still locked on the pale, lifeless face, lips parted, eyes shut, like sleep had simply overtaken him.

Morvena hovered just above the ground, wings still. Did he have the totem? She couldn't see it, but he could've hidden it, maybe he tucked it in one of those grimy, rune-stitched pockets. If she could stall, she might spot it, snatch it, and vanish.

But if he already had it... she'd need another plan.

Victor turned suddenly. "Well? Did she?"

Morvena raised an eyebrow, cool as frost. "I don't know."

"Don't lie to me," he snapped. His voice lowered to a growl, fingers twitching, spell ready. "I know what happened here."

"A wolf killed your son," Morvena said.

"Yes, a magical wolf summoned from my wolf totem," Victor said as he pulled the wolf totem from a pouch on his belt and showed her.

"It was mine," Morvena said, too quickly. "Teresa gave it to me."

"I gave that totem to Teresa!" Victor snapped. "It was a gift before she spat in my face and ran off with Rowan Winter."

"Where is Rowan?" he hissed. "He stole the love of my life, and I'll never forgive him."

Morvena's smile flickered—cold, calculating. This would be easier than she thought. "No need for theatrics," she purred. "I think you and I are going to be very good friends."

Victor held the totem tight, magic still crackling in his fingers.

Morvena drifted lower, moving slowly. "You're not wrong about Teresa," she said. "Rowan brought her to the court like a prize, and everything changed, but she couldn't handle fey life. She abandoned her child," she added. "Fled back to your world and left Escala behind."

She circled slightly, watching him. "After she vanished, I found the totem. I discovered its power, and my daughter Audrey and I—well, we tried to use it to get rid of Escala. And we nearly did," Morvena said, "until she turned her fey charms on your son."

Victor looked down at the wolf totem in his hand and then over to the bloodstained earth by his dead son.

"You married Rowan after Teresa left. Why?"

Morvena paused. That was an abrupt change in direction. Why did he care? She thought for a moment about how to answer. If a courtier had asked, she'd have given the noble version—fey traditions, eternal love, all of it. But here, with a warlock who might be useful, there was no need to pretend.

"For power," she said.

A smile crept across Victor's face.

"You want Rowan dead."

Morvena showed a wicked smile. "He's my husband. Why would I want him dead?"

Victor crouched by his son and gently closed his eyes. Then he stood.

"You want Escala gone."

"Escala is in the way," Morvena said.

"And you want to be the queen of the Court of Dreams." He said, "I can make that happen."

She smiled, folding her arms across her chest.

"And in return?" she asked.

"You help me get my revenge," Victor said.

"You mean Rowan."

"*Yes*, I mean Rowan," Victor said in an annoyed tone.

Morvena was silent for a moment, then said flatly, "You're talking about murdering the lord of the Court of Dreams—my husband."

Victor shrugged. "I'm talking about planting a seed."

"Don't be coy," she said.

"You just have to plant an item—you're only making a delivery for me in the Court of Dreams," Victor explained.

Morvena flew in a wary circle. "And what am I delivering?"

"A totem," Victor said. "It's a wooden stick, about two feet long. You'll plant it in soil in the fey realm, in your palace or central area of your court, and when the time is right… you will activate it."

She stopped moving. "And it kills him."

"No, it won't kill him."

"I don't understand then, what is the point of the totem?" Morvena asked.

"It will act as a beacon for me, so I can find the Court of Dreams. Once I know where it is, I will take care of Rowan personally."

Morvena's mouth curved into a thoughtful line as Victor said, "Plant the totem, and I will clear the way for you to become Queen of the Court of Dreams. I will get my revenge against Rowan and Escala."

She studied him as Victor extended his hand.

Morvena looked down at it, broad, human, and still smeared with fresh blood, before placing her own tiny pixie fingers against his palm. His skin radiated a rough human warmth; hers was cool and delicate, almost weightless. Old grudges and new power met there, sealing their wordless contract in the mingling of forbidden interference with the True Cycle and blood.

Chapter 16

After they finished sealing their partnership, Victor let go and knelt beside Jonathan's corpse. He opened a pouch; inside were two thin, rune-inscribed bracers. He fitted one onto each of his dead son's wrists and whispered an arcane word. The glyphs on the bracers glowed, dimly at first, then brighter. Jonathan's body jolted, then he slowly sat up and opened his gray, lifeless eyes.

Victor stood.

Jonathan did too.

The corpse moved obediently.

Victor didn't touch him.

"Come, let's go to my tower. I'll give you the totem."

A few minutes later, Victor cast a teleport spell, and in an instant, the three of them stood in his study at Blackthorn Tower.

He strode to a massive wooden chest and waved a hand over it, disabling the magical wards before lifting the lid.

From within, he retrieved a long, thin bundle wrapped in black cloth and handed it to her. It was about two feet long and as thick as a teakwood cane, its weight unsettling. Faintly pulsing runes and symbols wound along its length. Forged from black, spined metal, sharp, uneven, and threaded with jagged teeth, it looked as if it had been carved from the dying heart of a god.

"What is it?"

"The Vorrash Totem," Victor said. "I carved this from teakwood; it is the only one of its kind. All I need you to do is plant it about a foot deep in soil, ideally near the center of power in the court. Is there such a place?"

She nodded, thinking of the central gardens.

"You'll take it back," he said. "Plant it but make sure it is hidden. When the time is right, I'll activate it and deal with Rowan."

She nodded slowly. "And Escala?"

Victor handed her the wolf totem. "Yours to deal with however you please."

Morvena took the wolf totem and slipped it into a pouch on her belt.

And with that, they sealed their unholy alliance: a warlock hollowed by grief and a queen-in-waiting poisoned by ambition—each bearing a grudge that could tear the realms apart.

Chapter 17

When the fey guards came for Escala at dawn, she was already awake—she hadn't slept. All night, she'd stared at the crystal ceiling, haunted by Rihanna's screams and the wolf's snarls. Her heart was shattered, but her tears had long since dried.

When the door creaked open, she rose before they spoke.

Two guards entered silent, faces downcast. One stepped forward and extended a hand. "It's time."

She walked with them, her wing hanging useless at her side.

They passed the Hall of Petals, white blossoms swaying in preserved magic, where she once laughed with Rihanna. Then the Sapphire Corridor, walls aglow with pale blue light, floating gardens drifting beyond the windows, gardens where they had chased dragonflies.

The spiral path curved downward, opal tiles gleaming.

The last time she'd come this way, she'd been carried, broken, wrapped in bloodied cloth.

Now she walked alone, and it felt worse.

She felt a growing warmth in her skin, followed by a tightening in her stomach that bordered on pain. She straightened her posture as she walked, recalling her training, but it offered no relief.

The corridor widened abruptly into the Star Gallery. The doors, towering at least twelve spans high, were inscribed with ancient script encircling the True Cycle.

A guard stepped forward and pushed the doors open. Beyond them, the chamber was already full.

Every seat was occupied, the room's edges were lined, and even the upper balconies were filled with fey leaning forward to watch.

This was the Dream Weaver's court.

The Dream Weaver did not rule there; her father did, but he was here now, observing.

Her steps echoed sharply as she was led forward, louder than expected in such a large room. She kept her gaze lowered, focused ahead of her feet. Looking up felt too risky; if she met their eyes or saw their judgment, she might not be able to continue.

The chamber formed a wide circle, and overhead, the crystal dome scattered daylight into shifting colors across the smooth marble floor.

They were all watching.

The balconies curved around her, rising in tiers, filled with fey who had fallen into a kind of quiet that was not truly silence.

She stepped into the center of the court, and the guards withdrew silently, leaving her standing alone.

At the far end, the High Seat formed a pale crescent of moonwood and flame glass. Dream Weaver Volpe Inferna sat there with relaxed confidence, one leg crossed, his posture loose yet never careless. His white hair was tied back, his robes unremarkable, and he just watched.

Beside him stood Rowan.

She did not mean to look.

But she did.

The crown caught the light, silver and cold, its sharp edges clearly not ceremonial. It did not rest easily on him today.

She lowered her gaze again before she could think better of it.

Along the curve of the chamber, the judges waited.

She could not take in all the judges at once; her attention shifted from one to another. The blind judge faced her as if sight was unnecessary. Another tapped his fingers steadily on his seat. The armored woman watched with a fixed, unyielding expression. One judge smiled—

That smile lingered too long.

There was nothing there to read at all.

Then three chimes sounded; the trial had begun.

The Court Recorder stepped forward, a silver-barked dryad. In a loud, but emotionless voice, she said, "Escala of the Court of Dreams," she said, "you stand before this assembly charged with high violations of fey law. Your actions have destabilized the realms and resulted in two confirmed deaths: Rihanna of the Spring Vale, and a mortal man."

Murmurs rippled through the gallery. Escala's stomach knotted.

The Recorder continued, voice cold and echoing:

"You are accused of the following: unauthorized crossing into the material plane; breach of the Oath of Contact; concealment of prolonged mortal interaction; failure to report a binding ritual of emotional significance; and, most grievously, culpability in the death of a fellow fey brought on by reckless, gross negligence."

The murmurs grew louder, voices of outrage, until Lord Rowan raised his gavel and struck it with a sharp crack, silencing the Star Gallery.

The Recorder continued, "Lastly, you're charged with interference in the True Cycle itself, an act that caused the death of a mortal soul, and irreversible harm to the material plane."

She looked down at Escala from her high place. "How do you answer these charges?"

Escala lifted her eyes to the Dream Weaver.

Her voice was soft. "I'm sorry," she said, "I didn't mean for this to happen. I never meant to hurt anyone. Rihanna was my best friend." Her voice caught. "I loved her like a sister, and he was just a young man; he didn't deserve to die. I didn't know there was a wolf."

Her voice trembled, but she didn't cry. "I'm so sorry."

Some fey in the gallery shifted, and a few nobles lowered their eyes, but most remained unmoved. In the Court of Dreams, sorrow didn't erase mistakes, and emotion carried no weight against order.

Audrey rose without being called. Her pale robes swished as she stepped from the front row into the speaking ring. Her expression was calm, almost cool, and when she spoke, her clear voice carried the practiced ease of something well-rehearsed.

"Members of the court," she began, "you've heard her apology. You've heard her admit everything. The law is not unclear. We do not exist to feel. We exist to protect the balance. Escala broke the Oath that protects us all," Audrey said, voice cracking with sorrow. "Yes, she is my sister,"

She looked over at Escala. Audrey was crying, wiping her tears. She said, "I'm sorry, Escala, I love you."

Escala looked disgusted.

Turning back to the court, she continued, "I love her so much, and that is why testifying today is so hard. But I will not let family blind me to duty. That's why I reported what I saw at Dunwell Crossing when I found her nearly dead. I could've said nothing to protect her, but I didn't because the Oath matters more."

She wiped more tears.

"I was close to Rihanna, closer than anyone outside my family. She was kind, and she believed in the Oath, in the sacred balance of the True Cycle. And now she's gone, because of reckless disregard and, honestly, selfishness."

Audrey dabbed her eyes.

Escala seethed. They were never friends—Audrey had despised Rihanna. Such brazen lies!

"That loss will never stop hurting," Audrey said. "Not for me, not for any of us."

Audrey continued to dab at her wet eyes. "I tried to set an example for Escala, since I'm her older sister. I honored the court and kept the Oath. I even stood up for Escala when no one else would. And now," she said, her voice catching, "now I stand here, ashamed that I couldn't stop her. That I failed to guide her away from this reckless, selfish path."

She turned to the noble fey. "I owe this court an apology for not speaking up sooner. I thought she might change, that one day she'd understand what it means to be royalty. I see now I was wrong."

Escala clenched her fists.

Audrey sighed, her voice shaking with sadness. "For the good of our people and the balance we are sworn to keep, I call upon the Wane." Her words echoed in the hall. "If we excuse this and look away, we invite ruin into the court. Don't you see? If we value intent over consequences, others will follow. Other fey will think that meaning no harm is enough if their hearts are pure. But they won't notice the damage until it's too late. In their innocence, they'll undo everything we've worked to protect. The True Cycle could break from curiosity or carelessness. That's why we must remember what's at stake."

She looked at Escala, her eyes shining. "Sister, I'm so sorry for what is happening to you. But our laws are not suggestions, and they weren't written to punish. They were written to protect."

Escala had never been close to Audrey. They were too different, too often at odds. But this was something else entirely.

She took a sharp breath and stared across the chamber, frozen. Her wings trembled with disbelief. Audrey's voice still echoed in her ears, but no longer sounded familiar.

This wasn't rivalry. It was betrayal.

Audrey stepped back, wiped her eyes, and folded her hands. She glanced up at the gallery just long enough to see Morvena's approving smile and its clear message: *Well done, daughter.*

Escala kept her gaze fixed on the floor, hands still balled in fists in front of her, in quiet acceptance. She didn't expect mercy.

At the top of the chamber, the Recorder raised her staff and struck the ceremonial bell. Three times it rang through the hall.

"The evidence has been presented," she declared. "The accused has spoken. All bound to the authority of the Court of Dreams shall now enter deliberation."

Without a word, the six judges stood. Lord Rowan Winter was first. His silver-trimmed robes trailed behind him as he lifted into the air and flew from the Star Gallery, head bowed. One by one, the others followed.

Morvena, seated with perfect stillness in the gallery, caught the eyes of more than one judge.

Had Escala seen it, she might have understood how little hope remained, how far the betrayal reached.

Escala looked up at the crystal dome. Light drifted across the floor like stardust. She remembered lying beneath it with Rihanna when they were children, their wings touching as they dreamed aloud to the stars. Back then, the dome felt magical. Now it felt brittle and cold.

An hour passed before the judges returned, gliding in with solemn eyes. Hope faded from her. Everyone looked to Lord Rowan. He hadn't spoken to Escala or even looked at her, but now his gaze turned to where she stood.

She looked older than he remembered. He saw Teresa in her: wild, golden hair, bright blue eyes, a spark for adventure. He remembered her laughter echoing through ivy-lined halls, her endless questions, always asking why.

He had loved Teresa more than anything, but to protect the court and give Escala a chance at a normal life, he let that love go. Now their daughter stood alone before judgment. Once again, the same cruel choice rose before him: the law or the girl. The court or his blood.

He had lost Teresa to duty. Now the court demanded justice, and Escala would bear the cost. He had done what he could and could only hope that one day she might forgive him.

The Recorder stood again.

She now held a scroll, freshly sealed with the crest of the High Seat. Her voice filled the Star Gallery again, calm and cold.

"The court has reached its verdict."

Escala did not lift her head.

"The accused has been found guilty of gross violations of fey law, with consequences extending to both the dream realm and the material plane. The court recognizes these violations were not born of malice but of recklessness, naivety, and emotional instability."

A few scattered gasps moved through the crowd.

Audrey glanced at Morvena, who gave the faintest hint of a smile, so subtle it could have been a shadow. The Recorder continued, "However, this court has not ordered the Wane."

Gasps of shock filled the court.

Escala looked up at once. She blinked, unable to process what she had heard.

Audrey looked stunned, her composure slipping for the first time. Next to her, Morvena stood up quickly, eyes narrowed and lips pressed together.

No Wane?

Then what?

The Recorder went on, "Instead, the Court of Dreams, as allowed by ancient fey law, has voted to enact a sentence of Divine Reformation, a rare but lawful alternative, reserved for those who remain capable of balance, if not redemption."

Lord Rowan sat rigid, unmoving, like a boulder that would not move.

The Recorder unrolled the scroll with careful precision.

Her voice was calm and steady as she spoke:

"By decree of this court, Escala Winter of the Court of Dreams is stripped of title, rights, and station. Her claim to the royal line is severed. Because she chose the form of a female elf to trespass against the True Cycle, that form shall become her prison. She shall walk the material plane as a high elf, bound to mortal flesh yet still subject to fey mortality."

A hush fell over the chamber. Even the air seemed heavier. No one had expected this sentence, least of all Morvena.

"Escala Winter has disrupted the True Cycle through actions that led to the death of a mortal. She has introduced boulders into the Cycle, disruptions that burden its sacred flow. For this, she is sentenced to the material plane to remove the boulders from the True Cycle. When she has done so, she may petition the Court of Dreams for reinstatement.

"Until her task is complete, Escala Winter is banished to the material plane and forbidden from returning to the fey realm. Upon completion of her quest to remove the boulders, she may present herself at a fey crossing and formally petition this court for a review of her sentence. Until such time, she is exiled."

Escala was in shock. What did this mean? What were boulders?

The Recorder's voice rang clear and solemn through the crystalline chamber:

"Thus concludes the judgment of the Court of Dreams."

A gasp echoed, then a voice cracked through the stillness.

"Outrageous!" Morvena roared, rising like a viper.

On the dais, Lord Rowan Winter stood and raised the ceremonial hammer. "It is ordered," Lord Winter said, bringing the hammer down with a sharp crack as the Recorder lowered the scroll.

"This is not justice!" screamed Morvena.

The Dream Weaver's hand rose, and a beam of pale light rose from the center of the circle. From it, a web of ancient glyphs lit beneath Escala's knees, runes older than the court itself, drawn in the voice of the Song.

Escala barely had time to breathe before the transformation began. Her frame shifted, quietly at first, then with a strange, stretching pull. She grew taller. Her limbs elongated, her body filling out into that of a female elf maiden.

The glow of fey magic flickered away from her skin, as if unwilling to follow her into whatever came next. Escala's wings, once bright and translucent, crumbled into light and vanished. Her balance faltered. She felt the earth beneath her feet, solid, heavy, claiming her. Her ears reshaped, lengthening into the smooth, pointed edges of an elf. Her hands looked strange, longer fingers, broader palms. She turned them over slowly.

Her voice, if she spoke, would sound different now. Everything had changed except her long blonde hair and blue eyes. Her robe unraveling into light, then reweaving into a fitted navy-blue tunic trimmed with silver. A black leather belt cinched her waist, with pouches and a satchel at her hip.

A modest pack settled across her shoulders. At her side, a longsword hung in a plain scabbard. A shield formed in her hand. Its weight caught her breath, not because she knew how to use it, but because now she might have to.

No longer a pixie, Escala stood transformed at the center of the court. She rose slightly from the stone floor, arms at her sides, legs straight. Slowly, she turned in the air, as if to face the court one last time, but her eyes searched only for one person: Rowan.

He stood as well, lifting into the air to meet her gaze. And just before the spell's light flared and swept her into the veil, she caught something in his eyes—relief.

Then the light bloomed, and she was gone.

Chapter 18

A s the Dream Weaver's magic ebbed, Escala's senses returned. She could hear the whisper of the wind through the trees, see birds taking flight, and feel the crispness of the morning air.

She staggered, unsteady on long legs, the sword at her hip dragging heavy, the shield on her arm cumbersome. Clutching a low branch, she wobbled toward a pond a dozen paces away and knelt.

The still water showed a young female elf, five-foot-three, wingless. The face was hers, yet not: cheeks sharper, jaw more defined, ears pointed. Her golden hair still fell in waves down her back, and her vivid blue eyes remained unmistakable.

She touched an ear, trembling. She looked beautiful, striking, but like a stranger wearing her eyes.

The sword clanged against her thigh. She drew it, startled by its weight, the grip wrong in her hand, before sheathing it. The shield on her other arm was too heavy, and she tore it off, letting it thud into the dirt.

She wandered the clearing until a patch of brittle, brown grass caught her eye, as if the roots had been poisoned. Flies drifted above the ferns, their lazy buzz heavy in the air.

Without meaning to, she stepped toward it, and then she saw the stains: dried blood. Two patches—one small and dark, pooled beneath crushed ferns; the other larger, black at the edges, sunk deep, as if it had been clawed into the earth.

Escala dropped to her knees, hands hovering over the marks. This was where it happened—where Rihanna died. And the young man. She'd been sent back here, to the place where her kiss had unraveled everything.

Escala folded at the edge of the clearing, resting her forehead on her knees.

"I'm so sorry, Rihanna," she whispered, "I'm so—"

But she didn't finish, because a twig snapped behind her—then another snap—followed by the low shuffle of something heavy moving through the trees.

She rose quickly, drawing her sword and gripping it with both hands. It felt wrong, too heavy.

She turned in a full circle. "Stay back!" she barked. "I mean it! I'm armed!"

She pivoted again, scanning the trees, heart hammering. Nothing, just the wind whispering through the leaves. After a long, tense moment, she lowered the sword slightly.

"I'm not afraid to use this," she called out, though her voice faltered.

She glanced at the fern bush in front of her—the same one that had sprung her through the crossing. The same one where Rihanna had fallen.

Here, this exact spot, had been her best friend's final flight, her final scream, her final breath. It had happened here.

The ferns still leaned at odd angles, pressed down by the wolf. Escala reached out with trembling fingers and brushed one of the leaves, as if touching it might bring her closer to her lost friend.

She switched the sword to her right hand and gently stroked the leaves with her left.

"I'm so sorry, Rihanna. I miss you; I wish I could bring you back."

Behind her, a gravel-rough voice growled.

She spun, instincts flaring, gripping the sword again with both hands.

A hulking, shaggy orc emerged from the trees, smirking, flipping a massive battle axe between thick fingers. He smelled like old, rotten meat.

He gave her a crooked grin, pure evil in his eyes.

"Stay back!" Escala shouted, blade raised.

The orc circled her, axe swinging idly as he tossed it from one hand to the other.

Escala retreated a step, then another, trying to get behind a large nearby boulder, but the orc cut her off, forcing her back until she stumbled over a half-buried log.

With a guttural roar, he sprang forward, swinging the axe down in a vicious arc.

She ducked, rolled over the log just in time, sword flailing as she scrambled to her feet. The axe struck wood where her head had been, sending splinters flying.

The orc made a low rasp as he wrenched the weapon free. He swung again, this time straight at her blade.

She tried to parry, but the force of his swing shattered her guard. The impact rang through her arms, and her sword flew into the underbrush with a metallic thud.

She gasped, staring at her empty hands.

The orc advanced, teeth bared.

She scrambled over the log again, grabbing the first thing she could, a rotting branch. She brandished it like a spear, trembling.

The orc snorted and lurched forward, bringing his axe down in a wide arc, snapping the branch like kindling.

Escala fell again, scrambling backward through leaves and bramble.

The orc kept coming, growling as he sniffed the air.

She crab-walked frantically, hands and feet scrambling over the dirt, stomach to the sky, never taking her eyes off him. Her heels dug in until her back struck a tree.

She was trapped, and he'd be on her in seconds.

Instinct took over, her fingers clawed up a fistful of dirt and gravel.

The orc loomed, axe raised, his breath hot and foul against her face.

With a scream, she hurled the grit into his eyes.

He howled, staggering back, clutching at his face.

Escala rolled, sprang up, and bolted. She tore through the brush, branches whipping her hair, cheeks, and arms, ferns snagging her ankles, and didn't dare look back.

He came crashing after her, howling and swearing, smashing through the undergrowth like a boar.

But she was fast, far faster than him. Branches lashed her arms and face, brambles clawed at her legs, roots tried to trip her, but she tore through the underbrush, nimble and desperate. She ran until the trees blurred together, until the light grew soft and gray, until she couldn't hear anything but her own breathing.

Eventually, the crashing behind her faded as she ducked behind a moss-laced tree, her chest rising and falling in ragged bursts. She listened, heart pounding in her ears. She heard nothing—the orc was gone. She stood still, chest heaving, forcing herself to breathe until the edge of panic dulled. Then she took stock. Of all the things the Dream Weaver had given her, only a small leather pouch remained.

She opened it. Inside was a thin notebook and a flint pencil. Odd. She checked again, hoping for food, but found nothing more.

Night fell as she built a crude lean-to beneath a crooked tree. Sliding down the trunk, arms around her knees, she sat—cold, hungry, and afraid. Escala stayed motionless in the dark, sweat and dirt clinging to her, hair matted with leaves and twigs. She whispered, "I don't know how to do this."

Chapter 19

L ooking at the crowd, I say, "How many of you can identify with Escala's first day on Valla?" More than a couple of hands rise, and I notice some nods.

"I can't begin to grasp the full weight of it," I say. "Imagine, one moment you're banished from your home, and the next, you're alone in the forest, in the very spot where your best friend died because of your carelessness.

"You're in a body that doesn't feel like yours. You've never held a sword before, and suddenly you're face to face with an orc that wants to split you in two. You run and somehow survive. But now your weapon is gone, and you're cold, hungry, afraid, and alone. You know nothing—absolutely nothing—about survival or even where you are."

I sweep my eyes across the crowd. "Close your eyes for a second and try to imagine how terrifying that would be."

I let that sink in for a moment. "Well, let's see if her second day is any better as we return to her little lean-to."

I continue the story.

The scent of herbs and smoked rabbit woke her before the light. She lay still, stiff-legged and aching from the cold. Her stomach growled. Opening her eyes, she sat up, muscles protesting, and saw that her arms had been scratched during her flight from the orc. Following the smell down a narrow slope, she found a cabin tucked by a bend in the stream;

weathered but well kept, built from thick logs and rough stone.

Smoke rose from a crooked chimney. A stack of firewood leaned against one side of the cabin, and near the front step, a pot bubbled over a fire ringed with stones. Escala crouched behind a tree. Minutes passed, and Escala heard no voices and saw no movement. The stew's aroma clawed at her stomach, but caution whispered. She had no idea who lived here—bandit, orc, or worse. But she couldn't turn back. Not with her legs trembling and her belly hollow from hunger. She crept from cover toward the pot. Her plan was simple: grab it and run.

The door creaked open, and Escala was caught out in the open. An athletic woman in her mid-twenties stepped from the cabin, her black boots crunching against the packed dirt. Her armor—black leather, battle-worn, and close-fitted—hugged her frame, its red-trimmed seams tracing reinforced panels along the chest, shoulders, and elbows. A dark burn scar edged into view at the opening of her tunic, an old wound half hidden yet impossible to miss. A crimson sash rode her hips, its ends flicking in the air as she moved. The way the leather shifted with her stride reminded Escala of a predator—coiled, waiting to strike.

The woman's hair—jet black with a single white streak—was tied back in a short, unruly ponytail. Escala's eyes went to the scars: one cut through her right eyebrow as if a blade had tried to split her face, another pulled at the corner of her mouth, and the most striking ran from cheekbone to chin, giving her a dangerous edge. At her hip rested a finely wrought knife, carried as naturally as an extension of her hand.

The black-haired woman locked eyes with Escala, standing just feet from the fire, and her hand instantly moved to the knife. Her green gaze gleamed with sharp amusement and the wild edge of someone who would jump off a cliff just to see the bottom. It swept over Escala, quick, assessing, not entirely kind.

The woman took in Escala's empty scabbard, ragged tunic, and tear-stained cheeks. She eased her grip on the hilt and said, "By the hells, who are you?"

Escala's hands twitched at her sides, fingers brushing the empty scabbard. She looked like she hadn't slept—mud-caked, scratched arms, red eyes, leaves tangled in her long blonde hair. Then she straightened, shoulders back and chin up, trying to look like she belonged, and said, "I am Escala Winter, a pixie from the Court of Dreams."

The woman erupted into laughter, startling a crow in a nearby tree. "A pixie?" she choked out, clutching her stomach. "Oh, that's rich." She snickered. "Where're your wings?"

"They were… removed," Escala said stiffly.

"Removed?"

The woman, still giggling, began circling Escala, eyeing her from head to toe like she was searching for a hidden trick. Her gaze lingered on the cuts and scrapes on Escala's arms.

"You lose a fight with a bush? Or did you take a fall and bump your head? Maybe eat some hallucinogenic mushrooms?"

"No," Escala said.

The woman was unconvinced. "You sure? You're dirty, scraped up, weaponless, and talking nonsense about being a pixie. I'm just making sure that you don't have a concussion, or that we have some kind of mushroom thing going on here."

Escala lifted her chin. "I'm fine."

The woman cocked her head, lips pursed as if to say, "Really?"

"And I am a pixie," Escala declared.

"I thought pixies were tiny and had butterfly wings. I hate to break it to you, sweetie, but you're an elf."

"I wasn't always."

The woman gave her a long look.

"I'm on a quest," Escala added, more confidently, "to remove the boulders from the True Cycle, so I can return to the Court of Dreams."

"Say what now?"

"Do you have any boulders in your life I can help remove?" Escala asked hopefully.

The woman whistled. "What have you been drinking? I need some of that."

"I'm not drunk," Escala answered defensively.

"Well then," the woman said. She yelled at the cabin, "Roedyn!"

No answer.

She called again, louder, "Roedyn!"

A muffled male voice grumbled from inside. "What is it, Harper?"

"Get out here! You've got to see this. We've got a real live pixie out here."

A few moments passed.

She yelled again, "Roedyn! It's a pixie. Hurry, she wants to see your boulders!"

"A pixie?" came a groggy voice from behind the door.

The door creaked open, revealing a lean, pale man with broad shoulders and muscular arms, his sharp elven cheekbones and pointed ears mirroring Escala's. His long black hair was tied back in a tight bun, the tips of his ears peeking through. A jagged scar ran beneath one eye: under the other, a small tattoo—a black slash like a falling tear. Faintly glowing tattoos curled down his forearms like whispered incantations, pulsing softly in the low light. He wore scuffed brown leather armor, patched more for utility than show, and sleep still clung to his face.

"Boulders? What are you talking about?" he muttered, rubbing his eyes.

"Come on, Roedyn," the woman said with a wicked grin. "This pixie says she's from the Court of Dreams."

He glanced at Escala. Then at Harper. Then back at Escala. "Okay," he said dryly. "Where's the pixie?"

Harper pointed at Escala with both hands, rocking on the balls of her feet, her lips twitching, trying to keep a straight face.

"Right here," Harper said, barely holding back laughter.

Roedyn looked Escala up and down, then turned back to Harper and exploded into fits of laughter.

Escala's eyes flared. "I *AM* a pixie!"

Roedyn snorted. "Sure you are, and I'm a unicorn. Where're your wings?"

"They were removed by court order," Escala snapped.

"Which court?" Roedyn asked.

"The Court of Dreams," Escala said, impatiently.

"I've never heard of it, have you, Harper?" Roedyn said.

"Nope." Harper said.

"It's in the fey realm." Escala answered.

"Ok, then," Roedyn said, studying her closely and then folding his arms. "Where's your sword?"

Escala glanced at the empty scabbard. "I, um… lost it. There was an orc." She quickly added, "Really big—he took it from me."

"Did you lead him here?" Roedyn asked, his hand instinctively going to his dagger as his eyes swept the tree line.

"N-no!" Escala stammered. "I ran away and lost him yesterday. I found your cabin because I was hungry, and I smelled your cooking."

Roedyn and Harper shared a look, then studied Escala with wary curiosity, each trying to figure out what she was really after.

She looked at each of them in turn and added, "I'm hungry, but I'm sorry if I disturbed the harmony of your marital dwelling." She started to back away. "I'll just go."

Harper and Roedyn burst into laughter again—Roedyn slapped his knee while Harper clapped her hands, laughing so hard she doubled over, gasping for breath between fits of hysterics.

Escala looked confused. "What? What did I say?"

Harper wiped a tear from her eye. "Marital dwelling?" She clapped. "That's a good one!"

"I assumed you were a mated pair. You're living together in a single-room cottage. Isn't that what married couples do?"

Harper coughed, stifling another laugh. "We're not married."

"Oh." Escala tilted her head. "Well then, why not?"

Roedyn opened his mouth, closed it, and opened it again. "What's that have to do with anything?"

Escala raised her brows. "Look, I'm not from here, and I don't know your customs and ways, and I don't even know your full names. Perhaps that's the problem."

Harper, still giggling, gave a little bow. "Harper Darrow. Firestarter sorceress, sword master, and a walking headache to anyone who deserves it, and, on occasion, a monster hunter."

"I'm Roedyn Hammerfell," he said, folding his arms across his chest. "I'm a scout and tracker for hire, and for the record, definitely not her husband," he added, nodding toward Harper.

"Not her husband?" Escala said, her voice perking up. "Why not—don't you love Harper?" There was genuine surprise in her question.

Roedyn choked. "I—what? That's not—I mean—"

Harper turned on him, hands on her hips, smirking. "Yeah, Roedyn. Enlighten us—why don't you love me?" Clearly, she was enjoying this.

"I didn't say I didn't—" He groaned, rubbing his forehead. "Can we not have this conversation?"

Escala glanced at them, baffled. "But... you live together, and in just these five minutes I've heard you bicker and laugh like mated cliff birds. From your own words, you hunt together, share meals, and you're telling me you're not in love?"

"We're business partners," Harper said with a dry chuckle. "Monster contracts, killing beasts, dangerous errands, escorting caravans—basic adventurers for hire, that's it."

"And no romantic obligations," Roedyn added.

"Oh," Escala said. "In the Court of Dreams, you'd be legally soul-bound by now."

Harper snorted. "Then it's a good thing we're not in the Court of Dreams."

Roedyn muttered, "Thank the gods for that."

Escala folded her arms, still trying to make sense of it. "I just don't understand how can you spend so much time together, share your lives so closely, and not fall in love? Maybe it's because you've never kissed."

Seeing their confused looks, she said, "You haven't kissed yet, have you?"

"That's none of your business," Roedyn immediately snapped.

Harper laughed. "If my choices were between a drunk billy goat and him, I'd kiss the goat."

Roedyn glared.

"Well, that's why you're not in love," Escala said matter-of-factly. "You'll fall in love after you kiss." She nodded, as if that settled everything.

Harper and Roedyn exchanged another look that plainly asked, "Is she serious?"

Roedyn said, "I think there's a lot more to it than that."

"Oh, there is," Harper said playfully. "Otherwise, Roedyn would be head over heels for the large woman who darned his long johns at last year's harvest festival."

Roedyn turned beet red. "I just kissed her on the cheek!"

Harper said, "Ah, but you kissed her, though."

"And she was my aunt!" Roedyn yelled.

"Hey, I didn't make up these love rules, she did," Harper said, pointing at Escala. "She said you'd fall in love with a kiss," Harper added, straight-faced.

I look out at the crowd in The Stag and say, "Escala got into this whole mess because she was trying to understand love—with a kiss. And now she was even more confused. The first couple she met wasn't married, yet they lived exactly as married people in love might…and she couldn't understand why they denied it. Funny thing is, there are plenty who are married and live together without a hint of love, just saying. Maybe, just maybe, by the end of my tale tonight, if that's you, you'll think about love a little differently… maybe even remember why you wanted it in the first place."

I flash a grin. "But enough of that. Let's get back to Escala's meeting with Roedyn and Harper."

Roedyn was the first to change the subject. "So let me get this straight, you were kicked out of something called the Court of Dreams? Harper, have you ever heard of this place?"

"Nope," Harper said.

"It's in the fey realm," Escala answered. "And you haven't heard of it because we're not supposed to reveal ourselves to mortals."

Escala knew she couldn't remove the boulders alone, she would need help. And to get that help, she'd have to tell the truth, so she did.

"But I did reveal myself," she admitted. "I broke our laws, and I interfered with the True Cycle, and for that, I was banished. Now I've been sent here to fix it by removing boulders."

Harper leaned over to Roedyn and whispered, "She's definitely drunk."

Roedyn ignored her and clapped a hand on Escala's shoulder.

The moment his hand brushed her shoulder, Escala flinched, knocking it away. "*Don't touch me!*" she shouted, voice sharp as she jumped back, ready to run.

"*No one touches the faerie!*"

Roedyn's eyes widened, and Harper's hand went to her knife.

Escala quickly raised both palms, stepping back. "I'm sorry, please... don't touch me."

Roedyn held his hands up slowly. His voice was calm. "Didn't mean to scare you; it was just a friendly pat."

Harper didn't let go of the knife hilt, still watching Escala.

Escala's chest heaved once, then steadied. She lowered her hands. "I'm... I'm sorry I yelled. I don't like being touched."

Roedyn and Harper exchanged a glance, unreadable, but respectful.

"You've got nothing to apologize for," Roedyn said gently. "No one's going to touch you. Promise."

Escala studied his expression. Something in his face, maybe the calm in his eyes, helped her breathe again. The tension in her shoulders loosened.

Escala slowly softened.

Harper let her hand fall away from the knife.

Roedyn said, "Come inside and have breakfast with us. You can tell us about your quest, boulders and all."

Escala hesitated, then followed, drawn by the scent of rabbit stew and fresh bread.

As they entered, Harper looked at Roedyn, who shrugged.

The cabin was a one-room hunting shelter, plain but clearly lived in. Two beds sat opposite each other, piled with tangled wool blankets. A rough table and log benches filled the center. Cloaks and a few weapons hung from hooks. A kettle swayed over the fire. The air smelled of smoke, leather, and herbs.

They handed her a plate: soft bread and a steaming rabbit stew. She ate slowly at first, cautious, then faster, seemingly forgetting the uncomfortable talk about touching just minutes earlier.

Harper sat cross-legged by the hearth, poking at the flames with a stick that sparked red every time she muttered. Roedyn stood nearby, arms folded, quietly watching Escala with the wary stillness of a man who trusted slowly, if ever.

After the second bowl of stew, Harper asked, "So. What's your story, elf-girl?"

Escala wiped her mouth. "I'm not an elf."

Harper raised an eyebrow. "You look very elf."

"I already told you, I wasn't born this way," Escala said. "I was changed."

"Let me guess," Roedyn said, settling against the wall. "Cursed by a witch, raised by wolves, and now you're on a quest to avenge your beloved pet raccoon, probably named Nicky, or something equally tragic."

Harper cackled. "Oh gods, I hope it's that one."

"No," Escala said firmly. "I was born fey in the Court of Dreams, in the fey realm. I was a pixie."

Harper stared, mid-chew, as if trying to decide whether to laugh or choke.

Roedyn said, "You... really were a pixie? So you weren't just telling me a story to get a meal?"

"Yes, I mean no." Escala struggled. "I am a pixie, or was, but I did want a meal."

Harper laughed.

Roedyn, trying to be serious, asked, "And you had wings, fairy dust, sang songs in the moonlight, and could steal babies—that kind of pixie?"

"No!" Escala said immediately. "I do not steal babies! I was also a princess," she added, a touch of wounded pride in her voice.

Harper and Roedyn exchanged a long look.

"I know how it sounds," she said, "but it's true."

"Okay," Harper said slowly, setting her bowl down. "So, just to be clear, you were a tiny royal pixie, and now you're… what? An elf on some punishment quest?"

"The Court of Dreams sentenced me. They took my wings and my title, so technically, I am no longer a princess. They permanently polymorphed me into what you see now. So yes, Harper, I am an elf now."

Harper raised her cup in a toast and smiled.

Escala continued, "They cast me out and gave me a quest: to remove the boulders from the True Cycle."

Roedyn muttered, "She's lost it."

"Completely," agreed Harper.

"I'm not lying," Escala insisted. "There was a trial, and I was found guilty. I should have received the Wane, but…"

Harper arched a brow. "A Wane? That sounds like something made up by poets with too much wine."

Escala looked up from her third bowl of stew. "The fey realm is pure magic, and so are we. If the Wane deems you unworthy... you're erased."

Her voice caught, but she pressed on. "The Wane unmakes you—body, magic, name—every thread tying you to existence pulled loose. You dissolve into the realm. Your story is erased, and you are forgotten."

She looked up again, her voice hollow. "And no one remembers you lived, not even the ones who loved you most."

For once, Harper had no snarky reply.

"You're serious?" Roedyn asked.

Escala nodded.

Harper asked, "So... if you were found guilty, why didn't you get Waned?"

"I don't know," Escala admitted. "I stood there waiting... for the magic to take me. But it didn't. Instead, the Dream Weaver stripped my glamour and title, polymorphed me into this form, and banished me to the mortal plane with this quest."

Roedyn frowned. "And you can go back if you finish this quest?"

"I have to remove the boulders from the True Cycle."

Harper whistled low. "Well, that's new. Usually, when people snap and lose touch with reality, they claim to be royalty or from another world, but somehow, you've managed both."

"I'm not crazy!" Escala said, her eyes filling with tears. "I didn't ask for this. I just want to go home."

"You just said, 'remove the boulders from the True Cycle,' out loud," Roedyn deadpanned. "That's not exactly the phrase of a well-balanced person."

"It's part of my sentence," Escala said, frustrated. "I don't know what it means."

Harper tossed a twig into the fire.

"Well," she said, "you're either lying, delusional, or drunk, and I once met a guy who swore he was the god of shoes, so I think I'm a decent judge of which category this falls into."

Ignoring Harper, Roedyn asked, "So what happens if you don't fix the True Cycle?"

"I don't know," Escala said. "I don't think I ever get to go home."

Harper stopped grinning. Roedyn looked down at the fire.

Finally, Roedyn leaned back, arms behind his head. "Well, if you are who you say you are, then either Valla is about to end because of some boulder in the True Cycle, or you're our best shot at stopping it."

"And if she's not," Harper added, "we've got the best seats to watch a total mental breakdown—should be entertaining."

Harper smirked. "Either way, I say we keep her."

"Keep me?"

"Yeah," Harper said. "You're weird, and I like weird. Besides, you don't even have a sword. We can't let you leave this cabin alone—you'll die out there."

"She's not wrong," Roedyn added.

"So, you're letting me stay?" Escala asked hopefully.

"For now," Roedyn answered. "Unless you burn down the cabin or turn out to be secretly evil."

"Or lead orcs to our marital home," Harper said with mock seriousness. "My husband wouldn't take kindly to that."

Escala laughed.

Harper continued, "If any of that happens, he'll throw you in the stream."

"That's right," Roedyn deadpanned.

Escala smiled and stretched her feet toward the fire, warmth seeping through her stiff boots. The scent of stew, bread, and warm fire filled the hollow space in her chest, and for the first time since the trial, she didn't feel entirely alone.

Chapter 20

The next morning, Roedyn clanged a spoon against the iron kettle. "Up! Outside!" he called, lifting the blanket off Escala. "You want to remove boulders from the True Cycle? Then training starts now."

Escala groaned and rolled to her side, face buried in a lumpy bundle of rolled blankets. Her shoulders throbbed, her joints creaked, and the cot squealed as she shifted.

She sat up slowly, rubbing her face. She still ached and needed a few seconds to muster the strength to stand.

When Escala stepped me

into the cool morning air, Harper was already out front, hair tied back, and flames dancing on her fingers.

Roedyn handed Escala a stick sanded at the grip.

"What's this for?" Escala asked.

"Training," said Roedyn.

"But it's wood, shouldn't I be learning how to use a sword?" Escala asked with a hint of surprise.

"You're not ready for steel," Roedyn said. "You need to learn to move before you learn to kill."

Escala shrugged and took the stick, not sure how to hold it.

Roedyn drew a line in the dirt and faced her with his short wooden staff.

"First rule of surviving with a sword," he said, "is don't expect it to save you. Expect it to weigh you down, throw off your balance, and betray you when you get cocky."

He slowly and deliberately shifted his stance, raising the wooden staff into a defensive position.

"Now, show me what you've got."

Escala took a breath and swung. It was awkward—too wide. Her footing slipped, and Roedyn batted her attack away with ease.

"Again."

She swung again, he easily sidestepped, and she missed completely.

"Again."

This time, when she swung, he raised his staff, flicked his wrist, and knocked the stick from her hand.

She hissed and reached down to pick it up, but Harper beat her to it.

"That was… impressive," Harper said, tossing it back at her lazily. "In the way a chicken trying to dance is impressive."

Escala flushed.

Roedyn didn't smile. "You're using just your arms. Stop that. You fight with hips, feet, spine—everything must move. You must flow."

"I've never trained like this," Escala said, frustrated.

"I don't think you've ever trained," Roedyn said.

"Don't worry, though, I'm a great teacher," Harper said and clapped her shoulder.

Escala recoiled instantly, voice sharp. "Don't touch me! No one touches the faerie!"

"What—what did I do?" Harped asked in surprise.

"Please don't touch me."

"I thought you didn't want to be touched by him," Harper said, pointing at Roedyn, "because he's grumpy, likes to boss people, and smells like bark and sweat."

Roedyn rolled his eyes.

"But me?" Harper placed a hand over her heart in mock offense. "I'm charming, and I smell like fire and lilacs. I thought it was a sisterly love tap. Maybe even a royal honor, your majesty." She curtsied.

"Harper," Roedyn said flatly. "Enough."

Harper backed off, hands still raised, her mouth twitching in an almost-apology.

Escala stared at the ground, arms crossed, trembling.

Roedyn stepped in, voice low. "It's okay. We hear you; no one's going to touch you."

Escala looked at Roedyn. Her blue eyes were wide, and she still looked uncomfortable.

Roedyn studied her, seeing for the first time her beauty and vulnerability. Those eyes made it hard for him to look away.

I know what you're thinking, folks, looking around the Stag. ""How would you know this, Wigfrith? You weren't there."

A fair question, and you're right, I wasn't. Not at first. But unlike certain bards who make up half their material after the third mug of cider, I actually did the work. I tracked down everyone who lived through this tale, asked careful questions, compared their answers, and stitched the truth together piece by piece.

And I was with Escala for her adventure, trust me, she gave me enough details to fill three books and a pamphlet. I met the others too, so what I'm telling you tonight is as true as any story can be: gathered, verified, and polished just enough to keep you awake."

But this moment? I didn't have to guess. Harper told me herself, as she'd been watching closely. Why? You'll have to ask her that.

Speaking of Harper, she wasn't the patient sort. But she took it upon herself to train Escala in the ways of the blade. She told me it was like trying to teach a butterfly to brawl, but she tried. Drills at dawn, bruises by breakfast, and more than a few threats involving pointy ends, but day by day, Escala started to learn.

One afternoon, after a particularly tense sparring session, Escala collapsed on the grass.

"Why are you helping me?" she asked, breathless.

Roedyn sat nearby, stretching. "Because you won't survive if you set out into Valla trying to find boulders without this training," he said.

Harper dropped beside her, hand half raised for a friendly punch before she thought better of it and let it fall.

"And because you're sort of fascinating," Harper said with a grin. "Besides," she added, "I'll be the only master swordswoman who gets to brag she trained a real-life princess from the Court of Dreams."

As the days went by, even though she was sore and tired, Escala could tell she was making progress, she was steadier, more grounded. Her new body still felt strange, but she was starting to move in it without thinking, starting to learn what to do when someone swung a sword at her head.

One night, Roedyn made a fire outside the cabin. Harper flicked sparks from her fingertips into the embers. Across from her, Roedyn sat sharpening arrowheads with calm, steady strokes, the blade catching the firelight.

Escala sat between them. Her body ached, and her hands were sore from gripping the practice stick. Through all her training, one question constantly ran through her mind— what did "remove the boulders from the True Cycle" even mean?

"I need to figure out what the court meant about the boulders," she said.

"They could be metaphorical," Harper said, popping a roasted mushroom into her mouth.

"Or they could be literal," Roedyn muttered. "Maybe there's an actual boulder you're meant to push off a cliff or clear from some mountain pass."

Escala sighed. "You're just guessing, that's not helping."

Roedyn slid the arrow into his quiver and leaned back. "There might be someone who can help, though."

"Who?" Escala asked.

Now, good folks, brace yourselves. The story's been gripping so far, but what comes next catapults this tale into the stratosphere. For the character about to join is... well, unforgettable.

Escala asked, "Who?"

Harper sat up and said, "Wigfrith."

Yes, friends. I have finally entered the story.

"Who is Wigfrith?" Escala repeated.

"An old gnome bard." Roedyn shrugged. "From Misty Springs. Bit of a lunatic, depending on who you ask."

Harper said, "Wigfrith supposedly knows more about magic and cryptic prophecies than anyone we've met, and he claims to know something about everything," Harper said.

Looking at the crowd, I stomp my foot in anger. "What the blue hells," I yell, "Harper called me old? The nerve!" There is a lot of laughter.

"And Roedyn called me a lunatic? The bloody blue hells!" I feign mock outrage as the crowd roars and I add, "Well, Harper wasn't wrong in her introduction, at least. I do know something about everything. But there's one thing I still can't figure out. Do you know what that is?"

Before anyone can answer, I sigh dramatically. "I just can't, for the life of me, understand why *anyone* willingly goes to the Golden Goose to listen to the hussy bards' songs about kissing mermaids." The room erupts into waves of laughter and catcalls.

I sip my ale, a smug smile tugging at my lips, and wait for the laughter to fade before carrying on with the tale.

Escala was peppering Harper with questions about me—Wigfirth, the bard who knows everything. Grinning, Harper said, "He swears he once lived among the satyrs—those woodland folk with a man's chest and a goat's rump. And yes, I'm pretty sure they're fey."

"He didn't live with satyrs," Roedyn muttered.

"He might have," Harper shot back. "He knows a lot about grass."

Roedyn just shook his head. Escala, looking puzzled by the comment, asked. "Where is he?"

"City of Dunwell," Harper answered. "It is east from here, about three weeks' travel by foot. It's a big place. It has the best markets in the region, and it's where our so-called 'duke' keeps his seat."

Roedyn said, "We can probably find Wigfrith at The Stag and Hound."

"I'll go," Escala said.

"You mean we'll go," Harper said, standing and brushing off her pants. You're still one sloppy parry from being skewered by the next bandit. You're not going anywhere alone."

Roedyn nodded. "We leave at first light. Once we reach Dunwell, we'll gear you up properly. You can't wear just a nice tunic, pretty as the stitching is."

He motioned to her blue tunic and immediately blushed.

Harper raised an eyebrow. "Careful, Roedyn. Complimenting the outfit and checking the stitching? Should I leave you two alone?"

Roedyn blushed deeper. "I—no. I was just—look, it's a practical comment. I wasn't... I mean, it's a nice tunic. Just not for... bandit fighting, that's all." He quickly looked away.

Escala just stared at them.

Eager to shift the subject, Roedyn said, "I've got my sword, shield, and bow, but no spare blade that fits your size. Take the training sword you've been practicing with. It's about as sharp as a soup spoon, but it looks convincing while sheathed. With luck, no one will call your bluff and force you to draw it. Once we reach Dunwell, we'll get something better, and a real shield. For now, take one of my packs. I'll load it with what we need."

Harper grinned. "Any idea what tools you'll need Escala? Pickaxe? Crowbar? Maybe a sturdy rope for all this boulder removing?"

Roedyn gave Harper a warning glance.

Escala almost smiled and turned back to the fire. For the first time since her banishment, something stirred deep inside her.

Hope.

Chapter 21

Now, my fine and half-soused friends, before I tell you more about Escala's journey to find this so-called Old Bard—yes, Harper called me that, and I still haven't forgiven her—I must pause for a darker turn in the tale. You ought to know not everyone rejoiced when Escala was spared the Wane. And you know who I'm talking about.

That's right, her stepmother, Morvena. Deep in the Court of Dreams, she stormed off to find Rowan. When she did, she didn't knock. The tall doors flew open with a flash of magic and a wave of her hand. Rowan hovered with his back to her, facing the vast glass overlooking the Starfall Pools. In the reflection, he watched as she approached.

"I expected you sooner," he said.

"Then you already know why I'm here. You let her go," she hissed.

"I gave her a sentence that was allowed under our law," he said.

Morvena's voice thundered in anger. "That was mercy disguised as punishment. She violated the True Cycle! She took a mortal life and tampered with fate! That demands the Wane."

Rowan's voice stayed even. "Our laws provide other judgments. The First Oath says when the Cycle is disrupted without malice, a fey may be given a path to restoration."

"A path?" she scoffed. "You gave her a quest! That girl is reckless and untrained, and you sent her to the mortal plane to 'fix' the Cycle? Do you even hear yourself?"

"It's a path she will never finish," Rowan said, pain in his voice, "an impossible quest, one that keeps her from returning."

"You don't know what you've done!" Her voice shook with rage. "You've destroyed the only true deterrent we had. The Wane kept the fey in line. Fear of being forgotten keeps us from meddling. Now every fey will believe they can tamper with fate and bargain their way out. You've undone us!"

Rowan raised his voice. "The law allows for discretion—"

"No!" Morvena moved closer, trembling. "You've made this about her, you always do. You let your heart choose for you and wrapped the decision in legalese. You sent her to the mortal plane chasing something that doesn't exist. She'll ask everyone she meets about it, she'll reveal she's fey, and she'll expose her intent to return. Interference with the True Cycle? Rowan, you might as well stand at a Crossing with a horn and call the mortals to us yourself! You don't protect the Cycle anymore. You protect Escala."

Neither moved. Then, without a word, Morvena stormed out of the room and slammed the door behind her as she left. She flew back to her private chambers and yanked the curtains shut, drowning the moonlight and suffocating the room in shadow.

Rowan was no longer fit to rule, she thought. Not when he bent the law to protect Escala, a child of mortal blood. Morvena paced as her fury surged. Rowan had betrayed the court's fabric, all in the name of compassion. He'd coddled mortals, and now, with this sentence, he encouraged the fey to do the same. Worse, he'd sent a pixie in elf form to the mortal plane to spill secrets on some vain, ill-defined "quest."

Why not just banish her? At least she would remain in the fey realm. Why give her false hope? Now she would tell all of Valla she was fey and, in doing so, expose everything about the Court of Dreams. What kind of fool was he? Both Escala and Rowan had to be stopped.

The horror clawed at her throat. She opened a velvet-lined drawer with shaking hands. Beneath folds of scarlet cloth sat a leather-wrapped case. She opened it carefully, reverently. Within lay the Vorrash Totem, a thing of twisted wood and black iron veins, pulsing faintly with magic not of this realm. She held it with both hands, her fingers trembling. "He'll see," she whispered. "The court needs a ruler who isn't weak."

The door behind Morvena creaked open, and Audrey quietly flew into the chamber, already dressed for travel. Morvena turned, reached into the drawer, grabbed the wolf totem, and handed it to her.

"You recovered it?" Audrey said, accepting it with a slight bow.

"Of course I did," Morvena snapped. "I accomplish what I set out to do. Now go," she said. "Finish what the court refused to."

Chapter 22

Escala, Roedyn, and Harper were on their way through treacherous forests, marshes, and rough trading roads toward the distant city of Dunwell.

They traveled in a loose line: Roedyn ahead, scanning the path; Harper at the rear, watchful; and Escala in the middle, chatting with carefree energy and no discernible responsibilities for this trip.

The first leg took three punishing days through wild terrain—thorn-choked woods and steep ravines. Every step was a fight against roots and unstable ground. By the time they reached the narrow path near the Silverstand Forest, Escala was spent. Harper had been right—she'd never have survived this alone.

But Escala had enough energy for talking, and she never stopped. "What is the purpose of taxes if no one likes them?" she asked.

"Someone has to pay for all those gold thrones and royal banquets," Harper quipped.

Later, Escala asked, "Is marriage like a magical love contract?"

"It is more like a sword you fall on willingly," Roedyn said.

"Wrong," Harper snapped. "It's like a tavern brawl you keep going back to because you left your coat."

Later, Harper was explaining festivals, and Escala asked, "Why do children dress like monsters and scare adults on Halloween?"

"It's tradition," Roedyn answered. "They are hoping for a treat."

"No," Harper said, "it's to prepare them for adulthood where everyone still wears masks and pretends to like each other."

Escala looked confused. "Mortals are so confusing," she observed.

But Escala's questions kept coming, about life and death, ambition, friendship, betrayal, and love. She was enchanted and bewildered by the answers, especially when Roedyn and Harper disagreed, which was often. Their bickering didn't faze her. She soaked it all in, her expression shifting between curiosity, horror, and mischievous delight.

During the trip, Harper asked, "So... who's Rihanna?"

"She was my best friend," Escala answered. "We grew up in a place called the Spire," she added.

"Tell us about it," Roedyn said.

"The Spire is in the palace of the Court of Dreams and is simply beautiful. It overlooks the gardens," Escala said. "I miss all of it, the Spire, the lights, the gardens, the music at dusk, even the silence."

She stopped walking. "But mostly... I miss Rihanna. And I wish, I wish I could go back and fix everything." A tear traced down her cheek, but she didn't wipe it away.

Roedyn noticed the tears but didn't say anything. Harper, still walking ahead, asked, "What exactly did you do to get kicked out?"

Escala brushed the tears from her eyes. "I crossed into the mortal world… just to kiss a boy. Fey aren't allowed to do that, our Oath forbids us from interfering in mortal lives."

"So what?" Harper said. "What's the big deal about a kiss?"

Escala rubbed her nose, eyes distant. "A faerie's kiss can be magical, if we choose to make it so. And when we do, it binds a mortal's heart to us forever. No other woman could ever truly reach him again. By kissing him, I stole his chance at an ordinary life. He would've thought of me always, dreamed of me, and that longing would have twisted his fate in ways he'd never understand. He would've spent his days searching for something he couldn't name, something that would never satisfy the ache I left behind. That's why faeries keep to the hidden places. We're not meant to interfere. When I kissed him, I broke the True Cycle… even if he had survived the wolf attack."

"Then why did you do it?" Roedyn asked quietly.

Escala hesitated, her eyes downcast. When she finally spoke, her voice was barely a whisper, thick with shame. "Because I wanted to. I used to dream about it, whispering with my friends, wondering what it would feel like. If it would feel like love. My father once kissed a mortal woman, my mother… and they fell in love. I believed that's how it worked. I thought… maybe it could happen to me, too."

Harper frowned. "Okay, so… no offense, but if you were a tiny pixie and he was a full-grown man, how did you even kiss him? I mean, forgive me for asking about the logistics, but wouldn't that be like a butterfly trying to kiss a bloke? I'm just trying to picture the physics here."

Roedyn leaned forward, studying Escala with quiet curiosity, waiting for her answer.

Escala started walking again. "I changed forms to make myself bigger. Most fey can do that, polymorph into other forms. So I changed into an elf, what you see me as today, and I kissed him and used fey magic to charm him."

"And did you fall in love?" Harper asked, her tone laced with dry curiosity.

"I don't know what love is," Escala replied. "But then... the wolf came. I don't know how or why, but it went for me first. Tore my wing nearly off. The boy just stood there, still under my spell. I should have told him to fight. And Rihanna..."

She swallowed hard.

"She tried to save me..."

She paused.

"... and the wolf killed her..."

She was clearly emotional.

"... somehow I survived."

They walked in silence for the next hour or so until they took a rest at a stone bridge past midday. The shade was cool, the stream nearby shallow and clear.

Roedyn fetched water while Harper grimaced at stale bread. Escala sat on a rock, rubbing her sore calves.

Finally, Harper asked, "Okay, this might be rude, but I have to know: did you really think you were going to fall in love from just one kiss?"

"Yes," Escala said.

Harper doubled over with laughter.

Escala scrunched her nose, not understanding what Harper found funny.

Harper kept laughing until Roedyn cut in. "Harper, that's enough."

I stop the story and look around the Stag to see how the crowd is responding. I can tell the crowd is paying attention. I take a sip of ale and say, "Yes, Escala was naïve believing a kiss could spark real love, but I'd wager she's not the only one who's ever dared to hope."

Not everyone will meet my eye as I set my ale down and continue the story.

Later that evening, as they were setting up camp, Escala asked Harper, "Are you two always this coordinated?"

"What do you mean?" said Harper.

"I mean, you know each other's rhythms—you and Roedyn. You move like a team."

Roedyn handed her a canteen of water as he stood. "We've been adventuring together for five years now, ever since we had to leave Eronvale in a bit of a rush."

Escala took the canteen.

"You two stay here. I'm going to scout. I'll be back in twenty minutes," Roedyn said, and with that, he slipped quietly into the woods.

Harper stretched her legs and leaned back on her hands. "Roedyn and I used to be Gray Cloaks. Probably doesn't mean much to you, but back then, we were stationed in Eronvale." She nodded eastward. "That's at least six months on foot past Dunwell."

Harper continued, "Eronvale is the capital of the whole continent—it's an enormous city, maybe a million souls crammed behind those stone walls. King Orren Dor'Lean rules there now, from his polished little palace. But before him, we had Emperor Korveth; an evil warlord who seized the throne by slaughtering King Theren Dor'lean. But the emperor only lasted a short while, until the Dor'Lean family was able to reclaim the throne."

"So... the Gray Cloaks served the Dor'Lean family?" Escala asked.

Harper gave her a sharp sideways glance. "No, not at all. The Gray Cloaks weren't loyal to any king or emperor. We had a different mission, a higher order. We were charged with guarding certain extremely rare artifacts. If someone threatened those artifacts, well, let's say we didn't send letters; we climbed through windows."

"Oh," said Escala.

"When Emperor Korveth—may his name be deleted from every history book—decided he wanted one of those artifacts, I.... err... the Gray Cloaks stepped in and removed him. Permanently," Harper said.

Escala stared. "The emperor was murdered?"

A slight smirk crossed Harper's face, and she slowly said, "I heard that he drowned in his own chamber pot."

Escala gagged. "You're joking."

Harper's expression turned deadly serious. "I don't joke about chamber pots." She flicked a pebble into the brush.

"Anyway, Eronvale imploded after that—riots, fires, every noble house scrambling for the throne. After months of fighting, the Dor'Lean family eventually clawed their way back to power, but for a while, no one wanted to be anywhere near Eronvale."

"Is that how... well..." Escala trailed off.

"Well, what?" Harper arched a brow.

"Sorry, I don't mean to pry."

Harper's smile was quick and teasing. "Please. You asked if I'd ever kissed Roedyn the first day we met. For the record, the answer's still no. And trust me, nothing you ask could be worse than that."

Escala flushed. "I just wondered... did you get hurt in the riots?"

Harper blinked, then shook her head. "No. Why would you think that?"

"The scars," Escala admitted, fumbling. "I thought maybe you were cut, or, sorry. I shouldn't have asked."

Harper's hand brushed her cheek, tracing the long scar that split her lip. "No. Not the riots. But the person who gave me these isn't giving anyone scars anymore."

She took a slow drink of water, eyes glinting over the rim. "Generally speaking, picking a fight with a Gray Cloak is a poor choice if you like breathing."

Escala could only nod, unsure what else to say.

Harper leaned back, her tone softening. "Roedyn was a Gray Cloak, too. He's the one who got me out. When everything went sideways after the chamber-pot drowning, I found myself very much a person of interest. Once we were free of Eronvale, we went west. As far west as possible. We had more than a few reasons to put that place behind us. Over time, we became friends. Not that kind of friends, mind you. Eventually, we started taking up work as adventurers."

Escala nodded thoughtfully. "And that's why you live all the way out here? To escape the war for the throne?"

Harper raised an eyebrow, she'd basically just admitted to regicide, and Escala looked like she was hearing a bedtime story.

Harper shook her head, grinning again. "Partly. Also, Roedyn's paranoid, we have some very valuable treasure hidden in a nearby cave, and he won't ever leave it unguarded."

Escala tried not to laugh. "You don't need to tell me about your cave."

"Good," Harper replied, "because I'm not telling you."

Escala said, unexpectedly, "I think I trust you both."

"Took you long enough, but I'm still not telling you where the cave is," Harper said.

Escala laughed, and Harper grinned too, but for different reasons.

Chapter 23

They traveled two more days before reaching a river. Roedyn checked his maps and confirmed they should follow it. After a few hours along its banks, they reached the trade road. It was muddy from recent rains, but even so, their spirits lifted.

By mid-afternoon, they reached a bend thick with overhanging trees that blocked the view ahead. From around the corner came a low groan, a sharp crack, and then a string of curses in a language Escala didn't recognize.

"Did something just swear at us?" Harper asked.

Roedyn raised a hand for silence and crept forward. Escala followed, boots squelching in the mud. They rounded the bend and found the source.

A stout, red-faced man stood beside a crooked wagon, stuck in the muddy road. One front wheel had ridden up on a rock and now tilted absurdly, while the rear axle groaned under uneven weight. Two mules stood ahead, unfazed, flicking flies.

Likely a merchant, the man strained against the wheel. "Come on, you stubborn, tree-born hunk of timber!" he grunted, but the wagon didn't budge.

"It's a boulder!" Escala cried, pointing at the rock beneath the wheel, eyes wide with excitement.

"That's not a boulder, that's a rock," Roedyn said.

"It is an actual, honest-to-goodness boulder," Escala declared and rolled up her sleeves. "The Court of Dreams never said how big a boulder is—*this counts*!"

Seeing them, the man said, "Where did you come from?"

"Our mothers' wombs," Harper answered with a sly grin.

"Don't be weird," Roedyn muttered.

"I see you have a boulder blocking your way in the True Cycle," Escala announced. "I am Escala Winter of the Court of Dreams, and I am here to remove your boulders."

The man stared. "Right… I'm Brennock, I am an herb merchant. I'm stuck and going nowhere fast."

Escala nodded and crouched beside the front wheel lodged against the rock. She planted her feet in the mud, pressed her shoulder into the wagon, and pushed.

Her arms and legs trembled. The wagon groaned but didn't budge. Escala gritted her teeth and pushed harder, until every muscle in her back, legs, and shoulders screamed. Her boots sank deeper into the mud. Her palms burned against the rough wood.

Then, slowly, grudgingly, the wheel creaked up over the edge of the rock. For one moment, it looked like she might actually lift the wagon free.

But her foot slipped, she lost her leverage, and the wheel slammed back into the mud with a wet, heavy thud.

Brennock whooped. "By the gods! I thought you were going to snap in half!"

Escala, now covered in mud, panted as she wiped her forehead only to smear mud across her face.

Roedyn and Harper watched. Harper was visibly biting back a grin.

"I'm stronger than I look," Escala growled as she returned to the wagon, trying again to plant her feet in the slippery mud.

With Escala's attention focused on the wagon, she didn't see Roedyn quietly slip around to the far side.

Harper and Brennock exchanged a glance, but before either could respond, Escala let out a fierce grunt, braced herself in the slick mud, and heaved with everything she had.

And, ,miraculously, the wheel jolted free. The wagon rolled over the "boulder," forward onto dry ground.

Harper and Brennock stood in stunned silence.

"She actually did it," Brennock whispered. "By the gods..."

Escala stood panting, sweat-matted long blonde hair clinging to her muddy face, but her expression was triumphant. She tried to rub the mud off her hands onto her pants.

"I need you to sign something," she said solemnly.

"Come again?" Brennock said.

She pulled out a leather-bound book and a flint pencil. "Please write: 'I, Brennock, Herb Merchant, confirm that Escala Winter removed a boulder from my True Cycle.'"

Escala had her back turned as she handed the merchant her logbook, when Roedyn reappeared, boots covered with thick mud. Harper opened her mouth to comment, but Roedyn quickly raised a finger to his lips.

For once, Harper said nothing, but her grin widened, and her eyes sparkled with mischief.

Brennock held the book in his hands and looked at Escala. "Is this a religious thing?"

Harper shrugged. "Just sign and don't ask questions, it will be faster that way."

Still baffled, Brennock scribbled in the logbook and handed it back to Escala.

"Thank you," she said sincerely. "This helps more than you know."

She tucked the logbook away, sensing a strange glow in her chest that had nothing to do with magic just the satisfaction of doing something, anything, that felt like it mattered. And that boulder, whether literal or not, was one fewer in the Cycle.

I look around The Stag's common room. Not everyone here knows the weight of honest labor, but many do, and I see it in their eyes. Not everyone here knows the weight of honest labor, but many do, and I see it in their eyes. They understand Escala not just because they feel the ache of effort, but because they know what it means to try to help and to be unafraid to let others see it. I also spot a few "Roedyns" in the room—quiet types who carry the burden so others can rise, never asking for thanks or credit. And it's a good thing we have both kinds of people, because without them, Valla would be a far darker place.

Chapter 24

B y late afternoon, the forest began to thin, giving way to open fields of tall grass and the winding edge of a cobblestone road. Escala, who the day before had been talking aimlessly with no real responsibilities, was now scanning the road for opportunity.

Her fingers brushed her pouch, where the little leather logbook rested. She'd already flipped to the page with Brennock's note three times that morning, rereading his awkward handwriting like it might transform into something more official.

"I, Brennock, herb merchant, confirm that Escala Winter removed a boulder from my True Cycle."

She knew it sounded ridiculous, but part of her believed it mattered. The court had spoken in riddles: remove the boulders from the True Cycle. Wasn't that precisely what she was doing? Wasn't helping people the point?

She thought she knew her quest now: fill the book. Line after line of proof, virtuous deeds done, and people helped— all of them burdened by boulders needing removal. After all, the Dream Weaver had given her this book when he transformed her. Surely, he meant for her to fill it with evidence. And one day, if she returned, she'd walk into the Star Gallery, hold it up, and say, "Look, I did what you asked."

They came upon the second opportunity just before dusk.

A teenage girl with a brown ponytail stood by the road, holding the reins of a shaggy pony that clearly wasn't cooperating. Behind her, a wooden cart tilted in the mud— one wheel sunk deep in a rut, the others wobbling each time the pony jerked.

"Please, Bessy," the girl pleaded. "Please!"

The pony sneezed.

Escala walked straight toward the girl.

"I am Escala Winter from the Court of Dreams, and I am here to help remove boulders from your True Cycle."

The girl wrinkled her nose. "I—I don't know what you're talking about," she stammered. "There aren't any boulders here. And my True Cycle, well, that's not any of your business."

Harper burst out laughing.

Roedyn gave her a stern look.

Escala didn't understand the girl's concern. "I see that your cart's stuck. Do you need help?"

"Bessy won't pull. I've got to deliver this flour to the mill, or they'll dock my pay, and we won't be able to pay our rent to the manor lord next week." It all came out in one breath.

Escala smiled. "Then let's fix that."

"I can't pay you," the girl said cautiously.

"No pay is needed. There is a boulder in your True Cycle, and I remove boulders," Escala tried to explain.

"My mother said that only she and I can talk about my True Cycle," the girl said defensively.

Harper continued to snicker, and Roedyn gave her a disapproving glare.

Ten minutes later, Escala was in the mud again, her hands digging under the stuck wheel while Roedyn used a branch to lever up the other side. Harper mainly offered useless commentary.

With one final shove from Roedyn and Escala, the wheel popped free of the rut, and the cart thudded onto firmer ground. The girl clapped her hands.

"You did it!" the girl exclaimed.

Escala stood, trying to brush the mud from her leggings, and reached into her pouch for her logbook. "Could you write that down? In here?" She held it open, pointing to a blank page.

The girl looked at the page. Then at Escala.

"… You want me to write that you helped me?"

"Yes," Escala said. "Please write that I removed a boulder from your True Cycle."

The girl stared. "But you didn't remove a boulder, you only dug my cart out of a muddy rut."

Harper bit her knuckle to keep from laughing.

Still, the girl took the flint pencil, thought for a moment, and then scribbled:

"Escala helped me get my cart out of the mud. Thank you." —Silla

Escala read it twice and said, "Thank you."

Perhaps she could explain to the court that it was a bigger deal than what was written.

Silla waved goodbye as she and Bessy continued down the road.

Later, when they made camp beneath a crooked elm, Escala sat off to the side with her logbook in her lap.

Harper sat beside her, chewing a strip of dried meat. She glanced at the book. "Do you think that logbook is going to change their minds?"

"It might."

Roedyn sat across the fire and asked, "You really think the Court of Dreams is watching? Counting signatures?"

"I don't know," Escala whispered. "The Dream Weaver did give me the book. What else am I supposed to do with it?"

Harper had no answer.

By mid-morning the next day, they reached a small village clinging to the edge of a fast-moving river that carved through its center. The current was high, angry, almost, its churning waters slapping hard against the banks.

Escala spotted an old man kneeling at the roadside, shoulders hunched beneath the heavy weight of a large basket strapped to his back.

As they approached, he lifted his head. His face was pale, slick with sweat, but he offered a polite nod.

"What are you carrying?" Escala asked.

"Rocks," he replied with a grunt. "For the wall."

"What wall?"

"The flood wall," he muttered, nodding toward the river. "Down that way. The river's rising too fast. The villagers are stacking stones and sand before the river gets too high."

He tried to get up, but one of his knees buckled. He stumbled, catching himself on a fence post.

Escala stepped forward and reached for the basket's straps. "Let me carry it."

The man looked at her small frame. "It's heavy," he said.

"I can manage," she said as she strapped the basket onto her back. It was heavier than she expected, and the straps bit into her collarbone. The edges of the stones shifted with every step.

Roedyn watched, quietly impressed, as she managed to keep her balance down the slope toward the villagers.

The old man walked beside her, no longer burdened.

Harper, watching Roedyn, grinned and quietly said, "You like her, don't you?"

Roedyn kept his eyes on Escala. "No."

"Liar," Harper said, grabbing her pack and heading after them.

Roedyn exhaled, picked up his own pack, and followed.

At the river's edge, a low stone wall was slowly taking shape. The villagers moved with the sluggish rhythm of people already past the point of exhaustion, shoulders sagging, brows slick with sweat, hands caked in mud and grit.

A broad-shouldered woman waved them over. Escala stepped in without hesitation, unloading stones from the old man's basket. A villager handed her a worn trowel and pointed to a line of villagers spreading mortar and placing rocks. Escala wiped her brow and joined in the work.

Roedyn rose and joined Escala at the wall. She gave him a tired, grateful smile. Without a word, he stepped into the line, lifting heavy stones as others spread mortar.

Harper sat on the hill, eating an apple and watching.

After a while, Escala glanced at the old man. His hands trembled as he stacked stones. "You shouldn't be doing this," she said quietly.

"Then who should? If not me?"

"You're old," she said, not unkindly. "You've done your share. Why risk what time you have left for a wall of rocks?"

The man sighed and set a stone in place. "Because that wall protects what's left."

She looked at him, puzzled.

He brushed off his hands and stared at the rooftops. "A long time ago, I fell in love with a woman named Elira. Eyes like the sky, laugh like sunlight. We built a cottage by the river bend," he said, pointing downstream. "Had two kids, Theo and Thom, good boys. They grew up here, on the same patch where she used to hang laundry and sing."

He rubbed his chin. "Elira is buried out back now. Beneath the linden tree. She passed away last winter, an illness the priests couldn't fix."

"I'm sorry," Escala said.

"I loved her dearly," he said as he started to move rocks again. "And I'm grateful for the life we had. Our children are still here, living in the village that this river now threatens.

Sometimes I catch a look or a laugh from one of them, and it feels like she's still with us."

Sweat dripped from Escala's nose as she asked, "How do you know that was love? I don't know what love is. Could you help me understand?"

He stopped working again and looked at her, his intensity catching her off guard.

"Love," he said softly, "is carrying stones you know won't make a difference. It's knowing the wall may not hold, that the flood may still come, and the river might swallow everything you care about, but building the wall anyway."

Escala watched him, silent. She'd never heard anyone talk about love like that before.

He noticed the uncertainty in her expression and added gently, "I can tell it's weighing on you."

Escala said softly, "The stories always talk about a prince rescuing a princess from a dragon because he loves her, but what you're saying… it's nothing like that."

"Sweet child," the old man said kindly as he continued to stack stones, "love isn't found in the grand moments. It lives in the quiet ones, the hidden ones, where no one sees what you do. Love is choosing to help even when your back aches, love is choosing to stand when you'd rather rest. It's doing what must be done simply because you can't bear not to—that's love."

They worked in silence after that. Escala and Roedyn moved with quiet purpose, stacking stones along the riverbank, where the current lapped higher with each passing minute.

Roedyn had heard the old man's words. He thought of Escala's logbook and her few entries of humble, simple acts that, for her, were such big "boulders"—very much like the stones the old man was carrying.

Roedyn pondered the man's words as he stacked stones. Maybe Escala had been right—maybe that rock under the wagon wheel really was a boulder after all. He watched her work, more intrigued than ever. Who was she, really? It wasn't just what she was doing, it was how. No hesitation, no performance. Just a quiet, focused effort from someone who clearly believed this mattered.

There was a purity in her, a kind of sincerity that felt out of place in a world like Valla. He didn't know what to make of it. He only knew he couldn't look away.

Harper, meanwhile, took a nap.

I glance around the tavern. When I tell a story that lands deep—right in the heart—I can see it in their eyes. Tonight, they're not just hearing about Escala. They're thinking about what they value and for whom they would carry stones. Turning back to the story, I continue.

When they finished reinforcing the wall, the old man offered Escala a piece of honey bread, and she accepted it with a quiet thank you. Escala hesitated and pulled her logbook from her pouch.

"Would you sign this?" she asked gently. "I'm trying to get home. I can't return until I've removed enough boulders from the True Cycle."

The old man looked at the logbook, then at her. He didn't take it. Instead, he said, "Child, if you're measuring your worth in tally marks, you'll miss the weight of the stones that matter most."

She stood in silence, logbook still outstretched.

He gave her a small, kind smile. "Not every boulder needs to be remembered in ink—some boulders are written on the soul."

Escala lowered the book as he hobbled back to the village, to the things he loved most in life.

Chapter 25

I'm not about to bore you with every muddy step and bug bite they took on their journey to Dunwell. But I will tell you this: during that stretch, Escala told stories of the Court of Dreams—of her stepmother and stepsister, her father, and, of course, her dearest friend, Rihanna. She answered every question they had about fey life, customs, and their magic.

Moreover, she helped others. Again and again, as they passed by hovels, through villages, and lonely farms tucked into the folds of the countryside. By the time the next big moment in her journey rolled around, she'd completed—going by what Roedyn told me—more than twenty-two "boulder removal" tasks. Some small, some strange, but all sincere. I was also told that she had to sternly remind someone—only sixteen times—"Do not touch the faerie," when they tried to hug her out of gratitude.

They were still two days from Dunwell, trudging through woods where visibility was poor. Dense thickets, creeping vines, and hanging moss choked the trail, while twisted roots clawed from the earth. The path was little more than a game trail, winding between gnarled trees that arched overhead.

Suddenly, a wild beast burst from the underbrush with a snarl—it was as tall as a horse but hunched and wiry, all sinew and snapping teeth. It had an elongated snout, a bushy tail, and thick, matted gray fur. And its eyes—wild, gleaming—burned with a green light far too bright… and far too aware."

"A direwolf!" Roedyn hissed.

"They hunt in packs!" Harper barked, drawing her rapier. "Watch your backs."

The direwolf lunged. Roedyn fired an arrow, hitting the beast mid-stride, the shaft burying deep in its shoulder. It growled but kept coming.

Harper stepped in front of Escala. "Back!" she shouted. A blast of fire roared from her palm, catching the creature square in the chest.

The beast howled, stumbling backward, smoke rising from its fur. But it got up and continued charging, snarling.

Escala drew her training sword, hands trembling, heart pounding—her first real fight.

Roedyn loosed another arrow—it struck the beast's leg, but it didn't stop. Harper spun, flames swirling in both hands, her grin feral.

Roedyn barked out orders: "Harper, left! Escala, middle!"

"Middle?" she squealed.

"Move!" Harper yelled.

Escala moved, but did she reach the middle? Everything was happening too fast.

The direwolf attacked.

She raised her sword just in time, deflecting a claw swipe that nearly knocked her down. Her arms trembled, knees buckled, but she held.

"Legs!" Roedyn shouted.

She pivoted, swung low, just like he'd taught her. The blade hit its leg—real contact. The direwolf yelped. Steel met flesh. It didn't cut, but it stumbled.

Harper surged forward. "Let's see how fast you burn!"

Before she could finish the spell, a second direwolf leapt from the shadows behind her, fangs bared, eyes burning. A third followed, fast and deadly.

Harper spun, ready to cast, but she was too late. Instinct took over, and she dove aside as claws slashed through the air where her throat had been.

"Three!" she screamed.

Roedyn was already turning, bow up. One wolf barreled straight for him. The second veered toward Harper. The third made for Escala.

His pulse spiked. Escala wasn't ready—not for three. She was already in the melee. He had the shot, but no time. She wouldn't last much longer.

Shooting into a melee was risky. He and Harper had trained for it. Escala? He'd mentioned it once. Would she remember now?

Escala's eyes widened. She raised her training sword, scrambling to recall Roedyn's bracing tips. Her shield was still strapped to her back, useless. Gripping the dull blade with both hands, she mimicked the footwork Harper had drilled into her.

The direwolf snarled and lunged.

She swung with everything she had. The blade slammed into its shoulder, but the beast barely flinched. It barreled into her with one massive forepaw, sending her flying. She hit the ground hard. With a rush of air from her lungs, her ribs ached, and her vision became hazy.

Roedyn's voice cut through the ringing in her ears.

"Drop on my signal—"

"—Now!"

But Escala was already rising, dazed, blade still clutched tight. She hadn't heard him clearly. "Now?" What did that mean? She had no instincts, no training to fall back on. Had they covered this? She couldn't remember.

"Now!" Roedyn screamed again, sighting down the shaft of his arrow at the creature.

The direwolf closed the gap, its fangs bared, eyes locked on her throat. Escala raised her sword to meet it, steel clashing desperately with claw.

Roedyn loosed an arrow, but Escala was still standing!

"DOWN!" he shouted, but she stayed upright—still fighting, still not dropping.

His heart seized as the arrow whistled straight toward her.

"ESCALA!" he roared, fear rising in his throat.

She turned at the sound—too late.

The arrow hit hard, driving into her ribs with a dull, cracking force that knocked the breath from her before the pain even had time to register. Then it came, sharp and blinding, and her scream tore through the forest, cutting over the snarls of the direwolves.

She folded as she fell, hitting the mud on one side, blood already spreading dark across her tunic. Her back arched, fingers digging into the earth as if she could hold herself together by force alone. She tried to breathe, but couldn't get full breaths; she only managed a broken gasp that turned into a low, choking groan.

Roedyn's shout came raw and immediate. "No—!"

"ESCALA!" Harper's voice followed, high and strained, already breaking.

But Harper didn't have time to reach her.

The second direwolf lunged.

She twisted left on instinct, boots slipping in the wet leaves, just enough to keep its teeth from her throat, but not enough to avoid the claws. They caught her shoulder and tore through, deep enough to spin her sideways. She hit the ground hard, rolled, came up scrambling, and found the beast already on her again, jaws open, breath hot and foul.

It leapt.

She dropped low and drove her dagger upward without thinking. Steel met bone with a jarring impact that sent a shock up her arm. The wolf snarled, its weight crashing into her anyway, slamming her back against a tree hard enough to rattle her vision. Something in her ribs gave. The dagger slipped free and vanished somewhere in the leaves.

For a second, she had nothing.

Then she moved.

She threw herself forward as the wolf twisted, grabbing for its fur, hauling herself up along its side until she could hook an arm around its neck. It bucked immediately, snarling, trying to shake her loose, but she clung on, dragging a second blade from her boot with fumbling fingers.

She didn't aim.

She drove it down into the side of its face.

The wolf howled, snapping wildly, thrashing beneath her. She struck again, somewhere softer this time, and again, feeling the blade catch, tear free, then sink in deeper on the third blow. Blood ran hot across her hand, slicking her grip.

It slammed her sideways into a boulder.

The impact burst through her spine, stole what little breath she had left, but she held on, teeth clenched so hard her jaw ached.

She shifted her weight, wrapped her legs tight around its neck, and forced the blade forward again, this time into the eye.

The sound it made was high and broken.

It staggered, thrashed once more, then began to fail beneath her.

Still, she struck—once, twice more—until the movement stopped.

Only then did she let go.

She hit the ground hard, rolling onto her side, gasping, vision dimming at the edges.

Across the clearing, Roedyn had already loosed another arrow. It struck one of the remaining wolves behind the ribs, the force of it staggering the beast but not stopping it.

He tried to move but was too slow.

Claws raked across his back, tearing through cloth and skin alike. He lurched forward with a sharp intake of breath, barely catching himself as he turned, bow already coming up again even as the wolf circled back.

He fired.

The arrow drove into its flank.

The wolf didn't stop.

Roedyn released a final shot and sank deep into the beast's chest.

Three arrows in its body, yet it didn't stop. With a roar, it barreled into him.

His bow flew. The beast landed atop him, hot breath choking the air. He braced with one arm, kicked with his legs to keep its jaws away.

His free hand fumbled for his dagger, but was too slow. The direwolf bit his shoulder. White-hot pain shot through him, and he screamed.

At last, his fingers found the hilt. He wrenched the dagger free, turned his head, and stabbed up, deep into the beast's chest, straight into its heart.

The direwolf spasmed, gave one last growl, and collapsed on top of him.

For a moment, Roedyn couldn't breathe. Then, groaning, he shoved the carcass off and dragged himself free, arm limp, face pale, but alive. He crawled to his bow and stood.

The third direwolf loomed over Escala's limp form. She lay gasping, barely conscious. Blood soaked her pants, smeared her side. She inhaled sharply as the beast's shadow fell across her.

It struck; jaws clamping down on her forearm.

She screamed.

Harper got there first, slashing wildly with her rapier.

The direwolf roared, turned to pounce, and Roedyn, now upright, fired. One arrow to the flank and another to the side.

The wolf staggered and collapsed across Escala's legs, twitching.

It was over.

Harper dropped beside Escala, trembling. "Are you okay?"

Roedyn dropped beside them, ignoring the blood streaming from his wounds. "She's bleeding—her arm, her leg... and my arrow—"

His voice cracked. "Oh gods, Escala, I'm sorry," he whispered, grabbing her hand.

Her eyes flickered, lips moving but no sound. Blood pooled thick beneath her.

"Salve!" Roedyn barked. "Get the healing salve!"

Harper, ignoring her own injuries, tore into his pack. "It's not here!"

"Her bag—check it!"

"Got it!" Harper cried, ripping it open.

"Bring it here, now!" Roedyn pressed both hands to the wound. "When I lift, you smear—fast!"

Harper knelt, breath ragged. "Do it, now!"

Roedyn yanked the cloth away, and Escala's wound pulsed with blood.

Harper smeared the white salve on her wound, and it hissed and bubbled on contact.

Escala gasped in pain.

"That's it, stay with us," Roedyn whispered. "You're not done, princess. Not yet."

Was that sweat or tears on his face? Harper couldn't tell.

Though the bleeding had eased, Escala was unconscious now. They had no means to heal her further, and they didn't dare move her.

So, they crouched there, surrounded by direwolf corpses and blood-soaked earth.

Neither spoke because both knew they'd almost lost her.

.

Chapter 26

I don't know, maybe I'm one of the best bards alive. Or maybe I'm just another chainmail-clinking loudmouth, like the guy playing two inns over. Maybe my stories are worth hearing. Maybe they sound better after a few drinks.

But I'll say this—sometimes even I get caught up in the telling. And knowing what I know now—how close Escala came to dying that day—still gives me chills.

Escala was barely breathing. Roedyn's hands were slick with blood and salve as he tied off the last bandage on her shredded limbs. The direwolf hadn't just bitten her—it had ripped her apart.

Her thin blue tunic and canvas pants hadn't stood a chance. Hours later, the wounds were hot, swollen, oozing greenish pus.

But worse—far worse—was the arrow in her gut. Roedyn didn't have to say it. Anyone who'd hunted knew: a stomach wound like that meant slow, inevitable death.

"Why did you shoot at her?" Harper snapped, dressing Roedyn's wounds.

"I didn't mean to," he shot back. "I told her to drop on 'Now'—like we always do!"

"She's not us, Roedyn! We never taught her that; she had no idea what you meant!" Harper barked.

"I didn't have a choice; the dire wolf was going to kill her. And I figured she'd remember that move we practiced," Roedyn said.

"We only talked about it," Harper shot back. "Once. In passing."

"Do you have a healing potion?" Roedyn asked.

Harper shook her head. "No."

"Well, we have no way to heal her, and we can't move her; if we try, that stomach wound will open again."

"One of us has to go for help," Roedyn said. "Dunwell's only two days out. If I run—"

"That's four days round-trip, minimum. She isn't going to make it through tonight!" Harper stressed.

"Then what do you suggest?" Roedyn said, his voice tight with anxiety.

"I don't know!" Harper shouted, grabbing a fistful of her ponytail and yanking it in frustration. "I don't—"

Before she could finish, a sharp, splintering crack echoed through the woods—like a tree snapping in half—maybe seventy or eighty yards away. It wasn't a deer skittering or a startled boar crashing through brush. Whole trees shook. Something massive was coming. Something bigger than a direwolf—much bigger.

Roedyn was up in an instant, grabbing his bow. The runes etched along the limbs flared blue as he notched an arrow and stepped in front of Escala's limp form. Harper drew her rapier and long knife, grimacing in pain.

A grizzly bear the size of a wagon burst through the trees at full sprint; fur bristling, and eyes wide with terror. Its head snapped back toward the noise, but it didn't slow. It wasn't charging. It was fleeing. It thundered past without even glancing at them.

Harper and Roedyn exchanged looks.

Then came the roar.

A creature burst into view, towering more than twenty-five feet tall. It strode on two thick legs, each step slamming into the ground like a drumbeat of thunder. Its hide was sheathed in ridged scales of ash and slate, and its massive head lunged forward, jaws lined with jagged yellow teeth like shattered swords. Below, two clawed, stunted arms twitched near its chest, absurdly small on such a monstrous frame. Its tail, thick as a tree trunk, swept behind it with the force of a falling oak.

"What is that?" Harper gasped.

Roedyn's voice came tight and low. "Some kind of giant reptilian beast. We have to protect Escala!"

The creature's foot crashed down where the bear had stood moments before, shaking the ground beneath them. It snapped its jaws and let out a roar that split the air—then charged.

"I'll draw it off!" Harper shouted, adrenaline and fear twisting her words.

Before Roedyn could stop her, she gave a sharp, piercing whistle that cut through the trees like a blade.

"HEY, STUPID!" she yelled. "Yeah, you! The overgrown garden lizard—come get me!"

She bolted left, blades flashing, dirt and leaves exploding under her boots as she drew the monster's gaze.

Roedyn planted his feet, bow raised, arrow glowing. Every instinct screamed to run, but he didn't. He couldn't. Escala lay helpless behind him. If he missed, the beast would see her and crush her without a second thought. But if he waited too long, they'd both be dead.

The creature's tail swept through a tree like paper. With a sharp crack, the wood blew apart, and splinters sliced through the air.

Harper circled wide, hurling insults like daggers. "Come on, you lizard-faced coward!"

Roedyn whispered a prayer to a god he didn't believe in and took aim.

Beside him, Escala stirred, unaware of the death towering above.

The creature turned, its predatory eyes locking onto Harper. Muscles bunched, and then it lunged.

Harper spun on her heel and bolted, weaving between trees and boulders. Behind her, the beast thundered in pursuit, tail flattening trees and flinging rocks like pebbles.

"Run!" Roedyn shouted, tracking its movement with his bow.

"Oh, brilliant idea!" Harper yelled back, ducking just as the tail sliced the air inches above her head.

She dove between two jagged crevices and vanished into the dark. The creature skidded to a halt, snapping at the gap, jaws unable to reach her. After a few furious lunges, it turned and began lumbering back toward Roedyn.

His stomach dropped.

He couldn't run. Not with Escala unconscious behind him. But standing meant facing a creature ten times his size with nothing but arrows. A lucky shot to the eye might stop it, but if he missed, she'd die.

The monster drew closer, nostrils flaring, small arms twitching. Its tail swept in wide arcs, smashing through trees as it studied him. Roedyn didn't see Escala stir behind him, didn't hear her faint groan as her eyes fluttered open.

From the cliff, Harper peeked out and froze. Roedyn stood between the beast and Escala, bow trembling. Without hesitation, she squeezed through the rocks and sprinted toward them.

With a wild cry, Harper leapt onto the creature's back, scrambling up its ridged spine. The beast reared, shrieking in fury, thrashing as Harper clung tight.

She drew a dagger, aiming for its eye, but the monster slammed itself against a tree, and the blade slipped from her hand, tumbling to the ground below.

Roedyn loosed an arrow—clink! It ricocheted off the creature's skull. He fired again, the shaft whipping past Harper's shoulder. She shouted a curse but held fast.

Yanking another dagger free, Harper drove it deep into the creature's head. The knife sank to the hilt.

The beast let out a roar that shattered the air.

Then, an explosion of light.

Harper was thrown skyward, spinning, trying to grab a branch—missing—and slamming to the ground on her back. Stars burst across her vision.

Roedyn shielded his eyes from the blast. The last thing he saw was Harper's blade buried in the creature's skull, then a blinding light.

When the glow finally faded, the massive beast was gone. No blood or remains.

As he looked more closely, though, Roedyn saw a frog, round-bodied, two feet tall, with bulging orange eyes that took up half its face. It blinked up at him. The frog wore a blue tunic cinched with a leather belt and held a small wooden staff with a blue gem. He adjusted his belt, shook out his limbs, and gave a satisfied croak.

"Well, that was exhilarating. Painful, though the knife especially."

The group just stared.

Harper broke the silence. "Okay. What the actual hell?"

"I am Sticky," said the frog with dignified gravity.

"That's your real name?" Roedyn asked.

"No, but my real name is unpronounceable," said the frog. "So I go by Sticky."

Harper raised her rapier. "You were just a giant lizard trying to kill us."

"No," Sticky said. "I was a Tyrannosaurus rex, not a giant lizard."

"What's that?" Harper said.

Sticky rubbed his head where Harper's blade had struck. "That was a dinosaur form called the Tyrannosaurus rex. Technically, it is also known as the tyrant lizard, so I guess, yes, I was a giant lizard."

Roedyn kept his bow raised. "You going to explain that, or…?"

Sticky blinked. "I was trying to scare off the grizzly. It was trying to eat me."

His tongue flicked out, snatching a fly midair.

"I didn't want to be eaten."

"Well, we didn't either," Roedyn said flatly.

"I wasn't going to eat you," Sticky replied, mildly offended. "I smelled a fey and came to investigate. Then I saw you'd killed one."

He pointed to Escala's bloodied, motionless form.

"Roedyn shot her with an arrow because she was talking too much; he'd had enough," Harper said, deadpan.

Roedyn glared at Harper but quickly turned to Sticky. "It was an accident—she is very seriously wounded."

Harper cocked her head, still watching Sticky. "Wait... how do you know she's fey?"

Sticky blinked twice. "I could smell her fey magic because she was bleeding in my woods."

Roedyn's eyes widened.

Harper narrowed hers. "And what exactly do you mean by your woods?"

Sticky puffed up slightly. "I'm the caretaker of Never Glenns. And really, the entire Silverstand Forest. I speak for the trees."

"You're a druid," Roedyn said—it was more of a statement.

"Indeed. I keep the balance of the Silverstand attuned to the True Cycle. I can sense its threads. That's how I knew a fey had fallen and how I know one of you shot her."

Roedyn sighed. "I didn't kill her."

"But he did shoot her," Harper chimed in. "Just saying."

Roedyn quickly said, "Druids can heal. Can you heal her? Please?"

Sticky hopped closer. "Let me see her."

He squatted next to Escala, gumming his lips as he poked her shoulder.

"Don't do that!" Roedyn said protectively, extending his arm to stop Sticky. "She doesn't like being touched."

"I need to see her wounds, if you don't mind."

"Please, don't hurt her," Roedyn said.

Sticky examined her wounds. "She is indeed very ill."

"Can you help her?" Roedyn asked.

Sticky shook his head.

Roedyn's heart sank.

"But," Sticky said, "I can help her if I get her back to my lily pad. I can treat her."

"You can't move her," Harper said. "The wounds will reopen."

Sticky looked at her thoughtfully. Then, without warning, his tongue snapped out inches from her face and caught another fly.

"Mmm, crunchy," he said with a double blink, and as if he had not just eaten a fly, he continued, "Make a litter and tie a rope to each corner. I'll change into a giant eagle and fly her to my lily pad."

"You can fly?" Roedyn asked.

"I can change shape at will into any natural creature I have seen."

"You saw, what did you call that form, a tranno rex around here?" Roedyn asked.

"Oh no, not a tranno rex, a Tyrannosaurus rex" said Sticky, "I saw it in the Emerald Jungle on the continent of Zandara, which has a lot of interesting creatures."

Harper crossed her arms. "And why exactly were you in a jungle full of giant lizards?"

Sticky blinked once. "I was looking for the famed Magaambya University."

Roedyn turned toward him. "Why would you need to go there? I heard it was destroyed after the Purge."

Sticky nodded. "It was. But druids still guard what remains, to keep the Magocracy from trying again what caused it. It was my time to spend a season keeping the balance there."

Harper glanced at Roedyn. Their eyes met, a silent exchange of respect passing between them.

"I'll tell you this," Sticky said without looking up, cutting through the moment. "Lizards aren't the only giant creatures in the jungle. Did you ever see a spider the size of a wagon wheel? They're huge. And they've got opinions, loud ones."

Harper let out a shaky laugh, but Roedyn only gave her a steady look. "Come on," he said quietly. "Let's focus on Escala."

Harper nodded, the humor fading from her face. Together, they moved to Escala's side and got to work.

In twenty minutes, they'd fashioned a litter from branches and cloth, ropes tied at each corner. They lifted Escala gently onto it. Roedyn winced each time she whimpered.

Sticky raised his staff, muttered something primal, and the gem at the top flared blue. In a flash, the frog was gone, replaced by a massive golden eagle with broad, powerful wings.

He gripped the ropes in his talons and soared upward with surprising grace.

Roedyn and Harper grabbed their packs and sprinted after him, already falling behind as the eagle soared over the trees. For half an hour they scrambled over boulders, slid down muddy slopes, and skirted the edge of a bog before finally arriving—out of breath—at a small pond tucked into a quiet, misty glen.

Sticky, in frog form again, was brewing something in a copper pot. Escala lay beside him, her tunic pulled up just enough to reveal the arrow wound. The flesh around it was dark, necrotic. He held his staff over the wound, muttered words in a tongue older than leaves, and the blue gem pulsed with power.

Magic swirled from the staff, coiling like smoke, forming translucent blue tendrils that wrapped around Escala's ribs. Then, shockingly, the wound shrank, the skin pulling together until, within seconds, there was no blood, no scab, or even a scar.

He repeated the process on her leg and arm. This time, black pus hissed, bubbled up, and vanished beneath glowing threads of energy. The bite marks vanished too, completely gone.

Harper asked, "I thought you were going to boil herbs and slap on some poultices. You know, normal healer stuff."

Sticky double-blinked. "I was boiling water for tea. She'll want something hot when she wakes."

Right on cue, Escala stirred. Her eyes fluttered open, then flew wide as she jerked back. The first thing she saw was a frog crouched inches from her face, giant orange eyes blinking at her.

She gasped. "W-where... where am I?"

"You're in the Never Glens," Sticky said, his fingers tightening around his staff. "Why are you on the material plane, my fey child? You're not in your true form. Can you shapeshift?"

"Who... who are you?" she stammered, defensive and dazed.

"I am Sticky, Archdruid of Silverstand Forest." His tongue flicked out to snatch a passing bug. "I won't hurt you, in fact, I saved you."

Escala blinked at him. "I didn't know frogs could talk... and frogs can talk?"

"Yes," Sticky replied. "All tripkees frogs can talk, and most druids can shapeshift."

She hesitated, then added, "How did you know I'm… fey?"

Sticky tilted his head. "I can smell you."

Escala opened her mouth, closed it, then opened it again, unsure what to do with that information.

Only then did Sticky continue, his tone turning thoughtful. "I stopped chasing the bear when I caught your scent on the wind—your magic. You were bleeding. Faint, but definitely fey." He nodded toward Harper and Roedyn, who stood sheepishly behind her, Roedyn now a deep shade of red. "I thought these two had killed you."

Escala tried to sit up, her body weak and trembling. When she saw her friends, a faint smile broke through the pain. "Harper… Roedyn… you didn't leave me."

Harper smirked. "We don't usually ditch people Roedyn shoots. We bury them, it's the polite thing to do."

Roedyn groaned, dragged a hand down his face, and dropped to one knee beside her. He reached for Escala's hand, and to his surprise, she didn't pull away.

That's right, folks she did not pull away. It is important to note that that was the first time she did not tell Roedyn, "no one touches the faerie."

Roedyn knelt next to Escala, held her hand, and whispered, "Escala… I'm sorry, I didn't mean to hurt you. I was aiming for the wolf's chest, and I thought you were going to drop like we practiced."

Harper interrupted, "We didn't practice."

Roedyn's face reddened. "I'm sorry. I thought you would understand. I—I screwed up. If Sticky hadn't shown up, you'd be gone and I…"

His throat caught. "I…"

Escala gave his hand a gentle squeeze. "I know."

Her voice was thin. "I know you wouldn't hurt me on purpose."

"I wouldn't," Roedyn said quickly. "I mean, no, never."

She smiled faintly, her eyes soft. "You've already done so much for me. You're taking me to Wigfrith… so I can learn how to go home."

Home. The word hit Roedyn like a knife.

Before he could answer, Sticky waddled between them, tugging their hands apart with a grumble. "No touching the faerie—she needs rest. Shoo, shoo."

Escala turned to Sticky just in time to watch him devour another fly.

Roedyn reluctantly let go of her hand and stood up. "Escala, we've made light of your quest. We didn't believe you, I didn't believe you. I'm sorry. I promise I'll help you remove the boulders from the True Cycle. We'll stand by you."

"Hey, wait a second—" Harper started.

"You, too," Roedyn said, glaring at her. "You're helping."

Escala's eyes lit up. "Really? You'll really help me?"

Roedyn nodded. "Yes."

Harper let out a long sigh. "Well, since I'm not scheduled to drown an emperor in a chamber pot this week, count me in."

Sticky poured steaming cups from the pot and handed them around. The drink smelled like boiled nettles and regret.

Roedyn, as he took his cup, looked Sticky in the eyes and said, "Thank you for saving her."

Sticky nodded and continued to pass out the steaming cups.

Harper watched Roedyn's face but said nothing, for once.

Sticky looked at Escala. "So, you're going to fix the True Cycle?"

"I think so," she said. "I don't know what it means yet. The court sentenced me to remove boulders from it. I'm trying to figure it out."

Sticky plopped down with a loud, wet squish.

"Well, why didn't you say so earlier?" he croaked. "You're broken."

"I'm what?" Escala asked in surprise.

"Broken!" Sticky said. "Cracked open like a seed before spring. That's good, that's how new things grow."

He tapped her gently with his staff.

"If you're removing boulders," he said, "you're trying to return to the Dreaming Court?"

"Court of Dreams," she corrected. "But I don't know if I can go back."

Sticky nodded solemnly. "That's why I'm coming with you."

Harper coughed. "You're what now?"

"I'm joining your party," Sticky said proudly, raising his tea like a toast. "I've traveled across all of Valla—through its jungles, mountains, deserts, forests, plains, and seas. I've seen nearly every creature the gods ever set upon this world, and because of that, I can take their forms when I need to. You'll find that particularly useful, I think. Also, you need someone who can talk to boulders."

"You can talk to boulders?" Harper asked suspiciously.

"If they are sociable," Sticky answered, as if it were an established fact.

Escala asked, "Why help me?"

Sticky shrugged. "Because you're a mess. And messy things make the world interesting."

Chapter 27

They camped on Sticky's lily pad for a few days as Escala slowly regained her strength. Sticky filled the days with stories, tales of the Never Glenns and the wild woods of Silverstand Forest.

Escala shared her own, showing him her logbook and her plan to fill it with accounts of people she'd helped, and the boulders cleared from their paths, one by one. As Sticky listened, his thoughts kept circling the same idea: boulders in the True Cycle. A couple of days later, he finally said, "The Never Glenns may hold one of your boulders."

Escala sat up. "Really?"

He nodded. "A vinethrasher has grown too large. It's upsetting the balance."

Harper frowned. "That sounds made up."

"I wish it were," Sticky croaked. "Come. I'll show you."

He rose and limped to the edge of the clearing, motioning for them to follow. After a few hours of travel through the forest, they reached a twisted tree stump near a pool of dark water. Sticky tapped the bark once and whispered something in a language none of them knew.

The stump stirred, and bark peeled back like petals, revealing a glowing mural of tangled roots. Etched in glowing green lines was a towering vine-creature; limbs of bark and thorn, a cave-like mouth dripping with vine-teeth. Around it, smaller trees sagged and shriveled.

"It's not just alive," Sticky said. "It's starving."

Escala stared. "What does it eat?"

"Magic," Sticky said. "Not just from the ground—from birds, beasts, blossoms... even me."

Harper shifted. "And if it keeps feeding?"

"The Never Glenns will die," he said. "This is a boulder in the True Cycle."

"Has anyone tried fighting it?" Roedyn asked.

"You can't," Sticky said. "Blades are useless. Cut one limb, three more grow back. It's not evil, it's just a vine warped into something it was never meant to be."

He reached into his satchel and pulled out a small, clay vial that glowed faintly green.

"This is the cure. A purge made from dreamroot and moonvine. Touch the pistil at its core, and it'll unravel and go back to what it was."

He hopped forward. "Come."

An hour later, they reached a mossy clearing. At first glance, it looked like a boulder draped in vines. Then it moved. The vines pulsed and unfurled, and five slick tentacles rising like serpents through the mist.

Harper stepped back. "That's no rock."

"It's the vinethrasher," Sticky said grimly. "And it's grown."

"Great," Harper muttered. "Toss your magic juice and let's go."

Sticky shook his head. "The vial must be poured directly onto the pistil. But I can't get close. The tentacles swarm the moment I try. I need help keeping them busy—all of them."

Roedyn stiffened. "Help? From whom?"

Sticky turned to Escala. "The Dreaming Court sent you for a reason."

"It's the Court of Dreams," Escala corrected.

He waved her off. "Doesn't matter. This thing is a rupture in the forest's harmony. If we don't stop it now, it'll devour the Glenns, the swamps... maybe everything."

He suddenly looked older. Then—snap—his tongue lashed out, nabbing a dragonfly. Chewing, he said, "I'm a druid. I protect the balance. But I can't do it alone. I need you, and I need her."

Escala moved toward Sticky and said, "Then I'll do it."

"No," Roedyn said sharply, moving in front of her. "Absolutely not."

"I have to," Escala replied. "It's my quest. This is a boulder, and I came to remove it."

"You almost died a few days ago," Roedyn snapped. "I won't watch that happen again."

"Then don't watch," she said. "Help."

"This is suicide."

"This is a boulder," Escala said as she turned to Harper. "I need you too."

Harper said, "It beats sitting around here."

The vinethrasher's limbs thrashed louder, ripping trees and feeding on the magic in the air.

Roedyn exhaled. "What do I need to do?"

Sticky handed him a pouch of glowmote dust. "Blind its eyestalks with this if you can and keep moving."

Harper cracked her neck. "Guess I've got tentacle duty. Sticky, you'd better have a healing spell if I lose a limb."

Sticky's tongue snagged another fly while he pulled out the glowing vial and handed it to Escala.

Roedyn looked at her. "I did promise to help you move boulders. I just didn't think they'd be weeds."

Chapter 28

I f Sticky was to be believed, this wasn't some rock in the road or a mossy wall by a river. No, this was a living, roaring, magical beast. A creature swelling with power, throwing the Never Glenns out of balance. So dangerous that a druid whose sacred duty was to preserve the True Cycle had asked for help. Escala was about to move her first real boulder.

Now then… let me tell you what happened.

The four of them fanned out around the monstrous vine, which was tearing trees from the earth like twigs. Six massive tentacles whipped skyward—thick as ancient trunks, slick with sap and shadow, writhing with unnatural fury.

At the core, hidden behind the chaos of flailing limbs, was something far more sinister. Through brief, jolting glimpses, they caught sight of it—a jagged, vertical maw, like a wound in the world, ringed with obsidian teeth and half concealed beneath a flap of bark-like armor. That was the pistil—where Escala had to deliver the vial.

The vinethrasher roared so horrifically that I am not afraid to tell you, I would've been scared.

Sticky moved first, thrusting both arms skyward as he chanted in a strange, throaty tongue. Green runes burst from his fingertips and spiraled into the earth, glowing as they embedded into the mud like roots. From those sigils, thick, serpentine vines erupted—his own magic—snapping forward to ensnare two of the vinethrasher's tentacles. The summoned vines coiled tight, anchoring to the ground, straining with all their might against the beast's unnatural strength. The earth trembled from the clash.

"They won't hold long!" Sticky shouted. "Hurry!"

Roedyn was already sprinting left, loosing arrows with surgical precision, until one of the vinethrasher's free tentacles whipped through the air and struck him square in the chest. The impact launched him into a tree with a sickening crack, and he crumpled to the ground. Before he could move, another tentacle snapped around his torso and hoisted his limp form into the air.

"Roedyn!" Escala screamed.

Sticky, arms outstretched and trembling as he held his summoned vines in place, shouted through clenched teeth, "No, your weapons won't hurt it! Use the dust! Blind it—distract it!"

Harper didn't hesitate. She ignored Sticky's warning and charged into the fray, twin blades flashing, a snarl on her lips. She slashed into the nearest tentacle, ducked under a swinging tendril, rolled, and drove a dagger deep into its bark-like flesh. But before she could rise, another vine lashed around her waist and yanked her into the air—followed by a third that coiled around her arm, pulling her the other way.

Across the clearing, Roedyn thrashed against the tentacle, crushing his ribs. He fumbled for the pouch of glowmote dust Sticky had given him, but as he reached for it, another vine curled silently around his throat and jerked tight. His hands flew to his neck, trying to pry it loose—too late. The pouch slipped from his grasp and tumbled to the earth. Roedyn gagged, his chest heaving against the crushing grip as both vines constricted, stealing his breath.

Escala hesitated—just for a breath—and then vanished.

Not literally. But she moved like only the fey could—quiet, nearly invisible. She crept slowly, avoiding the vines' notice, but her eyes were locked on her goal.

The vinethrasher thrashed, fixated on the others. Its massive limbs writhed and flailed, but none struck her.

She crouched low and quietly picked up the pouch of glowmote dust that had fallen. Her fingers closed around it as she looked up. The vines trapped Roedyn, tightening around his chest until pain twisted his face. His skin flushed as he struggled for a breath.

She tightened her grip on the pouch and turned toward the maw.

She was deep within the vinethrasher's body—if it could be called that—a twisting mass of thick, pulsing stems coiling toward its monstrous center. Every movement was chaos. The plant thrashed blindly, madness in motion, its tentacles slashing through air and earth alike.

Sticky was losing. Two tentacles had just broken free, snapping his summoned vines. One slammed into him with brutal force, sending him tumbling into a shallow, marshy pool. Before he could rise, another vine wrapped around his small body and began driving him into the mud, burying him. Suffocating him. His limbs flailed helplessly.

Harper wasn't faring better. A thick vine had snared her leg and flung her like a rag doll, smashing her into the ground and nearby trees. She hung limp, blood trailing in arcs—unmoving, unconscious.

Sticky's struggles ceased, his small body now halfway submerged in mud. He wasn't breathing.

If Escala didn't reach the pistil, if she didn't pour the vial into that terrible, jagged maw, they were all going to die.

She crept closer, heart pounding, pulling the glowing vial from her pouch. The creature's gaping mouth loomed ahead, ringed with black, thorn-like teeth. She was only yards away.

Then a free tentacle snapped toward her—drawn by her scent, or maybe her magic. It struck with a vicious crack, slamming into her face and sending her sprawling.

Her ears rang, her vision blurred, but somehow, she still clutched the vial.

She pushed onto all fours, reaching for the pouch of glimmering dust—just as a vine coiled around her waist and yanked her into the air.

She felt it immediately, like ice through her veins. It was draining her, pulling at something deeper than blood.

The vine hoisted her high, holding her as if examining her. Below, the jagged maw opened and closed in hungry pulses.

She caught a glimpse of Sticky now wrapped in two vines, being shoved deeper into the mud, limbs twitching in slow, jerking spasms.

Roedyn dangled limp and choking, the tentacle around his neck glowing with a sickly green rot. His face had turned blue, eyes bulging, arms hanging uselessly.

Harper was still being whipped against the ground, again and again. Blood soaked her armor. She wasn't moving.

Escala knew she had only one chance.

She plunged her hand into the pouch of glimmering dust—fey magic was second nature, and she knew instinctively how to cast it. The vine around her waist was already coiling tighter, ready to whip her through the air while draining her fey magic from her veins.

She flung the dust in a wide, sweeping arc.

The dust caught the air and spread, coating the creature's gaping maw and the thick tentacle wrapped around her. The reaction was immediate. The tentacle spasmed, shuddered, then released her with a jerk and recoiled violently.

Something about the dust repelled it.

Escala crashed to the ground, landing hard on her back. Pain bloomed in her chest, but she was free, at least for the moment.

The other tentacles thrashed on, still locked in combat with her friends. She could barely breathe but forced herself to her feet.

The tentacle that had dropped her was already recovering, twitching and writhing as it reoriented. She had seconds—maybe less—to finish what she started.

She charged the one strangling Roedyn.

Ducking a swipe, she vaulted onto a fallen branch and launched herself like a silver blur. Her blade slashed through the tentacle just above the coil. Black sap burst out like tar. The vine spasmed and dropped Roedyn.

He crumpled, unmoving.

Escala spun and sprinted toward the maw. She grabbed a final handful of glimmer dust as two tentacles whipped toward her—the one she'd just severed and the one that nearly killed her before. She tossed the dust upwards and darted through the descending sparkle, much like a shadow moving in the moonlight. The tentacles recoiled, writhing in disgust.

She was just feet from the vinethrasher now. It snapped at the air, massive jaws gnashing just out of reach.

She reached for more dust, but the pouch was empty. The glittering cloud was already fading, and the tentacles were probing forward again, testing.

She pulled the vial from her belt and gripped it tight in one hand, training sword in the other. She lunged, slashing at the maw, trying to bait it open, but it was smart—too smart. It didn't fall for the feint. She couldn't get the right angle.

A vine wrapped around her ankle and yanked her into the air. Another struck like a whip, ripping the blade from her hand—it clattered near the maw. More vines snared her, hoisting her like prey. One coiled tight around her neck, squeezing.

Her vision darkened. But her right hand—her throwing arm—was still free. The vial was still clutched in her fist. She gasped for breath, barely conscious, memories flashing unbidden.

Rihanna and her, hiding in trees, hurling acorns at marketgoers, and ducking out of sight. Terrible aim at first. But over the years of pranks and mischief, they got good. Deadly good. If there was ever a time for it, it was now.

Escala locked eyes on the maw below, it gaped open, snapping hungrily. Maybe twenty feet. Maybe less. She hurled the vial. But just as it left her hand, the vine around her waist jerked her sideways—the throw went wide, veering left.

And that's when fate intervened. Harper's limp body, still clutched by another vine, was flung like a ragdoll—directly into the path of Escala's throw. The vial struck her boot with a sharp crack, bounced—

—and tumbled straight into the vinethrasher's gaping mouth. The vinethrasher snapped its jaws shut just as the vial shattered inside, releasing the potion. A second later, a shockwave of magic ripped through it, and every tentacle spasmed, flailed wildly—then went limp.

The vine no longer pushed Sticky into the mud. Harper was dropped unceremoniously into a bush and didn't move. Escala hit the ground hard, gasping.

The vinethrasher let out one final, awful screech, a low wail and then its body began to unravel. Leaves tore loose like paper in a storm. Stalks split and withered.

In moments, all that remained was a single, ordinary spider vine.

Escala staggered upright and rushed to Roedyn. He was groaning—alive. Relief surged through her, but there was no time to waste. She sprinted to Harper.

Harper was in terrible shape—bruised, bloodied, and deathly still—but somehow, miraculously, she was breathing.

Then Escala darted to Sticky. He sat dazed in the mud. "Croak," he muttered weakly, then hopped to his feet. He snatched up his staff and went to work, chanting low and fast. Healing magic flowed through his hands as he stabilized both Harper and Roedyn.

When it was done, he looked up, mud-caked but steady. "The spider vine is cured—it's no longer a threat."

He said, "Escala Winter from the Dreaming Court—"

"Court of Dreams," she gently corrected again.

Sticky ignored her. "You removed that boulder from the True Cycle. We'd all be dead if you hadn't used the glowmote dust and the antidote. The Silverstand Forest names you a friend."

"We did it," Escala whispered, almost in disbelief.

Roedyn looked at her, then Harper, then back to Sticky. "No," he said firmly. "You did it."

Escala pulled out her logbook and flint pencil, handed them to Sticky with a smile, and said, "Make sure you write how big the boulder was."

Chapter 29

Back at the lily pad, Escala lay beside the fire with her cloak drawn tight around her shoulders. Her body ached, but the warmth from the flames eased the pain. Roedyn sat across from her, head bowed, fletching a new arrow in silence. Harper, now recovered, thanks to Sticky's healing magic, had dozed off with her back against a tree, one half-melted boot drying near the fire.

Sticky crouched beside a small mushroom ring, whispering to the fungi.

"Sticky," Escala asked, turning towards the frog, "why do you care so much about this place?"

He turned his head, firelight glinting off his wide, orange eyes.

"Because it's mine," he said.

"I still don't understand," she said, "You say your job is to protect the balance of this place, but that wolf, the one that killed Rihanna, that was part of nature too, wasn't it? So how can you protect something like that? Why would you want to?"

Sticky didn't answer right away. He sat motionless, the firelight dancing in his wide, reflective eyes. When he finally spoke, his voice was measured.

"Because it's my family," he said.

"What is?"

"The wolf," he said, stirring the mossy fire with a stick. "The rabbits, the trees, the songbirds, the earthworm, even the vinethrasher—it's all part of the circle of life. And a druid's duty is not to judge that family by what comforts or frightens them, but to tend it all so the circle can continue. So, I protect every part, even the creatures that bite."

"But a wolf killed her," Escala said, pain in her voice.

Sticky nodded. "Yes, and I grieve that. If I had been there, maybe I could've stopped it. But protection doesn't mean preventing pain, nor does it mean taming nature or cutting off its sharp edges. And nature is sharp—it has teeth and claws. But nature is also beautiful—it has blossoms and birdsong, and you don't get one without the other."

Escala folded her arms. "So, you defend murderers now?"

Sticky's eyes flicked to hers. "Nature doesn't kill out of malice. That wolf didn't take Rihanna's life because it hated her. It probably was hungry or felt threatened; it was just being natural. I can't pick sides when animals are being natural. Druids don't say, 'this one's good, that one's evil.' Instead, we say 'What is this, and where does it belong?'"

Escala's voice dropped. "And if it doesn't belong?"

"Then I remove it from the family I protect," Sticky said, "and guide it back to where it was meant to be."

He looked away, toward the dark trees beyond the firelight.

"It hurts when one of my creatures turns savage under my watch," he said, tossing a bit of moss into the fire. "But I still love it."

Sticky glanced at the others. "People think love means safety—that if you love something, it won't ever hurt you. But that's not love—that's convenience. Real love sticks around, even when it's risky and even when it hurts. If I only cared for the creatures that obeyed me and if I started deciding who gets to stay and who gets cast out based on whether they follow my rules, then I wouldn't be a druid anymore. I'd be a tyrant in a flower crown."

Sticky added, "If you think nature should be tame and soft, then you've mistaken it for a garden. A garden is what mortals do with nature when they are afraid of it. I don't protect nature from danger. I protect nature as it is— beautiful and dangerous."

He leaned forward, nudging the fire with the end of his staff, and sparks leapt into the air like startled fireflies.

"When you love something—when it's your family— you don't just protect it. You belong to it, and you give yourself to it, whatever it asks."

They sat in silence, the fire crackling between them.

Escala loosened her cloak as she thought on Sticky's words. They had taken root, deeper than she expected. Love wasn't kisses or starlit promises beside a pond.

Love was a choice you made to protect the beautiful and dangerous things you care about and those people you call family.

She'd never thought of it that way. Now she couldn't stop thinking about it.

Chapter 30

———

As Escala and her companions pushed on toward Dunwell, things were happening in the Court of Dreams.

A figure in shadow glided past the Pearl Arch. She passed through the long-mirrored corridor and down past the moss-stone pillars that no longer hummed.

She wore no perfume tonight or jewelry to catch the light. Her robes were dark so she could blend with the shadows—she did not want to be seen.

The garden gate creaked once, then fell still.

Moonlight cascaded over the marble urns lining the quiet path, each resting like an offering above carefully tended soil. No guards at this hour.

There would be no witnesses.

She moved to the center of the garden, where silver blossoms curled toward the stars. She knelt by a patch of bare earth between two old urns.

From beneath her cloak, she withdrew the Vorrash Totem.

Victor had told her it would slumber—that its time would come later. All she had to do was plant it. And wait.

The totem pulsed once in her hand, almost eager. She pressed it into the soil with both hands, burying it deep. Then she placed a plain urn over the spot, carefully matching the others in shape and weathering. It vanished into the row like a coin into water.

She rose, adjusted the folds of her robe, and disappeared down the corridor like smoke curling beneath a closed door.

By nightfall two days later, after passing through the veil by bleeding, she stood in the lower chamber of Blackthorn Tower.

Victor didn't look up from his table of glass instruments and bone-etched runes.

"Well?" he asked.

"It's there," Morvena said.

"Good." He touched the edge of a mirror and watched it ripple like water. "It won't be long now."

Morvena nodded.

Victor knew the totem would stir when called—when he had enough power to activate it—and the court would never see it coming. Not even Morvena, the fool.

Chapter 31

I reach for my pipe, a quiet invitation, in case anyone else fancies a smoke. As I pack the bowl with tobacco from the rolling fields of Kelly's Pride, I nearly launch into the tale of how it got its name. Something about a woman named Kelly who seduced a wealthy old miner, took over his town, and inherited everything, after he "accidentally" tumbled down one of his own goldmine shafts.

But that's a story for another night.

As I puff, I continue Escala's Wish.

When they arrived at Dunwell, the first thing Escala noticed were the vivid colors. Everything was painted, doors in faded reds and deep greens, shutters in lavender and storm blue. Even the cobblestones were splashed here and there with dye and chalk, remnants of old festivals and careless children.

They passed a bakery with golden rolls steaming on the sill, a smithy with a horseshoe nailed crooked over the lintel. Street vendors called out wares. Sticky walked beside Escala, arms folded behind his back, scanning every flowerpot for bugs to snatch with his tongue, and he was not disappointed.

Escala wasn't used to being surrounded by so many people. Almost immediately, there were some "no one touches the faerie" moments that Roedyn had to defuse.

They followed a cobbled lane to a three-story inn with a crooked sign swinging out front: The Stag and Hound.

They stepped inside by the very door you all came through tonight. It looked the same back then, maybe with fewer folks inside, but on stage was a certain dashing gnome performer, finishing a tale as they walked in.

He struck a pose and recited:

"—and with a roar, she tore the wing from the firedrake's spine and fanned herself with it; the way only a queen of the Summer Court might!"

The gnome was me, of course, and I bowed so deeply that I nearly tumbled off the table.

"Wigfrith?" Harper called out, grinning.

I snapped my head up and took in Harper and her companions.

I lifted my mug as if preparing to deliver the toast of a lifetime. This was the very first time I laid eyes on Escala. And my, oh my, was she beautiful.

She wore tan canvas pants tucked into black boots that rose to her knees. A royal navy-blue tunic, trimmed with silver, hugged her frame. A black leather belt circled her waist, with a travel pouch on one side and a short sword on the other. Her pack was slung casually over one shoulder. I even noticed a small patch near her ribs where the tunic had clearly been stitched, like it had once been torn in battle.

But what struck me was her presence. She carried herself like someone who belonged in a court, she was no peasant. Of course, I recognized Harper and Roedyn immediately. But the frog? I didn't know him. I had questions, oh so many questions.

Harper nudged Escala forward, of course, but I did not yet know her name. "She's looking for you," Harper said. "We told her you know everything."

I looked at the crowd for confirmation that perhaps Harper was not wrong. It took a moment, longer than I would have liked, but eventually, applause developed, and when I was satisfied, I gave a courteous nod.

Smiling at Harper, I said, "Well, now, I can see you definitely didn't inflate her expectations."

Turning to Escala, I bowed with an elaborate flourish. "My dearest elf maiden, it is my honor to meet you. I'm Wigfrith Foreverbloom, Bard Medic of Misty Springs, spinner of a hundred tales, and survivor of at least thirty-five. And you—"

And that's when she said those nine words I would come to hear hundreds—if not thousands—of times throughout our adventures together: "I am Escala Winter from the Court of Dreams."

Now, I'd heard of the Court of Dreams, most bards had. But she was claiming to be fey, even though she looked like an elf. Interesting.

I stroked my chin theatrically. "Then come, we have much to discuss."

We took the corner table by the hearth. Escala sat across from me and watched me closely, her eyes searching my face. And I, well, I was doing the same to her, looking for any hint of madness.

I pulled out a leather-bound notebook, a fountain pen, and prepared to take notes.

"Now," I said, "we must establish that you are who you say you are. Let's begin."

I squinted suspiciously at her. "First question. Name the three most dangerous edible mushrooms in the Deep Briar, which, as you know, is a hollow four valleys southwest of the palace of the Court of Dreams, and tell me what they whisper when picked under a full moon?"

"What?" Escala said.

Roedyn leaned over to Harper. "Is he serious?"

"Oh yeah," Harper muttered. "He's in full Wiggie mode."

Escala thought carefully. "This is a trick question."

"How so?" I asked, knowing she was right.

"Well, the mushrooms that are dangerous to some are also a boon to others. For example, firecaps can burn your blood, and if you eat too many, you can explode from the inside. But they're used by healers in small quantities to treat certain infections. And what they whisper depends on how fast you pick them. If you pick them fast, they scream. But if you pick them very slowly, they don't whisper anything."

I raised an eyebrow, surprised. She was right.

"And then there are the purple-stemmed heartspore mushrooms," she continued. "They're deadly to mortals and can kill almost instantly if consumed, but they're not poisonous to fey. We use them for stomach aches. So, I'm

209

not sure whether that counts as a dangerous mushroom or not. And they don't whisper anything, well, I guess they do, but no one knows what they say because they speak a language no one understands, and then—"

I cut her off. "Very good!" I quickly scribbled her answers into my notebook.

"But I didn't finish the answer," she said, almost annoyed.

"You did fine, just fine," I said. "Question two: What is the third law of moonlight according to sprite tradition?"

Escala didn't hesitate. "Moonlight reveals only what wishes to be found."

I grinned wider. "Excellent. Question three: How many names does the wind have in the Court of Dreams?"

"Eighteen," she said. "Nineteen, when a crossing is open."

Harper raised an eyebrow. "What does that even mean?"

"It means she knows what she's talking about," I said, my eyes never leaving Escala's. Maybe it was because she was so unbearably beautiful, those striking blue eyes impossible to look away from or maybe I was trying to spot a 'tell,' some twitching lip or suspiciously sweaty forehead that would reveal a lie.

All I can report is this: she had none of those things. Just those impossibly beautiful blue eyes.

I leaned forward across the table. "Last question, the real test." My voice dropped to a conspiratorial whisper. "In your truest form, before the banishment, how tall were you?"

I pause the tale and take a slow sip of ale, rubbing my chin as if pondering some grand mystery. Then I lean in and say, "Now listen closely, friends, that last question I asked Escala was a trick question. The fey don't measure things the way we do. No pounds, feet, or meters for them. They measure by nature, petals, raindrops, moonbeams, that sort of thing.

If she'd said something like 'one foot' or 'sixteen inches,' I'd know she was faking it. This is the moment of truth. If her answer sounds like a lie, the story ends right here, and you can all head over to the Golden Goose, hells, I'm going with you!

"But," I tap the table for emphasis, "listen to what she tells me."

Escala immediately answered, "I was two red apples and a green grape tall."

I must admit I howled with laughter and slapped my knee, and the audience did too.

Harper choked on her drink.

"Two red apples!" I was nearly crying. "And a green grape!" I thumped the table. "By the gods, she's genuine!"

I nearly toppled off the stool, catching myself with a wobble and a curse. Then, recovering with all the grace I could muster, I swept my arm in a grand arc across the table.

"Escala of the Court of Dreams," I proclaimed, "welcome to the material plane, to Dunwell, and to The Stag and Hound!"

I extended my hand with a theatrical flourish. "How may I, Wigfrith Foreverbloom, be of service?"

She did not shake my hand. To be honest, I thought she was being rude. However, Roedyn quickly said, "She doesn't like to be touched; it's nothing personal." I withdrew my hand at once.

I leaned forward, elbows on the table, hands folded beneath my chin.

"So," I said, "what can I help you with?

Escala told me her story, which you have already heard, and I focused on the boulder part.

"Tell me exactly what the Court of Dreams said, word for word." I said, ready to take detailed notes.

Escala nodded slowly. She took a breath, closed her eyes for a moment, and recited her sentence from the trial I told you about earlier. I stopped her at the part about the boulders and made her repeat it.

Now, I am a smart gnome, I think you'll agree, but I did not know what a boulder was in the context of her punishment.

"Apples and pears," I said. "They went full poetic punishment."

"I've been trying to figure out what it means ever since," Escala said. "At first, I thought the court meant real boulders, physical things I had to move or destroy. Then I thought maybe it was about people's obstacles, dreadful things in their lives they needed help with. I've been keeping a logbook, I have people sign it every time I help someone."

"She's not kidding," Harper said. "She even has a signed page from some guy saying she helped him negotiate a peace treaty with a swarm of bees."

"Do you think what I'm doing is right? Is helping people with their troubles and obstacles the boulders the Court of Dreams meant?" she asked.

"No," I said. "But," I added, holding up one finger, voice laced with stubborn brightness, "I have theories."

I flipped through my notebook and stopped with a flourish on a page—crinkled, ink-stained, singed at the corner.

I tapped a passage with my knuckle. "This one always stuck with me. A forest warden I met in the Cindermarshes said it came to him in a fever dream. He woke screaming and didn't speak for days. When he finally did, all he said was, 'The Cycle's jammed. Too many boulders, the wheel's stuck.'"

That line sent me spiraling. Some scholars, those unhinged enough to study dream-sentencing, believe the True Cycle governs more than life and death. They think it governs intention and balance, not just how life moves... but why.

I traced a small circular sketch beside the passage. "The fey courts, especially the Dreaming Court—"

"Court of Dreams," Escala corrected.

"Yes, the Court of Dreams," I said, "are obsessed with the idea of balance. Dreams, stories, seasons, they all turn like wheels. But when a wheel is blocked... everything can get warped."

"So…" Roedyn frowned. "Boulders could be disruptions?"

"Exactly," I said, nodding firmly now. "Blockages or interferences. Some obstacle that prevents the Cycle from moving cleanly. It could be anything, unresolved pain, misplaced power, unnatural magic, or festering guilt. Something that doesn't belong but won't move."

"If enough of those stack up… the wheel stops."

"Like corruption?" Harper asked. "Or monsters?"

"Sometimes." I shrugged. "But the 'boulder' could be a lie, a secret, or even a regret. Something stuck in someone's heart that refuses to move forward."

"That could be anything," Escala exclaimed.

"Exactly," I said. "That's the point, it's not a checklist. It's a test of the soul."

Escala looked down, the reality hitting her for the first time.

"They gave you an open-ended sentence. That means the court doesn't want you to solve a riddle. They want you to change. To see the world. To touch it and let it touch you."

"But I don't understand. I was sent here for interfering. It doesn't make sense, why would they want me to interfere with the True Cycle now?"

"I don't know," I said.

"So, the logbook… won't help?" she asked quietly.

I knew I had to be careful not to crush her spirit. I smiled gently. "It might. I think it says more about you than you realize."

Escala looked down again.

"That's the worst part of fey justice," I added, settling back on my stool. "They don't hand you chains, they hand you a mirror."

Chapter 32

That night, we gathered in the common room of The Stag and talked long after the others had gone. The fire had burned low, its last embers pulsing in the hearth. I sat on a barstool with my feet propped on a stack of books, sipping my third blackberry cider and thumbing through my journal—searching for anything, any reference at all, that might help with Escala's boulder-removal quest.

Escala sat across from me, arms folded. Her drink was untouched. Harper lounged, boots up, picking at a tart. Sticky snored under the table. Roedyn stood against the wall, polishing his bowstring.

I looked up. "I've thought more about it—the boulders in the True Cycle. I think it's both a personal transformation and a disruption in the magical balance. You're not just being punished—you're being tasked."

"Tasked with what?" Escala asked. "Fixing the world?"

"Not all of it," I said. "Just the parts the court can't reach. But I am simply guessing here."

Escala sighed, seemingly defeated.

I raised a finger in triumph, hoping to raise her spirits. "But there's someone who might know more."

Harper raised an eyebrow. "Who?"

Now, I wish I could say I was wise and perfect. I wish I'd named anyone else. But I didn't. And in hindsight, I feel terrible. I swear, I didn't know what I'd done.

Roedyn asked, "What's his name?"

"Victor Graves," I said.

"Who is that?" Escala asked.

"The most powerful wizard this side of Eronvale. He lives in Blackthorn Tower, in the mountains north of Black Bay. If anyone can unravel the court's quest, it's Victor."

Harper and Roedyn exchanged a glance.

Escala stood. "I'm going."

"We're going," Roedyn corrected.

Then added, "Escala needs better gear. She has improved, but she'll need more training, too, before we leave."

Harper nodded. "I'll handle provisioning—food for two weeks and camping gear. I'll start at the market tomorrow."

"Good," Roedyn said. "We leave in a few weeks after we are provisioned, and Escala's training is complete."

The next day, we headed to the market district. Roedyn led Escala through guild shops, testing weapons and gear. After a few stops, he handed her a silver longsword. "Try this one."

She gave it a few test swings. It felt perfect—light, balanced, like it belonged to her. She looked at him. "How did you know?"

"I watched you spar with Harper," he said with a shrug. "You're fast, not strong. That blade won't slow you down, and it frees your other hand for a shield. That'll keep you alive."

The list grew. They picked out a shirt of mithril chain mail—fine, silver-bright, and so light. Escala gasped. "It weighs nothing."

"That's the point," Harper said, arms crossed like a seasoned quartermaster. "Better than leather, none of the bulk, and you won't jingle like a tavern dancer."

Next came a royal-blue tunic, embroidered in silver thread, with flared sleeves and a tailored cut—elegant but made for battle, not ceremony.

Harper held the fabric up for Roedyn's inspection. "Do you think this will match her eyes, Roedyn? You care about those things, you know."

Roedyn turned bright red, and Escala giggled.

"I love the blue and silver," she said, holding the tunic against her chest and spinning in a small circle. "What do you think, Roedyn?"

"I... err... it's... uh..." Roedyn stammered, his cheeks deepening in color.

Harper burst out laughing. "He means you're beautiful and he can't wait to see you wearing it over your new armor."

Roedyn groaned and covered his face with his palm.

Once they'd finished teasing Roedyn, they moved on to another smithy—one that specialized in shields. After much inspection, Roedyn found a steel shield: rounded and polished, its edges trimmed in white and its surface painted a deep blue. At its center, a silver crescent moon cradled a cluster of stars. Escala traced it with her fingers, visibly moved. "It's beautiful," she whispered. "It reminds me of the Court of Dreams."

"Wait—how are we paying for all this?" she asked.

Harper waved a hand. "My treat. You need gear if you're going to survive. That chain mail turns a deathblow into a bruise. Call it a team investment."

Later, as they walked back to The Stag, Escala leaned toward Roedyn and whispered, "How can Harper afford all this?"

Roedyn quietly said, "Let's just say she used to be in the chamber pot business. And trust me, chamberers are paid quite well in certain castles."

Escala blinked, completely lost.

Chapter 33

——————————

We spent the next few days continuing to gather supplies, weaving through Dunwell's bustling streets. As expected, tension flared in crowded markets—any time someone brushed against Escala, she snapped, "No one touches the faerie." The line earned her confused looks, as if she were drunk or unstable. Roedyn would step protectively between Escala and the townsperson, Harper would crack a joke, and we would move on. But it became pretty clear that crowds rattled her, and even casual contact sent her into a panic attack. Most folks value personal space, but she treated it like sacred ground. When we were alone—like when she bathed or slipped away to change—we often discussed it among ourselves. None of us could understand why she recoiled so sharply from the simple, familiar customs of touch.

Each morning before exploring the city, we trained by the river on a patch of flat, pebbled earth.

"Again," Roedyn said flatly.

Escala groaned, arms slick with sweat. She adjusted her grip and squared her feet.

"Too wide," Roedyn said. "You're bracing like a mountain. Be a stream—flow, move."

She tried again, slicing the air, but Roedyn had already stepped aside. Her follow-up strike met his staff and twisted her blade off course, sending a jolt up her arms. She stumbled but reset.

He didn't counter; he just stood there—steady, unreadable.

"You're better than you think," Harper said later.

During their sparring sessions, Harper taught her to handle multiple attackers. She summoned a ring of illusions and launched a flurry of strikes. Escala parried, dodged, rolled, and blocked, but her cloak was scorched, and a boot was smoldering by the end of the session. "Really?" she gasped.

"You're not dead." Harper grinned. "Huge improvement."

After a break, they sparred again. Escala lunged low— Harper spun behind her, flicked a flame at her shoulder. Escala dropped, rolled, and came up facing the right way, sword ready.

Harper clapped once. "See? That's new!"

"I think I burned my elbow," Escala muttered.

"Marks of glory," Harper smirked. "Or proof you zigged when you should've zagged. Either way, you're learning."

Each day, Escala moved with more fluidity. She still dropped her guard and led with the wrong foot, but her instincts were shifting. She no longer thought about movement; she just moved. Her arms understood the sword's weight. Her balance steadied. Breathing grew easier.

Roedyn drilled her on shield work. At first, she swung too wide, held it too low, but he guided her patiently. "Tuck your elbow, let the shield work for you," he said, tapping it with his sword. Bit by bit, she found her rhythm—deflecting, adjusting, grinning after a clean parry. "Okay." She puffed. "I'm starting to feel like a real knight."

Roedyn handed her a cloth. "Good job."

Harper ruffled her hair. "Almost like you were born in that body."

Escala swatted her hand. "No one touches the faerie."

Chapter 34

During the week of preparations, I worked my contacts and sifted through forgotten archives and field notes until I finally pinpointed the location of Blackthorn Tower. It lay to the east—roughly two weeks' journey—tucked deep within the mountains north of Black Bay, a region notorious for its landslides, lurking beasts, and treacherous terrain. Through a friend in the cartographers' guild, I managed to secure a rough map that was faded, incomplete, but enough to plot a course through the wilderness.

That evening, Roedyn called a quiet meeting in the shaded courtyard behind the inn. He spread a weathered map across the stone bench, weighing down its curling edges with stones.

"It won't be easy," he said, tracing a line with his finger. "We can follow the trade roads about halfway, but after that, we'll have to leave them and then cut through the forests and climb into the mountains. The map shows a few trails, but none that reach the tower. We'll have to scout our way through."

I leaned over the map and said, pointing to the area without roads, "The terrain gets rough once we leave the forests." He looked at each of us, as if testing our wills, "And there are monsters and wild beasts."

Harper folded her arms. "Perfect. I love a trip where the roads just stop and the monsters start."

Sticky tilted his head, gazing at the map. "All roads stop somewhere," he said softly. "That's where you find out who you really are."

We agreed to leave in two days and spent that time making our final preparations. Since our path would take us into the mountains, we decided to travel on foot since none of us was certain the terrain would favor horses.

The days passed quickly, and before long, we departed Dunwell, walking on the trade road east. The road wound through open fields and shadowed forests, across shallow creeks and past crooked stone fences half swallowed by grass. Morning mist clung to the hollows, silver and cool, and the dew sparkled on every leaf.

We passed quiet farms and sleepy villages, greeting farmers hauling their goods to market and traders trudging by with the dust of the road on their boots. The scent of fresh-baked bread and woodsmoke drifted from cottage chimneys, a reminder that life went on, even after all we'd seen.

By midday, the sun burned away the fog, and the countryside brightened into the soft gold of late autumn. The fields hummed with crickets; a hawk circled high above as if keeping watch.

"So, what was it like?" Harper asked as they walked.

Escala glanced over. "What was what like?"

"The Court of Dreams," Harper said. "Before you were cast out."

"Beautiful," Escala said softly.

Sticky perked up. "That describes my swamp."

Escala offered a tired smile. "I used to sneak into the rooftop gardens at night. Rihanna would be waiting with candied strawberries—sticky, way too sweet—oh, so good. I was just so happy to be out, away from my stepmother and sister... I would've eaten a toad."

She caught herself and glanced at Sticky. "Oh—sorry, Sticky."

Sticky double-blinked and kept hopping.

Roedyn glanced back. "Sounds like you were close with her."

"She's my best friend—we were friends since we were three," Escala said softly. "One time, we dared each other to fly up to the Starlight Towers. I got caught in a wind pocket and slammed into a crystal wind bell, shattering the whole thing. We hid in the laundry halls until morning, giggling the entire time."

Roedyn raised an eyebrow. "And?"

"We never got caught." Escala chuckled. "And we laughed about it for years."

Later that day, we made camp just off the road in a small grove. Roedyn set a small perimeter with string and bells. Harper started the fire with a snap of her fingers and a muttered rhyme. Sticky foraged nearby, returning with two mushrooms, a beetle, and something he insisted was edible, though no one was brave enough to confirm.

Escala sat beside the fire, deep in thought, until Harper nudged her boot. "What are you thinking about?"

"My stepmother married my father when I was one," Escala said. "They called her kind, but she wasn't. She barked insults, criticized everything: my laugh, my wings, my voice, even my nose. Always with that flawless, hollow smile—like I wasn't worth genuine cruelty."

"She sounds like a joy," Harper muttered. "Too bad you didn't have any chamber pots around."

Roedyn shot Harper another look.

Harper shrugged, all innocence. "What? Did I say something?"

Escala stared at her hands in the firelight. "And then there was Audrey, my stepsister. A year older, always spying. She spoke like she was quoting someone and made me feel like the outsider."

"Jealous?" Roedyn asked.

"No," Escala said. "She didn't want what I had. Worse, she wanted me gone."

"Why are you thinking about them?" Roedyn asked. "They don't sound like positive people."

"Because, before the trial," Escala said slowly, "Audrey said something. I haven't been able to forget it."

She paused, then repeated it word for word: "'You were never meant for the throne, Escala. You're a thread that was always meant to be pulled.'"

Roedyn's whetstone stilled.

"That's... a strange thing to say," Harper said.

"She smiled when she said it," Escala added. "Smiled like it was already over. Like she knew the verdict before I even entered the gallery. I didn't think much of it at the time. I was too scared. But now, I wonder."

Roedyn finally spoke. "You think she had something to do with it?"

Escala nodded. "Or maybe Morvena did. Audrey never had thoughts of her own, she just echoed whatever Morvena wanted. But I don't know what they did. And I can't stop thinking, what if they were behind it? What if they wanted me out of the court?"

We talked for hours until we all retired for the evening.

Sticky snored beneath his mossy blanket, tucked into a suspiciously neat pile of leaves. Harper slept with one arm over her face, boots still on.

Roedyn stood at the edge of camp, motionless, as he took the first watch. I curled up near the roots of an old oak and pulled my cloak over my head, cradling my lute.

Escala lay wrapped in her blanket, staring into the dying fire. She closed her eyes, willing herself to sleep, but the questions circled—tight and relentless—refusing to fade. At last, sleep crept in, dragging her into dreams filled with snarling wolves and Rihanna's screams.

Chapter 35

———————

The next morning, after Roedyn and Harper's now routine pre-breakfast training session with Escala, we set out. A few hours into the journey, we crested a hill and Escala's eyes widened in delight.

Bright colors blanketed the valley. Banners fluttered in the breeze. Smoke rose from firepits, rich with the scent of roasted nuts and sugar glaze. Tents of all shapes and hues filled the field, ringed by painted wagons and the distant sound of cheerful, clumsy music.

"What's that?" Escala asked.

Harper grinned. "That, my wingless friend, is a traveling circus."

Escala's eyes widened. "I've never seen one."

"Never?" Roedyn asked.

She shook her head. "In the court, our festivals were dazzling... but everything was polished and perfect. This feels..." She trailed off. "... so chaotic and wonderful!"

Her eyes danced as she scanned the swirl of color and noise. "This," she said, her voice lifting with wonder, "this is messy, loud, and alive—I love it!"

Roedyn couldn't help it—his mouth curled into a soft grin.

Harper hummed with amusement. Roedyn flushed, scowled, and said, "We don't have time for this circus."

Harper kept smirking.

Escala, oblivious to Harper, asked eagerly, "But can we stop, just for a little while?"

Roedyn's stare remained fixed. "This is a waste of daylight."

"Roedyn," she pleaded, placing her hand on his forearm, "please, just an hour. We haven't laughed in days."

Did you notice what happened there? Escala placed her hand on his arm, and she didn't say, "No one touches the faerie!"

Roedyn looked down at her hand and up at her face, surprised.

I turned to my party and said, "I've seen this circus before—it's been to Dunwell. They put on a good show; there's a dwarf who juggles flaming scimitars with his feet."

"Really?" Escala exclaimed.

"Yes, but it's expensive to see that show," I said.

Escala looked confused. "Wait—it costs money?"

Harper snorted. "Of course it does. This isn't some magical fey performance where unicorns prance around for free. Welcome to the material plane, princess."

Escala turned to Roedyn, her voice soft. "Could you... maybe lend me a coin? The Court of Dreams didn't give me any."

She looked up at him with that wide-eyed wonder and hope. He glanced toward the gates, then down at the coin pouch on his belt.

Harper, leaning against a fence post, watched with quiet curiosity, clearly interested in how the ever-practical Roedyn would handle this.

"You're on a mission, remember?" he asked. "Do you think we really have time for this?"

Escala tilted her head playfully and offered a shy smile, batting her blue eyes. Her blonde hair spilled over her shoulders in soft waves, making her look every bit the storybook princess.

He sighed, the fight draining from his voice. "This is a distraction," he muttered, then, softer, almost to himself, "A beautiful, ridiculous distraction."

I'm not sure if Roedyn meant the circus was ridiculous or just a distraction, or if he was talking about Escala. But the way he looked at her? I'd bet my horse he meant she was a beautiful distraction. And I think Harper would back me up.

Regardless, Roedyn's hand found its way to the coin pouch.

Escala beamed. "You're the best!" she chirped, snatching the coins with glee.

As she bounced toward the entrance, Harper leaned toward Roedyn with a grin. "You just bought her tickets to a traveling show, are you going on a date?"

Roedyn said, perhaps too sharply, "No," as he hurried after her. I think I saw him smile but don't quote me.

As we passed through the gates, Escala spun in a slow circle, drinking it all in. Jugglers tossed knives in perfect arcs. Fire-breathers dazzled wide-eyed children. Overhead, acrobats twisted between silk ribbons, muscles gleaming in the lantern light. A slow violin tune drifted from deeper in the camp, and a bear cub napped belly-up beside the path.

Escala's eyes sparkled with wonder while Roedyn stayed close, quietly explaining everything. He bought her a candied lemon on a stick, and her face puckered in delight as she bit into it. Roedyn laughed.

Then, without quite meaning to, Escala wandered into a red-and-yellow tent where a man was trying, with great intensity, to hypnotize a chicken.

It was not going well as the bird blinked in the opposite direction while the man waved a shiny coin and muttered, "Chikk-chikk… you're getting very sleepy…"

Escala watched for a moment, then burst into laughter, real, helpless laughter. She doubled over, gripping a tent pole as the chicken flapped onto the man's head and he shouted, "No, Gregory! Not again!"

Roedyn trailed behind, as stoic as ever. But when he saw Escala wiping tears from her eyes, her laughter echoing through the tent, even he couldn't help it, and a quiet chuckle slipped out. Then another. Soon, his shoulders shook with laughter of his own.

When they exited the tent, they couldn't find Sticky; it was as if he had vanished. They searched for nearly an hour, weaving through fire-breathers, contortionists, stilt walkers, and one deeply unsettling mime.

They called his name. Roedyn even checked under a snake charmer's stage. Harper climbed the rigging of the main tent for a better view—nothing. Sticky had melted into the shadows and was gone.

Frustrated, they regrouped near the snack stalls.

Harper narrowed her eyes toward the petting zoo. "Okay," she said slowly, pointing across the field, "see those kids riding that two-humped camel over there?"

Roedyn followed her gaze.

"I've walked this place twice," she continued. "And I definitely don't remember any camels when we arrived."

The group watched as the giggling children slid off the camel's back. A second later, with a flash and a grunt, the camel shrank and shifted into a very smug-looking Sticky.

He stretched like nothing had happened. "Being a camel? Not bad—got pampered, petted, and didn't have to hear Roedyn drone on about responsibility while Escala pretends to listen, and Harper keeps score on who's more dramatic." Picking hay out of his teeth, he added, "Also, kids drop snacks. Bonus. Plus, I haven't used my camel form since I was visiting the Magaambya University south of Per-Bastet."

"Where's that?" I asked.

"It's on the continent of Zandara," Sticky said, "a land of jungles and deserts, about halfway around Valla, across the Moonwake Sea."

"What's the Magaambya University?" I asked. "Never heard of it."

Roedyn replied, "It was founded centuries ago by a runelord named Old-Mage Jatembe, sometime after a cataclysm called the Purge. It's a place where powerful mages study ancient arcane secrets from the fallen Magocracy, but always under the guidance of archdruids, to keep things balanced."

"Wait, what's the Magocracy?" Escala asked.

"It was an ancient kingdom ruled entirely by mages and wizards—runelords, they were called," Roedyn said. "They grew too powerful, angered the gods, and were wiped out."

I frowned. "Okay, but why are you protecting their secrets, Sticky?"

Harper jumped in. "Because maniacs are always trying to find and misuse those lost artifacts and magical secrets."

Sticky nodded. "The Magaambya exists to safeguard those secrets. To study them. To keep them from falling into the wrong hands."

"So you joined to help protect that balance?" I asked.

Sticky gave a solemn nod. "That's the idea."

Sticky blinked. "But I also wanted to see the animals that lived in the jungles and deserts, so before it was my season to keep the balance, I traveled to the Emerald Deep jungle first to learn how to become a baboon and a panther and then to the desert, of course, to observe camels."

I had no idea what Sticky was talking about, but at least I now understood where some of his more exotic animal forms had come from.

There is one event I need to tell you about. It happened maybe twenty minutes after they left, while Sticky was still commenting about giving camel rides. We were weaving through the crowd past a booth of glassblowers when a large man stumbled out of the crowd, colliding hard with Escala. He grasped her shoulders for balance, his weight nearly dragging her down.

Roedyn was on him in an instant, stepping between them with a growl. Harper's hand went to her knife, eyes narrowed, scanning the man's posture for signs of a cutpurse or worse.

Escala cried out, voice sharp, "No one touches the faerie!"

The man looked startled, flustered. "I—I didn't mean—she stepped—I mean, I slipped—"

Roedyn shoved him back with a protective arm, fully shielding Escala.

From the crowd's edge, Sticky emerged like a shadow gaining form. He slid between them with practiced ease, palms lifted. "Easy now, just a stumble, right? No need for sparks."

The man stepped back, hands raised. "Didn't mean to startle her, just lost my footing, I swear it, m'lady. My deepest apologies."

Sticky gave a slight nod and turned to the gathering crowd. With a grin and a flick of his fingers, he waved them along. "Show's that way, folks!"

He turned back to Escala, the grin fading. He watched her closely now, real concern in his eyes.

"You alright?" he asked gently.

Escala nodded, but her breathing was shallow, and she didn't quite meet his gaze. She stood there shivering, hyperventilating for a few minutes, while we tried to reassure her that everything was okay, but no one dared do anything like put a comforting hand on her shoulder.

Sticky frowned, more to himself than anyone. A stranger bumping into someone in a crowd? Normal. But her reaction hadn't been. That troubled him.

It took a few minutes to calm her down, but the sights and sounds quickly lifted her spirits. Soon she was back to her curious self, and she was the first to notice a tightrope strung between two old wagons, a thin silver line swaying slightly in the wind with no safety net.

High above, a figure balanced atop it—tall and sleek, fur dappled in soft stripes, moving like wind.

"Look." Escala pointed up.

A male catfolk acrobat, in loose red pants and a sleeveless vest, walked backward along the rope, his tail curled for balance. With a fluid motion, he cartwheeled across, light as air.

He stood just over five feet tall; lean, wiry, built for speed. His black-and-white fur looked painted in moonlight and shadow, one eye jet black, the other ghostly white; mesmerizing and a little eerie. At the rope's center, he paused, stretched, and lifted into a one-arm handstand, holding it for a full fifteen seconds before dropping soundlessly to the grass.

The crowd clapped politely and began to wander off, but Escala didn't move.

The catfolk turned, caught her stare, and grinned. "Enjoy the show?"

Escala clapped, eyes bright. "That was wonderful!"

"I am Crurri," he said, bowing with a flourish, tail curling behind him. "And you are?"

"I'm Escala Winter, from the Court of Dreams."

"Strange name... but pretty. Where is this Court of Dreams? I don't believe I've heard of it."

"It's in the fey realm," she said, still beaming.

Crurri tilted his head, intrigued. "Truly? How fascinating. Come, do you have a moment? I've never met anyone from the Court of Dreams."

Escala glanced at Harper. "See? He believes me."

Harper shrugged. "He works in a circus. Everyone here is weird—he's used to it."

Roedyn punched Harper in the arm. "Enough," he growled. "She's not weird."

"Okay, okay, I won't insult your girlfriend," Harper mocked.

Roedyn glared. Escala ignored the comment.

Crurri smiled. "I chose this life because it's the best way to see Wallo. To gather stories, witness beauty. I'm a philosopher, you see. I seek the meaning of life."

Harper raised a brow. "All right, then. What is the meaning of life?"

But Escala and Crurri had already wandered off, deep in conversation, and we had to hurry to catch up. They walked side by side. Crurri wove between wagons while Escala followed. The rest of us trailed behind, keeping our distance.

Crurri spoke of growing up in a traveling troupe, how he learned to balance before he could walk and to breathe with the rhythm of the drumbeat.

To him, performance wasn't just art; it was meditation.

"The silence," he said once, "is where the soul speaks loudest."

I'm not certain of everything they discussed—well, I am—but Escala told me I could only share this part:

"May I ask you something?" Crurri said.

Escala nodded.

"This time, I ask as a collector of wisdom," he said, placing a hand to his chest. "You're of the Court of Dreams, are you not?"

She nodded.

"Then you carry the heritage of the ancient fey," Crurri said, his voice thoughtful. "Your kind holds stories that go back further than empires. I've spent my life studying truths in quiet corners, but I've never had the chance to walk beside one like you."

He looked at her with soft sincerity. "Would you be offended if I asked questions? Not to test you, only to learn. Fey wisdom is rare in these parts, and I confess I'm greedy for it."

"I… I don't know how much wisdom I have," she said. "And I'm not sure I can answer everything."

"But you'll try?"

She gave a small smile. "I'll try."

Crurri nodded. "That's all anyone can do."

"Why are you here in an elf form?" he asked.

Now, folks, for the sake of time, I won't repeat Escala's whole tale—you know it well enough by now. She told Crurri everything: the crossing with her friend Rihanna, the kiss, the wolf, the trial, the banishment, and that absurd quest to remove boulders from the True Cycle.

Crurri listened with rapt attention, eyes wide, and he slowly stroked his whiskers and asked, "Did you really think you'd fall in love from just one kiss?"

"Yes," Escala admitted. "But I know now that isn't true."

"Oh?" Crurri asked. "And how do you know?"

"Because people I trust"—her eyes drifted to Harper, lounging near a knife thrower's tent—"told me so."

"So, you don't know from experience?"

"I didn't fall in love with the boy," she said with a shrug, then added, "At least, I don't think I did. But my parents fell in love after just one kiss."

"Did they now?" Crurri mused. "As the fey understand it, what makes Valla go around—love, wealth, power?"

"Is that a riddle?"

"Maybe." His smile deepened.

Escala thought for a moment and said, "We fey don't care at all for coins. But from what I have observed, some fey are motivated by love and others by power, but it is not wealth."

Crurri nodded and said, "I think the answer is love. The love of wealth. The love of power. Or—on rare and reckless days—just love."

She didn't speak, so he continued.

"Is love always romantic?"

"I don't know," Escala said.

"Then maybe that's where we begin," he said. "What if love isn't a shape, but a motion? Not about who you lie next to but for whom you show up?"

Escala frowned. "Like a duty?"

"No," Crurri replied. "A choice."

"I've met some in Valla who say fulfilling your duty proves love," Escala said. "But a soldier might be ordered to guard a murderer. Just doing his job to keep the jail operating safely doesn't mean he loves the prisoner."

"No, it doesn't," Crurri agreed. "But his duty isn't to the murderer, it's to the people of the town. If he loves even one person in that town, then fulfilling his duty protects what he loves. Do you agree?"

Escala didn't answer.

Crurri pressed on. "Would you say love is loyalty?"

"Yes."

"Then is it still love when the loyalty's broken?"

"I don't know."

"Can you love someone who hurt you?" Crurri asked, watching her intently.

"Yes."

"Can you stop loving someone you hurt?"

"I hope not," she answered.

"Is love something you feel or something you do?"

She thought for a moment and then said, "I used to think it was something you felt, but I have learned from others that it can be something you do for others. I hope it's both?"

"And when they don't match? When the feeling is strong, but the doing is gone—or the actions remain, but the feeling fades—is it still love?"

Escala scrunched her eyebrows. "I don't know."

"Have you ever loved someone who didn't understand you?"

"I don't know if I've ever loved anyone."

"I see," he said contemplatively. "That's too bad. Being in love is a wonderful thing. Do you think love grows stronger the more you give it away?"

"I think so."

"Then is love infinite?"

"I hope it is," Escala said, trying to smile.

"And if it is, why do people act like it's scarce?"

She looked at him, her expression raw. "Because they're afraid. That's what my stepmother says."

Crurri nodded. "Fear. That's an interesting answer."

"My stepmother says mortals use love to control each other by promising happiness if the other person would just like them or be with them. Is that true?" Escala asked.

It was Crurri's turn to pause before answering. "There are those who twist the emotions of others under the guise of love, using confusion and control to get what they want. But that is not love, and I doubt it brings contentment or even happiness.

"Tell me… do you believe contentment is the same as happiness?"

"No."

"Which lasts longer?" Crurri asked.

"Contentment."

"Which feels better in the moment?"

"Happiness," Escala answered.

"Which one do you chase?"

She let out a quiet laugh. "Depends on the day."

He smiled. "Then are you chasing joy or comfort?"

"Isn't joy a kind of comfort?"

"Does laughter always come from joy?"

"You can laugh because you're happy," she said, "but you can laugh to mock or hurt. So, no, laughter isn't always joy."

"Do you think happiness is earned?"

Escala looked around at the crowds enjoying themselves, experiencing the wonders and delights of the circus, and said, "I think... we're taught that it has to be."

"But is it? Is joy a reward or a seed?"

"A seed," she said slowly. "Something you plant."

"And tend," he added. "And sometimes, it doesn't bloom in your garden, but in someone else's. And you must be content just to see it grow."

Crurri looked at Escala and smiled. "Do you think you deserve love, Escala?"

When she didn't answer, he performed and handstand and asked, "Do you think love requires proof? Or that you must become someone worthy of it?"

Her eyes filled with tears. He was asking too much, too fast—she had no time to breathe.

"Does love only come when you're perfect?" he asked. "Or does it meet you exactly where you are? Do you think," he added gently, "that maybe love is what heals us?"

Escala gave the faintest nod.

Crurri nodded back. "I'm sorry, I asked too many questions. I didn't mean to upset you."

He shifted his weight. "Let me tell you something I do understand. I love performing. Not for the applause, and not because I'm the best. I do it because, for just a few minutes, I get to give someone joy. That's enough."

He glanced at her, one black eye and one white, catching the dappled light through the trees. "Even if the joy lasts only a song. Even if they forget me by morning, it still matters."

"Why?" Escala asked.

"Because life is heavy for most," he said. "Grief, loneliness, regret… they cling like shadows. But when someone laughs—really laughs—or weeps at a melody, for just a breath, the pain lifts."

He paused. "Art does that. So does music and even a well-told story. It's not an escape, but a reminder… that beauty still exists."

Escala smiled, warmth rising in her. "The fey dance for the same reason."

Crurri nodded.

"We sing and dance not just because we can," she said, "but to shape beauty out of air. Sometimes to celebrate. Sometimes to mourn. But always to feel."

"Then maybe that's why you and I understand each other."

She smiled, brighter. "Maybe we do."

"Come with me," Crurri said. "I want to introduce you to my friends."

They walked slowly through the circus, Crurri cheerfully making introductions. Roedyn followed a few paces behind, silent but watchful.

She asked, "Crurri, are you happy here?"

Crurri gave a small smile. "That's the wrong question."

"What's the right one?"

"Am I content?"

She nodded. "Okay, are you?"

He took a slow breath. "I am… when someone really considers the questions I ask."

His eyes sparkled. "I've spent my life chasing meaning—not answers. Just the pursuit. And when someone listens—really listens—and dares to think with me… those are the days I'm content. That's why I travel with the circus. Not for the stage or the coin. But because each day brings someone new. And sometimes, someone humors me. Wonders aloud."

He gently took her hand, and she didn't pull away.

"Today, Escala, was one of those days."

She smiled.

Crurri rose and gave a graceful bow. "Now, if you'll excuse me, I've got a tightrope to walk. Maybe you'll come watch."

And with that, he slipped away toward the tall tents.

We stayed to watch, and we were genuinely impressed. But too soon, it was time to head back to our camp beyond the circus edge.

Escala lingered a moment and said softly, "Goodnight, Crurri."

That night around the fire, she brought up his questions, repeating them, turning them over.

And later, curled in her blanket, she realized it had been one of the most honest conversations she'd had since Rihanna died.

She found herself replaying Crurri's words, and she wasn't sure what they meant—not yet.

But she couldn't stop thinking about them.

And the fact that she had no answers to his questions.

Chapter 36

The next morning, Escala was reluctant to leave the circus, but she knew we had to press on toward Blackthorn Tower. Crurri met us at the edge of the grounds as we left.

"I came to say goodbye," he said. "But I hope you find your boulder—whatever it turns out to be."

Escala stepped forward and hugged him tightly.

Harper raised an eyebrow and pointed wordlessly at the hug. Roedyn shrugged.

As Escala stepped back, she said, "I still do not have answers to your questions."

"Neither do I," Crurri said and gave a small bow.

Then, with a wave that somehow felt like a blessing, he turned and strolled back toward the tents, already calling out to the fire-eater as he vanished behind the striped flaps.

We left the circus, following the eastern trade road. To make better time, Sticky took the form of a two-humped camel and plodded along the path with Escala and Harper on his broad back. I also rode, because my legs are short and it beat walking.

Escala pointed out every squirrel, cloud, and oddly shaped rock as if they were sacred signs. Harper mostly looked unimpressed, though she didn't climb down.

Roedyn flatly refused the offer of a ride. "I'll keep my dignity, thanks," he muttered, marching ahead to scout the road.

We walked for a few hours before Harper got bored and leapt off the camel. Escala followed a moment later, stretching her legs. I stayed put—riding high was a rare luxury.

All day, Escala's words about her trial and sentence turned over in my mind. As we moved along, I asked, "During your trial, Audrey said she found you half dead at a crossing, right?"

Escala nodded. "Yes."

"How many crossings are there?"

"No one really knows."

"I mean, how many could be open at any one time?"

"Oh, dozens—sometimes more," she said. "It changes constantly. That's part of what makes them so exciting—and dangerous."

"And where do they go? Are the destinations predictable?" I asked.

"Some are," she said. "We call those 'static' crossings—they always open to the same place in the material plane. But many are random."

I nodded. "And the crossing that day was that one random?"

"Yes," Escala said. "That's why Rihanna was so desperate. The crossing was already closing, and she knew we'd be trapped if we didn't leave quickly."

"Tell me," I said. "How often would you and Rihanna find a crossing?"

Her face brightened. "That was the best part—we would find one almost every day," she said. "Not all of them were safe, and not all were empty—sometimes other fey were already using them. But when we found one that was quiet and abandoned," she said, laughing, "it felt like discovering a secret only we knew."

I watched her closely. Her joy was real. I wasn't the only one who noticed.

Roedyn was watching her too. When our eyes met, he quickly looked away and returned his gaze to the trail ahead.

She continued, "The crossings were wildly unpredictable, which made everything ten times more exciting! We never knew what—or who—we were going to see. Every time one opened, it was like the start of a grand adventure. Part of the thrill was that we never knew how long we had. Crossings don't exactly come with a schedule. Sometimes they last days, sometimes only a few hours. You might get a warning—five, maybe ten minutes before they collapse—but that's it."

"Well," I said, "how is it that Audrey just happened to be at the crossing the very moment you got flung out?"

Escala stopped so abruptly that Harper ran into the back of her, and Escala snapped, "No one touches—"

Harper interrupted. "The faerie... I know... I know."

At this point, I had jumped down from Sticky, who had transformed back into a frog and was hopping alongside us.

"I don't understand," Sticky said plainly. "I saw you hug the acrobat cat, who was basically a stranger. And you held Roedyn's hand before—"

Roedyn stiffened instantly, cheeks flushing crimson.

"—but someone accidentally bumps into you in the marketplace, or pats you on the shoulder, and you come to pieces, almost having a panic attack. What exactly are the rules?"

He wasn't accusing—he was curious; honestly, we all were.

All of us looked at Escala, everyone except Roedyn, who was still bright red and extremely focused on retying a suddenly loose pack strap that hadn't needed fixing a moment ago.

Escala didn't answer right away. Her eyes dropped to the ground, and for a moment, it looked like she might just brush it off, make a joke, do that little half-smile she always did when something hit too close.

But instead, she stood still, her fingers trembling as they reached up and began to twist a lock of her long blonde hair.

When she finally spoke, her voice was so soft it barely reached us: "I'm scared."

She swallowed hard. "I'm scared of doing more damage to the True Cycle. I'm scared of touching someone and accidentally charming them, altering their life in a way the court will say damages the Cycle. That's… that's why I flinch when people touch me."

Her eyes flicked up for a second, searching our faces. Her body deflated, shoulders sagging as though the weight she'd been holding finally settled onto her.

"But how am I supposed to fix the Cycle if every step I take might hurt someone or break it again? How do I help without wrecking the very thing I'm trying to protect? And it's not just the Cycle I'm afraid of damaging."

Tears welled in her eyes.

"I lost my best friend because I was reckless. And now… now that I've met all of you…"

She looked at each of us, her eyes lingering longer on Roedyn.

"I'm terrified of messing you up, of being the reason something awful happens to you. I'm scared of waking up one day and realizing I ruined the only people who ever gave me a second chance."

She hugged herself, arms crossed tightly over her chest, like she was trying to hold herself together.

"You all mean so much to me. I don't even know when that happened. But I can feel it—you matter. And that means I could lose you, and I don't think I could survive that."

She turned slightly, wiping a tear from her cheek with the back of her hand.

Silence followed, and it was uncomfortable—wow, was it uncomfortable.

Harper shifted her weight, eyes flicking to the ground and back. Roedyn stared ahead, the muscles in his neck tense, like he wanted to speak but couldn't. Sticky sat still, then suddenly his tongue flashed out, snatching a passing bug. He gulped it down and blinked—but said nothing.

It was obvious she needed comfort, some reassurance, but we were limited. Under normal circumstances, if it had been one of us, we'd offer a hug, a hand on the shoulder, a quiet gesture that says you're not alone.

But with Escala, touch wasn't really an option. Not with the fear of causing more damage weighing on her, heavier than any of us could truly grasp. So even though we wanted to reach out, all we had were words—and no one could seem to find the right ones.

We just stood there. And the silence turned awkward—not because we didn't care, but because we did, and none of us knew how to show it without making things worse.

Finally, I took a careful step forward. Just one step, and then another. When I was close enough, I extended my hand—open, welcoming, no pressure—and said, "I accept the risk."

She looked down into my eyes. Yeah, I know how that sounds. Breaks the dramatic tension, doesn't it? But she's well over five feet tall—and I'm just a touch over three. So yes, she had to look down. That's just physics.

But in that moment, our eyes met, and something passed between us. It's hard to put into words—maybe it was understanding maybe it was relief. Whatever it was, it was real.

I kept my hand extended, steady, and open. And after a long, aching pause, she slowly raised hers and gently took mine.

We shook hands, slowly at first. A small smile crept across her face, so I pumped her hand a little harder. Then a little more. And just when it veered from sincere to slightly ridiculous—I yelped, threw my arm back with a dramatic flourish, tucked it under my other arm like I'd been bitten by a timber rattler, and shouted, "No one touches the gnome!"

For a second, no one reacted.

Then we all burst out laughing, even Escala. It came bright and sudden, like sunlight breaking through a storm, and it was exactly what we needed in that moment—maybe more than we realized.

Chapter 37

We were still a few days out from Blackthorn Tower, but we'd been making good time. That evening, we camped beside a shallow, fish-filled river, barely two feet deep but lively with movement. Roedyn and Harper offered to catch dinner, but when Harper pulled out the fishing gear—a hopeless tangle—she sighed and tossed it to Roedyn.

I wandered off to answer nature's call, still chuckling at the sound of Roedyn's increasingly colorful commentary about people who "pack like goblins in a bar fight."

When I returned, to say I was startled would be generous—I nearly lost a decade of my life. A massive grizzly bear was barreling into the stream, sending up a spray of water. My heart pounded wildly until I realized it was just Sticky, who had decided bear form was the most efficient way to help with dinner.

I watched in awe as he lumbered into the current and began swiping through the water with his massive claws with terrifying precision. Within minutes, he'd tossed five fat salmon onto the shore with practiced ease.

Roedyn, meanwhile, was still trying to untangle his fishing line and hadn't even gotten his hook in the water.

Sticky lumbered out of the creek with a satisfied grunt and shook himself like a dog—drenching all of us in freezing river spray.

Escala and Harper shrieked in disgust, though only one of them used language I can't repeat. Without a word, Sticky casually shifted back into his frog form and plopped down next to the fire, waiting for someone to cook the fish.

Sticky looked at Roedyn, who was still working on untangling the fishing line, and said, "Why do you use a string and a hook when you could just be a bear?"

Roedyn, still battling the snarled fishing line, grumbled without looking up, "Because, Sticky, I'm *not* a bear."

Harper smirked and said, "I don't know about that. You're grumpy, mean, and hairy... I'd say you're pretty much a bear."

I laughed and Escala giggled, and Roedyn went quiet and blushed.

It was one of those moments where a bit of mercy seemed in order, so I cleared my throat and said, "Roedyn, we'll need something to go with the fish. Think you could head into the woods and see what you can find?"

I gestured toward the trees, doing my best to make it sound like a practical request, rather than the rescue it plainly was.

Roedyn nodded. But before he could take two steps, Harper—ever the mischief-maker—called after him, "Take Escala with you. She could use some lessons in foraging."

Roedyn gave her a long look and turned to Escala, who was beaming and brandishing a stick that she said was her "foraging wand."

"... Sure," he said, not quite sighing. "Let's go, Escala."

And the two of them slipped into the forest, Roedyn scanning for herbs and vegetables.

Escala followed close behind, light-footed and curious, occasionally jabbing at roots and leaves with her "foraging wand," declaring her findings like she was on a treasure hunt.

"So," Escala said, "you're really good at this plant-hunting thing. Did someone teach you?"

He nodded. "My mother was an elf. Taught me to move quietly, see patterns, read the land."

"That makes sense. What about your dad? You said you're half elf, so he must've been human."

"Yes, my father's human. He's a blacksmith, like my brother."

Roedyn pointed to a patch of green off the trail. "There, see those feathery tops?" He knelt and gently brushed away the soil. "These are wild carrots; they grow in loose soil, often near a stream. The tops look like parsley, but if you rub the stem, it'll smell like a sweet carrot."

Escala crouched beside him, did as instructed, sniffed, and grinned. "Carroty!"

He smiled.

"Harper said you were both Gray Cloaks."

"Yes, we are, I mean were, Gray Cloaks. I joined because... well, it's complicated. It wasn't exactly a choice; it was something I had to do."

Escala tugged up more carrots, brushing the dirt from the roots. "What do the Gray Cloaks protect?"

"Very rare artifacts," he carefully said.

"Like the Dream Orb," Escala said, as if she expected him to know it. "No one's allowed to touch it. We have fey guards stationed around it day and night."

Seeing a way to steer the conversation elsewhere, Roedyn nodded quickly and said, "Same idea—the Gray Cloaks do that sort of work on the material plane. That's what we did before settling in Silverstand Forest."

They kept talking as their foraging led them deeper into the woods.

Escala glanced at him again. "So why the Gray Cloaks? Why not follow your father into blacksmithing?"

Roedyn exhaled through his nose. "My older brother took to the forge like a hammer to steel. He actually enjoyed it, and everyone assumed I'd follow. But I didn't, and with him handling things, I could slip away without drawing notice. I think I learned to disappear before I even knew why. So, when… other responsibilities came up, no one questioned why I wasn't at the forge."

Escala wrinkled her nose. "But you're always making arrows at night. Isn't that still blacksmith-y?"

He shook his head. "It's not the same. Arrows are part of something larger—tools that help you move through the world. The forge… that was staying put. Same walls, same fire, same rhythm every day. I didn't hate it, but I didn't belong there either."

Escala nodded slowly. "That's what court functions felt like. If my stepmother showed up, she stole the attention. If she didn't, I had to be the princess, and I hated those nights more."

He glanced at her, his voice gentler now. "I just needed room to breathe. Space that wasn't boxed in by stone and expectation. I wanted trees. Open sky. A world that didn't press in. And more than that, I needed something ahead of me I hadn't seen before."

Escala wandered a few steps up the path, twirling her so-called foraging wand. "I know what you mean," she was getting excited, "That's why I started crossing to the material plane. Every day with Rihanna, we found something new. Even the smallest, strangest things made life feel... alive. Like just walking into the world made me part of something bigger."

Roedyn looked at her, really looked, and nodded. "That's how I feel about scouting. Discovery feels... necessary."

"It's the thrill of the unknown," she said, her voice bright and bubbly. They had just stumbled onto a shared core belief—something that shaped who they were and how they lived. The last person Escala had felt this with was Rihanna.

A rare smile crept onto his face. "Exactly."

They walked in silence for a while. Eventually, Roedyn slowed, crouching beside a patch of brush at the base of an old hardwood. "Here. Wild potatoes. They grow in damp soil near trees like this. Look for broad, fuzzy leaves. You'll feel them more than see them."

Escala knelt beside him, fingers brushing the leaves he'd uncovered. "You know, I've been thinking... I still don't understand why getting me to Blackthorn Tower became your mission. You didn't have to care, but you did."

She glanced sideways. "I just wanted to say thank you for staying close. You, Harper, Sticky, even Wigfrith...

you've all been there for me. But I've leaned on you more than most."

His ears turned slightly red. He stood quickly, clutching a few of the potatoes.

Escala was quiet as he stood, brushing a thumb over one of the leaves.

"What will you do... after?"

"After?" Roedyn asked.

"After you get me to Blackthorn Tower," she said, meeting his eyes.

Roedyn studied her. "I don't know," he said. "I thought I did. But now... things feel different."

She looked at him, waiting for him to continue.

"I guess," he said slowly, "it depends on what needs doing. And maybe... who still needs me around. I mean, aren't there boulders left to move?"

She smiled. "That's a good answer."

For a while, they just foraged together in comfortable silence. Once they had enough carrots, potatoes, and herbs, they returned to camp.

Dinner turned out wonderfully. Harper, ever the surprising culinary talent, cooked the salmon to perfection over the fire, pairing it with the foraged roots and herbs for a bright, earthy finish. For the first time in days, maybe weeks, it felt like a proper campfire evening.

The fire burned low, shadows dancing across the clearing as stars appeared overhead. We'd eaten well, and the mood was light. As bards do when spirits are high and bellies full, I pulled out my lute.

The first chords rang out bright and quick, playful notes that scampered like foxfire through the trees. Escala perked up immediately. Harper clapped once, and Sticky spun in a slow, delighted circle.

"Don't just sit there!" I grinned. "This one's meant for dancing."

I strummed harder, and the rhythm caught the air like wind in sails. Escala stood, her hair catching the firelight, and in a single motion, fluid and effortless, she began to dance.

Not the playful spinning and swaying we'd seen before. This was different.

Her feet barely touched the ground. Her hands traced symbols I didn't recognize, each motion part of a pattern older than language; this was fey dancing.

Roedyn stared, unmoving on his log. His eyes tracked Escala's every motion. Harper nudged Sticky with her boot. "He's smitten," she said, just loud enough for me to hear.

"I noticed," I said, plucking a flourish.

Sticky leapt up and joined Escala, catching her rhythm mid-motion. She laughed and spun into his arms. They clasped hands and kicked side to side in sync; his was a joyful, chaotic whirl 'dance' that was as charming as it was ridiculous.

Not to be outdone, Harper marched over. "I will cut in," she declared.

And she did, twirling between them and taking Sticky's hands in her own. Escala burst into laughter and stepped aside, cheering and clapping in time.

The music was fast and bright, my fingers flying across the strings.

"Roedyn!" I called. "Your turn!"

He shook his head. "I don't dance."

"Oh, come on," Harper shouted. "If Sticky can do it, you can do it!"

"I'm not Sticky," Roedyn grumbled, though I swear I saw the ghost of a smile.

Escala stepped in front of him, graceful and glowing, and extended her hand.

"Please?" she asked, voice soft. Her smile was the kind that made "no" impossible.

Roedyn hesitated. And then, like it physically pained him, he stood.

He took her hand awkwardly, and she pulled him gently toward the open space near the fire.

"It's easy," she said. "Like sword training, it's all footwork. Flow with the music."

"I'm terrible at this," he muttered.

"Then you'll need a patient teacher," she said, beaming.

And that's exactly what she became.

From one song to the next, Escala guided him, gently correcting, showing him the steps, laughing when he stumbled, but never mocking. Slowly, Roedyn began to relax. His movements lost their stiffness. His feet stopped fighting the beat. He wasn't good, but he was trying. And to her, that was enough.

I saw it happen, the moment dancing stopped being an obligation and became joy. He laughed, really laughed, the kind of rare sound that makes everyone stop and look. His eyes lit up. Escala clapped for him mid-spin.

And then, without warning, I changed the song, and the tempo slowed, the melody deepened. I was playing something softer and older as I wove the chords. Maybe there was a bit of magic in it, who's to say?

Escala tilted her head, closing the distance between them and placing a hand gently on his shoulder.

"This one's slower," she whispered. "You'll need to put your hand on my waist."

He said cautiously, "I thought… I thought no one could touch the faerie."

Her tone was gentle but instructional. "You've already got my hand, that's the first part. Now follow my lead. Don't overthink it. One step at a time. Stay with the rhythm."

With all the care in the world, Roedyn gently placed his hand at her waist. She stepped into him, their bodies closer now, the fire casting a golden ring around them.

The others stopped dancing and sat on a log, watching, but I kept playing.

Roedyn and Escala moved in slow circles, arms wrapped around each other. Her eyes fluttered shut as she rested her head against his chest, the song's rhythm guiding her breath. Roedyn looked down, startled at first, but then, slowly, he lowered his cheek to the top of her head. His arm drew her in a little tighter, holding her like he didn't want to let go.

They danced like that through two whole songs. No one said a word, and nothing else mattered.

As the final notes drifted into the air, I let the music fade naturally. The spell—if there was one, I'll never say—broke gently.

Roedyn opened his eyes as if waking from a dream. He saw Harper and Sticky watching. He tensed immediately and took a quick step back.

"I—uh—I didn't mean—"

Escala looked up at him and smiled. "If that had been a Court of Dreams dance competition, we would've been eliminated in the first round. But perhaps you'll get better next time."

Chapter 38

L ooking at the crowd, I say, "I may be a decent storyteller, but even I push things too far sometimes. That night, I switched to slow tunes, maybe added a touch too much charm to the melody. Because the next morning was awkward. Roedyn kept himself busy with the fire, the gear, anything that didn't involve Escala.

"Harper, of course, noticed everything."

"So," she said, biting into a biscuit, "anyone planning on dancing again tonight, or was that a one-night-only performance?"

Roedyn stiffened as he pulled on a pack strap. "It wasn't a performance; we were just practicing balance," he muttered. "For sword work."

Harper planted a hand on her hip and cocked it dramatically. "For sword work, right. You're sure that wasn't grappling training?" she added with a smirk.

Escala laughed softly, a faint pink rising to her cheeks. But she was watching Roedyn now, and she didn't miss the way he shifted, clearly uncomfortable. She didn't press it. Instead, she grabbed her soap and headed for the creek, calling over her shoulder with a hopeful smile, "I really like dancing... maybe we'll get to do it again sometime?"

As her footsteps faded into the trees, Harper turned on Roedyn. "Okay, what's your problem? She dances with you once, and you act like she handed you a marriage contract."

Roedyn yanked a strap, far harder than needed. "She doesn't understand what this is. This is an escort mission. We're getting her to Blackthorn Tower, that's it."

"An escort mission? Oh, don't give me that," Harper snapped. "Don't feed me that 'just a job' crap either, not after everything we've been through. You didn't have to take her to Dunwell. You didn't have to guard her night after night; you did have to teach her to fight or throw yourself between her and death. You didn't have to shoot her with an arrow, oh, too soon? But you did. And now you're standing here pretending she's just cargo?"

She was visibly upset, speaking in a low, furious voice. "That girl worships the ground you walk on. If you hurt her just to protect your own feelings, I swear I'll break you. By the gods, Roedyn, you nearly killed her, and you even promised to help her remove boulders that don't exist. This is not 'just a job.'"

Roedyn shook his head, voice tight with frustration. "You don't get it, she's fey. This isn't her world, and once she removes these... 'boulders'"—he gestured vaguely— "she's gone. Back to wherever she came from. I don't even know if any of this matters to her,"—again he gestured nebulously in the air—"the way it does to us. I can't afford to get attached. I have one job: get her to Blackthorn Tower. That's it. She's the job."

"Oh, and when did she hire us? Did we agree on a fee?" Harper crossed her arms.

Roedyn started to reply, faltered, and forced it out. "Look, we never set a fee, but she knows this is a job. I'm a scout, this is what I do. I get people where they need to go. It's a business arrangement. We'll sort payment later."

Harper was usually very observant—*very*. But this time she wasn't, and neither was Roedyn. While they were arguing, Escala realized she had forgotten something before she had gone fifty paces toward the creek and returned to the camp. Hearing them, she ducked behind a tree and caught almost the entire argument. Saying nothing, she turned and walked back toward the creek, eyes burning, towel clutched tight in one trembling fist.

Chapter 39

I f you thought breakfast was awkward, the rest of the morning? Brutal.

Escala returned from the creek twenty minutes later, armor on and pack tight. She said almost nothing. I glanced at Sticky, who blinked and shrugged.

Neither Roedyn nor Harper had seen her during their argument, but I had. I saw her face when Roedyn called this "just a job." She looked crushed.

We broke camp in tense silence and headed east. The road was gone, replaced by twisted forest trails winding toward the Gray Mountains—toward Blackthorn Tower.

Roedyn warned us that this stretch held no farms or villages. Just beasts, worse things, dense woods, ravines, and cliffs.

We marched in silence, alert. Roedyn scouted ahead often, then returned and rerouted us, muttering that something felt off. These detours earned steady complaints from Harper; honestly, it was the only conversation all day.

One reroute brought us to the base of a ten-foot cliff. Roedyn climbed first, then Harper, grumbling. Sticky shifted into a gorilla, hoisted me like a sack of oats, and climbed with ease.

Escala was last and she struggled. Sticky, still a gorilla, offered a hairy hand. She swatted it away.

Roedyn dropped down, crouched, and laced his hands. She stepped in, reached up. He reached to steady her, and she snapped.

"*No one touches the faerie!*" she shouted, voice sharp, eyes fiery.

Roedyn stepped back, stunned, as she slid back down.

"Here," Harper said, firmly, extending a thick branch. "Grab it."

Escala begrudgingly took the branch and kicked upward. Harper, Sticky, and I hauled her up. Roedyn waited below and followed once she was safely up.

When he joined us, Harper dusted her hands off and glared at him.

Roedyn wisely didn't say a word and moved ahead to scout the trail. As the rest of us followed, Sticky plodded quietly beside Escala, his long arms swinging low in his latest form—a shaggy red panda this time.

"Escala, what's wrong?"

"Sometimes people see you a certain way," she said, eyes forward, "and when they finally say it out loud… it stings."

"Sounds like what people say about my skunk form," Sticky said—and I'm not entirely sure he was joking—as he gently bumped her shoulder with his fuzzy head. That, at least, managed to make her laugh.

That night, I didn't touch my lute. While the others worked by the fire, Escala slipped off to the brook. A fallen tree formed a smooth bridge. I followed and found her perched on it, legs swinging, toes skimming the water. I climbed up beside her.

"I know what happened."

She glanced over.

"Why does it bother you?" I asked. "You need help, don't you?"

She didn't answer right away—just stared down at the water.

"I didn't expect to care," she said at last. "I don't know what I feel, but I care, and I'm confused."

She hugged her knees. "I don't know what's wrong with me, Wigfrith. I just want to be near him. When he's around, everything feels right. I notice dumb things, like how bees make him nervous, or how he squints when he thinks. And when he's gone off to forage or scout…" She trailed off.

"Sometimes I catch him looking and then he's back to fussing with straps like I'm invisible. Maybe I imagined it. But after what he told Harper—that this is just a job— everything I felt suddenly seemed stupid. Like I was the only one dreaming."

She swatted a mosquito away from her face. "It hurt, Wigfrith. Like I was foolish to believe I could ever be anything more than an obligation to someone like him."

She turned toward me. "And that's what scares me the most. I wasn't pretending, while he was. And that is exactly what my stepmother does."

I stop the story and look at the gathered crowd in the Stag; it's crowded in here tonight. I pace the stage for a moment and then say, "Now, friends, I'm not usually at a loss for words—you know that—but I swear to you, I didn't know what to say. So, I said, 'Sometimes the river doesn't flow around the rock... it just politely ignores it and becomes soup.'"

She scrunched her nose. "Wigfrith, that is the dumbest thing I've ever heard."

I clutched my chest. "By the gods, you wound me! If my eyes were closed, I'd swear Harper just said that, her sharp tongue's rubbing off on you."

She laughed, gave me a playful shove, and we headed back to camp.

Chapter 40

———————

The next day was better—well, slightly. Escala and Roedyn resumed their morning sparring sessions, and I swear she was really trying to hit him. Harper, naturally, kept up her running commentary—none of it helpful, all of it loud. But you get the gist of how those sessions go.

After breakfast, we traveled like before—off trail, slow, cautious. Strange sounds echoed through the woods. Once, Roedyn had us duck into a cave as something winged circled overhead. It didn't land, and eventually, it moved on.

By dusk, we made camp but with no creek nearby, fishing was out. Sticky said nonchalantly, "I'll handle dinner," turned into a bobcat, and vanished into the trees.

An hour later, a massive, long-limbed monkey with a powerful jaw and a bare face framed by thick fur lumbered into camp and dropped a deer beside the fire. It was Sticky, back from his hunt. He explained that this form was called a baboon, a creature that lived in tight-knit troops on the continent of Zandara.

As we prepared the deer for our meal, I noticed Sticky had shifted back into his frog form. He turned toward the dark line of the woods and bowed his head. "Thank you," he said so softly I almost missed it. It struck me how deeply he respected the balance of things. While the rest of us saw only meat and survival, Sticky saw the cycle—life returning to life, one thread feeding another. For all his quirks and grumbles, he was the truest druid I'd ever met.

That night, we dined on fresh venison while trading the kind of small talk travelers share, nothing serious. But I caught Roedyn sneaking glances at Escala. And just once, I saw her do the same.

Later, when Harper and I were off collecting firewood, away from the camp, I got nosy. "Are you two really just helping her for coin?"

"He's an idiot," Harper said.

That didn't really answer my question, so I pressed again. "Are you two going back to your cabin once you get her to Blackthorn Tower? What if Victor Graves doesn't have answers? Or what if he says the boulder she's after is on the other side of Valla? Then what?"

"Well, Roedyn did swear an oath to help her move the boulder..." She left the sentence unfinished and kept packing.

Back at the fire, Roedyn settled beside Escala. She didn't look at him, just kept staring at the stars, arms draped loosely around her knees.

After a moment, Roedyn said, "You've seemed... off since..." He hesitated, like he didn't want to say it. "Since the night we danced—since we all danced. What's wrong?"

"Audrey."

"What about her?" He sounded surprised, maybe even a little relieved.

"At the trial, she described things she couldn't have known. I didn't even question it—until Wigfrith did."

Escala added, "She told the court details about the noises being made by the wolf. How could she have known that?"

"Maybe the court has seers? Maybe they used magic," I suggested.

Escala shook her head. "That would've shown what happened. But Audrey didn't describe the events like a vision. She told them like someone who was there."

Roedyn's eyes narrowed. "You think Audrey was there with you when the wolf attacked?"

"I don't know," Escala said. "But she's always tried to get me in trouble. Ever since we were little, she'd run to Morvena the moment I broke a rule. Always watching, always waiting for me to slip. And now? I'm sure they want me to fail this quest, too."

Roedyn's voice came from across the fire. "Then maybe we prove them wrong."

Her eyes narrowed. "What do you mean... we?"

I sprang to my feet. "Sticky, Harper—I need your help over there," I said, pointing to a tree about fifty paces away. "There's a rare owl's nest, and I need one of its feathers, urgently."

Harper stood immediately, catching on to the ruse. Sticky, however, remained planted on the log, eyes wide and unblinking as he watched Escala and Roedyn, his expression a perfect picture of amphibious curiosity.

Harper and I were already halfway to the tree when I turned and called, "Sticky, come on—I need you."

He looked at me, then finally hopped to his feet and bounded after us with a reluctant sigh, casting one last glance over his shoulder.

Roedyn watched us walk away, then turned to Escala.

Harper and I stared at the non-existent owl's nest, though we were clearly eavesdropping.

I suspect Roedyn was glad for the delay, it gave him time to form a response. Finally, he said, "We—as in all of us— are going to help you get home. Back to your Court of Dreams. I promised I would help you."

"Right, just get me home—that's it and then goodbye." Her tone carried a sharp edge, hurt but masked in sarcasm.

Roedyn was caught off guard. "I don't understand—I thought you wanted to go home."

"I do."

"Then what's wrong? Why are you so... distant suddenly?"

Harper whispered to me, "He doesn't know."

Sticky, louder than he should have, asked, "He doesn't know what?"

I raised my voice and said, "Since the red-tail owl *can* and *will* bite, we need to be extremely careful." I mimed an owl with my hands; fingers curled like talons. Roedyn and Escala both looked over.

Harper whispered to Sticky, "Roedyn doesn't even get it—she's not mad over some slight. She's mad because he danced with her like it meant something... then acted like it didn't."

Sticky blinked twice. "Oh, got it."

I turned to Harper. "And how do you know that?"

She gave me a look like I was the daftest bard in Valla. "Please, I'm a woman. Roedyn's clearly taken with her, whether he admits it or not. But he's too proud or scared to show it. Escala thought the dance meant something. Now he's pretending it didn't, and she thinks she imagined the whole thing."

I nodded my agreement and looked back at the pair.

Roedyn, trying to steady himself, said, "Ever since the dance... nothing's felt the same. This is exactly why I don't like dancing—it's never just dancing. It always means one thing to one person and something entirely different to the other."

"Really?" Escala asked, her eyes narrowing. "Then tell me, what did it mean to me?"

"I... I don't know."

"Alright, then what did it mean to you?"

He hesitated again. "I... I don't know that either."

"You don't know what it meant to you?" she said, incredulously.

Harper groaned. "By the gods, just say it already."

Sticky, too loud again, asked, "Say what?"

Escala glanced back at us, so I started miming an owl mating ritual in the trees and began explaining to Harper the complex owl courtship behaviors in absurdly serious tones.

Roedyn flushed. "Fine. At first, I was embarrassed. There, I said it. I don't like dancing."

Sticky turned to Harper. "He said it!"

Harper rolled her eyes. "No, he didn't."

Escala cocked her head, eyes narrowing as she stared at him, unimpressed and clearly not buying a word.

Roedyn rushed to fill the silence. "But after I got the hang of it... I didn't hate it."

"Didn't hate it," Escala parroted, folding her arms.

"I actually started to enjoy it," Roedyn added, with some enthusiasm.

She arched a brow.

"I was having fun," he said, and then shifting his eyes to the fire, he added, "With you."

Sticky excitedly whispered to Harper, "Did he say it?"

Harper shook her head. "No."

Escala flipped her hair over her shoulder and, in a tone both defiant and a little bossy, said, "Well then, Roedyn Hammerfell, let me tell you what that dance meant to me. It was special. I felt safe with you. The music took me somewhere beautiful, and I wanted you there with me."

She uncrossed her arms, and he turned to meet her gaze. Her blue eyes studied him closely.

"And I used to really like you," she said, losing the defiance and almost trembling, like a child bracing for a scolding after speaking a hard truth.

"Used to like me?" Roedyn repeated. He was stunned. He studied her eyes for answers. "But... not anymore?" He sounded almost fearful of the answer.

For a moment, it looked like he might say more, but instead, he just gave a small shake of his head and looked away toward the fire.

"I don't know, Roedyn," she said, her voice tight. "Am I just a client to you?"

And there it was.

Roedyn looked like he'd just been struck.

Harper covered her face and groaned. Sticky looked up at her, puzzled.

"You're a friend," he said.

"I don't like being lied to, Roedyn," she snapped, frowning. "You forget—my stepmother's a professional liar. I grew up surrounded by deceit. I know when someone's lying."

"I'm not lying—you are a friend!" Roedyn pleaded.

With a huff, she stood without another word, walked to her sleeping blanket, lay down, and pulled the cover over her head.

Sticky looked at Harper hopefully and asked, "Did he say it?"

Harper crossed her arms and said, "Nope."

Chapter 41

"Now then," I say, lifting my mug but holding it just short of a sip. "Before I lead us any deeper into the wilds on the road to Blackthorn Tower... allow me a brief detour.

"I know what you're all thinking: 'Wigfrith, you saucy fox, don't leave us wondering what happened next between Roedyn and Escala.' And I tell you—if you came looking for bawdy tales without heart, full of tawdry nonsense and no hint of romance, then march yourselves right over to the Golden Goose. Go on now, off with you—get!"

Laughter rolls through the room while I stand with my back to the common room acting annoyed. After a minute I turn and face the room and say, "Okay, I see that you have decided to stay," I say, surveying the crowd, confident that no one has left.

"Good, now let me share one of the stories Escala told me during that long journey—back before things grew cold and distant between her and Roedyn. It was the story of her first crossing."

It started on a clear morning, years before she left the court. Escala was thirteen. She and Rihanna crept through a crack in the Moonvault wall—where tangled roots concealed a long-forgotten crossing.

The crossing pulsed gently. Even standing near it made Escala's wings twitch. The air around it smelled different, like turned soil and firewood. Not wrong, just other.

They had read about it. Crossings were rare and usually guarded, meant for emissaries, not for pixie girls with overgrown curiosity.

"Are you scared?" Escala asked.

Rihanna nodded. "Terrified."

Escala held out her hand. "Then hold my hand."

Rihanna did, and together they stepped through.

It felt like falling through honey, as though time itself had slowed. Then they stumbled into a waist-high field of yellow flowers swaying in a breeze untouched by magic.

Escala had never seen a sky like this. She gasped before she could stop herself. Just an endless sweep of blue, with huge, white, billowy clouds.

Rihanna stood beside her, hair tousled, eyes wide with wonder. "It's ugly," she whispered.

Escala's blue eyes were wide. "I think it's beautiful."

They turned slowly, taking in the landscape. To the north, a hill rose, its top covered in exposed stone. To the east and west, trees lined the horizon. To the south, rolling hills of crops stretched out, dotted with distant farmhouses.

They wandered for what felt like hours. Everything was different, but so foreign and fascinating. At one point, Escala leaned down to touch a beetle crawling along a rotten log. It didn't speak to her or flutter its wings in recognition. It just kept walking, unaware or uninterested.

"They don't know who we are," she said, a little stunned.

Rihanna nodded.

They found a small stream and followed it. The water was cold and clear, and when Escala dipped her fingers in, she felt her fingertips go numb. Not magic-numb, real numb. Like frostbite. It startled her.

"This place could kill us," Rihanna said warily.

"Probably." Escala grinned. "That's why it is so exciting!"

They stopped at the edge of a clearing where a leaning stick fence enclosed a scraggly garden. Carrots and beans fought to grow in crooked rows.

A cottage door creaked open, and a middle-aged woman stepped out. Brown dress, apron, graying hair tied in a scarf.

She spotted them and hobbled toward the gate. Tilting her head, she said, "Well now, I haven't seen your kind since I was a girl leaving teeth under pillows."

Escala and Rihanna bolted, wings thrumming as they tore through the trees. They didn't stop for fifteen solid minutes, diving deeper into the woods, hearts pounding like war drums. Neither dared to look back.

Only when they were sure the woman hadn't followed did they slow and then they collapsed into laughter.

When they stopped giggling, Rihanna said, "We have to stay hidden." Rihanna panted.

"Yeah," Escala said, still grinning. "That was too close."

They kept exploring until they reached a small village. A village might have been a generous description as it was just a few buildings clustered around a dirt road, with a crooked bell tower, water troughs, and a laundry line between a bakery and a stable.

To Escala and Rihanna, it felt like a stage, and they were ready to perform.

The baker was first. He was a large man with flour in his beard and a laugh like thunder. He'd just set down a sack of flour when Rihanna whispered something and flicked her fingers toward it.

It shuddered once, then burst—boom!

A white cloud erupted into the air, covering the baker from head to toe. His apron vanished beneath the powder. His eyebrows disappeared entirely. He looked like a ghost who had taken a wrong turn through a bakery.

Rihanna snorted, and Escala burst out laughing, doubled over behind a barrel.

The baker sneezed hard enough to make more flour puff from his shirt.

"What in the devil—!"

They flew as fast as their wings would carry them, darting behind a fencepost and around the corner before he could figure out what happened.

Next came the seamstress. She was older, serious, and deeply concentrated on her sewing.

Escala waited until she wasn't looking, then whispered to the pins in the velvet cushion by the window.

"Dance."

The pins shivered and rose. One by one, they twirled through the air like silver dragonflies, spinning loops in front of the startled seamstress, who dropped her scissors with a yelp. Her eyes went wide, and her chair tipped over. She shrieked as the pins formed a perfect ring above her head and pirouetted in midair.

The pixies struggled to hold in squeals while hiding behind a lavender bush just outside the window.

"Is this mean?" Escala snickered.

Rihanna was giggling too and shook her head. "No."

Their next prank? The pickles. They found the jar sitting outside the general store—fat, green pickles floating in brine, probably a gift between shopkeepers. Escala barely hesitated. She hovered her hands, whispered three improvised syllables, and the brine began to glow.

Pop… Pop… Pop.

The pickles twitched, then sprouted legs, bulging eyes, and warty green skin. Toads.

Rihanna slapped a hand over her mouth, stifling a laugh. Escala tipped the jar. The toads leapt—one onto a windowsill, another into the street, a third under a wagon. Chaos bloomed, and a woman shrieked as a toad dashed between her feet. A man tripped, trying to shoo one off the tavern steps.

And a small boy grabbed a pot lid like a shield and shouted, "I'll save the town!" as he charged after them.

More villagers spilled into the square—someone dropped potatoes, someone else slipped on them, and a goat broke loose, to make things worse.

Escala doubled over, bracing against a wall as tears streamed down her face. Across from her, Rihanna was slapping her knee, giggling uncontrollably. They crashed into an embrace, then lifted off, spinning through the air in wild, breathless laughter.

And in that moment, something bloomed in Escala's chest—joy, not just because the human world was a playground, but because she was in it with her best friend.

"That," I say, "was the first time Escala crossed into our world. I share it now because she was often confused about love, at least the kind between a man and a woman. She asked about it often, puzzled over it regularly. But to those of us who knew her stories about Rihanna, it was clear she already understood a different kind of love—the kind that expects nothing, that's built on laughter, loyalty, and time.

"She loved Rihanna, not romantically, but deeply—the way you love someone who sees your soul and walks beside you through every storm. They were best friends, and I hope everyone in this room has someone like that.

"You could hear it sometimes, that ache—the way her voice caught when she remembered something small that reminded her of Rihanna. You could feel it in her pauses, the unfinished thoughts, the smile that never quite reached her eyes. I think she told us those stories not just to entertain us, but to keep a part of Rihanna alive"—I tap the side of my head—"in here"—I rest my hand over my heart—"and in here.

"You don't need to be a bard to tell stories, friends. Just speak of the ones you love—tell their stories while they're here and keep telling them when they're gone."

I look slowly around the common room and say, "Don't let them be forgotten."

Chapter 42

The next morning it was still awkward. Roedyn and Escala sparred after breakfast, and it was the closest I'd seen them come to a real fight. There were no lessons, no coaching—just the sharp ring of steel on steel as they tried to knock each other's heads off.

For nearly an hour, their weapons clashed and echoed through the trees. Roedyn's blade slammed repeatedly into Escala's shield, but she was holding her own. She'd gotten better, much better. She blocked, parried, and countered with an intensity that matched his. By the time they finally stopped, both were drenched in sweat and panting hard.

After breaking camp, we pushed on. The terrain had steepened as we entered the high hills leading to the mountain passes. One of them, Roedyn said, would take us to Blackthorn Tower. He spent the day studying maps, searching for a route, but every ravine ended in cliffs.

The best option we found required scaling a forty-foot wall of stone.

Harper shrugged. "I'll climb up and drop a rope."

Roedyn nodded.

Harper scaled the cliff with ease, anchoring a line for the rest of us.

Roedyn climbed up and studied the pine-choked ridge, but he didn't see the massive shape dropping silently behind him.

Escala and I were halfway up the rope—I was climbing above her. Sticky had just crested the top when Harper yelled, "Incoming bird!"

A shadow blotted out the sun as a monstrous roc—thirty feet of muscle and feathers with a wingspan wide as ship's main sail plunged toward us, talons curved like scythes and eyes burning with predatory rage. Gray-white feathers blurred in the sun, talons outstretched, eyes locked on me.

Escala's shield was strapped to her back, so she drew her one-handed long sword while clinging to the rope with her other. I held on, heart hammering, frozen in place.

"Roedyn!" Harper shouted, pointing upward.

He turned and drew his bow in a single motion.

"It's a roc!" Roedyn yelled, firing an arrow that whistled past the bird's wing.

The roc swooped low, and Escala slashed at its flank, her blade tearing through feathers. It extended its talons toward me. I dropped a few feet in panic, nearly landing on Escala.

Harper hurled a fire spell that singed its back, barely slowing it. Sticky began casting, morphing. Roedyn readied another shot, tracking the roc as it soared away.

"Climb!" he barked. "It's circling back!"

We scrambled. I climbed ten more feet, Escala just behind. The roc returned, slamming us into the cliffside with a wing blast. Pain lanced through my ribs. Roedyn fired again—hit—but the roc barely flinched.

Harper's fire spells kept landing, igniting feathers, only enraging the beast.

On its third pass, I clung to the same spot, dazed. This time, it grabbed me. Escala struck again, but the roc didn't let go. I screamed.

Roedyn had the roc in his sights and loosed an arrow. But just as the arrow flew, Harper's fire bolt struck the creature's head. The roc shrieked and recoiled, jerking away from the cliff with a violent flap, dragging me with it.

That sudden shift turned Roedyn's perfect shot into a disaster. Escala saw the arrow at the last second. She twisted mid-swing, just enough to avoid death, but not enough to avoid the hit. The arrow punched through her mithril chain mail and buried deep in her sword arm. With a cry, she dropped her blade. It spun away into the chasm as she clung to the rope, blood streaking her grip.

The roc's wing struck her. She lost her hold of the rope and spun through the air. Blood trailed behind her. She hit the cliff wall, fell thirty feet, and struck the rocks with a thud, next to her sword.

She lay still.

Above, the roc flapped hard and ascended, dragging me in its talons. I screamed for help, voice ragged with panic, as the creature climbed into the open sky.

Sticky's transformation was complete as he now stood as a regal griffin, eyes glowing.

"Get on!" he shouted. "We're going after Wigfrith!"

Harper vaulted onto his back. Roedyn rushed down the rope, shouting Escala's name, his voice raw with panic.

Sticky and Harper launched into the sky. I wish I could say I was brave, but I was too busy being crushed in a pair of talons, barely conscious.

The world spun as the roc tore through the mountain air, a living thunderclap. Its wings carved the sky with brutal force. Wind stung my eyes. Ravines twisted below like blades. I dangled helplessly, blood rushing to my head, every wingbeat rattling my bones.

Far behind, but closing fast, came a blur of feathers and fury. Sticky, now a griffin, rode the air like a predator. On his back crouched Harper, eyes wild, rapier drawn, knuckles white.

The roc's feathers were scorched, its right wing faltering. That gave Sticky the edge. Bit by bit, he closed in on the roc.

I tried to stay conscious, but hanging upside down, every spin blurred my vision. My fingers were numb, ribs screaming with each jolt.

Somewhere behind, Harper shouted—maybe a command, maybe a curse. Sticky lunged, and Harper launched from his back like a bolt. She slammed into the roc's neck with a thud, steel flashing. One dagger buried deep, serving as an anchor. With the other, she clawed upward, driving blades into flesh and feather, climbing toward the roc's head one stab at a time. The roc shrieked, wings flailing like sails in a storm. It slammed into a cliff wall, tried to roll and crush her.

Harper cried out in pain but didn't let go.

Above me, she climbed, driving her blades in like pitons, each strike pulling her closer to the roc's head. It twisted violently, banking hard enough for Sticky to pull back or be dashed on the rocks. The roc scraped the cliffs, boulders tumbling, but Harper held fast. At one point, she dangled by a single dagger, legs flailing over a thousand-foot drop.

Then, with a furious cry, she jammed her blade into its eye.

The roc's scream was raw and unbearably loud. The roc climbed in panic, blood streaming down its beak. Harper clung to the hilt buried in its skull. Her second dagger slipped free, vanishing into the chasm. Sticky, unable to hold on, was thrown back. With a violent shake, the roc released me, and I fell.

Wind howled past as I plummeted, the sky and ground spinning in a dizzying blur. I flailed, bracing for death.

Then, I wasn't falling. Sticky's talons clamped around me, knocking the air from my lungs. Gasping, I looked up to see Harper still clinging to the roc's face, limbs whipping wildly in the wind. Blood streamed from the beast's ruined eye in crimson arcs.

"Hang on!" Sticky called out as his talons tightened even more around me.

"To what?!" I screamed. "You're the one holding me!"

Sticky's wings strained as he climbed, muscles trembling. Above, Harper was driving her remaining dagger into the roc's skull repeatedly. The bird shrieked, thrashed, blood streaming down its feathers, high above the gorge.

Sticky lunged, snapping at its wings, while I dangled from his talons, the world spinning beneath me.

Then the roc let out a final screech and its wings went still.

It went limp and dropped. Harper clung to its neck as they fell, wind tearing past her, blood whipping across her face.

Sticky surged forward. Harper scrambled to plant her knees.

"Get closer!" she shouted. "I'm jumping!"

Sticky swooped in, with me still in his grip.

"Now!" Harper braced and leapt.

Her cloak snapped in the wind as she somersaulted through the air, perhaps a thousand feet above the jagged cliffs and barren crevices below. One miscalculation, and Harper would plummet to her death.

Sticky dropped beneath, twisting mid-flight to catch her. She slammed into his back and slid across his feathers, barely hooking an arm around his neck.

Sticky's wings flared, tilting to balance the weight. We dipped hard, fast—but Harper clung tight, pulling herself upright through the wind.

Somehow, impossibly, she stayed on.

The roc plunged the last thousand feet in eerie silence.

Sticky, wings trembling and breath ragged, circled back toward the ledge. Harper clung to his back, barely upright. I swung limp in his talons, fingers burning.

But whatever victory we thought we'd won vanished the moment we spotted them. Roedyn was still kneeling beside Escala, face ashen, hands trembling—she wasn't moving.

Chapter 43

Sticky released me from his talons, and I hit the ground hard, shoulder first, rolling twice and skidding to a stop. I didn't check for bruises. I sprang to my feet and sprinted toward my lute case, which had fallen with Escala and me. Somehow, it had landed beside a jagged stone near her. I dropped to my knees and popped the latches open with trembling fingers, dreading what I'd find.

But it wasn't broken. It opened with a soft click. Inside was my lute, undamaged, thank the gods. I lifted it with reverence, as if cradling a sacred relic.

Behind me, Harper was furious. "What the hells, Roedyn?"

He was kneeling beside Escala, hunched over her as if shielding her from the world. His face was pale, drawn tight with grief.

"She has internal bleeding, broken ribs—she won't wake up," Roedyn said slowly.

He brushed dirt from her cheek with trembling fingers. "Escala… It's me. I'm here. I'm not leaving. Stay with me."

She didn't move.

Sticky collapsed nearby, already back in frog form, slumped against his staff, breath shallow and skin dull.

Roedyn turned to him, voice desperate. "Heal her, like you did in the swamp. *Please*."

Sticky met his gaze, then looked at Escala. "I… can't. I used all my magic fighting the roc. I won't have magic again until dawn."

Roedyn reeled back like he'd been punched. "She won't last 'til dawn," he choked out. "I promised I'd protect her. And now she's—"

His voice broke. "She trusted me."

Harper knelt beside him, placing her hand on his shoulder. Roedyn shook his head. "She's coughing blood. It's her lungs; I don't know how to stop it."

That was when I strummed the first note. The sound wasn't like any tune I had ever coaxed from my lute, it was deeper, older, a resonance that seemed to vibrate through bone as much as air. The chord swelled with impossible layers, as if a choir of unseen voices had joined me. The air itself shivered, each pulse rippling outward like rings on water, bending light and shadow in its wake.

The magic rose. Ribbons of melody took form, glowing strands that coiled upward and wove themselves into arcane symbols, notes etched in silver fire, hanging in the air as though the world itself had become parchment. Roedyn's head snapped up, his knuckles whitening as he gripped Escala's hand tighter. Harper's dagger was half drawn before she stilled, eyes darting from me to the glowing runes with something between suspicion and wonder. Sticky's mouth dropped open wide enough to catch the sparks themselves, then, with perfect absurdity, his tongue flicked out to snatch a passing moth, crunching it mid-glow.

The music deepened, every harmony a clash and release that rattled the stones underfoot. Sweat streamed down my temple, my hands trembling from the sheer current coursing through strings and wood. The symbols spun faster, rising in glowing bands that spiraled around Escala's still form. They orbited her like a constellation being drawn in real time—circles within circles, runes flowing like a storm caught in slow motion. Her body flickered, faint blue at first, then violet, until the edges of her form gleamed silver-white, as though she were being reforged in light.

Roedyn's whisper broke through the music, ragged with awe. "By the gods… what is this?"

The melody swelled to its peak, a final crashing wave that left the hairs on my arms bristling. My vision blurred. The last note left me like a cry torn from the world itself. Then silence. The runes guttered out like smoke on the wind. My arms fell limp across the lute, breath dragging in my chest as I slumped against the stone, every muscle hollowed by the strain.

And then Escala's fingers twitched.

Roedyn gasped. "Escala?"

Her eyes fluttered, barely at first, then wider, flickering with confusion and pain. Her gaze moved from Roedyn… to Harper… to Sticky… then to me.

Her voice, raspy and slurred, carried more defiance than breath.

"I said no one touches the faerie… and stop shooting me with arrows…"

Harper smiled. "She'll be fine."

Chapter 44

W
e spent the night at the base of what's now called—depending on who you ask—either Escala's Ledge or Harper's Leap. Escala nearly died there. Harper did leap from a griffin onto a roc's face. Fair enough, either way.

"I'm sure you, just like the party, are wondering what kind of magic I used to heal Escala." Tapping my lute, I say, "First, I'm a bard, an extraordinary one. That's magic enough. Second, true bards can shape reality through song. Some learn fire, some healing, and others, illusions. Me? I dabble in everything, naturally."

The crowd in The Stag laughs, and I explain, "I can play tavern songs all night. But the kind of music I used to heal Escala? That drains me. I can only sing a handful of magical songs like that before I need a nap, a drink, and maybe a long hug.

"You probably think we bards are just traveling musicians. Most are, but that day at Escala's Ledge, Roedyn, Harper, and Sticky saw what bardic magic looks like. It is rare and is enormously powerful, and in my case, extremely good-looking." The crowd laughs with me, or at me—sometimes I can't really tell—but I grin and give a mock salute.

"And if, for some reason I can't fathom, you want to see a non-magical bard, head on over to the Golden Goose. They have the most non-magical entertainment in all of Dunwell," I say, my tone mocking.

There's more laughter. "Now, back to the story. But first, I need a drink. Saving the life of a princess left me quite parched." I take a long, theatrical swig, half for the joke, half for the thirst, and it earns a round of chuckles and a few claps.

Setting the empty mug on the small table, I say, "Escala stirred not long after my music faded. She was groggy, but alive."

Roedyn immediately became Valla's most overbearing nursemaid: fetching water, fluffing her cloaks, offering food, and constantly asking what she needed. Roedyn did pull me aside and thank me profusely for saving her life. He also asked me not to share that part with you, but Harper told me it was really important for my audiences to know the 'soft side' of Roedyn, and yes, she did the air quotes, so here it is, in the story." The crowd roars with laughter.

Eventually, we made it back up the cliff—whether you call it Escala's Ledge or Harper's Leap—and pressed on into the mountains.

If I never see a cliff again, it will be too soon.

Chapter 45

T he next day, we climbed deeper into the Shadowspire Mountains. The cliffs softened into forested slopes, and by midday, the ridgeline broke, revealing our destination. We saw it long before we reached it—Blackthorn Tower.

It loomed between the peaks like a thorn jammed into the spine of the mountains. Its central spire rose crooked and high, shaped for menace over symmetry.

The outer walls were twenty feet tall, capped with crumbling parapets. Arrow slits marked them at irregular intervals. The lone gatehouse jutted like a broken tooth. The gate hung open, daring us to enter.

Harper let out a low whistle, eyes fixed on the rust-colored spikes crowning the tower. "Subtle place," she muttered. "Real warm welcome."

The wind was stiff and constant, and yet the clouds didn't drift. Instead, they circled the peak, making slow spirals around the tower like cliff birds that wouldn't land. I looked up, wary of another roc.

"Do you find it odd that there are no guards to greet us?" I asked.

"Or stop us," Harper added.

Roedyn nodded, scanning the walls.

The outer gate loomed; arched, blackened stone, its iron portcullis raised. Vines clung to the walls. I swear some moved.

We stepped into a narrow hall. The air shifted; it seemed colder, heavier. The walls were the same dark stone, veined with glowing crystal that refracted torchlight like bright candles.

The corridor stretched ahead before branching into stairways; some climbing up, others spiraling down. Blue flames flickered in wrought-iron sconces, casting twisted shadows.

We stood still and listened, but heard nothing.

Carefully, we moved deeper into the tower. Some passages stretched impossibly far before vanishing into the dark; others ended at sealed doors etched with faintly glowing runes.

Beyond a second archway, the corridor opened into a vast vaulted chamber. The ceiling rose into shadow, marked with silver sigils and stars.

At the center, a great brass brazier hung suspended by unseen forces, slowly rotating and casting golden light. Blue and violet flames licked upward in spirals, smelling of lavender and cedar.

Bookshelves curved along the walls, packed with scrolls, tomes, and crystalline memory orbs pulsing with quiet light. A wrought-iron staircase spiraled upward into shadow. Strange artifacts hovered in glass globes overhead. One of them contained what appeared to be a miniature thunderstorm sealed in a bottle.

The floor was made of black stone, polished to a mirror finish, etched with a vast, magical circle.

In the center stood a tall, gaunt man. His black robes were layered, worn, and heavy, and seemed to absorb light. His cheeks were hollow, his face carved with deep lines. Pale skin stretched over sharp bones. His hair, dark at the crown and silver at the tips, hung loose down his back. In one hand, he held a twisted and petrified staff, veined with silver. He didn't look healthy. Or happy.

"Visitors?" he said, tasting the word like it was foreign. "That's rare."

He didn't seem startled, and there was no edge to his voice.

Escala bowed slightly and said, "I'm Escala Winter, from the Court of Dreams."

The cloaked man studied her. "Are you now?" he said. "You look like someone walking between truths."

Roedyn shifted, stepping slightly closer to Escala's right, hand brushing his hilt. Harper hovered to her left, alert and watching, like always.

And me? I stood behind Escala with Sticky.

"I'm looking for a wizard named Victor Graves," Escala asked, her voice curious, maybe even hopeful.

"I am a keeper of relics." His eyes drifted across us but settled on Escala. "You're fey, aren't you?"

"I am—I mean, I was," she said.

"Still are, in essence," he replied. "Polymorphed. I can sense the magic."

She frowned. "How did you know?"

He didn't answer, only gave a genial wave, and smiled. "Come now, you've traveled far, where are my manners?"

Straightening, he said, "I am Victor Graves, Grand Master of the Black Order. And this"—he gestured around— "is my humble home. Some call it Blackthorn Tower."

We introduced ourselves and followed him into a wider hallway. Runes lined the floor, lighting beneath our steps, but it wasn't from torchlight; the light was glowing from the stone itself.

We entered a chamber clearly meant for entertaining; its high-arched ceilings, polished stone walls, and a long darkwood table inlaid with arcane runes that glowed.

It was already set with silver plates, crystal goblets, and utensils arranged with obsessive precision, as if he had been expecting us.

Victor clapped twice, and from alcoves in the stone, robed servants emerged, silent and fluid. Without a word, they laid out a lavish spread: roasted meats, glazed vegetables, jeweled fruits, and deep violet wine.

Victor took the head seat and raised a flute.

"Come," he said warmly, gesturing to the chairs. "I seldom have guests. Please share what news you have from Dunwell—eat, rest, and tell me your tales."

Harper muttered as she sat, "Well, if you had a proper road, maybe you'd have more visitors."

Victor chuckled, especially when we recounted our run-in with the roc. "Ah, that would be Hayyana, one of my guardians. She watches the high passes. And yes, there's a road on the eastern side. You climbed the west. No one's ever survived that... until now."

I glanced at Roedyn, but he did not react. I hoped he wouldn't make us go back to Harper's Leap on the way back to Dunwell.

The conversation wandered through bread, stew, and honey cakes. When hot tea was poured, Victor turned to Escala.

"So, Escala Winter of the Court of Dreams," he said, "I understand Rowan Winter is Lord of the court. Are you part of his house?"

"I was born a pixie in House Winter," she said. "My father is Lord Rowan Winter."

"And your mother? Victor asked.

"My mother," Escala paused. "That's complicated."

"Why are you here?" Victor probed.

"Fey law in the Court of Dreams forbids interfering with the True Cycle." She picked at a honey cake with her fork. "I broke it when I interfered. My closest friend, Rihanna, another pixie, and I crossed over. We saw a young man, alone. Then a wolf attacked. It killed him."

Victor studied Escala; he knew she was not telling him the whole story.

"It would've killed me too, but... Rihanna intervened. She saved me."

Grief swept across Escala's face, or was it guilt?

"But the wolf turned on her. It killed her." She said as she looked away. "I was tried for breaking the Oath. Banished to the mortal realm and given a quest."

Victor already knew the answer, but he asked, "What quest?"

"They said boulders are blocking the True Cycle. I must remove them, but I don't know what they are. I only know I can't return until they're gone. Roedyn and Harper offered to help, and we met Sticky on the way—"

"After Roedyn shot her with an arrow," Harper interjected.

Roedyn tilted his head back, looked at the ceiling, and sighed.

Escala ignored this and continued, "The three of them took me to Wigfrith because they said he knew everything." She gestured to me. "But Wigfrith didn't know everything because he didn't know what the boulders were."

I tilted my head back, looked at the ceiling, and sighed.

I took it from there and said, "Wizard Graves, I told her I only knew one person in all Tor'Vaen who was studied enough to help her, and that would be you, good sir." I gave a little bow, which I regret to this day.

Victor looked intrigued. "Tell me, Escala, if you could find the boulders mentioned in your sentence, would you remove them? Why go back?"

"Because it's still my home," she said. "And it's all I have."

Harper glanced at Roedyn, who looked uncomfortable.

Victor steepled his fingers. "That is… beautiful. Naïve, but beautiful."

He smiled gently, "I'd very much like to help you, Escala Winter, from the Court of Dreams. If you'll let me."

Escala beamed.

Chapter 46

After dinner, Victor led us to his study filled with leather chairs, a fireplace, and lined wall-to-wall with more books than I've ever seen.

Escala asked, "Do you know what the Court of Dreams meant by boulders?"

Victor folded his hands. "I've seen them mentioned in prophecy. And based on your story, I don't think the court sees them as metaphors. I think the court believes the boulders to be real."

"Boulders are real!" Escala exclaimed, turning to Harper who only shook her head then back to Victor as she held out her logbook. "I've been tracking them, helping people remove them from their lives."

"Oh, they're very real," Victor said. "*Very real.*"

Escala flashed Harper a triumphant little smile and clasped her hands together in delight.

"And documenting them is wise," Victor continued. "Tell me about the ones you've removed."

Escala eagerly flipped through her log, recounting tales of the people she'd helped. Harper and Sticky chimed in with color, Roedyn adding quiet corrections. Victor listened patiently.

When she finished, he said, "That's a very good start. I'm sure the court will be interested. But I don't think you've yet found the boulder your sentence requires you to move.

Yes, you've helped individuals but their boulders were personal. Yours is greater. It distorts the True Cycle for all of Valla."

Escala asked, "Do you know of such a boulder?"

Victor stood and crossed to a tapestry on the far wall. He pulled it aside, revealing a carved stone relief—a circle of interlocking symbols with a jagged crown suspended between two hands at its center. It looked evil to me.

"This," Victor said, tapping the image, "is the Crown of Dreams, a fey creation. Have you heard of it?"

Escala shook her head as she studied the image.

"Not surprising," Victor said. "It wasn't exactly the brightest moment in fey history, and probably not one they like to talk about. The crown was crafted by the Dream Weaver eons ago, but it fell into the wrong hands and has been lost to the court for centuries. It's an incredibly powerful artifact. When worn, it grants the wearer the ability to send dreams—visions of hope, comfort, and healing... or nightmares laced with dread, despair, even madness."

Victor went on, "It vanished from the Court of Dreams long ago. Most recently, Emperor Terrance Korveth used it to take the Eronvale throne by unleashing nightmares so vivid his enemies woke screaming, tearing at their skin, even murdering their own families. Entire houses and armies fell without a battle. With the Crown of Dreams, he bent the kingdom to his will and crowned himself Emperor until he somehow drowned in his own chamber pot."

Roedyn shot Harper a sharp look, but she just scratched her neck and took a long sip of wine.

Victor said, "After Korveth's death, the fey failed to recover the crown. I'm sure the court now seeks to remove it from the True Cycle. And I agree that such power in the wrong hands could twist the dreamscape beyond recognition. Based on what you've told me, I don't think you were sent just to find the crown... I think you were sent to destroy it."

"But how can I destroy it?" Escala asked.

"I can see to its destruction," Victor said. "But you must bring it to me. When you do, I'll testify before the court that you removed this boulder and saved the material plane from the madness Korveth once spread."

Escala practically vibrated with excitement. She grabbed Sticky's hands and bounced in place. "Sticky, this is it! This is the boulder I have to remove!"

Sticky joined her without hesitation, hopping up and down, swept up in her joy.

We should've seen it—the way he spoke about the court and the boulders like they were both common knowledge. What should've tipped us off—especially me, the one who's supposed to be clever—is that he didn't ask a single question.

Victor showed no curiosity about the fey realm, her sentence, or the court's justice. Instead, he identified her boulder immediately and was far too confident.

That should've set off alarms. But Escala was so relieved—he had information about a real boulder. And he seemed so sure. And we... well, we were just happy for her, and it never crossed our minds that Victor Graves might have his own agenda.

Harper and Roedyn shared a glance, and Roedyn asked, "How do you know where it is?"

Victor remained calm. "Oh, I know where it is."

"Where?" Harper asked, suspicious.

Victor clasped his hands and said, "In a red dragon's hoard at Bulan Castle, far west of Dunwell."

Roedyn exhaled deeply.

"I hope you like the material plane, Escala," Harper said dryly, "because I don't think you're going home."

Chapter 47

Victor Graves gave us directions to Bulan Castle, and Escala was so eager she nearly left that minute. I don't think she noticed how quiet we all went at the mention of a red dragon.

We stayed the night at the tower, and by first light, she was packing. Roedyn insisted on morning training, but unlike recent tense sessions, Escala was bright, talkative, buoyed by the thought of progress. Roedyn looked grim. She didn't see it, but the rest of us did.

After breakfast, Victor told us a safer route to Dunwell— one that did not involve cliffs. As we left, he stood at the gates, hands folded, watching silently. Halfway down the eastern slope, Escala glanced back. He didn't move but just raised a hand in farewell before turning toward the tower.

Back in Victor's study, two small figures emerged from the stone corridor. Morvena flew in first. She wasn't smiling. Victor didn't smile either. He opened his arms in a mock greeting. "Morvena."

"You lied to her," Morvena said sharply. "The Crown of Dreams has nothing to do with the Court of Dreams—it is not a fey artifact."

"Of course I lied," Victor said. "I needed her to believe the crown was the boulder she had to move. She's naïve, and I had to prey on that."

Morvena narrowed her eyes. "Then what is this crown?"

"*It is* called the Crown of Dreams—that much is true. But it wasn't crafted by the fey. It was forged by Nazzurel the Withering, an ancient lich who conquered Void magic— the raw, unbounded power between realms. When activated, the crown opens a portal to the Void."

His eyes gleamed, almost feverish. "Once I wear it, the Void will obey me. I'll feel the Vorrash Totem singing through the dark between realms. When the totem responds to my call, I will be able to sense its location in the planes, and I'll tear the veil between the realms, forcing a crossing into the fey realm where you planted the totem. Then I'll split my soul, become one with the Void, and step into your court as a Void demon made flesh… to kill Rowan with my own hands."

Rubbing his hands together in anticipation, he asked, "Is the totem in place?"

"It is," she replied coolly.

"Excellent." A sinister grin spread across his face.

"Rowan suspects nothing," Morvena added.

Victor nodded. Another set of wings echoed down the corridor—it was Audrey. Morvena turned sharply. "What are you doing here?"

"I want to kill her!" Audrey said.

Victor snapped, "No!"

Audrey frowned and said, "Why not?"

Morvena's voice was firm. "Because we need her. She's retrieving something for us."

"Escala is our tool," Victor said. "And we don't throw away tools until they've served their purpose."

Audrey's eyes narrowed, but she said nothing.

Victor clasped his hands behind his back. "If you truly want to be princess of the Court of Dreams," he said, "you must think beyond anger. I need Escala to retrieve the Crown of Dreams. With it, I'll secure the throne for your mother. And once Morvena is queen, you'll be princess."

As Rowan Winter's daughter, Escala was next in line to rule the Court of Dreams—she would become queen when Rowan stepped down or died. But her banishment stripped her of that claim. However, if she completed this quest to remove boulders from the True Cycle and was reinstated, her title and place in the line of succession would be fully restored. That was why Morvena wanted her dead but only after she retrieved the crown for Victor. Then, using the Vorrash Totem, he would channel part of his soul into the court, kill Rowan, and let Audrey finish Escala. With both gone, the throne would pass to Morvena.

A slow smile of understanding crossed Audrey's face as she looked to her mother. "Fine," she said slyly. "But I want to be the one to kill her."

"In time," Morvena said. "In time, my daughter."

Victor turned back toward the inner chamber. "Audrey will return to the court. She'll wait for my word. You should return as well," he said to Morvena.

"Why?"

"You'll be needed," he said. "The moment the Crown of Dreams is delivered, and Escala completes her journey, I will awaken the Vorrash Totem. When I strike down Rowan, the court will need leadership, they will need to see you present and in command."

Morvena nodded once. It made perfect sense—she had been waiting for this day to rule the court. Adjusting her cloak, she flew from the chamber with Audrey close behind. Only when the soft flutter of their wings faded down the corridor did Victor allow his smile to return. What Morvena didn't know—what she could never know—was that Victor wouldn't stop with Rowan. No, he would purge the Court of Dreams and kill every last faerie. He could already hear their screams, and he rubbed his hands in gleeful anticipation.

Chapter 48

I t took two weeks to reach Dunwell by the route Victor had shared, and while longer, it was almost all trade roads and no cliffs. The trip was uneventful and quiet, except for Escala, who buzzed with excitement, chattering nonstop about the crown, her logbook, and going home.

None of us had the heart to temper her excitement, and we agreed to save any talk of dragons for Dunwell.

Sticky beamed the whole way, thrilled for her, and honestly, so was I. Roedyn was polite, protective... but distant. Harper noticed, of course.

One evening, while Harper and Roedyn fished, Escala laughed and rode Sticky—transformed into a warhorse— across a sunlit meadow, within view but out of earshot. Harper didn't look over at Roedyn as she asked, casually enough, "So... when are you going to tell her you care about her?"

"I did," Roedyn said as he cast his line.

"No, you didn't."

"Sure I did, when she was at the bottom of the cliff and another time when we were at Sticky's lily pad."

Harper stopped reeling and looked at Roedyn. "Oh, when she was unconscious both times... after you shot her with an arrow? That's when you told her you cared?"

"She wants to go back anyway," Roedyn said.

"Well, she has nothing here, does she? You haven't given her a reason to stay, have you?" Harper said sarcastically. She raised a finger. "I've got it—just never let her recover the crown, and she will be here forever! That's it—that's your plan, isn't it?"

"Stop it."

"No, you stop it. I'm done with the excuses," Harper snapped, slamming her fishing pole down. Her voice hardened. "Look at me."

Roedyn turned to meet Harper's gaze.

"What do you really feel about her? I mean it, be honest. After everything we've done together, everything we've hidden and protected—you and me, and what we buried in that cave—you've trusted me with secrets that could shake the world. So why can't you trust me with this?" Harper said.

She pointed at Escala and Sticky riding in the field and added, "Look, she can't hear you; she's a quarter mile away playing knights with Sticky."

"I've never met anyone like her," Roedyn said softly as he watched her ride across the field, his voice laced with something that sounded a lot like longing.

"None of us have. I mean, who goes around constantly saying their full name and where they're from?" Harper said, adding, "But that is not what you feel about her. What do you feel in your heart? I already know what your brain thinks. You think she is going to leave soon, and you will never see her again, so why get involved, right?"

Roedyn nodded.

"But what does your heart feel?"

Roedyn watched Escala galloping across the meadow on Sticky's back, her golden hair streaming in the wind. She was close enough that he could hear her laughter as she rode.

Roedyn found himself smiling. Turning to Harper, he said, "I'm crazy about her," he said quietly. "Gods, she's beautiful, but it's so much more than that. It's her spirit, her drive, her optimism. Her innocence, too—the way she looks at the world like it's all new and worth discovering. The way she questions everything, never content to just accept what she's told. The way her curiosity pulls her toward everything she doesn't understand. The way she laughs, the way she dances, that smile… and how she talks about life as if every moment is an adventure waiting to happen. It's intoxicating, and I can't stand being away from her. I nearly died inside, thinking she wasn't going to make it when she fell off the cliff, and when…. and when I shot her with the arrow."

"Arrows," Harper corrected.

Roedyn ignored the comment. "But I can't tell her that."

"Why not?"

"Because she's leaving soon… as soon as we get this crown."

"Please don't tell me that you're worried she'll kiss you like the guy the wolf killed. Are you worried you're going to get attacked by a wolf?" Harper was half laughing.

"No."

Roedyn stood and started walking back to the fire. "I'm afraid no kiss will ever satisfy me again," he muttered to himself as he went.

Chapter 49

I wish I could tell you we were suspicious of Victor Graves from the start, but we weren't. He was using us long before we knew it. Unbeknownst to us, Morvena and Audrey were in the tower that day, cloaked in illusion, listening to every word we said.

A few hours after we left Blackthorn Tower, Audrey defied Victor's orders and followed us. Her plan was simple: once the Crown of Dreams was recovered, she'd kill Escala.

We had no idea at the time, but Audrey was following us. I remember Roedyn muttering that something was out there, but he never found any tracks.

As we traveled, Escala kept talking, you know how she is, filling the silence with stories. She spoke of the Court of Dreams, her duties, old friends, and the ache of losing Rihanna. She spoke of her father, Lord Rowan Winter, with reverence and distance. She spoke of Junel, the elder faerie who raised her. Not quite a mother, more a governess. But deeply, fiercely loved.

But in all her stories, she never once mentioned her real mother.

Not until Sticky asked.

About a week into our trip, we were sharing smoked fish and apples around the fire. Sticky, in his blunt way, asked, "Escala, who's your real mother?"

She didn't hesitate at all. "I don't know, and I don't care," she said, taking a bite of her apple like the matter was closed.

That answer sat wrong with me, and I said the first foolish thing that came to mind. "You don't care? Everyone cares about their mother, well, except stepmothers."

I was hoping for a laugh.

None came. Everyone, even Sticky, glared at me.

"I hate her," Escala snarled, taking an aggressive bite of the apple.

Roedyn, calm as ever, tried to reason with her. "Hate's a strong word."

Escala turned toward him, eyes blazing. "She left me, Roedyn. She abandoned me, I didn't mean anything to her."

"Wow," Harper muttered, caught between surprise and sympathy. "That's rough."

Sticky frowned, stirring the embers with a stick. "But how do you know? You said you don't even know her."

"I don't need to," Escala spat. "I know what she did. I don't know much about love—and yes, Harper, I thought a person could fall in love with just a kiss—but I do know that mothers don't abandon their babies… they are supposed to love their babies. Even if she fought with my father and they broke up, why didn't she…"

She was starting to lose it.

"… why didn't she ever come back to see me?" She hurled her half-eaten apple into the bushes, tears welling.

Harper started to speak but stopped herself. "Escala…" she whispered softly, then just shook her head, helpless.

She was crying. Roedyn moved to her side and placed an arm gently around her shoulders; amazingly, she did not pull away.

"She left me alone… I hate her." She turned her face into Roedyn's chest, sobbing, and he carefully cradled her.

No one said anything for the rest of the evening, and we never brought up her real mother again.

Chapter 50

W
e arrived back in Dunwell under slate-gray skies and the distant sound of bells. Roedyn took charge with quiet efficiency—organizing supplies and mapping routes. He'd been more reserved since the mountains, definitely hiding his emotions.

Escala and Roedyn resumed their morning sparring, though the edge that once crackled between them had dulled. She no longer seemed like she was trying to take his head off.

Harper, sensing the silent truce between them and wisely choosing not to poke it, shifted her attention to a subject far more entertaining: interrogating Sticky about his animal forms.

"So Sticky," she said, nudging him with her elbow as they walked. "What's your favorite animal form?"

Sticky tilted his froggy head. "That depends entirely on my mood."

"Oh boy." Harper grinned. "Okay then. What mood puts you in the form of a—let's say—one of those wild four-tusked pigs that roam the Hingahan plains north of here?"

"You mean the babirusa?" Sticky said.

"I don't know if that's what they're called." Harper shrugged. "All I know is they're fast, and their tusks are sharp. So when would you use that form?"

"Ah," Sticky said, nodding thoughtfully, "that's my diplomatic brunch form."

Harper raised an eyebrow. "I'm sorry, what now?"

"Diplomatic brunch," he repeated. "You want to show you're wild but refined." He looked at Harper and double-blinked.

Harper choked on a laugh. "Right, of course. What about one of those small bald-faced monkey creatures from Zandara whose face looks like an arse?"

"Don't insult the bald uakari like that," Sticky lectured. "That's my romance form."

"Really? The bald uakari—a red-faced monkey with the soul of a haunted maraca—is your romance form?"

Sticky nodded with earnest conviction. "Exactly. That bright red face is not just for show; it's an evolutionary power move. Strong lymph nodes are the cornerstone of any proper seduction ritual; the old scrolls are very clear on this."

"What scrolls?!"

Sticky waved dismissively. "You wouldn't know them."

Harper snorted and pressed on, curiously studying the frog. "Alright, last one—the duck-billed platypus. What possible mood makes you think, 'Ah yes, now is the time for egg-laying, venomous, web-footed creature of confusion?'"

"That's my sneaky form," Sticky replied proudly, as if it were the most obvious answer in the world.

"No one suspects the duck-billed platypus," he continued.

"I first encountered one in the Silverstand Forest and was amazed at how hard it was to find and track. They are naturally solitary, nocturnal, and elusive creatures that prefer to avoid confrontation. That's why they are my stealth form—part duck, part beaver, all mystery."

Harper looked dumbfounded, "You're making this up. You're telling me you actually have used that form before?"

"Of course," Sticky said, "Once, I was cornered by a whole troop of maddened hill giants who were, of all things, washing laundry in a river. I had nowhere to run—so I shifted, slipped into the water, and swam right past them. One saw me, called me a 'silly little river god,' and went back to scrubbing his underthings."

"Sticky," Harper said, shaking her head, "I am both horrified and delighted by you."

"I strive for balance," Sticky said as his tongue flashed out to grab a passing dragonfly.

Chapter 51

I grab a honey cake from a passing tray and take a big bite, nodding my thanks to Pints as the sweetness fills my mouth. Swallowing, I resume the story.

"It was our second night in Dunwell when they, not me, they, decided I had to be the one to tell her. Evidently, they felt that as a bard it was my job to break Escala's heart. Gods help me if I gain a reputation as a bard who breaks hearts. That's what I would expect from the bards at the Golden Goose, with their songs of flirts and firebrands. I'm sure those hussy bards overpromise to pack the place. Half the fellas there tonight are about to get their hearts stepped on."

The crowd reacts just as I hoped, laughter, whistles, the correct dose of scandalized amusement. I grin. "Oh, I'll be insulting the Golden Goose all night."

Truth be told, I don't hate the two women who perform there. They are friendly enough, and not the worst-looking either. But they have no heart for the craft. To them, music is filler, noise to drink to, from first sip to final stumble.

But that's not barding to me. I want to fill your mind with a tale that lingers, to let you see the characters, feel their joy and pain, root for them, laugh with them… maybe even cry. What I do isn't noise. And I certainly don't aim to be a heartbreaker, but what I had to tell Escala was about to put that reputation at risk.

Turning back to the crowd, I say, "If I lured you into The Stag tonight with promises I'm not delivering on, now's your chance, you can still get to the Golden Goose. I won't judge, I'll even make it easy and close my eyes. Go on, I won't be offended."

I close my eyes, count to ten, and open them.

Not one person has left. I smile and rock back on my heels.

"Well, thank you, that means an awful lot, it really does. And yes, I am stalling, because when I get back into the story, I have to break Escala's heart." The crowd laughs, and I continue with the tale.

To Escala, it seemed simple: find Bulan Castle and retrieve the Crown of Dreams. What she didn't grasp was that it was guarded by a red dragon, making the task not just dangerous, but nearly impossible.

Escala didn't understand, how could she? She wasn't from this plane. She didn't know about the history of Valla, the Boxes of Kestrel, or the fragile Dragon Truce we all lived under. So, in a quiet side room of The Stag (yes, the one just off the balcony), I told her the story. Not the whole saga, that would've eaten an evening and half of a keg. I gave her the abridged edition.

"Escala," I began, "the Crown of Dreams may very well be your boulder."

She clapped her hands. "Then I'm going home soon!" She beamed.

Roedyn and Harper exchanged a look.

"Victor said the crown is in the red dragon's treasure hoard at Bulan Castle," I said.

"Yup, that's what he said," she confirmed.

I pressed on, more gently this time. "I need to tell you a story. One that explains why even thinking about facing this dragon is..." I was searching for the right word when Sticky supplied it.

"Dangerous," he said.

"Suicidal, more like it," Harper muttered.

I continued, "In the beginning, when the gods first shaped Valla, it was so beautiful that Virelle, goddess of harmony, wept with joy. Where her tears struck the surface, they crystallized into dragon eggs, the firstborn of Valla, creatures of divine magic made scales, and for a time, utterly alone."

Escala smiled. "That's beautiful. It that sounds like the First World."

"Yes, very similar," I said. "Later, the gods brought forth the lesser races: humans, elves, and dwarves. Magic was abundant then, woven into every corner of Valla, and all beings could wield it. The younger races, curious and bold, soon discovered ways to traverse the planes. They accidentally tore open gateways, crossings, as you call them, Escala, into realms of unspeakable evil.

"Through one such crossing came Zharulek, the Nameless One, and with him came corruption. Furious at the defilement of their perfect world, the gods cast Zharulek into the underworld. But even when he was imprisoned, his darkness seeped into Valla, poisoning the land, twisting mortal hearts, and turning a third of the dragons against their kin."

"He sounds horrible," Escala said, frowning in disgust.

"He is," I agreed, "and from that rot rose the runelords—once-mortal mages now fully consumed by Zharulek's influence. Arrogant beyond measure, they forged Orbs of Power and dared to wield the gods' own magic against them in a bold attempt to usurp them.

"The gods, outraged by this defiance, responded with the Purge; a sweeping act that stripped Valla of magic so their creations could never again rise against them. But such divine retribution came at a cost."

I took a sip. I was talking a lot and was thirsty, and honestly, I was getting to the part that was going to break her heart.

"You see, Escala, dragons are magic. Their essence is woven from the fabric of Valla. If the gods had gone through with the Purge, they would've wiped out the dragons entirely. Since fey are also pure magic, I'm sure you can understand how serious a problem this was."

Escala nodded. I believed she understood the story so far.

"The gods debated for weeks. The good dragons pleaded for mercy, begging the gods to spare them. The evil dragons, enraged by the devastation wrought by the god's creations, lashed out, laying waste to cities and towns in a furious attempt to wipe out all life and remove the need for a Purge. In effect, they sought to eradicate the lesser races.

"Amid the chaos, it was Kestrel, a lesser god, who offered a bold solution. He forged three arcane boxes, each capable of containing a dragon's essence: one for good, one for neutral, one for evil. To prove it was safe, he sealed a faerie dragon inside and released it unharmed the next day."

I pulled a small, ornate box from my pack, eight inches long, gold filigree, glowing faintly with runes.

"This," I said with a grin, "is a Box of Kestrel."

Harper's face went white. She immediately looked at Roedyn, who stood frozen.

"Oh! I mean it's just a replica," I added quickly, raising a hand. "A harmless prop modeled from the historical tomes, right down to the enchantments. It even has illusions."

I began to lift the lid, and everyone flinched—everyone except Harper and Roedyn, who watched me closely, as if wondering whether I actually had one of the three Boxes of Kestrel.

"When I open it," I continued with a grin, "there's a little flash, a fireworks pop, just like at festivals, and a fake dragon emerges."

With a soft click, I opened the box. A whoosh of light exploded from within, followed by the roar of an illusory dragon that soared around the room in dazzling colors before vanishing through the ceiling in a blaze of sparks.

Escala and Sticky were delighted; she clapped with glee, and Sticky hopped. Roedyn and Harper locked eyes but said nothing.

"Great for tavern storytelling," I said, snapping the lid shut and slipping the box back into my bag. "Anyway... after the dragon was sealed in his test box, it lived. And the next day, Kestrel reversed the ritual, and the faerie dragon returned, whole. The gods were stunned—but desperate to preserve the dragons. So, they agreed."

"That sounds like Kestrel's box was going to save the dragons," Escala observed.

"That was the hope," I said. "The good dragons went first, surrendering their power. Then came the neutrals. But when it was time for the evil dragons, everything unraveled.

"The betrayal came mid-ritual. Kestrel, caught off guard, watched in horror as the box meant for evil dragons overflowed with magic beyond control. The surge threatened to tear Valla apart. In desperation, he funneled the excess magic into the other two boxes, linking all three. The gambit worked, and Valla was saved, and the evil dragons were sealed.

"But then came the Purge. Divine magic tore through the realm like a storm, ripping away much of its power and rending great fissures that split open the Underdark and the Underworld. From those wounds in the earth, monsters surged forth, spilling onto the surface in endless waves.

"Kestrel opened the boxes to summon the dragons back, begging for their help. But the magic wouldn't fully return. By linking the boxes, he had broken something. The dragons emerged weakened, no longer immortal.

"Outraged, the gods turned on Kestrel. So did the dragons. Shamed and afraid, Kestrel vanished into the planes, leaving the Boxes behind."

"How rude!" Escala said.

"I think the dragons would agree," I said. "And as monsters swarmed Valla and the dragons refused to help, the mortal races—elves, dwarves, and men—united and drove back the demon tide together. During the battles, a half-elf ranger named Jurikii, wielding a sentient sword named Bride, used the boxes' power to forge a great lock. Together, they sealed the gateway to the Underworld.

"After the demon threat was quelled, the lesser races turned on the dragons for refusing to help, hunting them one by one. Thus began the Dragon Wars. But the conflict was short-lived. Both sides saw the danger: reopening the Boxes would once again banish the dragons, but it would also weaken the seal on the Underworld. If all three were ever opened, the gateway would collapse… and the demon horde would return. Valla would end. Thus, the Dragon Truce was born."

"So, the dragons agreed to stop attacking?" Escala asked.

"Well, they're allowed to defend themselves if their lairs are invaded," I said. "But under the Dragon Truce, the dragons, now diminished and mortal, swore never to make war on the races of men. In return, the mortals vowed to honor the dragons and never open the Boxes. To preserve that balance, the gods decreed a sacred duty: elves, dwarves, and humans would together appoint a single order to guard the Boxes for all time. They became known as the Gray Cloaks."

Escala's eyes grew large. She quickly looked to Harper, then to Roedyn, shock on her face. Had they once protected the Boxes of Kestrel?

I continued, "If the dragon truce were ever broken, by dragon or mortal alike, there would be only one option: open the boxes. And if all three were opened, the end of Valla would follow."

"Okay, so there are three boxes of Kestrel." Escala said, "We just don't open them, and the dragons should not attack us. We can sneak into the dragon's lair, get the crown, and leave. We must be *very careful* and *quiet*; I'm particularly good at that."

Harper spoke first. "Two of the Boxes of Kestrel have already been opened, Escala."

"Who would do something like that?" Escala asked, surprise in her voice.

"The first Box was opened a few years ago by a warlord named Barak Vassak," I explained. "A cruel, ambitious tyrant, drunk on the dream of empire. Reckless beyond measure, he lifted the lid of the Box—and in that instant, the good dragons vanished from Valla."

Escala's brow furrowed. "And what became of him?"

"He did not hold power long," I said. "For heroes rose against him, an unlikely fellowship whose names are still sung in the halls of the brave. Argone Deepwater, the dragonborn warrior whose shield stood firm against armies; Kriick Brightseer, the kobold swashbuckler rogue, quick with a grin, a quip, and quicker with a blade; Kiervasan, the tiefling grave cleric who called the dead to rise in chains against their tyrant; River, the catfolk cleric whose magic was granted by the god of tricks and burned brighter than torchlight in the darkest hours; and Zordanus Mul, the gnome necromancer whose art turned death itself into a weapon.

"They came at last to the Gray Citadel, Vassak's stronghold, black stone rising from the cliffs like the teeth of some buried beast. His banners, crimson and iron, snapped in the wind above walls bristling with spears. For three days

325

and nights, the warlord's forces hurled fire and steel against them. Argone's shield bore the scars of ten thousand arrows; River's voice grew ragged from prayer; Zordanus's skeletal thralls shattered and rose again under his command. Still, they pressed on.

"On the fourth night, when the storm clouds split and rain lashed the battlements, Kriick scaled the sheer wall like a shadow, slipping past the guards to fling open the gates. The others charged within, a thunderclap of steel and spell. They carved their way through the citadel's heart, step by bloody step, until they reached the throne room where Vassak awaited them.

"The tyrant was a giant of a man, clad in iron and fury, the cursed Box chained to his side. He fought like one possessed, shattering Argone's spear, hurling River across the chamber, driving Kiervasan to his knees. But Zordanus whispered a word to the grave, and the bones of Vassak's own ancestors clawed free from beneath the stone to tear at his limbs. In that moment, Argone seized a broken blade and drove it into the warlord's chest.

"Vassak fell, but too late—the Box had already been opened, its curse spilling like poison into the world. Still, the fellowship seized it from his bloodied hand, locking it once more, and with his death, the Gray Citadel fell silent.

"Their names—Argone Deepwater, Kriick Brightseer, Kiervasan, River, and Zordanus Mul—are remembered as the fellowship who struck down a tyrant. Legends say their courage saved Valla from the empire, though not even they could undo what the Box had unleashed.

"As for the second Box," I continued, my voice low, "it was opened more recently, in the burning wastes of the Nuria Desert, in Zandara. Unlike the first, this time it may have been an accident—but the consequences were no less ruinous. For when its lid was lifted, the neutral dragons, those who kept the balance between light and shadow, were ripped from Valla, gone in an instant."

Escala frowned. "An accident? Who would be so reckless?"

"A fey druid," I said. "One who did not know what she carried. Her name was Belladonna."

Escala shook her head. "I don't know her."

"No," I agreed, "few do. She was young, eager, and far from the courtly halls of your realm. She wandered with a strange company of heroes, each of them outcasts, bound together by chance and circumstance. There was Aswan, a fire genasi grave cleric whose prayers rang like tolling bells over battlefields; Zephry, another fire genasi, a bard with a voice that could cut through despair and call forth courage; Nixian, a dhampir sorcerer who always wrestled with the darkness in his blood; Karwl, a gnoll monk, who always seemed to be drunk but had strikes as swift as sand serpents; Zithgar Hammerfell, a towering minotaur fighter who longed for his minotaur kingdom to rise again; and Belladonna herself, a fairy druid with a heart more curious than cautious.

"Their path led them into the Nuria Desert, across dunes that stretched like oceans of fire beneath the sun. It was there, in the ruins of a forgotten temple, half-buried in sand, that they found the Box and had to wrestle it away from two runelords drunk with desire for immortality as they defeated the Queen Reborn, a runelord who sought to become a Dream Weaver. Remember the Magocracy? These two were part of that group, wizards who challenged the gods. To their eyes, the second Box of Kestrel was only an ancient relic, humming faintly with power. Belladonna, drawn by its voice, laid her hands upon it. Some say it whispered to her. Some say it sang. Whatever it was, she opened it, thinking it would help against the Queen Reborn. Valla changed in that instant as a shockwave tore across the desert, as the skies split, and the neutral dragons cried out one last time before vanishing forever. Their absence unbalanced all things, neither good nor evil could be checked, and the scales of the world tilted wildly. Belladonna fell to her knees, broken by what she had done.

"But her companions rallied to her. They fought through the storm of chaos as the Box's unleashed power twisted the temple into a nightmare, stone walls sagging and melting like wax, desert sand spiraling into jagged glass. Aswan's solemn prayers raised barriers of light to shield them from the curse's fury. Zephry's song rang out, a defiant melody that held despair at bay. Nixian poured every drop of magic in his veins into holding back the raging tempests, his body trembling on the brink of collapse. Karwl darted through the ruin with impossible speed, dragging his companions clear of falling stone. And Zithgar Hammerfell planted his hooves and braced the collapsing gate on his massive shoulders until the last of them had passed through.

"In the heart of that maelstrom, they wrenched the Box from Belladonna's trembling hands, slamming it shut before its corruption could spread further. Their struggle not only ended the catastrophe but also the schemes of the Queen Reborn, who had sought the Box to fuel her blasphemous rise to become a Dream Weaver.

"Now that cursed relic lies in their keeping. Whether they guard it out of duty, guilt, or fear, no one can say. But all know that Belladonna carries the heaviest weight, the faerie who, by one tragic mistake, destroyed the neutral dragons. You've probably never heard of her because she doesn't dare return to the Court of Dreams—talk about interfering with the True Cycle.

"And the others remain by her side because they share the grim burden of what can never be undone."

"Okay, but we aren't dealing with a Box. We just want the Crown of Dreams," Escala said, not understanding the connection.

"Don't you get it? Two boxes have already been opened, Escala." Harper said.

"Why does that matter?" she asked.

Sticky tried to explain: "If the evil dragons were gone, we might have had a chance either to parlay with a good dragon or sneak past a neutral dragon, because those dragons wouldn't want to break the truce. But red dragons are the worst of them, the evil ones. Even before the Purge, they burned for vengeance. They won't bargain or negotiate. If it wakes while we're in its lair, we will die."

I added, "Sneaking up on a dragon is nearly impossible. Even asleep, they're aware."

Roedyn crossed his arms. "Dragons radiate fear. If we get too close, we could become too scared to fight or even run."

"And then there's dragonfire," Harper warned. "It breathes a roaring cone of fire that melts walls, armor, and flesh right off your bones."

Sticky's throat clicked. "I'm sorry, Escala. That red dragon will be furious, even more furious now that two boxes have been opened. Anything coming near its hoard is as good as dead. It could even be patrolling, looking for someone to punish. We might not even get close to the castle."

Harper folded her arms. "No wonder Victor hasn't gone after the crown. It would take a hundred seasoned knights, archers, and wizards to take down a dragon, and they'd still take heavy losses."

Tears filled Escala's eyes. I had done it, I had broken her heart.

Her hands trembled as she set the teacup down with care, as if letting it go meant letting go of hope. She stood slowly, her voice breaking, raw with pain. "You've brought me this far. And I'm grateful. Truly."

She swallowed hard. "The Crown of Dreams is my boulder, and I know where it is. I have to remove it to go home. I don't blame you for staying behind."

She paused and rubbed an eye. "But I must go... I'll remove it alone."

She turned, her words barely a whisper. "Good night."

She left before we could speak. Harper glanced at Roedyn. Roedyn stood, pain in his face. "I made an oath to help her remove the boulders. I don't break oaths; I'll be in the stables in the morning." He headed to his room without another word.

Harper exhaled. "Guess I'm going too." She stood and followed. Sticky croaked, "I can turn into a fire salamander, which I think is immune to fire. I'll be okay. I'm going too."

That left only me. There was no way I was not going to observe this; what a tale it would be, so long as I survived. So I downed my ale and went up the stairs to pack for what felt like a journey straight into the jaws of death.

Chapter 52

The next morning, Escala stepped into the common room, pack over her shoulder, ready to leave alone. But she stopped and stared in disbelief, because we were already there, geared up and waiting.

It was emotional—too much to capture in the little time we had. Roedyn reminded her, gently but firmly, that he'd sworn an oath to help remove the boulders. One by one, we spoke, each offering reasons. None of us wanted to face a red dragon... but letting Escala go alone was something with which we couldn't live.

Deep down, we all hoped we could sneak in, steal the crown, and slip away. A full assault wasn't an option.

Her eyes brimmed, but she didn't cry. Instead, she bit her lip, smiled faintly, and mouthed, "Thank you."

Roedyn cautioned her that we still needed to plan, so we remained in Dunwell three more days—just long enough for Escala to rest, resupply, and grow restless. She was eager to move again.

Victor's map would take us past the village of Marlow, through Sticky's beloved Never Glenns, around Osar's Spire, and up into the Koor Peaks. Our destination: the ruins of Bulan Castle.

Fortunately, much of the route followed established trade roads, and this time, we'd be traveling by horseback. Harper, ever the miracle worker when it came to coin, secured us mounts just as Roedyn and Escala were finishing their final morning spar.

"Look what I found." Harper grinned, patting the side of a sturdy gray gelding. "They were priced just right after I reminded the seller that our former emperor is no longer around to collect taxes and that he should be grateful, particularly once he knew who to thank."

Escala turned to Sticky and said, "Thank you so much for the riding lessons last week. I'm so excited to ride my first real horse!"

Sticky puffed up with mock pride. "You're welcome. I've now trained exactly one blonde elf and three confused goats and you're by far the fastest learner."

Before anyone could respond, Escala gave her mare a gentle nudge and took off at a canter, her golden hair streaming behind her like a banner. Laughing, she leaned forward with joyful abandon and gave the horse its head.

Harper looked at Roedyn. "You going to let her just ride out of your life like that?" She didn't wait for an answer; she just clicked her tongue and galloped after Escala.

The rest of us had to spur our mounts to keep up, laughing and calling out for Escala to slow down. With a resigned shake of his head, Roedyn kicked his horse into motion and took off after her.

Chapter 53

W
e rode for two days before, to everyone's surprise and Escala's delight, we spotted the circus pitched at a fork of three trade roads near the bustling town of Tarnwick. Without waiting, she hopped off her horse and vanished among the colorful tents, calling, "Crurri! Crurri!"

She found him quickly, sprawled atop a circus wagon, dozing in the sun. Hearing his name, he opened one eye and sat up.

"Well, well," Crurri purred, stretching. "What a pleasant surprise. Did your search bear fruit?"

"Yes!" Escala beamed. "We found Victor Graves, and he told us where the boulder is!"

Crurri cocked his head in surprise. "It's real?"

"Yes!" Escala said, "It's called the Crown of Dreams— a fey crown that controls dreams. It's in a red dragon's hoard."

Crurri's whiskers twitched. "That does sound dangerous."

"I know! But Victor offered to destroy it if I could get it away from the dragon."

"Gracious of him," Crurri said evenly.

We spent the rest of the day with Crurri, mostly listening as Escala breathlessly recounted our travels. But the old performer wasn't fooled—he sensed something beneath her excitement. As Roedyn and Harper readied the horses, Crurri gently pulled Escala aside.

"I'm glad you've found purpose," he said kindly. "But something in you is still stirring. Like a question you haven't figured out how to ask."

Escala shifted. "How can you tell?"

"I watch people all day," Crurri said. "I see pain or worry behind their delight—I see the same in you."

"I don't know what's wrong," she admitted. "I should be happy. I found my boulder and my friends are helping. But something feels off."

"How so?"

She exhaled. "I thought going home would make me feel happier. But instead... I feel sad when I think about leaving. And that confuses me."

She glanced over—Roedyn was adjusting his saddle straps.

Crurri followed her eyes. "Is it because of him?"

Escala nodded. "I keep wondering if I'm just a mission to him. He made a vow—and he takes oaths seriously. But sometimes... I wish it was more than that. I don't know how he feels—he shows he cares through actions, not words."

"And that makes leaving harder?"

She slowly nodded.

"Oaths are heavy burdens," Crurri said. "Some honor them out of duty or pride—but sometimes, it's for reasons they won't admit, even to themselves."

"What do I do, then?"

"Nothing," Crurri said. "Some people tuck their feelings away like secrets in locked boxes, and they might never open those boxes."

"Just do nothing," Escala repeated his instructions, clearly disappointed.

"Does he know how you feel?"

"I don't know."

"Think on that. He could be just as confused as you."

Escala nodded, lost in thought. She had always believed it was obvious she was drawn to Roedyn—that she wanted to be near him. But her nose crinkled, and doubt crept in. Maybe it hadn't been obvious. Maybe he hadn't seen it at all.

Crurri gave a slight bow. "If you come across my circus again, stop by. Tell me how it turned out."

"I will," she said, patting his arm. "Thank you, Crurri."

She turned, steadier than before, and walked back toward the horses—toward Roedyn.

Chapter 54

W e left the circus behind and rode west, the road narrowing as we entered the Silverstand Forest. For the first two days, we made excellent time. At the end of the second, we left the main road and followed a nearly invisible path Roedyn had spotted; it was overgrown, forgotten, and unused for years., and honestly, awful.

By midday on the third day, the path vanished entirely, and we continued through the forest on foot, relying on Roedyn's tracking and Victor's map. Eventually, the trees began to thin, giving way to steep, stony bluffs—just where Victor had marked the ruins of Bulan Castle.

By late afternoon, we arrived.

The ruin clung to the cliff, but it hadn't fallen to age or siege—it had been torn apart, scorched, and in places, melted. Towers lay crumpled, stone blackened and warped, and one wall looked as if it had simply liquefied under intense heat.

Harper said what we were all thinking: "Dragonfire."

We searched for a dungeon entrance, but if one had existed, it was buried under scorched rubble. By sundown, we made camp in the trees south of the ruins.

At dusk, Sticky—restless—convinced us to let him scout. He turned into a bat and disappeared into the night.

He returned hours later, flapping into camp. "There's a cavern high in the cliffs east of the castle," Sticky said. "It runs deeper than I dared go. I didn't reach the bottom, but it's near the ruins and wide enough for a dragon."

He added, "It'd be nearly impossible to climb down from above. But if the cavern at the bottom connects to the dungeons under the ruins, there might be other entrances along the cliffs."

"We'll search the ridge by daylight," Roedyn announced.

After our evening meal, as the fire dimmed to embers, Escala stood. Her cloak shifted in the breeze, golden hair catching the firelight.

"I need to say something," she said, looking at each of us.

"First, I want to thank you for helping me get this far and for putting up with me."

Harper smirked. "Oh, we've been keeping score. You owe us at least three drinks and a kingdom."

Roedyn glared at Harper.

Escala smiled and shook her head. "This is my quest. If any of you turn back tomorrow, I won't hold it against you. I understand."

Roedyn stood. "No," he said firmly. "I'll be at your side. I made an oath—and I don't break my oaths."

Something flickered across Escala's face—hurt, maybe—but before she could respond, he softened.

"But even if I hadn't... I'd still be here because you're my friend. And that's enough. I won't let a friend face this alone."

Escala swallowed hard. Her eyes glinted in the firelight—wet with something unspoken. Or maybe it was just the flames. Then again, what would I know? I once swallowed a watermelon seed and cried for an hour.

Harper grinned. "You think I'd miss this? I want to see if you can actually fight. Plus, I bet Sticky you'll go full berserker if something touches you."

Sticky sat still, double-blinking. That earned a laugh from Escala.

He adjusted his cloak and said matter-of-factly, "There are great larvae in dragon lairs, and I'm very hungry."

Escala just shook her head and smiled.

All eyes turned to me.

I raised a hand. "Are you kidding? This is going to be the greatest story ever told. I'm not going back to Dunwell—not until I get my masterpiece."

Escala sat back down, the worry on her face softened by the fire's glow. For the first time in days, she looked like she believed we'd truly stay.

We would probably all die tomorrow—at least some of us—but tonight, we were still together.

Chapter 55

Audrey had trailed them all the way to the ruins of Bulan Castle, watching from the shadows as they spent the day searching for an entrance.

She had nearly acted when the frog vanished into the underbrush and Harper wandered off for firewood. Her fingers brushed the wolf totem in her pouch. But Escala was never alone—Roedyn, the ranger, always hovered close.

Audrey could tell he was protecting her. And he was good—too good. A week earlier, under the velvet black of the new moon, he'd nearly caught her.

He'd taken third watch and, without warning, slipped from the fire and into the forest. He moved so quietly that he startled even her. She darted into the dense pine branches, heart pounding, just as he notched an arrow and scanned the tree branches. Audrey froze, wings tight, limbs pressed to the bark, hoping her small frame cloaked in night shadows might pass for a startled crow or owl.

He stared up for far too long before finally turning and heading back to camp. When Audrey's heart rate settled, she grew more cautious in her approach but still crept near their camp each night, eavesdropping and waiting for a chance to deploy the wolf totem, even though Escala hadn't yet recovered the crown.

Not that Audrey cared about the crown. She just wanted Escala dead—Audrey wanted to be a princess, and that would happen as soon as Escala was dead.

The night we reached the ruins, Audrey perched in the withered branches of a tree, just thirty feet from our fire. Of course we didn't know it, but our voices drifted easily through the still night air and she heard every word.

"I don't expect any of you to join me," Escala had said.

Audrey's heart quickened. Finally, this was it. Escala would enter alone. Audrey would follow right behind her and release the wolf totem.

But Roedyn stood immediately—blast him—and ruined everything by declaring he'd made an oath to help her and didn't break oaths. Audrey almost groaned aloud.

Shaking her head, she whispered bitterly into the leaves, "Roedyn, you'd better hope she never makes an oath with you; all she does is break them."

Chapter 56

The next morning, we tethered the horses in a grove of trees near our camp and began searching for an entrance to the dragon's cave. Sticky had spent the night as a squirrel, chittering with the local wildlife. He said, "The animals will watch the horses. Word's been sent to the predators, wolves, and such, that I'm here and the mounts are under my protection."

Harper raised an eyebrow. "You talk to animals, and you believe wolves will pass on a free meal because you croaked at them?"

"Yes, and yes," he said. "I am the archdruid of Silverstand Forest, and I speak for the trees, the bees, and all things that hum in harmonies. If they ignore my request..." He looked meaningfully toward the forest. "Then I stop speaking for them."

We exchanged confused glances, but no one pressed further. Sticky's nature-magic business was best left unexplained.

With the horses secured, we turned toward the jagged cliffs near the castle ruins and began our search for an entrance. By mid-morning, we found a jagged cleft on the east side facing the bluffs Sticky had scouted the night before. Sticky peered into the blackness and muttered, "Feels like something's watching us in there."

Harper smirked. "Charming, isn't it?"

Cautiously, we squeezed into the narrow gap in the cliffside and stepped into a stone corridor. The ceiling arched ten feet above us, the floor paved with worn flagstones. The walls were rough stone, hewn from the bedrock, and I wondered how many years it had taken to carve these passages. It seemed like a lot of work to create a place to put political prisoners, if indeed this was a dungeon beneath the castle.

The passage stretched north and south. A stairwell to the south curled upward, disappearing into darkness, and we figured it might connect back to the ruined castle above. But our focus turned north, toward the bluffs and the likely dragon lair.

With torches lit and Harper in the lead, we advanced in wary silence and soon reached a fork.

"Which way?" Harper asked.

Sticky sniffed each branch. "Given our entrance point and where the cliffs run, I'd say right. That should lead toward the deeper caverns."

Trying to be helpful, I pointed to a door straight ahead. "Well, there's a door right here—"

I opened the door and stepped in—then the floor disappeared. I was falling. Thirty feet below, iron spikes waited. I was going to die.

Escala lunged and caught my wrist just in time. My legs kicked above the pit, heart pounding. She grunted, bracing herself. Thankfully, I'm a gnome, light and nimble. Roedyn was there in a flash. He grabbed my shoulders and hauled me back.

Once I could breathe again, I said nonchalantly, "Okay, it's not that way."

Roedyn said firmly, "Don't just open doors."

We chose the left path, winding through various twists and turns and passing several doors, which I ignored, before descending two steep staircases.

The corridor narrowed the deeper we went. Then came a sound, faint at first, like a hum buried in the bones. It grew louder with each step, becoming a slow, grinding scrape of metal against stone.

Roedyn raised a hand, signaling us to stop.

Harper tilted her head. "That didn't sound good."

"No," I said. "It didn't."

The stairs led to a large chamber, about forty by twenty feet. Three tall granite statues stood at the far end, each bearing an unknown sigil on its chest. Their heads were smooth and helmeted with vertical eye slits, but no faces.

Escala whispered, "Are they alive?"

As if in answer, the sigils lit up with a soft blue glow, the hum deepened, and they began to move. Much faster than we could have anticipated. The first lunged at Roedyn, who ducked just in time, rolled behind a pillar, and nocked an arrow.

Harper flung a burst of flame at the second, catching its shoulder. The fire rolled across its body like water, dissipating with only a faint hiss. It turned toward her, unfazed.

Sticky began to cast a spell, and I moved behind Escala, lute in hand.

The third golem came straight for Escala, but she raised her shield quickly, instinctive now, after all those hours sparring with Roedyn.

Holding her sword in her other hand, she didn't back away.

As the golem raised its massive stone arms to strike, she stepped inside its swing arc at an angle, the same footwork Roedyn had drilled into her every morning. Her shield rose high, her sword drawn back, then she slashed downward in a brutal arc. Steel shrieked against stone. The blade crashed into the golem's leg, sending sparks and stone chips flying, but it did not appear to slow it in any way.

The golem retaliated with a crushing blow. Escala caught it on her shield and drove her back a step.

Her boots slid, knees buckling, but she didn't fall.

She straightened and shouted through gritted teeth, "No one touches the faerie!"

The second golem lunged at Escala—now two were on her. She pivoted between them, shield raised to deflect their stone strikes, her sword flashing in quick counters.

She absorbed the second hit with a grunt, shield braced, feet planted. Each blow echoed through her bones, but she stood firm. Her sword darted out again and again, though her strikes seemed to do little damage.

Still, each swing drew another attack, and if she had the strength to keep her shield up, keeping their blows from landing clean, she could hold them. Two constructs, locked on her alone.

Sticky finished his spell and suddenly transformed into what I can only describe as a fifteen-foot walking landslide.

Still vaguely humanoid–wo legs, two arms, a head—his form was a churning mass of black, oozing mud.

The landslide charged the third golem and slammed into it. The golem struck back, but each blow sank harmlessly into Sticky's muddy body, which warped and reformed.

Sticky's landslide form wasn't doing real damage either, but Roedyn saw it immediately: this was a distraction, just like Escala's shield work. Both had become living targets, holding the golems' attention so Roedyn and Harper could figure out how to bring them down, while my song slowed the enemy's attacks and hopefully made ours hit harder.

Roedyn kept his distance, eyes sharp. He loosed an arrow just below one golem's shoulder plate. The arrow struck with a dull thud, and the thing jerked, stiffening.

"Target their joints!" he called.

Harper snapped her fingers, and a column of stone erupted beneath one golem, knocking it off balance. She dashed forward, dagger flashing, and drove it into the back of its knee. It groaned—a deep, grinding sound—and toppled sideways.

Escala was still fending one off, ducking and blocking. Roedyn glanced her way, saw she was holding her own, and loosed two more arrows at the one Sticky had engaged, one sank into its shoulder joint, the other into the back of its knee. Its leg buckled.

Harper was already there, flames dancing up her arm. She struck cleanly at the base of its spine. The construct shuddered, then dropped, shaking the floor.

The walking landslide lurched toward the last golem locked in combat with Escala. His muddy form swarmed over the back of the golem, pulling its attention from Escala. The golem raised its arms, turning its stone head to track the shifting mass.

Escala didn't hesitate. She drove her blade up into its neck joint with a mighty thrust. Stone chips burst into the air as her blade found purchase. The light in its chest flickered, then went out. The golem collapsed, and she leapt back just in time to avoid being crushed.

Escala stood, chest heaving, her knuckles white on the hilt of her sword. "I hit something," she said. "I actually hit something."

"And you didn't get hit by an arrow either," Harper quipped.

Roedyn shot Harper a glare and turned to Escala. "You were incredible. You held off two of them while we figured out how to hurt them—that's what a knight does."

Escala beamed.

After we caught our breath, we moved on.

Chapter 57

W e followed the corridor as it sloped steadily downward, the air growing cooler with each step. Eventually, the passage ended at a door, though calling it a door felt wrong.

It wasn't wood or stone, but a black, obsidian-like material, polished so smooth that it looked like dark water. There were no hinges, no frame; it was just a seamless slab, set into the wall like a coffin lid.

From its center, six faintly glowing runes spiraled outward, each tracing a perfect line in a different hue. Six paths, etched with eerie precision to matching runes on the floor.

Harper examined the patterns and, after a few minutes, said, "This isn't that complex. This is a hexlock gate."

Roedyn nodded.

"What's that?" Escala asked.

"A hexlock gate requires six people of like mind to open it," Roedyn explained. "Each must willingly stand on one of the six runes. It's a safeguard designed for cooperation and secrecy. You can't sneak six people into a vault without someone noticing. That's the point. They're used by kings, churches, secret orders to protect something truly valuable." Roedyn added, "My guess is the castle's former occupants placed this hexlock gate to guard their treasure vault. The Crown of Dreams is likely beyond it."

"And probably the red dragon," Sticky said.

"And don't forget certain death," Harper quickly added.

Roedyn glared at Harper.

Ignoring their banter, I said, "But there are only five of us—we're one short. How are we supposed to open the hexlock gate?"

For twenty minutes, we tried everything—stacking gear to weigh down the sixth rune, thinking we could trick it. We even had Sticky take elephant form and try touching two runes at once—one with his foot, the other with his trunk— but none of it worked. The hexlock gate stayed firmly shut.

"We could go back," Roedyn suggested. "Find Crurri, bring him here."

That was when Sticky spoke, his tone quiet but resolute. "I have an idea."

We turned to him.

"We need to empty your canteens into two of our cooking pots," Sticky said.

I pulled the cooking pots out of my pack.

"Perfect." He nodded. "Fill them with water and place each one on a different rune."

I did exactly that.

Roedyn cautiously asked, "Sticky... what are you planning?"

"I'm going to ask Harper to do something that might go against every instinct she has. Something that may violate her moral code."

Harper narrowed her eyes. "What is it?"

"I want you to cut me in half."

Before anyone could speak, Harper's blade was halfway drawn.

"Whoa, whoa, WHOA!" Roedyn shouted, grabbing her arm. "Sticky, what in the nine hells are you saying?"

I didn't know what was more shocking—Sticky's idea or Harper's disturbingly fast readiness to carry it out.

Sticky held up both hands. "Let me explain. When I traveled into the depths of the Driftwood Gulf, south of the Silverstand Forest, I discovered the starfish. I learned that when a starfish is cut cleanly in two, each half can regenerate into an entirely new starfish. So I'll turn into a starfish, and Harper will cut me in half then there'll be two of me."

I thought about it and it wasn't so different from splitting your soul. Not far off from what Victor Graves was attempting with his Spirit Split spells and soul-bound totems.

Sticky looked at Harper. "You'll need to make one straight cut. If it's clean, both halves should survive and regrow. There will be two of me."

He turned to the rest of us. "You'll place each half into a separate pot of water—but you need to do it fast because starfish don't last long out of water. If we're quick, we'll have six bodies. Enough to open the hexlock gate."

Escala went pale. "But what if it doesn't work? What if one half dies? What if both do?"

"I know the risk," Sticky said.

Harper ran her fingers along the flat of her blade. "I can do it," she said slowly. "Clean and straight." But even she looked nervous.

Escala stepped forward, knelt beside Sticky, kissed the top of his head, and whispered, "Thank you."

Harper, trying to ease the tension, smirked. "It's a good thing Escala's not a princess right now, or you'd be a prince and Roedyn would have competition."

I laughed, but no one else did.

Sticky turned to us all. "Are you ready? I can't be out of water for long once I transform. As soon as the cut is made, you must move fast."

We all nodded.

With a flash of magic and a pop of air, Sticky transformed into a foot-long, yellowish starfish and flopped to the floor.

The sword was already falling.

Harper's timing was perfect, too perfect. Before the starfish had even landed, her blade struck in a flawless arc. But Sticky flipped mid-fall, and instead of slicing top to bottom, the cut went sideways.

There was a wet, tearing sound. Pale ichor sprayed across the stone. The starfish twitched—then sagged, deflating with a soft puff, a blue spark of light, and a faint tremor through both halves.

"Stop!" Escala screamed.

Roedyn's face turned bone white. Harper stared, stunned.

I rushed forward, scooping one half into my arms. "Harper—grab the other, now!"

She snapped out of it and moved. Together, we raced to the pots and dropped the starfish halves into the water but mine didn't stir.

"Get on the runes!" I shouted.

Everyone ran.

And then—nothing.

The hexlock gate remained closed.

Harper's hands trembled, her sword dragging limply at her side.

Escala bolted to Harper's pot, boots skidding on stone as she dropped to her knees and peered in, eyes wide. Then she scrambled to my pot, frantic. Her gaze met mine—pleading. Her face crumpled.

Grief tore through her. "No—no, no, no," she said, shaking as she clutched the pot's rim. "He said it would work—he said he'd come back—he promised—" She sobbed, collapsing forward until her forehead touched the cold stone.

Sticky was dead.

Chapter 58

W
e stood in stunned silence, unable to fully comprehend what had just happened. Sticky was gone—really gone. We couldn't believe it.

We kept peering into the pots, trying to will some sign of movement, hoping for the regeneration he had so confidently promised. But there was nothing—just two lifeless halves of what had once been our companion.

Escala was still sobbing. Roedyn gently placed a hand on her shoulder. When she didn't pull away, he added his other hand, and then, wordlessly, drew her into an embrace. Her head came to rest against his chest in the same posture they had shared while dancing only this time, there was no joy. Her petite frame trembled against him, wracked with sobs, while Roedyn rested his cheek against her golden hair and stroked it softly, as if whispering to her.

As we watched, I heard the faint buzzing of a gnat near my ear and instinctively swatted at it, annoyed and then, somehow, heartbroken. Sticky would've caught that bug in midair without a second thought, maybe even joked about how plump it was. He had told me just a few days ago about how he expected the larvae to be wonderful here.

I kept swatting absently as Roedyn continued to hold Escala, rocking her gently as her sobs slowed. She didn't let go, not this time. She wrapped her arms around his waist like a child clinging to a parent, and for a long moment, they stood there.

Harper had gone quiet, which was unusual. She wiped and sheathed her blade, then began checking each pot, again and again, as if sheer willpower could coax Sticky's halves back to life.

Eventually, I found my voice. "We should say a few words to remember him. And maybe decide if we go back to the surface."

Another gnat buzzed around Harper's head. She swatted at it. Roedyn still held Escala, her tear-streaked face pressed to his chest.

"Yes," she said, barely audible. "We should go back— it's too dangerous down here."

Roedyn looked down and gently asked, "Is that what you want?"

Escala didn't lift her head. "I don't know what I want," she whispered.

Harper finally spoke, her voice caught between guilt and restraint. "I'm sorry—I thought I could make the cut, but I failed." She hung her head. "We should take his remains back to the swamp. That's where he would want to rest."

I nodded. So did Roedyn and Escala. The mission, it seemed, was over.

And then, a high-pitched voice—familiar and impossible—said, "It's not what I want."

I spun around, heart in my throat. Another gnat buzzed past my nose, and I brushed it away.

"Stop trying to hit me!" the voice squeaked.

Escala pulled back from Roedyn, eyes darting as she turned, confused, scanning the air.

"… Sticky?" she asked hopefully.

"Do you know any other gnats who talk?" the gnat snapped, then zipped into a quick loop-de-loop around her head.

Harper's mouth dropped open. For a moment, we all wondered if we were finally losing our minds.

The gnat landed on my staff. "It's me, Sticky," it said matter-of-factly.

"B-but… how?" Harper stammered. "I—I cut you in half, and not the right way."

"I know," Sticky replied with exasperated cheer. "I saw it coming. Just as the blade was about to hit, I polymorphed into a gnat. It's not quite the same as my usual shapeshifting—it's a spell, like what Escala does."

"You're alive!" Escala cried, her voice rising with excitement.

"We can still do this. Come back on the runes," Sticky said. "But please stop trying to swat me."

The gnat buzzed around Harper's face. Harper stood perfectly still—annoyed but saying nothing. It was too soon.

"You nearly did kill me when you slapped the back of your head," Sticky added, before buzzing over to the buckets. He landed on the rim of each one, eyeing the bisected starfish with what I could only describe as pride.

We stood on our runes, watching as a tiny gnat landed on one of the buckets.

"I'm going to drop polymorph and return to this half of the starfish. That should trigger regeneration. Harper, you'll need to cut me again—but slower this time, while I'm lying flat."

Roedyn frowned. "Are you sure, Sticky?"

"Yes. Harper can do it. Just hurry, before this half stops being able to receive me."

Harper took a steadying breath, dagger in hand, and approached the bucket. Sweat gathered on her brow.

"Ready?" Sticky chirped.

She nodded.

There was a flash of blue light and the gnat was gone. Inside the pot, the half-starfish twitched. Harper gently lifted it out and laid it on the stone floor.

I crouched nearby, ready to grab my half.

Harper lined up the blade, then, with a smooth, precise slice, cut the starfish cleanly. "Now!" she shouted.

I scooped up one half; it wiggled in my hand as I gently placed it in my pot. Harper did the same with her half, which was also wiggling this time. We all rushed back to our runes.

Instantly, the runes began to glow, light streaking like spokes toward the hexlock gate. With a grinding rumble, the gate split open, revealing a staircase spiraling into darkness.

Chapter 59

O nce Sticky returned to his frog form, we continued our descent deeper into the dungeon.

This level was crawling with monsters. Ogres, orcs, kobolds, and even a gelatinous cube. I could spend an evening describing the battles in rich, harrowing detail, but instead, I'll summarize:

Wigfrith was incredible; he handled all the monsters single-handedly while Roedyn and Escala made out in a corner, Harper offered snarky comments, and Sticky kept interrupting to ask if Roedyn had "finally said it." That's my tale, good night!

The Stag erupted into laughter, and I turned back to the crowd and said, "What? You don't believe me? Fine, the real version was this:

"Escala took the front line in most fights, shield up, yelling, 'No one touches the faerie!' Harper and Roedyn cut down enemies with bow and blade, and Sticky transformed into creatures tailored to the threat of the moment. I sang songs of encouragement and healed when needed, and yes, maybe hid once or twice.

That is how we spent the day—we cleared rooms, and it was exhausting work, and eventually we rested in a chamber with a single entrance we could secure off a long hallway.

I strummed my lute and told the group, "This song casts an illusion over the doorway—it'll look like solid stone from the outside. It also cloaks us in silence so we can talk and sleep undisturbed. We've got eight hours of peace."

"Why don't you do that every night?" Roedyn asked.

Harper smirked. "Because he wants to play songs, so you'll dance with Escala."

Roedyn turned bright red and wisely dropped the subject.

During the rest time, Escala said, "Why are you all risking your lives for me?"

Harper, again eating an apple, said, "I was bored, plain and simple. When I first met you, you were helpless and don't get mad, Escala, but I honestly thought you were crazy and bound to get yourself killed."

Escala laughed. "I probably would have been killed."

Harper continued, "But that first day at our cabin, you were so serious about boulders which seemed ridiculous, and I got curious. I wanted to see if you really were crazy. Turns out you're not as crazy as I thought."

Escala shook her head and laughed.

"Then it became a challenge to train you, help you succeed. And I've had fun—I live for this kind of thing," Harper finished.

"Fine—I'll admit it," I said. "I'm here selfishly— because I plan to turn this adventure into the most epic tale ever told. I'll charge admission, naturally. But I have to see how it ends, so I'm staying until you say that I am not contributing."

She smiled at me, probably thinking I was just being funny. I wasn't.

"I told you why I'm here back on my lily pad, after you got hit with Roedyn's arrow," Sticky said.

"Really, Sticky?" Roedyn groaned.

Sticky ignored him. "The creatures of the Silverstand are my family. You faced the vinethrasher for them—that was a boulder. I named you a friend of the Silverstand Forest, and you are now part of my family. Now you're facing one that threatens the True Cycle. If you're fighting for it, I'm with you whether we face danger, pain, even death…because your family."

Escala smiled and hugged Sticky and said, "I was so naïve when I met you, Sticky. I didn't understand love could mean so many things. Protecting the wolf that killed Rihanna? That's still hard for me. But you love them—they're your family. I used to think love was just romance and happiness. I still don't know what it is… but it's more."

Harper suddenly got serious—which was rare for her—and said, "Love is the quiet choice to give something of yourself for someone else's good—it's not a transaction. It's making their life better than it was—just because you want to."

She turned to Roedyn. "Right, Roedyn?"

Roedyn turned bright red. He stood and said, "I'd like to speak with Escala alone, please. Could you all give us a moment and maybe move back up the hall for a few minutes?"

Escala looked puzzled, but Harper and I got up immediately. We had to drag Sticky with us.

We headed up the tunnel a bit but you all know us. We're experts at pretending not to eavesdrop.

Roedyn sat beside Escala, staring at her, taking her in.

"What are you staring at?" she asked suspiciously.

"I wasn't staring," he said.

"You were."

"Fine, I was," Roedyn said.

"Why?" Escala asked, tilting her head to the side and flipping her hair over her shoulder.

"I'm trying to memorize what you look like," he said at last.

That caught her off guard. "Why would you do that?"

His eyes met hers, and for a moment her beauty washed over him, leaving him utterly still. He stared, captivated by the depth of her blue eyes. After a long breath, he said softly, "Because I don't want to forget what you look like when you go back to the Court of Dreams."

She was silent for a long moment. Then, quietly, she asked, "You think I'm going back?"

"You're fey," he said. "That's your world—your home. Of course you'll go back... once we finish your quest."

He hesitated and said, "I'm going to miss you, Escala Winter of the Court of Dreams."

Her eyes swept his face, searching. "Did you always feel this way?"

"Not that I was willing to admit."

She looked at him. "But I heard what you said to Harper—that I was a job, you just had to fulfill your oath."

He blinked—then realization struck. She had overheard the conversation he'd had with Harper weeks ago, the one where he'd called this whole journey "just a job." Regret surged through him, and he said quietly, "I didn't mean what I said."

"Then why did you say it?" she challenged.

He sighed. "Because Harper was getting under my skin. She asked if I liked you—really liked you—and I panicked. I said whatever it would take to shut her up."

Escala crossed her arms. "So… do you?"

"Do I what?"

"Do you like me?" There was hope in her voice.

"Of course I do. We all do."

She sighed. He never seemed able to say what he truly felt; he always folded others into his answers—*we all do*, never *I do*. Disappointed, she looked down. "Since when?" she asked, her voice revealing disappointment.

"I don't know. There wasn't one moment—it just built. We've trained, camped, cooked, and nearly died—we have spent a lot of time together," he explained.

She just stared at him, waiting for him to continue.

He flushed. "I'm not good at this. I told myself I wouldn't let this happen."

"Let what happen?"

"Tell you the truth," he said.

She sat straighter. Was he finally going to say it?

"Why not?" she asked, hope again rising in her tone.

"The more time I spend with you, the harder it'll be to say goodbye." Roedyn said. "But Harper's been badgering me for days, so here it is: Either we find your crown and you return to the Court of Dreams, or we die trying. And, well, you see, I, uhm…well I just don't know what you…. You know…what you…feel."

"You really don't know how I feel?" Escala asked, surprised.

He shook his head.

"Roedyn Hammerfell," she said, her voice bossy, "do you want to know how I feel?"

She studied his face. His eyes were warm and steady, thoughtful in a way that always made her feel seen—and yes, he was handsome. And he cared for her well-being and for her quest. He'd done so much for her already: put his own life on hold to train her, traveled beside her all the way to Wigfrith, and helped her find Victor Graves so she could finally understand the boulder she was meant to move. She had never met anyone like him before.

Something fluttered inside her—excitement and dread twisting together until she could barely breathe. For the bricfest moment, she wondered what it might feel like to kiss him. The thought lit a warmth in her chest... and terror just beneath it.

But she couldn't. Not ever.

A kiss would bind him, ruin his chance at an ordinary life in the material world. He would dream of her, ache for her, never fully understand why nothing else ever satisfied him. And she—she was returning to the Court of Dreams without him when this quest was over.

Making a mortal fall in love with you was one of the cruelest ways to break the True Cycle—just shy of taking their life.

And she was already being punished for that. She could never risk it again. He didn't answer her question, and after a long silence, she spoke softly.

"I want to be around you all the time. I've talked to Wigfrith—"

Roedyn mouthed "Wigfrith?"

"—and Crurri—"

"Crurri?" he said, surprised.

"—and Harper."

"Harper!" He threw his hands up in mock frustration.

She smiled. "I feel safe with you—being near you makes me feel happy. It's the same feeling I had with Rihanna," she added.

Roedyn's smile faded. So that was it—Escala saw him like she saw Rihanna. He was just a friend.

The words landed harder than he expected, and his cheeks flushed. What a fool he'd been. Why had he listened to Harper? Why had he told Escala how he felt when he knew she didn't feel the same way? He was crushed and embarrassed. Roedyn shoved his feelings down and retreated into the only place that ever felt safe—being the commander. Giving orders was easier than being vulnerable. He had been such a fool to think that this beautiful fey princess could ever fall for him, a simple scout.

"We must finish this," he said. His voice was different, more distant. "You need to prove you're worthy to return to the Court of Dreams. I want that for you—I promised I'd see it through."

"I don't know what happens next," she said. She could tell the moment had passed.

"Neither do I," he said, distance growing in his voice.

From around the corner, Sticky whispered, "Okay, now he definitely said it."

Harper gently smacked him upside his large green head. "No! Neither one of them will really say what they feel."

Sticky shrugged, and I just shook my head. We were probably going to die in a few hours, and these two still couldn't admit they were falling for each other. Whatever happened to romance?

Chapter 60

W e regrouped with Roedyn and Escala. Roedyn seemed flushed, and Escala… I don't know—disappointed? We ate some terrible rations, I'll have you know, and Roedyn declared it was time to move on.

We'd been underground for over twelve hours—at least, according to my stomach—but we pressed forward.

We descended two more long staircases and came to a fork. Sticky sniffed the air and pointed left. "If my calculations are right, the cavern I scouted earlier should be this way."

We took the left passage, which sloped down through a widening corridor nearly twenty feet across. By now, we had to be half a mile underground. At the bottom stood a pair of heavy oak doors, banded in iron with thick pull rings.

Roedyn turned to me. "Don't open it."

I quickly nodded in agreement—after my narrow escape with the last door, I wasn't about to open another door. For the first time, I felt genuine envy for women whose men still practiced chivalry and opened doors for them.

Harper stepped up, scanning for traps. After a few careful minutes, she nodded—it was clear. Roedyn pressed his ear to the wood, listened, then shook his head.

"I'm opening it slowly. Be ready."

He eased it open, and since no pit, poison needle, pot of boiling oil, or guillotine blade was triggered, we stepped through into a vast cavern. Our torchlight sputtered uselessly against the dark, swallowed by the sheer size of the chamber. The walls lay beyond sight, the ceiling lost overhead. A jagged break in the stone ceiling revealed a sliver of moonlight and stars, just enough to hint at the immensity around us.

"This is the cave I saw," Sticky whispered.

We quietly slipped inside the cave and shut the door, hugging the wall and waiting in breathless silence.

Then we heard it—a sharp snort, followed by a slow, deliberate puff of breath echoing deep in the cavern fog.

It was the unmistakable sound of a dragon.

Chapter 61

———————————

We crept into the cavern. "Vast" didn't begin to cover it. At first, our torchlight barely pierced the dark, but as we moved deeper, pools of magma glowed like molten eyes, casting shadows across ancient stone. The chamber stretched five hundred feet wide and nearly as high.

Far above, moonlight poured through a jagged break in the ceiling—cut by time or claw—casting a pale beam like a divine spotlight. And what it revealed stole our breath. Weapons, enchanted armor, rings, helms, and relics lay strewn across a sea of gold, silver, and gemstones, piled into dunes.

Atop it all, at the heart of the hoard, lay an ancient female red dragon—so massive, she made the cavern feel suddenly small.

We didn't know her name yet, but we later learned it was Myrrh. She was magnificent. Her scales were deep, ancient red like old blood soaked into obsidian. Near her spine, her scales faintly reflected veins of black and ash. Along her flank, I counted a dozen scars, some pale and jagged, others so deep they twisted her plating into cruel ridges. One scar looked as though a siege engine had left it.

Her wings were folded tight, but even at rest they loomed like leathery sails the size of village rooftops, spined with barbed hooks that looked more like weapons than bone. Her tail, thick as an oak tree and easily forty feet long, curled around her. If you had asked Escala how long, she would have told you the tail was forty-two watermelons, two cantaloupes, and a lemon long.

The dragon's chest rose and fell with slow, seismic rhythm. Steam curled from her nostrils, winding through the air like incense smoke, sweet and sulfurous. Even asleep, her presence saturated the cave. It smelled of scorched stone, molten copper, and charred bone.

Her claws caught the moonlight like polished steel, each one nearly a foot long, thick at the base, and tapering to needle-fine points. They looked freshly sharpened, curved slightly like a predator's hook, and capable of rending armor as easily as silk. Her forearms, larger than a man's thigh, gleamed with black scales in the magma glow.

And her head... her horns arched back in twin ridges, fluted like obsidian blades, scarred in places, chipped at the tips, one slightly cracked. Her snout was long and lined with rows of ivory teeth beneath scaled lips. Even in sleep, she looked like she was smiling.

I'm telling you all this in such excruciating detail because no bard alive has ever stood this close to an ancient red dragon, really any dragon, if truth be told, and lived to sing about it. So yes, I may be long-winded, but you need to understand that as beautiful as Escala was, Myrrh was the most beautiful and breathtaking creature I've ever seen.

Now let me tell you what happened next, because this part? This part is where the story... well, listen.

As we crept through the cavern, moonlight spilled from the shaft above, glinting off the hoard. Weapons, wands, armor, and relics lay scattered across dunes of gold and gems.

367

Despite that, I was only looking for one particular item—the Crown of Dreams.

Victor had told us it was a slim golden diadem set with diamonds and sapphires, etched with shifting sigils that pulsed faintly beneath the surface. At its center hovered a dark, rune-veined gem, suspended just above the gold.

So, I did what I always do when the moment calls for something more than mortal eyes, I played my song of finding, a composition crafted to reveal lost things. A quiet, enchanted melody that stirred no air and made no sound, save for a faint vibration in my bones. Only I could hear it. Only I could see its magic. If the object were near, it would shine so that only I could see. I focused on Victor's description and began to play.

A shiver threaded through my spine, and I felt the cave thrum; a deep, silent chord that plucked my nerves and made my teeth ache.

My eyes opened, but Harper was already tapping Roedyn's shoulder and pointing. Roedyn gave one slow nod.

That… wasn't right. Only I should've sensed it. And yet they were looking right at it.

Confused, I rose onto a nearby pile of coins to see what they saw, and what my magic had found. The gold clinked underfoot, but Myrrh didn't stir. Her vast body loomed before me, a fortress of flesh and scarred scale, wings folded tight. And at the center of it all, on the end of her tail—the way you or I might wear a ring—radiant and unmistakable: the Crown of Dreams.

My heart sank. I'd foolishly hoped the crown might be loose, tucked between a war banner and a rusted elven glaive, so we could slip in, grab it, and be gone before the dragon stirred.

But no, she was wearing it. To get that crown, we'd have to pry it off the tail of an infernal dragon. And that meant one thing: we'd have to kill her.

Chapter 62

I shifted my lute's melody to an enchantment that cloaked our footfalls in silence. No crunch of gem, no clink of gold, not even the whisper of dust disturbed the air. But while it silenced what we stepped on, it wouldn't silence what we knocked over, so I cautioned the group to move carefully.

Harper glided forward, scanning the hills of gold for a clear path to the dragon. She stepped, crouched, and reached into a pile of treasure—emerging with a golden chamber pot in hand.

Harper turned it slowly, a grin spreading across her face. Then, beaming, she tucked it into her pack like a priceless artifact.

And that's when it happened.

Two coins, perched on the rim, slid loose and tumbled down the mound.

Clink.

Clink-clink.

A swarm of fire bats burst from the shadows, diving in a searing spiral that sent us ducking. They didn't strike—just swept past, their cries echoing through the cavern. We froze, hoping they hadn't woken the dragon... or planned a return. But they did—this time with claws and teeth. We scattered. One clipped me, sank its fangs into my shoulder—and let me tell you, the burn was real.

But Myrrh just lay curled atop her hoard, asleep. Or maybe just pretending.

After the bats' second wave, they vanished into the shadows above and didn't return.

Roedyn gestured: *Fan out.* Sticky darted off, staying low, padding between stalagmites, gold piles, and rubble. Escala and Harper split in opposite directions, vanishing behind massive pillars. Roedyn crouched behind a pillar, arrow nocked, watching the tail and crown. And me? I hid behind a pillar and nervously waited.

Above, the bats wheeled and danced, casting flickers of light through the smoky air—but they didn't dive again.

Then the dragon's tail twitched—just slightly.

Chapter 63

In the palace of the Court of Dreams, Junel found Rowan seated beneath the weeping moonbark tree, its pale silver leaves falling gently around him.

"How did you get the court to issue a banishment instead of the Wane?" she asked. "I thought that wasn't possible."

"Before the trial, I spoke to each judge," he said. "Not to plead her innocence, but to remind them how the Oath began. I showed them lesser-known punishments under fey law."

Junel nodded. "So fey law provided for banishment?"

"Yes," Rowan said, his voice low but unsteady. "The judges agreed—reluctantly, with suspicion in their eyes. They saw the danger, and so did I."

He thought for a moment and continued, "I risked everything to argue for an alternative to the Wane, to buy her even a chance at life on the material plane. If Morvena discovers what I've done, she'll seize it as proof of favoritism, demand my removal, perhaps even exile. I know the risk, but what choice did I have? To stand silent while my own child was condemned? No crown, no court, no law could bind me to watch her fade. She is my daughter—my blood—and I would burn every law of the court before I let her go without a fight."

His shoulders were strung tight with tension.

Junel nodded and asked, "Are the boulders real? Will she be able to find and remove them?"

Rowan shook his head. "No, not really."

Junel sighed.

"You must understand, Junel. In persuading the judges to forgo the Wane, I had to accept a sentence just as harsh and final. But I could not tell her the True Cycle cannot be mended, boulders aren't real—they are a word used in the ancient laws to describe how mortals view troubles and challenges in their lives."

"So her exile has no end?" Junel asked.

Rowan nodded and said, "Boulders will never cease to exist in the material plane, so yes, her exile is without end. But I could not have told her that—it would've destroyed her."

He breathed out slowly.

"I negotiated the wording of the quest, so it gave her purpose. She'll never remove enough boulders—no one could because there really isn't a boulder—the True Cycle is full of boulders and always will be," he said quietly. "But you know her, she'll try anyway. To find them, she'll have to walk among mortals, learn their lives and their troubles. And she will help them because helping them means becoming part of their lives. She'll find friends... maybe even a new life. The quest was never about success. It's about motion. You know she can't sit still."

Junel nodded. She knew Escala.

Rowan continued, "If we'd told her the truth that she was banished permanently I don't think she'd have made it. She needs a goal. Something to chase."

"But you gave her false hope," Junel said cautiously.

"She's my daughter, and she may not believe it, but I love her deeply—and I couldn't let her face the Wane. So yes, I gave her false hope... but I also gave her a quest. One that tethers her to the mortal world, drawing her into their lives—their joy, their pain, their failures. And maybe, in time, their love."

Junel flew over to him. "So Valla will be her new home?"

Rowan rubbed his chin as his wings slowly fanned the air. "Maybe, after enough seasons have passed, she'll stop searching for a way back to the court and realize she's already found a new home. Because if I'm honest with you, I fear that's the only home she'll ever have."

Chapter 64

Friends," I say, raising a finger. "Why did I tell you about Rowan's and Junel's talk about Escala's hopeless quest? It's not for the reason you might think. You're probably thinking, 'Wigfrith, I get it—Escala's not going back to the Court of Dreams. She'll stay in Dunwell, run into Roedyn's arms, and they'll live happily ever after, right?'"

I waggle that same finger. "Wrong again, dear friends, this tale is anything but predictable. Think back, two hours ago, I promised a strange story about a mischievous pixie from the Court of Dreams. Have I not delivered such a story so far?"

The crowd roars, clapping and stomping.

"Stay with me a little longer, folks, there is still a lot left to the story, and the risk Rowan took trying to save Escala from the Wane will all make sense soon enough. And yes, I paused here in the middle of the dragon encounter, mostly because it still haunts my dreams, and frankly, I needed a breather."

I gesture grandly. "So now stretch your legs, light your pipe, grab a drink, or visit a man about a dog. When I return in just a few minutes, the pace will quicken, the danger will rise, and you'll know you picked the right tavern tonight. Sound good?"

Murmurs of agreement ripple through the room as I see more than a few stand, stretch, grab a pipe, or head to the privy. Serving girls weave through the crowd, refilling mugs, swapping platters, and adding firewood.

"Excellent. Back soon." I hop from the stage.

Less than ten minutes later, I crack my knuckles, return to center stage, sling my lute into place, give it a fierce strum, and launch into a battle tune, fast and fierce.

Chapter 65

I'm sure you've heard the old sailor tales—ships dragged under by monstrous octopuses, their tentacles as long as horses, teeth sharp enough to split a hull. Well, every word is true. How do I know? Because I saw one myself in the dragon cave. It happened just after the fire bats scattered us through the cavern. I turned to see Sticky—yes, Sticky—shifting into one of those sea monsters that live in the Driftwood Gulf, where he learned of the starfish!

His flesh pulsed in deep maroon and oily midnight, slick and dappled with shifting patterns. Eight massive tentacles sprawled outward, thick as tree trunks, coiling and uncoiling with eerie silence. Each one was lined with a double row of suckers—huge, pale, rimmed with tiny barbs—that flexed and clicked, tasting the air.

At the center of that horror was a bulbous, rubbery head, and set into it were two enormous eyes, gleaming, intelligent, and red with something between rage and resolve. I suppose the mouth was underneath; I didn't see it until the thing—Sticky, I mean—lifted and skittered—yes, skittered—across the treasure-strewn floor.

There was very little sound when he moved, just the faint slip of wet tentacles over gold. Sticky flowed rather than walked, his boneless form adapting instantly to every rise and dip in the treasure mounds.

Now you might be thinking, "How does an octopus survive out of water?" Good question, I didn't know either. Sticky explained later, quite matter-of-factly, that an octopus can survive outside the sea for nearly thirty minutes. Long enough to do something mad, which he was about to attempt.

He was going for the crown perched on the tip of the dragon's tail. But as Sticky crept closer, the dragon shifted in her sleep, and the tail swept across her body with sudden, terrifying force, nearly catching him mid-step. The octopus sprang, coiling midair, and latched onto a stalagmite with all eight tentacles, holding fast in the shadows.

Sticky waited, motionless, as the dragon settled. Then, slowly, he slithered down the rock and began his second approach, now from the other side, where the tail had come to rest. The great beast's bulk blocked Escala's view, so she crouched behind an open chest spilling sapphires and gold. Harper crept along the far side of the cavern, hugging the wall, blades drawn.

Roedyn and I had a clear view of the crown, still balanced like a halo on the wyrm's tail. And we could see what Sticky meant to do. I raised my lute and began to play a lullaby—a children's tune to cradle the dragon deeper into sleep, in case a single clink of coin betrayed us.

Sticky arrived at the tail. With four tentacles anchoring him to the floor and two wrapped around either side of the dragon's tail, he reached up with the last pair—carefully, steadily—probing the crown. It was breathtakingly brave. Even Roedyn, arrow nocked, glanced at me with wide eyes. Escala had her shield raised, and we watched in awe.

Sticky twisted, and at first, the crown didn't budge. Then, with eerie precision only a cephalopod could possess, he shifted his weight, and that's when it happened.

He made contact, sitting, or what passed for an octopus sitting, directly atop the dragon's tail. In an instant, the dragon exploded into motion, her tail snapping like a thundercrack, flicking out with lethal force.

Sticky didn't stand a chance. The gigantic octopus was launched through the air like a wet rag, tentacles flailing, flying toward the far wall with horrifying speed. He struck the stone with a sickening, wet smack and slid down in a boneless heap, leaving a smear in his wake.

My eyes snapped back to the dragon now towering to her full height, tail whipping in wide, furious arcs. The crown still gleamed tight around her tail, catching the molten light with every lash. My gaze darted to Sticky. He lay crumpled and unmoving on the stone, his daring bid for the crown ended in failure. Sprawled on the cold rock, he had reverted to his frog form, small and fragile against the cavern's vast fury.

The dragon let out a deafening roar, and I could feel fear rising in my chest, we were in serious trouble.

Chapter 66

As Sticky lay still on the coins. Roedyn rose and fired—his arrow struck the dragon's chest, only to glance off her gleaming scales. The wyrm's eyes flared open.

Escala emerged from behind a chest of jewels and charged. This was the same girl who had once run from a lone orc, now sprinting at one of the most feared creatures in Valla; if I had not witnessed this, I would not have believed it.

Harper was already scrambling up the dragon's massive back, trying to get to her head.

But Myrrh shrugged, and Harper slid down her back, clipped a dorsal fin, tumbled along the tail, and crashed into a bed of gold.

The dragon's foot slammed down. Harper rolled clear as talons split stone, sending treasure scattering.

Escala charged straight for the giant wyrm, shield up, catching her gaze as she swung. Her sword struck the dragon's snout with a ringing blow that echoed through the cavern like a struck bell.

Roedyn fired again and again; most arrows glanced harmlessly off the dragon's scales, but a few found their mark slipping into soft gaps, drawing smoke and a furious roar.

I darted between stalagmites to Sticky's crumpled form. Clutching my lute, I strummed a healing chord, glowing notes swept over him. As his chest began to rise and the magic took hold, I won't lie, I was just grateful I'd saved him.

But there was no time to celebrate. The fire bats returned; black streaks ripping through the air. Escala raised her shield, swinging wildly, swatting some away, but others sank into her neck and shoulders, trailing smoke and blood, and she cried out in pain.

Roedyn dropped his bow and dove, shielding his face as several fire bats tore into his arms and cheek.

My song still played. Sticky rose, blinking at the chaos.

The dragon turned to Escala, lashing out with her talons. She raised her shield as the dragon's talon slammed against it. Her arms shook as she tried to absorb the blow. The dragon swung a second talon, and this one punched through Escala's shield, stopping inches from her face. The dragon yanked back, trying to rip it free from her grasp, but Escala held tight until the wyrm finally tore it away.

Still bleeding, Roedyn snatched his bow and fired beside the dragon's nose. The dragon roared and turned on him. Escala tumbled back, shieldless, as the dragon lunged, jaws wide, impossibly fast.

Harper was already climbing again. She scrambled up the dragon's back, gripping a dorsal ridge, swinging as the beast stormed forward.

I leapt behind a gold-buried throne and switched songs mid-verse—this one to boost speed and reflexes. The tempo surged.

Roedyn tried to rise but stumbled. The dragon's jaws snapped inches from his head. He lunged sideways, tumbling toward Sticky and me.

Escala scrambled toward her shield, flung far when the dragon tore it away.

Then came Myrrh's roar, it was deafening. Then the dragon's voice rang out in the common tongue: "You will all die!"

Escala shouted back, "I am Escala Winter of the Court of Dreams! I only seek the crown from your tail, and we'll leave you in peace!"

"Peace?" The dragon snarled. "Your kind broke the truce!"

The dragon whipped her tail at Escala in fury. Escala jumped aside just in time as the tail smashed into the pillar shielding me, sending a cascade of stone shards flying. A massive crack split the column, crawling upward like lightning. The whole thing groaned, then gave way. The pillar collapsed, toppling down on me.

Then a massive shape appeared beside me—it was an elephant. It was Sticky!

He wrapped his trunk around the falling pillar, stopping it inches from crushing me. His legs trembled under the weight. The stone slipped.

I'd just started crawling clear when the dragon's tail swept back at terrifying speed. I had no chance to dodge. It slammed into my ribs and hurled me at full force into the base of the collapsing pillar Sticky was still holding up. Pain exploded through my midsection.

Sticky faltered, one massive knee buckling as the full weight of the collapsing pillar bore down on his elephant trunk.

Roedyn crawled over, seized my tunic, and dragged me out of the way. "Let it go!" he shouted at Sticky, urgency crackling in his voice.

The elephant dropped the pillar, and it landed with a deafening crack. Sticky collapsed, flanks heaving. I was alive, barely. Sticky had saved me.

The dragon surged upward, wings unfurling in a blast of wind as Harper clung to her back. Gritting her teeth, Harper climbed the dragon's ridged spine, each movement a battle against the dragon's thrashing strength. With a fierce yell, Harper lunged toward the dragon's head and drove her dagger at the left eye. But the dragon's eyelid snapped shut, armored scales sliding over like a trapdoor of steel. The blade struck and skittered harmlessly aside.

Instantly, the fire bats descended, swarming Harper in a frenzy of wings, claws, and teeth. Blood streaked her face as she clung to the dragon with both hands, unable to fight them off. With a cry of pain and frustration, she let go, plummeting forty feet. She twisted in midair and slammed into the gold below, landing hard on her back with a sharp clink. Stunned, yes, but alive.

The dragon spread her wings and roared, and a wave of terror slammed into all of us. It was dragon fear, and it struck like a wave of ice through my chest, stripping away every shred of courage. My limbs locked up, useless, even as my mind screamed to run. If you were lucky, you could drop what you held and flee. If not, you just stood there, shaking… waiting to die.

Around me, the others were overcome with dragon fear as well—Sticky and Roedyn were wide-eyed, trembling. Escala stood frozen, rooted by pure panic.

As the waves of terror crashed through me, it took everything I had not to turn and run. But I'd heard the bard tales—hells, I was the one who told them. Running meant death. That was the dragon's trick: scatter the prey with fear, then chase down the runners like a cat toying with mice or incinerate the frozen ones with dragonfire where they stood. If I didn't do something, we were going to die.

If I could strum three chords on my lute—a calming melody—I might break the effects of the dragon fear.

My hands shook. My legs begged to run. Every instinct screamed: *Flee*.

I bit my lip, drawing blood, and forced down the crippling fear, just three chords, I kept telling myself.

I locked my fingers around the lute and strummed. The notes rose, shaky but clear, twining with the dragon's roar, pushing back the magic. The fear cracked, then shattered. Though the dragon still roared above us, her massive form hovering thirty feet in the air, wings spread wide and jaws agape, a terrifying sight on its own—the magical grip of dragon fear had broken; we could move.

But it didn't save us from what came next.

The dragon, still hovering, gave a single ferocious beat of her wings, unleashing a thunderous gale.

A hurricane of gold exploded, turning thousands of coins, debris, weapons, and gems into a roaring storm of shrapnel.

Escala crouched low, shield raised against the torrent. It protected her head and chest, but gold, weapons, and debris pelted her exposed legs and midsection, bruising and battering her until she cried out in agony.

Roedyn vaulted over me, his body shielding mine. I could hear him grunt as he absorbed the blows, his leather armor tearing under the relentless barrage.

Sticky roared as the storm of treasure slammed into him. Harper curled into a tight ball, screaming as shards and shrapnel pummeled her from every side.

Hovering above, the dragon laughed with a deep rumble. "This is only the beginning of your punishment," she roared. Then she inhaled, and the air began heat. The temperature spiked, sweat beading on my skin.

Dragonfire was coming, and I knew this was the end.

Chapter 67

H arper groaned in pain and slowly uncurled, bloodied and dazed, just as the air seemed to drain from the chamber. A crushing pressure settled over us—the hush before death. Above, the fire bats shrieked and scattered as the dragon inhaled. The dragon's chest expanded, glowing like a living forge. She pulled her wings back, ready to snap them forward, adding force to the firestorm building in her throat.

Escala was on her knees, shield raised, eyes locked on the ancient terror about to incinerate us. I lay sprawled on my back, vision swimming, fingers inches from my fallen lute. Every breath burned. Sticky, back in frog form, crouched nearby, chest heaving, his bruised body glistening with sweat. Coins had battered him like hail.

We'd accomplished nothing; just a couple of Roedyn's arrows were wedged in her scales like decoration, not wounds.

Her eyes blazed with fury, her gaze itself a death sentence. Deep in her throat, dragonfire swelled—castle-melting, wall-shattering fire. I could hear it building, a low, grinding roar like stone splitting under a mountain's weight. Heat rippled through the air, turning every breath into a lung-scorching sear. In the molten glow of her jaws, I saw our deaths reflected.

I seized my lute and clutched it to my chest. Bloodied fingers struck the strings, hard and fast, forcing sound into radiant arcs that flared outward. Notes cracked like thunderbolts as a glowing dome unfolded, wrapping Roedyn and me in trembling light.

Then horror struck me—Sticky was outside the dome.

He knew it too. Bless him, he did not hesitate. With a desperate croak and a burst of strength, he hopped himself forward. The dragonfire came then—a tidal wave of flame that roared like a hurricane, searing stone into glass and turning the cavern into a furnace. Sticky took one more giant hop and made it inside a breath before it hit.

The fire slammed into the shield with a sound like worlds colliding—an endless, screeching howl as flame and magic wrestled. The dome shuddered violently, and cracks of sound rang through it, high and sharp. The air inside trembled, hot wind buffeting us as sparks and embers rained down and the barrier strained to hold. But it held.

By sacrifice and by miracle, Sticky lived, sprawled, gasping, while the shield glowed red-hot around us, defiant against annihilation.

And gods forgive me, my shield magic could not reach Escala or Harper. They were too far away.

The dragon drew a second breath, deeper, hungrier. A torrent of flame, deep red, ravenous, erupted from her maw, roaring toward them like divine wrath. Harper lay limp, eyes wide and unfocused, staring up at the advancing inferno.

Time seemed to fracture.

Escala's head turned, her face lit by the first glow of fire spilling across the cavern walls. Her eyes widened, and she sprang to her feet, legs pumping, every muscle straining as the roar swelled around her. The ground shook beneath each step, the heat peeling at her skin, yet she did not falter. Her shield came up as she ran.

To me, it seemed she ran forever, hair whipping, chain mail flashing, her shadow stretching across the stone. But in truth, it was only heartbeats. She dove, twisting in midair, and crashed down across Harper, yanking the shield over them in an attempt to cover them both.

But it wasn't enough.

The shield barely sheltered their heads and torsos. Harper's right arm and both her legs lay exposed, and so did Escala's, unguarded even beneath the mithril chain mail.

Flame, white-hot and roaring, swallowed them whole.

The sound—the screams—were the most harrowing thing I've ever heard. Two voices, raw, human, and breaking in agony, rose above the roar of fire.

And then silence.

I was sure I'd just watched them die.

Chapter 68

Roedyn went pale as death. He knelt beside me, chest heaving, and tried to see through the thick curtain of smoke left hanging in the air from the dragon's breath. The chamber reeked of scorched metal and charred flesh.

Somewhere above, we still heard the rhythmic whump of the dragon's wings cutting through the dark.

"Escala!" he cried, voice cracking. "Harper!"

No answer. Only silence and the soft, hissing crackle of molten coins cooling on stone.

Sticky staggered to his feet, battered and limping, his hops uneven and pained as he made his way toward the spot where they'd last been. But the gold was no longer just gold, it was fire. Each step sizzled beneath his webbed feet, burning raw grunts from his throat.

The smoke began to thin.

And then we heard it.

THUNK.

The dragon had landed again. Likely back atop her hoard. Then came the sound—creaaaashhh—of treasure shifting, groaning beneath ancient weight. The slow, deliberate scrape of claws dragging through mountains of wealth as the red death made her way toward us.

Roedyn leaned down, voice low but urgent.

"Give me the Box of Kestrel."

"What?" I said.

"We're going to die. It's our only chance!"

I fumbled through my pouch until I found the small, enchanted box, the prop we'd spoken of yesterday. I placed it into his outstretched palm.

Another gust—BOOM—as the dragon's wings crashed down. Coins and gems lifted like a tidal gale, slamming into us with brutal force.

My magic shield was long gone. I tried to raise my arms, but it was too late, the volley hit like a war hammer. A barrage of coins and jagged gems tore into my face—my nose was broken, lip split, one eye swelling shut.

Roedyn took the brunt of it in the chest, the impact hurling him backward into a stone pillar. He gasped, clutching his side, and the fake Box of Kestrel slipped from his grasp, clattering beneath a pile of debris.

Sticky had just reached Escala and Harper when the gale of treasure hit. A tidal wave of coins slammed into him, and a massive chest spun through the air, smashing into the side of his head with a sickening crack. He flew backward, crashed onto his stomach, and tried to rise but, only made it to all fours. Blood misted the air as he let out a weak, rattling ribbit.

Escala lay draped over Harper, her scorched shield still clutched over their heads and torsos. It had saved them, mostly. Harper's right arm and both their legs were severely burned, the skin blackened and blistered. Harper didn't move. Escala groaned, her face smeared with ash and blood, hers and Harper's. The armor on Escala's legs was charred and warped; the burns beneath had to be excruciating.

The dragon was still advancing. We had nothing left.

The dragon loomed above them, claws scattering treasure with each step. Then, without a word, she stared down at the battered shield and flicked it away with a single, contemptuous swipe.

Escala groaned in pain and rolled off Harper, who let out a pained moan. Harper's arm hung limp, a burned ruin. Her legs twisted beneath her, face and neck torn by fire bat bites.

Escala's mouth bled freely. Her once-golden hair was soaked and matted with Harper's blood. Blackened mithril chain clung to scorched skin. She tried to crawl—to reach her sword—looking terrified.

The dragon lowered her head. Smoke poured from her nostrils, curling around them like a serpent. Escala rolled weakly, trying to escape—then SLAM—the dragon's claw pinned her arm to the stone. Escala screamed in terror.

The dragon tilted her massive head, eyes narrowing.

"Court of Dreams?" she hissed. "Liar. You're just an elf. A mortal liar —like all your kind." The dragon's jaws opened wide, fangs glistening, neck pulled back, preparing to rip Escala in two.

Chapter 69

H arper staggered upright, pain etched into her bloodied face, her burned legs trembling. The dragon loomed over Escala, jaws descending toward her terrified face. With a defiant cry, Harper hurled the golden chamber pot at the beast's head. It struck with a solid clank, bouncing off the dragon's temple.

The dragon froze, jaws inches from Escala, and turned toward Harper, murder in her eyes.

Roedyn was already tearing through molten coins in search of the Box of Kestrel. I dragged myself to my knees, grabbed my lute, and strummed the opening chords of an illusion spell.

Four more Harpers instantly appeared, rapiers drawn. The dragon's eyes narrowed as the clones circled and retreated in unison. The dragon withdrew her claw from Escala, who was panicking, now focused on the ring of challengers.

Sticky, barely upright, blinked through blood. The fire bats had returned, swarming him, biting, clawing, piercing with needle-like beaks. He flailed, croaking, trying to communicate, but it wasn't working.

Escala groaned, rolled away, and rose shakily. Her shield was scorched, her sword slick with soot. She reclaimed both, eyes locked on the beast. The dragon, distracted, didn't see her coming.

The dragon's tail lashed—a blur. One clone popped, and Harper lunged, her blade skimming harmlessly off the dragon's underbelly.

The dragon snorted, spun, and her tail slammed into Escala before she could raise her shield. She flew across the chamber and crashed into a wall. Her sword dropped from limp fingers as she crumpled to her knees, gasping.

Then the dragon turned to me.

I dove behind a pile of tapestry rolls, still strumming. Harper and her illusions darted, stabbing and dodging, but it was like bees stinging a giant.

With a growl, the dragon swept the carpets aside.

I rolled clear—barely—but my lute went flying. The instant it hit the ground, the illusions vanished. Harper stood alone at the dragon's feet. She tried to leap back, but she wasn't fast enough—the dragon lunged and seized her in its claws.

Everything was unraveling.

Escala lay crumpled, bloodied, and burned. Harper dangled limply in the dragon's grip, barely conscious and badly burned. Sticky was buried beneath a storm of shrieking bats, dragged to his knees, his skin shredded and raw.

I was dazed—one eye swollen shut, mouth thick with blood, too weak to crawl, let alone reach my lute.

It was over. We had failed.

And then Roedyn rose.

Bleeding, one arm wrapped tight around cracked ribs, he stood tall. In his other hand, he held high the fake Box of Kestrel.

His voice rang out clear, steady, unshaken:

"I am Roedyn Hammerfell Dor'lean, Ghost Warden of the Third Box of Kestrel. Stand down, great one or I will open the box!"

Chapter 70

I grab my mug and say, "What Roedyn just did was, how do I put this delicately, reckless beyond belief. He just stood before an ancient red dragon—Harper in her claws, the rest of us half-dead and tried to bluff with a stage prop."

I shake my head. "Roedyn Hammerfell Dor'Lean," I say, hoping someone will recognize the surname.

"Yes, that Dor'Lean. As in our King Orren Dor'Lean of Eronvale. As in poor former King Theren Dor'Lean, butchered when Korveth named himself emperor. Which means our moody scout—the one Escala is clearly developing feelings for—is actual royalty.

"But was that it?" I ask.

"Oh no, Roedyn threw in one more twist, he claimed to be a Ghost Warden!"

I shake my head. "Most of you probably don't know what that is,, but lucky for you, I'm a bard, and I know things."

I gesture with my mug as if saluting myself.

"Ghost Wardens are the most secretive sect of the Gray Cloaks, an elite order sworn to protect the Boxes of Kestrel. Warriors, spies, mystics, wizards, scouts, and assassins."

"But Ghost Wardens?" I ask. "They erase their past. No name, no record, total disavowal. Even the Gray Cloaks deny they exist."

I pause, swirling my drink.

"So, when Roedyn says he's a Ghost Warden, he's basically telling the dragon, 'I am protecting the very magical artifacts that keep your existence safe.'

"There you have it, folks, we're seconds from death, and our lives rest in the hands of a brooding ranger who can't tell a pretty elf he's in love with her. And now, clutching a stage prop, he's about to spin the greatest lie of his life, about himself and that fake box, straight to the most furious, most dangerous creature in all of Valla.

"What could possibly go wrong?"

Chapter 71

The dragon stared at Roedyn, studying him. Her eyes flicked to the box he held aloft, her tail twitching. I could still see the crown looped around her tail.

Sticky's cries changed—high-pitched squeals softened into low, rhythmic pulses. The fire bats still swarmed him, but they'd stopped attacking—now they circled above in lazy, hypnotic arcs as he moved his arms in sweeping gestures.

Escala was battered and bloodied, but she struggled to her feet. Her sword and shield lay forgotten. She took a slow step toward Roedyn, confusion and pain writ across her face.

His eyes were locked with the dragon.

"You're lying," the dragon hissed, stepping closer.

"I do not lie," Roedyn replied calmly. "Per the dragon truce, I ask you to name yourself, great one."

The dragon narrowed her eyes.

Suddenly, the box flared, glowing a soft blue. The dragon had cast Detect Magic—that was why it glowed. While the box was fake, the illusion runes still lit up because they were magical. If it had no magic, it would have glowed white.

"It's fake," the dragon growled.

My heart sank. We were going to die. She had seen through Roedyn's bluff.

But Roedyn didn't flinch. He turned the box over and pointed to a cluster of faint markings.

"Here, runes of shadow," he said. "Carved in accordance with the Book of Shadows."

His voice was steady, confident. How did he know those details? But one thing was clear: he wasn't bluffing about dragon protocol under the truce.

The truce required mortals to show respect by asking dragons to name themselves, then offering deference. Roedyn was walking a razor's edge, parlaying for our lives with courtly ritual.

Escala took another step toward him, limping in pain as she moved, eyes shifting between Roedyn and the dragon.

Harper stopped struggling as the dragon held her tight in her claws. She just stared, trying to catch his eye. But Roedyn's focus was unbroken. The dragon stepped closer too. She was less than ten feet away; close enough to bite, crush, or burn him with ease.

Roedyn lifted his other hand from his ribs, grimacing as he did and flipped open the clasp on the box.

"Great one," he said with more authority, "name yourself."

The dragon lowered her head to his level. Smoke billowed from her nostrils, wrapping Roedyn in a choking shroud. I thought for sure she'd strike. But instead, she let out a low grunt. "Myrrh," she said in a deep gravelly voice, lifting her head high as her wings unfurled in a slow, regal display.

Without hesitation, Roedyn dropped to one knee, box still raised. "I, Roedyn Hammerfell Dor'Lean, do honor you, Myrrh," he said, bowing his head, "and acknowledge the Dragon Truce made at the Purge."

Myrrh exhaled a plume of smoke through her nostrils and grunted. "Why are you here?"

Harper coughed. "Um, great, Myrrh, could you maybe put me down?"

Myrrh ignored the request and continued to hold Harper high above the piles of treasure.

Roedyn stood. "We do not seek to harm you—"

"You can't harm me," Myrrh interjected.

Roedyn nodded in agreement.

"We do not seek to harm you," he repeated. Perhaps this was formality under the Dragon Truce.

Roedyn added, "I seek to help this fey"—he gestured toward Escala—"return to the Court of Dreams. To do so, we need an item in your hoard."

"What item?" Myrrh asked.

Escala stepped forward. "The Crown of Dreams that is on your tail."

Myrrh turned away, clearly bored with the exchange. Without a glance back, she said, "No. You've honored me by the Truce. Now leave."

She continued to lumber deeper into the chamber, Harper still clutched in her claws.

Harper shot us a panicked look. Roedyn stepped forward.

"Wait! I propose a trade," he called out, raising his voice.

The dragon halted but did not turn. "What kind of trade?"

"I offer you this Box for the crown and my friend's life. With it, you alone can protect your kind with the power this contains as you see fit."

Myrrh's tail swished, and she turned slowly. "Why would you trade something so valuable for this crown? If you lie, I will know."

Roedyn was silent.

A careless answer would expose the bluff.

Sticky had finally calmed the fire bats and sent them back to the ceiling. He was a wreck—blood oozed from welts and bruises; I had never seen him this battered. Barely able to stand, he gasped, "Do not break the True Cycle, Roedyn. Keep the balance."

Roedyn looked at Escala. Blood and ash streaked her hair. Scratches and bites marked her face and arms. One eye was swollen. Her armor was scorched. Her legs burned. She could barely stand.

And yet, she looked at him with wonder and hope.

He stared back, and his heart ached.

Turning back to Myrrh, Roedyn said, "Myrrh, my kind has lied enough. I will not lie to you now. Would you hear the truth?"

Myrrh snorted. "I doubt your kind can speak truth."

"You asked why a Ghost Warden sworn to protect the Boxes would trade one. It is because I made an oath. An oath to bring Escala Winter home to the Court of Dreams. And to do that, I need that crown."

There was heartbreak in Escala's eyes. To her, it must have sounded like "you're just a mission."

Roedyn continued, "I also swore to protect the Boxes. However, as you are aware, two have already been opened. Twice, my kind has failed yours. I confess; I don't know what power lies in this Box. As a Ghost Warden, I merely protect it. But if I give you this box, I will have given you what power exists in this box for you to use as you feel proper to protect your kind better than we have."

The dragon's head tilted, molten eyes narrowing. "Is that the truth? I will know if you lie. And if you do, I will kill you all long before you can open the Box."

Roedyn's heart pounded as he weighed the risk. Myrrh's molten eyes burned through him, and he knew—knew—that she could sense even the faintest tremor of falsehood. Dragons thrived on lies; they tasted deception on the air, like sharks smelling blood in the water. If he tried to bend the truth, if he dared to cloak his heart behind half-measures, she would see it, and she would kill them all.

He swallowed hard. To save them, to preserve the plan, he would have to bare his soul. The thought seared worse than the dragon's fire. To speak it aloud, here, of all places, with Escala watching, felt like walking naked through the crowded Dunwell market.

"But there is one more reason," Roedyn spoke with a steady voice, undeterred by the fear inside him. "I would give anything—everything—so that Escala Winter can return home because…"

Escala's eyes widened in surprise.

"… I have fallen in love with her, and I want nothing more than for her to be happy."

Escala's face went pale; her lips parted in shock. She drew in a trembling breath. "Roedyn…" she said softly.

Roedyn looked at Harper, still dangling in Myrrh's claws.

"There, I said it."

Harper grinned, dried blood on her face. "Telling Myrrh is sweet and all," she said, "but you still haven't told Escala."

Chapter 72

Well, Roedyn did it. I'll admit—I didn't think he could pull off the bluff, but he did. After twenty tense minutes of negotiation—and no shortage of bickering—Myrrh finally agreed that having the Box of Kestrel served her best interests.

It took another twenty to convince her to release Harper—and honestly, I don't think Roedyn tried that hard. Maybe he was still sore about Harper's earlier remark.

The exchange itself was a marvel, all thanks to Sticky. Neither Roedyn nor Myrrh trusted the other for a direct handoff of the crown for the box, so Sticky, in a flash of druidic brilliance, suggested using the fire bats.

He split the swarm—half with Myrrh, half with us—and fitted them with leather harnesses Harper had cobbled together. One group would carry the Box of Kestrel, the other the Crown of Dreams. Then he communed with the bats in his strange druid way, instructing them to release their cargo only when both sides were safely out of reach. Myrrh would get the Box once we reached the horses; we'd get the crown once we were clear.

The only reason it worked, I suspect, was because Sticky isn't one of the three races bound by the Dragon Truce and, more importantly, not one of the races that had violated it. Myrrh tolerated him in a way she didn't tolerate the rest of us.

Finally, with both artifacts secured in their harnesses, the fire bats flew to their waypoints, and we began our long walk back up through the cavern.

As we passed the edge of the treasure hoard, Myrrh spoke. "Roedyn of House Dor'Lean, I will give you six hours as part of these terms. I will have kept the truce."

It wasn't a threat, just a statement of fact: we had six hours to leave after the transfer, or she'd kill us.

Roedyn nodded. We hurried back to the horses so Sticky could command the bats to begin the transfer and start the six-hour clock.

Chapter 73

———————

As we made our way to the surface, we were in rough shape—bloodied, bruised, battered, and some of us severely burned. Harper's limbs had been scorched by dragonfire, and the fact that she could still walk was a miracle.

If not for Escala's quick thinking, Harper would've died in that lair. Her arms and legs were in terrible shape—skin blackened, blistered, in places simply gone. The pain must have been unimaginable. Escala's legs had been burned as well; her mithril chainmail absorbed part of the blast, but she still limped, clearly hurting.

All of us had been battered, slammed again and again by Myrrh's tail and pelted by hurricane-force waves of gold coins that left welts, black eyes, bruises, and cuts on every inch of exposed skin.

Escala walked beside Roedyn, one arm wrapped carefully around his probably broken ribs as they trudged on in silence, both wounded, both exhausted. Whether their quiet came from pain or something deeper—the shock of surviving a dragon, or the dawning truth of who Roedyn really was—it was hard to say.

Either way, this wasn't the moment for serious talk. We just needed to get away.

As we walked, it finally became clear how Roedyn and Harper had recognized the Crown of Dreams on Myrrh's tail.

They hadn't seen it through any spell or secret magic; it was memory. They'd seen that same crown years earlier, perched on the head of the emperor Korveth himself during their time in the capital of Eronvale. Of course, they would know the Crown of Dreams anywhere.

The realization brought an odd sense of relief. At least my secret song wasn't revealing hidden enchantments to anyone but me. No, this was simply sharp memory and good observation on their part. Typical Roedyn and Harper, really.

When we reached our camp, we found our horses were gone. Harper spun on Sticky. "I thought the animals listened to you? You said the horses would be safe, but they're gone, and we can't outrun Myrrh on foot."

Sticky ignored Harper and directed the fire bats, who delivered the Crown of Dreams as planned. Escala limped forward, hair wild, tunic scorched, smeared with dirt and blood. But her face lit up as she took the crown. She stared at it in awe, held it at arm's length, and hugged it to her chest, grinning through the grime. The contrast was striking.

She limped over to Roedyn and wrapped her arms around his waist. He groaned, his ribs still broken, and she loosened her grip. Her face was a mess, bloodied, one eye swollen shut. She looked up and said, "Thank you."

Now, I know what you romantics were hoping for—a kiss. That didn't happen because suddenly, wings rushed overhead.

Harper dove for a bush, yelling, "Myrrh broke the truce!"

Escala released Roedyn just as he gently pushed her aside and reached for his bow. She scanned for her shield. I looked skyward, bracing for dragonfire.

Sticky stood calm. He blinked twice and lazily flicked his tongue to snatch a mosquito.

Roedyn barked orders, shouting for us to move. Wings thundered above, and we all looked up, bracing for death.

But it wasn't Myrrh.

Instead, five Pegasi—gleaming white, majestic horses with wings—landed in a half-circle around Sticky, whose staff was glowing faintly. The largest tossed its head and neighed.

Sticky lifted his staff. "Welcome, Veleryn Kin of the Silverstand. Thank you for coming."

He turned to Harper. "The animals listen. I asked them to escort our horses back to Dunwell, and I sent two especially chatty sparrows to find the Veleryn Kin, a family of Pegasi I have known for eight winters. I figured Escala would want to return to Blackthorn Tower quickly, and a Pegasus is much faster than a horse, plus the Veleryn Kin owe me a favor."

Roedyn glanced at Harper. "He speaks for the bees and trees. I wouldn't cross him, or you might find a snake in your bedroll tonight."

Harper limped over and gently patted Sticky on the head. "I'm sorry I doubted you."

Sticky waved Harper off and introduced us to the Pegasi—powerful creatures that, despite their grandeur, were wonderfully gentle.

After a few quick instructions, we mounted and soared above the treetops. It was one of the journey's true highs, because none of us, aside from Sticky, had ever seen Valla from the air. And what a sight it was. Rolling hills, golden fields, winding rivers—it all looked new from above, breathtaking in ways I can't quite explain.

But the flight gave us more than scenery. It gave us silence. Space to think of what we all had just been through together and how close to death we had come.

Roedyn and Escala often flew side by side, saying nothing. The rest of us kept quiet, too.

We couldn't make it back to Blackthorn Tower in one night, so we had to land and camp.

The first order of business was healing. We were a wreck—scars, blackened eyes, burns, some of them nasty, bruises, broken ribs, and probably more than a few concussions. Before we even thought about eating, Sticky and I poured every bit of our combined healing magic into the group. And when I say heal, I mean heal—with the right spells and the right songs, even burn scars vanished. The angry marks on Escala's legs and the ones along Harper's arms and legs were gone, as if they'd never been there. Every bruise faded, and even broken bones knitted back together.

The memories, though—those stayed. And so did the nightmares I still get from time to time.

Once we felt whole again and had eaten, we sat around the fire. That was when Sticky brought up the question I'd been dying to ask. "You're really part of the Dor'Lean royal family?"

"Not anymore," Roedyn said.

"I don't get it." Escala said, "If you're born into a family, you're always part of it."

"It's true that I was born into the House Dor'Lean and that my birth name was Thorne Dor'Lean, not Roedyn."

All of us except Harper immediately looked at Roedyn, completely surprised by this news.

"What?" Escala said.

"All this time," I said, "we've known you as Roedyn Hammerfell, not Thorne Dor'Lean."

Roedyn wiped his mouth. "It's complicated. I was born Thorne Dor'Lean—the same family that rules Eronvale. The Dor'Leans founded the Gray Cloaks because they were tasked with guarding the Boxes of Kestrel. I joined at seventeen, that's when I met Harper."

"You told Myrrh you were a Ghost Warden. What's that?" Escala asked.

"We're the elite of the Gray Cloaks," Harper said, "—the ones directly charged with guarding the Boxes of Kestrel.

"You're still a Gray Cloak?" Escala asked.

"Yes," said Roedyn.

Harper added, "We both are."

"I still don't understand what the Gray Cloaks are." Said Escala.

"The Gray Cloaks are a large organization with many roles." Harper said, "Think of it like a knight and his squires. The squires support, but only the knight mounts the horse. Ghost Wardens are that knight—we alone bear the direct responsibility for the custody and protection of the Boxes. And because that burden is so great, our identities must remain secret to protect against bribery or corruption. That's why we can't exist, or at least, why no one can know who we are."

Roedyn added, "Our former lives ended the day we accepted the responsibility. Thorne Dor'Lean died in a hunting accident when I was sixteen. There was a funeral. I became Roedyn Hammerfell, Ghost Warden of the Third Box."

"Your death was faked, and your name was changed?" Sticky asked.

"It was the only way to serve. But Roedyn is who I am now. Only a few in the Dor'Lean family know the truth."

"Roedyn, didn't you lie to the dragon, though? Doesn't that violate your oath somehow?" Escala asked.

"I didn't lie," Roedyn said.

"But you held up a fake box and said it was the Box of Kestrel," I said.

Roedyn looked at me in frustration before answering, "I said, 'Stand down or I will open this box.' I never said it was the real Box of Kestrel."

"But you deceived her," I said, more challengingly this time. "You led her to believe it was the Box."

"I didn't lie." Roedyn looked at me, narrowing his eyes. "How did I lie?"

I tried again. "You told her you had the box and if she didn't stop attacking, you'd open it."

"I showed her a box, and I told her I would open that box. What she chooses to believe about the box is her business. How is that a lie?" Roedyn asked.

"The box was a fake."

"Wigfrith, I never said the box I was holding, as much as it looked real, was the Box of Kestrel." Roedyn set down his knife; he was getting a little annoyed. "Wigfrith, I don't lie."

What Escala heard was different from what the rest of us heard, and I suspect Harper already knew. When Escala heard that Roedyn didn't lie she knew that everything he told Myrrh was true, so she heard: "I'm falling in love with you."

While we all heard: "I have the real Box of Kestrel in my possession."

"So, giving her a fake box, doesn't that break your oath?" I asked.

"How so?" Roedyn said.

"Well, what's to stop her from razing Valla? The Boxes were meant as deterrents. Dragons feared being banished; mortals feared unleashing demons," I said. I was on a roll, so I kept going. "The system worked because both sides were terrified. But now you've given up our leverage. What's left to stop her?"

Roedyn said, "Remember what I told her, because with dragons, words matter. I said I didn't know what power was contained in that box I held, but I was willing to trade it with her so she could use whatever power existed in that box to protect her kind as she saw fit, and meanwhile, I'd continue to protect what I've sworn to guard. Wigfrith, you're clever, I trust you caught what I did."

I stop the story and take sip of ale. I set the mug down on the small table on the stage and say, "You all know I'm smart—obviously—but I didn't get it. It was Escala who figured it out, and I've got to admit, I was impressed."

"It's not that hard," Escala said. "Myrrh's going to cast spells on the box, trying to figure out how to bring back the other dragons—or at least, that's what I'd do if I were her. That's when she'll realize the box Roedyn gave her is a fake. And that Roedyn, the Ghost Warden, is still guarding the real one."

Escala looked at Harper, puzzled and surprised at my dimwittedness. "I thought you said he knew everything?" As she pointed at me.

That was when it hit me like a thunderclap. Roedyn—by Kestrel's bones—had the last Box of Kestrel, hidden away somewhere far from here. One of the most sacred, most dangerous relics in all of Valla. And in all our time together, not once had he let slip the weight of that burden. Never a word. Never a hint. Nothing to betray the monumental charge laid on his shoulders.

Suddenly, it all aligned—Harper and Roedyn's life in the middle of nowhere had never been chance. He wasn't a scout, and he and Harper were indeed not living as a marital couple. Harper's cryptic talk to Escala about a treasure in a cave, Roedyn's silence heavy as stone—it all fit.

And then it snapped into place: of course, they recognized the Crown of Dreams. They had seen it before. By the gods, they had been there when the emperor died, when he still wore that very crown. Every secret, every half-answer, every weighted silence collapsed together into one terrible, undeniable truth:

Roedyn was the guardian of the last Box of Kestrel.

And in that instant, I understood Escala's meaning—that the Dragon Truce would still hold even after Myrrh discovered the box she'd been given was a forgery. Because she knew Roedyn carried the true one. And as long as he did, the threat to her existence—and the deterrent that held her wrath in check—endured.

Roedyn had chosen every word with Myrrh carefully, deliberately. He had not made a single mistake. The deterrent of the Dragon Truce still stood. And because of it, Valla was safe from a demon swarm on one front, and from annihilation by the evil dragons on the other.

What Roedyn did took real courage standing before the most vicious creature in Valla, revealing his identity, and explaining why he was willing to trade a fake Box of Kestrel for the Crown of Dreams—all without breaking his oath— was brave enough. But the most challenging part? Admitting his love for Escala. Those of us who knew Roedyn understood how difficult that was for him.

Myrrh would've grown suspicious the moment she sensed Roedyn was withholding something. Dragons can detect lies, and even half-truths. Her patience was razor-thin, and if Roedyn had tried to conceal his true motivation, the dragon would've snapped. One flicker of deceit, and she would've shifted back into violence and killed us all.

Looking back now, I honestly believe that it wasn't the fake box or clever words that saved our lives, it was Roedyn finally being willing to say aloud that he loved Escala.

That night, as I crawled into my bedroll, I realized something: Roedyn Hammerfell wasn't just a scout. He was a protector. A guardian of Valla. And he'd just outwitted one of its oldest, deadliest creatures, all while awkwardly

413

confessing his feelings for a faerie girl in front of the entire party.

Too bad she was going to leave him in a few days and absolutely break his heart. I wasn't sure I could bear to watch that goodbye.

Chapter 74

T he Pegasi left us at the gates of Blackthorn Tower. We all thanked them and then turned to face what lay ahead.

Escala was nervous but excited. The Crown of Dreams was secured in her pack, and as we stepped inside, she carried one thing, hope.

Her logbook held a string of small "boulders" she'd cleared from the lives of ordinary people: reuniting pets, helping travelers, catching loose animals, building flood walls, and dealing with the vinethrasher. But Victor Graves had told her plainly: this crown was the real boulder—the one the Court of Dreams meant her to remove. Stolen from the fey realm, the crown had fallen into the hands of a brutal emperor who used its magic to usurp Roedyn's family's throne.

The crown of dreams didn't just channel nightmares; the emperor had twisted minds and summoned madness with it. Victor couldn't be more delighted that he had easily manipulated the fey to participate in setting up their own demise.

Inside the tower, servants greeted us in hushed tones and led us to the receiving chamber, where Victor waited. Refreshments were offered, pastries and cider, and Victor, ever the formal host, asked to hear our tale.

I recounted the adventure in unpolished bardic fashion, my first draft of the story you're hearing tonight. Victor listened with rapt attention. Despite being wrinkled like a baked apple and wearing a frown that could sour milk, even he couldn't suppress a crooked smile when Escala presented the crown.

She was radiant as she handed him the Crown of Dreams—hopeful, almost innocent again.

Victor took it with reverence and set it beside him, his face radiating something that looked like joy, but in hindsight, knowing what I know now, I'll tell you it was early signs of madness. He told us he would see to destroying it right away and would be glad to sign her logbook so she could return to the Court of Dreams.

Escala nearly bounced with joy as she handed Victor her logbook, and Victor, Grand Master of the Black Order, scrawled an elaborate entry praising her for removing a colossal boulder, the boulder, from the True Cycle, signing with a flourish that nearly filled two pages.

Escala read it aloud, and she clutched it to her chest like a prize ribbon, beaming, and I must admit I was filled with a certain sense of accomplishment. We had survived a dragon fight, and our friend Escala was going home; my story was going to be amazing!

But then something changed.

Victor, now eager to conclude our visit, began urging us, gently but firmly, to escort Escala to a crossing at once. He stressed the urgency of her return, insisting every hour counted. Escala, still glowing from praise, agreed.

But Roedyn said little. He stood apart, unreadable.

Since Roedyn's confession to Myrrh, the two of them hadn't spoken directly about their relationship. Yes, they were polite to each other, and she continued to thank him, and all of us, with the occasional lingering glance by a campfire, but no words had passed between them regarding their relationship. He had declared his love in the dragon's lair.

She had told me about her feelings for Roedyn before, so her silence now seemed strange. Harper and I had spoken privately during the trip, both hoping Roedyn's bold confession would spark something similar from Escala. But instead, she was the one who'd gone distant. It was confusing, and neither of us could make sense of it.

But we both kept quiet while we cared for both of them; it wasn't our place to pry any further. Well, it wasn't my place—I can't speak for Harper.

Finally, Victor got his way, and we were ready to leave. After formal goodbyes said, we departed Blackthorn Tower and headed for the nearest crossing, where Escala would finally return to the Court of Dreams.

Chapter 75

The moment we departed Blackthorn Tower, Victor Graves set his plan in motion. In his sanctum, which was on the highest floors of the tower, he moved like a man possessed. He'd waited nearly twenty years for this moment—the Crown of Dreams finally in his grasp, and the Vorrash Totem buried deep within the Court of Dreams. With the crown, he could now command Void magic, tear a hole in the veil, split his soul, and step into the palace to kill Rowan Winter himself. At last, his plan was becoming reality.

Tonight, he would begin casting a spell to find the Vorrash Totem's beacon in the Void, pulling power from the obsidian orbs in the dungeon of Blackthorn Tower.

His hands trembled with anticipation. For years, he had dreamed of vengeance against Rowan Winter, the self-righteous fool who crossed into the mortal realm and stole what was rightfully his: Teresa.

And now their spawn, that fluttering, reckless little pixie, Escala, had followed in her father's arrogant footsteps, meddling in mortal affairs she barely understood. Through her foolishness, and with Morvena's daughter, no less, she had gotten his son killed. And with his own totem!

The injustice of it scorched his soul and the fey would pay, all of them.

"Morvena," he sneered in thought, "you were useful, yes, I couldn't have done it without you. But you were so easy to manipulate, so blinded by your quest for power. And Audrey, such a cheap echo of your mother's ambition… You dared touch what was mine and you murdered my son. Now, you'll all die."

Behind him stood his boy, Jonathan, or what remained of him. Once vibrant, he now moved only by the black, pulsing magic holding his rotting body together. His arms, bound in the glowing bracers Victor had forged, twitched faintly. His eyes were dull, empty.

Victor touched his son's decaying cheek. "Soon, Jonathan, they'll understand what it means to lose everything."

The zombie didn't react; it just stared ahead.

Victor summoned two men-at-arms, their faces shadowed beneath blackened helms.

"Yes, master?" one said.

"Double the patrols," Victor said. "And release the Underdark creatures into the lower halls. I won't risk interruption. What I'm about to begin may take days, maybe weeks. If the spell breaks even for a heartbeat, the consequences will be catastrophic. Understood?"

The warriors saluted. "Yes, master." They vanished into the halls.

Victor turned and descended from the sanctum, following the four flights of magnificent spiral stairs down into the dungeon, into the chamber of the obsidian orbs. With a gesture of magic, he awakened the massive orb at the room's center. Power flared through it, surging upward toward the three smaller orbs in the sanctum above. Those upper orbs were nothing more than conduits; the true power was here, in the great sphere he had fed for decades.

For years, Victor had poured his magic into this orb, slowly, methodically, like inflating a festival balloon one painful breath at a time. Now it held nearly twenty years of accumulated energy: rage, grief, betrayal, and his unending hatred for Rowan Winter.

And with the Crown of Dreams—capable of opening the Void—he intended to use every drop.

He would draw out those twenty years of magic, split his own soul, cross the Void, breach the Court of Dreams, and kill every last fey.

Victor began the ritual, casting the complex spells that would extract his magic and channel it upward through the tower and into the three waiting orbs in his sanctum, and from there, into the Crown.

When the extraction started to flow, he ascended the stairs again, passing patrols of orcs, hobgoblins, goblins, and other twisted creatures that roamed the lower levels. Satisfied that they would guard the great orb in his absence, he continued upward.

At last he reached the sanctum. At its center stood a three-foot obsidian pedestal carved with faded runes that hummed with ancient, forgotten power. Around it, three dragonbone stands held crackling orbs of chaotic purple and blue energy, each one sparking with the magic now rising from the depths below.

He laid a square of black velvet on the pedestal and set the Crown of Dreams atop it, aligning each jagged gem with its corresponding orb. Many levels below, deep beneath the tower, a massive obsidian sphere—his Void magic conduit—reached up from the dungeon where the obsidian orb's power stretched into his sanctum and the three orbs.

Soon, he would cast the binding spell: Void energy would channel through the crown, pass into the orbs, and funnel into the obsidian core. Once enough magic gathered, he'd reverse the flow and pull it back through the crown, wear it, split his soul, and become the Void demon.

He held his breath. With a flick of his fingers, a heavy, leather-bound tome appeared. He carried it to a stand, opened it to a page marked in blood-red ink and symbols older than Eronvale, and began to chant. The room darkened. Power rippled outward in slow, pulsing waves. It was going to be a very long night.

Chapter 76

O ur trip to the Dunwell crossing felt strange. At first, it felt like this moment would be the victory Escala had longed for—the one we'd all wanted. A banished pixie, cast from her home, had done the impossible. And an unlikely band of heroes had helped her do it.

It should have felt triumphant. So why wasn't anyone smiling? Why did we walk in silence? The mood felt more funereal than festive, but none of us dared say it aloud.

At last, we found the crossing about a mile outside Dunwell and three hundred yards off the road, buried in a dense snarl of thickets and wild grapevines.

Escala had to point it out or I would have walked right past. It was smaller than I expected. Instead of a glowing archway or a grand portal, it was just a hovering, door-sized opening of pale energy, almost hidden by the overgrowth.

It was four bells past noon when Escala found a clear creek just beyond a small grove of trees. Harper stood guard while she washed up, Escala said she wanted to be fresh and clean before going back.

When she returned to our small camp, she had changed into a clean blue tunic, the same one she wore the day we met. She brushed her hair until it fell like sunlight down her back and tucked a lily behind her ear. The soft white petals made her eyes seem bluer. Her hair gleamed like spun gold.

She looked stunning. But this was still her elf form, none of us had seen her true pixie self. If she were reinstated and allowed to return to her natural form, what would she look like? We knew she'd be tiny—"two apples and a grape," as she'd said. This meant she would be small and delicate, with blonde hair and blue eyes, just as she was now. But would that beauty remain? Would she still look like the Escala we knew?

I glanced at Roedyn, wondering how much of his love for her was tied to her beauty. What if Escala looked like a bog witch in her proper form? Would he still love her? I didn't dare ask.

Escala turned to us and asked nervously, "How do I look?"

We all talked over one another, but our response was unanimous: "Beautiful."

She smiled, though it seemed very tight. "Well," she said, glancing around. "I guess… this is where I say goodbye." Her voice wavered, just a little. "Thank you, Wigfrith, for getting us to Victor Graves. Without you, I would never have found the big boulder I needed to remove."

She turned to Sticky. "And you? Sticky… there's no way to count all the things you've done on this journey to help. I'm going to miss you, a lot." She reached out and gently patted his head.

Then she looked at Harper. "You were the first person I met in Valla—well, besides that orc, but I don't think he counts. You were my first friend. You taught me to be brave. And I loved your snarky comments—Rihanna and I used to joke like that too. You made me feel like I belonged."

Finally, she turned to Roedyn. He stood perfectly still, arms at his sides. A tear traced down her cheek. Oh, how she longed to tell him what he meant to her. But to speak the truth would be to do exactly what she had been accused of: tampering with the True Cycle, breaking the Oath, bending fate itself. Already, she feared her bonds with her friends had altered their paths, placing their lives in peril, just as that young man had lost his life to the wolf because of her.

And if she confessed her true feelings to Roedyn? What if her words bound him to her, kept him from ever marrying, from ever finding love or happiness again? How could she live with herself knowing she had stolen his future, crushed his chance at joy if she told him how she really felt and then left? Better, she thought, to walk away without a word than to burden him with a truth he could never bear. Let him believe she had never loved him at all, rather than confess her heart and condemn him to the torment of knowing he could never have her, never see her again. Better the clean wound of silence than the lifelong ruin of forbidden love.

"Roedyn Hammerfell," she said softly, "you kept your oath and your promise. You brought me home to the Court of Dreams."

Her eyes swept his face. "I wish I could tell you what's in my heart. But I took an oath, and while I've broken oaths before, I can't break this one."

There was pain in her voice, real pain. My heart broke for her.

Roedyn didn't speak. He stood there watching her. He was stoic; I could see he had buried his feelings.

"What you've done for me," Escala continued, "I can never repay, and I wish I could. I wish there were a way to show you what your words, your actions... what you... have meant to me."

She rushed forward and hugged him, burying her face in his chest, but folks, no... no, she did not kiss him. I know some of you were expecting the storybook ending, but I am sorry, that isn't what happened. She just hugged him—tight and long—like she couldn't let go, and he hugged her back.

Finally, the hug ended, and Roedyn looked down at her. There was pain in his voice as he said, "Escala Winter of the Court of Dreams, it was an honor to help you remove boulders from the True Cycle. You're a remarkable soul, with a heart bigger than any boulder we've ever faced—I'll miss you."

She smiled, another tear sliding down her other cheek. Then she turned and stepped into the crossing.

Chapter 77

E scala stepped into the First World for the first time in months as a wave of homesickness washed over her. The colors were too vivid, the songs of the fey birds too rich. Valla paled in comparison.

She looked around, and just beyond the hills stood the spires and crystalline towers of the Court of Dreams. She knew this land, every curve of it, and her heart longed for wings to carry her home. But still trapped in elf form, she walked. It didn't take long to reach the palace outskirts, where nixie guards stopped her. They didn't recognize her—an elf stranger, not fey, made them instantly wary.

Only after a tense delay and the summoning of higher-ranking fey was her case reviewed, her identity begrudgingly confirmed, and her entry allowed. But she wasn't welcomed, nor permitted into the court's heart. She couldn't speak or embrace old friends.

Instead, she was led to the Star Gallery, the chamber for trials, formal hearings, and, today, the appeal of a banished daughter. As she walked the sacred halls, she scanned corridors she'd once flown through, laughing. She searched for friends—Junel, her father, any familiar face—but found only whispers, sidelong glances thick with suspicion, or silenced frowns.

She did not feel welcome. She stood in the very spot where she'd once been sentenced, where her wings were stripped, her form altered, her name erased from the noble rolls.

The judges arrived one by one. Then came her father, Rowan. This time, he met her gaze, and in it, she saw relief that she was alive. Sticky's magic and Wigfrith's songs had mended the burns, the shattered bones, and even the inner wounds. But if he knew what she had truly endured, that relief might vanish.

When the last judge took their place, a solemn bell tolled through the chamber. The fey rose, hovering. Above the central throne, a glowing sphere of pale blue energy coalesced, pulsing and expanding until it took shape as a man of immense, ancient presence.

It was the Dream Weaver, Volpe Inferna. Volpe Inferna was older than memory, the one who forged the Court of Dreams and shaped the fey who were pure of heart, sworn to protect the True Cycle. Though largely absent, he entrusted governance to the House Winter, now led by Lord Rowan Winter. But when a banished fey sought reinstatement, only the Dream Weaver could decide.

Dream Weaver Volpe took his seat, crossed his legs, and said in a kind voice, "What matter do we have before us today?"

The Recorder arose and hovered before the court, wings slowly flapping. "It is the appeal of Escala Winter."

"And what was her sentence?"

The Recorder unfurled a scroll and read, "Escala Winter has disrupted the True Cycle through actions that led to the death of a mortal. She has introduced boulders into the Cycle, disruptions that burden its sacred flow. For this, she

427

is hereby sentenced to the material plane to remove the boulders from the True Cycle. When she has done so, she may petition the Court of Dreams for reinstatement.

"Until her task is fulfilled, Escala Winter is banished to the material plane and forbidden from returning to the fey realm. Upon completion of her quest to remove the boulders, she may present herself at a fey crossing and formally petition this court for a review of her sentence. Until such time, she is exiled."

The words, though known to Escala, struck with renewed force, like a blade reopening an old wound.

The Dream Weaver turned his eyes toward her, his gaze impossibly deep. "What evidence do you present to us today regarding your efforts to remove these boulders from the True Cycle?"

She hesitated only a moment, then lifted her chin to face the judges. She searched each one for an ally, a clue, a hint of compassion. Her father's eyes offered nothing. Audrey, ever smug, tilted her head in a satisfied little shake that whispered, I told you so. And Morvena, arms crossed, lips curled in amusement, looked upon her with the certainty of someone who already believed the outcome was sealed.

Escala turned back to the Dream Weaver and began to speak.

"Dream Weaver," she said, thick with emotion, "when I was sentenced, I was guilty. I am still guilty. I crossed into the material plane against the will of my father, of the court, and of fey law. I ignored every warning—my father's, my stepmother's, even Rihanna's. I was reckless, and I interfered with the world of mortals. I violated the Oath. And because of that, a young man died, and so did Rihanna. I failed to listen to her warnings regarding odd noises in the bushes, which I now know was the wolf."

"It wasn't, it was the sound of the crossing closing," Audrey interjected.

Escala turned, startled. Morvena shot Audrey a look of pure fury. Escala said nothing and turned back to the Dream Weaver.

"I have never denied my part in their deaths," she said. "And I accepted the punishment. When I arrived on the material plane, I was scared. I was sent to the clearing where Rihanna died. It nearly broke me. But within minutes, I was attacked by an orc, and he nearly killed me. I was able to get away, and I sat alone in the woods, hungry, cold, and scared, and I've never felt more humbled. I'd give anything to undo what I did. But I quickly learned there's no room for self-pity on the material plane."

Morvena smiled; she was enjoying this.

Escala told her story—how Harper, Roedyn, Sticky, and Wigfrith taught her to survive, to care, and to hope. Then she reached into her pouch and drew out the logbook.

"At first," she said, "I thought that if I did enough good deeds—saved enough people, built enough walls, pulled enough wagons from ditches—that maybe I would balance the scale, so I started keeping this log."

She flipped the book open.

"I thought that was the point of it all. Until Wigfrith took me to meet a wizard named Victor Graves. He told me about a fey artifact called the Crown of Dreams that was stolen from the Court of Dreams, and I found it!" She was getting excited. "And Victor is going to destroy it, just like you want. He even signed the log right here." She pointed to the entry.

But the faces staring back at her held only confusion.

"The Crown of Dreams," she repeated. "The artifact stolen from the Court of Dreams. The one Emperor Korveth used to poison dreams—don't you know of it?"

The judges whispered. The Dream Weaver slowly shook his head.

"The Crown of Dreams," she repeated. "The crown that sends dreams… or nightmares. Wasn't it stolen? Victor Graves claimed it was taken ages ago, and that we might need to search the archives."

The Dream Weaver shook his head gently. "I'm afraid he's misinformed. We have never possessed a Crown of Dreams. We have no need for such a thing—our power comes from the Dream Orb. I'm sorry."

Waves of disappointment crashed over her—this wasn't the boulder. She had failed.

The Dream Weaver looked down at her with sorrowful affection and shook his head again.

"Little spark, you've done beautiful things for the material plane. I can hear it in your voice, and I see it in your logbook. You are beginning to understand why the True Cycle must be protected. But you have not even glimpsed the true boulders yet. Helping little girls with cats in trees, wagons in mud, old men with their stone walls… even this crown—whatever it is—is not what your sentence was about.

"There are greater weights in the river of life, immovable stones that strain the current and alter its flow. And one day, little spark, you will learn that such boulders are not always what we expect."

His eyes lingered on her, sorrowful yet unwavering. "It will take more than goodwill. This cannot be accomplished in a few months. It will take a lifetime to truly understand the weight of your task."

The words filled Escala's heart with dread, and tears blurred her vision. The Dream Weaver's gaze softened, though his decree did not.

"Your appeal is denied."

Chapter 78

I n Blackthorn Tower, Victor continued to cast spells of tremendous power. The chamber stank of arcane smoke, heat rippling as Victor hunched over a glowing pedestal, violet energy crackling from his hands. Runes swirled in the haze, circling the Crown of Dreams— hovering, pulsing with a sickly light.

Beside him, a massive tome lay open, its pages fluttering in the power-charged air. He was eight hours into a day-long spell, his voice hoarse, his robes soaked with sweat.

Morvena burst in, her wings scattering ash and parchment. Smoke curled in her wake, but Victor didn't flinch. He kept chanting, fingers slicing the air in dangerous arcs.

"What are you doing here?" he snapped, his voice raw with agitation—yet the spell's rhythm never faltered.

Morvena hovered, eyes narrowing. "I'm here because you asked me to come."

"No, I didn't," he barked. "I told you to stay in the Court of Dreams."

She sighed, more tired than angry. There was no arguing with a man this far gone. "She was rejected," Morvena said with satisfaction in her voice, but as she talked, she saw a small round totem, about the size of an orange, near Victor's spell books. Victor had told her about its power—she wanted it. As she talked, she carefully slid into her pouch. "She's back in the material plane... and we're going to kill her now."

Victor barely reacted, not looking at her. "I don't care. But first, return and activate the Vorrash Totem. Only then can you kill her."

Morvena's jaw tightened. "Fine, but once that's done, Escala will be killed, and Audrey will be the princess of the Court of Dreams."

She drew a blade from her belt. Without hesitation, she sliced her forearm. A line of blood welled bright, and with a whispered word, the spell ignited. But before she did, she grab

The blood crossing hummed to life. Wings folded tight, eyes burning with malice, Morvena stepped toward it.

Chapter 79

W e were still camped at the Dunwell cross and after dinner, as the fire dwindled to glowing embers and the sun dipped behind the tree line, I took up my lute and began to strum. Soft melodies wandered into the clearing, a gentle balm against the heaviness left in Escala's wake.

Roedyn sat unusually quiet by the fire, letting the music dredge his heart, his gaze fixed on some distant place. Harper, ever irreverent, tried her usual snark to spark a reaction. She even offered to spar in the morning, an olive branch wrapped in sarcasm, but he declined with a polite nod.

Sticky, unbothered by the emotional weight, contentedly snatched bugs from the air with his long tongue. This part of the forest was thick with insects at night, and he was making the most of it.

Eventually, my fingers stilled. Silence returned until Harper broke it with a sharp sigh. "I miss her," she said. "I know we all do. But we can't mope around like sad puppies. She's back in the Court of Dreams now, and let's face it, we're never going to see her again."

Harper continued, "Tomorrow, we head back to Dunwell to drop off Wigfrith. Then we're off to the Never Glenns to take Sticky home, and Roedyn and I, well, we're heading west, back to our so-called 'marital cabin' in Silverstand."

She made air quotes, but no one laughed.

I laid my lute across my knees. "I'm turning this entire journey into one of my tavern tales, one of the good ones, the kind people remember. So no one forgets what we did or forgets her."

Sticky nodded in agreement.

Harper leaned in with a devilish grin. "Roedyn, how much are you willing to pay Wigfrith to skip over those times you accidentally put arrows in Escala?"

Normally, Roedyn would have met her jab with a glare or snapped back with a growl of protest. But this time he only stared into the fire, as though he hadn't heard her at all. My heart ached for him.

Harper fell silent, and the rest of us followed, lost deep in our thoughts.

Nearly ten minutes crept by before a sudden rustle in the grapevines near the crossing snapped us to attention. Roedyn rose at once, bow in hand, every muscle drawn tight. Harper was right behind him, dagger flashing in the firelight as her eyes swept the shadows. Only Sticky remained unbothered, lazily flicking his tongue at insects as though peril were a foreign word.

The vines tore apart, and Escala emerged in her elven form. She looked almost spectral in the fire's glow, eyes raw and red, cheeks streaked with tears, and her whole frame was trembling.

Harper's stance eased first; she slid her dagger back into its sheath. Roedyn lowered his bow, face showing concern. I stared, stunned. Something had gone terribly wrong.

"Escala?" I said, barely a whisper. "What happened?"

"There is no boulder… they don't want me back," she blurted out, her eyes welling with tears.

Roedyn was there in an instant, pulling her into his arms as her grief broke loose in uncontrollable sobs.

Escala was back and shattered.

udrey stepped through the crossing into Valla, the evening chill brushing her skin. Escala had done precisely what Victor wanted—retrieved the crown, handed it over, sealed her fate.

Her appeal denied, Escala had been cast back to the material plane. The Dream Weaver said it would take a lifetime to return and fey live forever. Escala was still in the way—as long as she lived, Audrey's claim to the royal succession would be threatened. She had to be eliminated.

Morvena had been explicit: no more mistakes. This time, Audrey was cautious. She watched and waited, even before the appeal was denied, biding her time for the perfect chance.

Roedyn was always too close. Using the wolf totem then would've been suicide. But Audrey didn't need to rely on that alone, she could be just as cunning as her mother. She had other pixie tricks. Her hand brushed the dagger at her hip. Oh, she'd kill Escala one way or another.

The veil closed behind Audrey as she stepped into a grapevine thicket a mile outside Dunwell. It was late evening, and the woods were quiet. Escala had made it too easy, during her appeal she had told the court she was staying at The Stag and Hound in Dunwell.

Audrey smiled. *Let the hunt begin.*

Chapter 81

In the Court of Dreams, the palace stood silent as Morvena moved like a shadow through its beautiful halls, her wings soundless as she slipped into the gardens. She found the decorative urn, the one she had placed weeks ago, and, after making sure no one was watching, slowly lifted it. There, just where she had planted it in the soft soil of the fey palace garden, was the Vorrash Totem, a slender, dark staff etched with cruel symbols and half buried in earth.

She knelt, pressed her palm to the totem, just as Victor had instructed. She winced as it bit into her skin. Dark with fey magic, her blood welled and slipped into the carved grooves. The totem pulsed red as it absorbed the blood. Satisfied, she replaced the urn and vanished into the night.

An elder fey, weathered and sharp-eyed, drifted silently from behind a trellis buried in a tangle of morning glories, violet and blue blooms veiling the lattice in leaves and shadow. She had seen Morvena doing something suspicious with the urns, and her instincts flared; something was wrong. She checked the urns one by one until she found the hollow one. Lifting it carefully, she peered into the soil and froze. A red glow throbbed at the tip of a buried wooden totem.

She turned and bolted toward the Winter chambers as fast as she could fly. Lord Winter had to know.

Chapter 82

I do ten toe touches and stretch my arms high toward the ceiling, joints popping for all to hear. "Ever since Myrrh smacked me with her tail, my back's never been the same," I tell them, half grinning. "So forgive the stretches, got to keep loose." I rise onto my tiptoes in an exaggerated stretch, holding it a beat longer than needed. "There. Much better. Now, back to the story. Where was I?"

I pace the stage trying to remember, and Tully yells out, "You were telling us that Junel had found the Vorrash Totem and was rushing off to tell Lord Rowan Winter."

"Ah, yes, thank you, good sir." I nod appreciatively in his direction.

"Yes, indeed, Morvena and Audrey have sprung their traps, and Rowan and Escala are in trouble. But things are about to get significantly worse for the Court of Dreams as Victor Graves has something far more sinister planned for all fey. Let me take you back to Blackthorn Tower to see how his master revenge plot is shaping up."

In his sanctum, Victor chanted, well into the twelfth hour of the spell. His voice was raw, and the air was thick with magic. The Crown of Dreams sat on an obsidian pedestal, pulsing blue and violet, bridging worlds, but not yet fully open, not quite ready to wear.

Beside Victor, his ancient spellbook fluttered and dragonbone spires thrummed in harmony, reaching down into the lower depths of the tower, their magic connecting to the obsidian orb.

The crown was the key, a conduit for harnessing the Void as a bridge between realms, allowing Victor to create crossings wherever he desired. Once infused with enough Void magic, the crown would let him sense the Vorrash Totem buried in the Court of Dreams, piercing through the veil that separated the material plane from the fey realm. Wearing it would be like steering a ship through fog, with the totem as the distant lighthouse, and only with the crown could he see it.

But the crown alone lacked the power to perform this task. So, deep in the lower chambers, Victor had forged an obsidian orb and connected it to the dragonbone gems embedded in his sanctum. Through an intricate Void spell, he linked the crown to the gems. When activated, the crown would open a narrow gateway to the Void, drawing its raw energy into the obsidian orb. Once filled, the process would reverse, channeling the stored power into the crown itself, allowing the wearer to "see" into the Void and lock onto the Vorrash Totem's location.

From there, Victor could cycle Void magic between the crown and the orb at will, building a surge strong enough to tear open the veil at the totem's position, ripping reality and forging an unnatural crossing in the palace gardens.

Then, as a master of Spirit Split, he would divide his soul, become two Void-born entities, and enter the fey realm through the breach—one to hunt down Rowan Winter, and the other to annihilate the rest of the fey.

Victor smiled. Morvena had done her part. It was a shame that she'd die too, she'd almost been likable. He brushed the thought aside and turned back to the crown, which was now pulsing with Void magic.

Soon, he would wear the crown and tear a hole in the fabric of the fey realm just large enough for Victor to enter, kill Rowan Winter, and destroy the Court of Dreams.

Chapter 83

―――――――

"Gimm'me 'noth'r one…" Escala slurred, slamming her glass on the counter in The Stag. She was drunk and wanted to be left alone, so we gave her space and let her sit at the bar by herself.

We'd never seen her drink before. But after everything that had happened, I couldn't blame her, and we didn't even try to stop her. Still, things might've gone a bit too far, because Escala didn't just have one… or two… or even three drinks—she had nine dragonfire brandies.

You heard me, nine. And you all know how strong those things are. Let's just say she got really sassy that night. And by the end of it, nobody dared touch the faerie—hells, nobody even wanted to talk to her.

We'd tried to cheer her up, but what do you say to someone whose entire life got shattered in one day?

Roedyn had tried the hardest, and I know it tore him up inside. Just days before, he'd told her he was falling in love. Having her back must've felt like a miracle only to see her shattered. And knowing this was absolutely the wrong time for romance? That trapped him in emotional limbo.

Harper and Sticky tossed out theories about the Dream Weaver's words, trying to offer hope. But Escala knew better now—this punishment had no end. Her father's goodbye might have been all he could give, maybe even a way to spare her from the Wane. But if so, why give her false hope?

She'd risked everything—her life and ours—for a lie. The boulder never existed. The roc attack, the battle with Myrrh... all of it, for nothing. Furious at the court and her father for hiding the truth, she also felt crushing guilt for dragging us into it.

Loudly lamenting to Pints, she swore she couldn't have lived with herself if any of us had died chasing a boulder that wasn't real. So, she drank dragonfire brandies, and plenty of them.

And that was when a plainly dressed woman stepped into the bar. She looked like any other working woman in town—strong arms, scarred hands, clearly shaped by hard labor. She sat beside Escala, who was still tossing back dragonfire brandies like they were water.

The woman looked Escala up and down. "Ah, would ya look at yerself," she said, in an accent from the southern farmlands. "What's got ya turnin' the bottle upside down, lass? You're far too bonnie to be drownin' sorrows. You should be breakin' hearts and sendin' the poor lads off to the pub to patch up what's left o' their egos."

Escala turned her head slowly, her neck wobbling as she struggled to focus. I'd never heard her be cruel before. Maybe it was the drink, the grief, or a dozen other things—but tonight, she was mean. And while she slurred every word, her tone couldn't have been clearer: get out of my face. What she actually said—well, more slurred—to the poor new arrival was:

443

"Who inna bluhhdy hells d'you... d'you thi'ks you're? Go tak' a f'in' leap an' git—git them 'am berries outta m'face."

If I were to attempt to translate, I think Escala said, "Who in the bloody hells do you think you are? Go take a flying leap and get them berries out of my face."

Of course, I don't know for certain, and I don't know why Escala would mention berries, but in any event, the woman's frown deepened, her tone sharpening as she began to ball her fist. "An' what was that you just said to me now, lass?"

Escala turned again, badly slurring her words and almost falling off the stool. "I say"—as she nearly spit on the woman—"... go on... gets' lost... d'you rat-face bit—" And then she fell right off the barstool, flat on her back with a thud. Sticky hopped over and lifted her up.

The woman looked furious now, convinced Escala had insulted her. She grabbed up Escala by the collar.

Roedyn stepped between them. "Now, now, m'lady— she's had far too much to drink. Doesn't even know what she's saying." He offered a disarming smile.

"Let me buy you a drink, start your night off right. Forget her." He waved Escala off with a casual flick, while behind him Sticky—only two feet tall—struggled mightily to hoist a staggering, swaying Escala back onto her barstool. She wobbled like a ship in a storm, one hand clawing for the bar. She sent empty shot glasses skittering away—one spun off the edge, shattering against the floor in a sharp explosion of glass. Every time Sticky got her halfway up, Escala slid right back down in a heap, nearly toppling him with her.

444

Meanwhile, Roedyn was in the foreground, trying to calm the furious woman, who looked about two seconds from throwing a punch, completely unaware of the disaster unfolding just over his shoulder.

Finally, Escala—awkwardly, and in a manner no one would call ladylike—climbed back onto the barstool. She blurted out her next words, clearer this time though still heavily slurred: "Yu'look like my'rat-face'd steppshisster...!"

The woman reared back and punched.

Roedyn caught her fist in midair. "No need for that, trust me, she'll have a raging headache tomorrow. Your punch won't add much. Pints! Get my new friend here a drink—on me."

The woman lowered her arm but kept her glare fixed on Escala. She took the drink Pints handed her and muttered, "I don't take kindly to insults—no matter how bonnie the lass, eh? I was only makin' conversation. Someone oughta teach this one a bit o' manners. Y'd swear she was queen o' the bloody ball."

Harper muttered under her breath, "You would indeed."

Roedyn glared, and Harper suddenly chugged her brandy.

The woman took her drink, glared one more time at Escala, and moved to the far end of the bar.

We tried to convince Escala to go up to her room, but she refused; she can be incredibly stubborn when she wants to be. We did get her to eat some soup and bread, hoping to sober her up. But Pints served her onion soup cooked in red wine. So much for sobering her up.

445

We returned to our table while she ate at the bar alone.

That was a mistake.

None of us saw what happened or were close enough to stop it. But we heard a sharp scream and a thud.

Escala had fallen off the stool—again. But this time, a knife was in her back.

The woman from earlier was already at the front door.

Sticky raced to Escala's side. Harper flipped her chair over and barreled after the fleeing woman.

Escala was crying out in pain as blood streamed from the deep wound in her back. I didn't have my lute—I couldn't sing my healing spell.

Gasps rippled through The Stag. Pints fumbled for towels, but they were useless for this wound was deep. Roedyn was already at her side, clutching her hand, whispering, begging her to hold on.

Sticky pulled the knife out of Escala's back, and blood gushed. Roedyn shouted for him to hurry with the healing. Sticky stared at the flow for a while, then finally began casting, and it took longer than expected, but at last the wound sealed and the bleeding stopped. Escala's pain eased, though she was still clearly in shock, or drunk, or both.

I asked Sticky why he had taken so long to heal her.

"She was drunk," he said. "I wanted some of that alcohol out of her blood before I healed her. She'll be sober a lot faster this way."

I couldn't help but smile. Sticky, our sweet, simple frog… might just have been the wisest of us all.

Meanwhile, Harper burst out the Stag's front door into the night, scanning the street—left, right. Nothing.

She stopped two men who were stumbling down the street. "Did either of you see a woman leave The Stag just now?"

"No," they slurred.

Impossible. She was gone. Harper checked the alley and rooftops—nothing, no sign of her.

She returned, baffled.

"Did you catch her?" I asked.

Harper shook her head. "She vanished. No way she ran that fast."

Escala was sitting up now, Roedyn holding one hand for balance. She reached behind her, feeling where the knife had gone in. Slowly, she said, pain in her voice, although she sounded more sober, thanks to Sticky, "I think my back hurt her knife."

Harper burst out laughing, and soon we were all laughing.

Perched in the branches across from The Stag, a small pixie, perhaps two oranges and a prune tall, hovered in shadow, her wings barely stirring the air. Audrey's eyes burned as she stared at the tavern, heart pounding with the thrill of what she'd done. She had driven the blade into Escala's back, felt the resistance, and heard the scream. Oh, how satisfying that scream had been.

But was Escala dead?

She still didn't know, and she wasn't about to wait around to find out. If Escala somehow survived, Audrey

447

would wait for another chance. She would not stop until Escala was dead.

Chapter 84

Junel led Lord Rowan through the shadowed garden to where the strange wooden object lay half-buried in the soil behind the palace.

Rowan knelt beside the totem and examined it closely. A faint pulse radiated from within and he knew instantly this wasn't fey magic and it didn't belong here.

He grabbed the totem and pulled, but it didn't move.

He tried again, harder this time but he still could not budge it. It was anchored, like it had grown roots into the rich fey soil.

Scowling, he dug into the soil to see just how deep this thing had buried itself.

Back at the Blackthorn Sanctum, Victor Graves had been weaving a spell for hours to scan the endless dark of the Void, searching for a single signal—the beacon of the Vorrash Totem. He had been casting for over twelve hours, and the magic had ravaged his body, pushing him to the brink of collapse. But at last, he felt it—a faint pulse threading through the fabric of the fey realm.

He couldn't tear the veil yet, not without wearing the Crown of Dreams to channel the Void magic. But before he risked that kind of power, he had to be certain this was the correct location.

Drawing on his formidable focus, he layered a scrying spell into the Vorrash Totem while continuing to pull Void magic into the obsidian orb in the chamber below his sanctum.

As the scrying spell took hold, a floating magical window unfurled before him and the mists within parted to reveal a shadowed garden. Figures began to form—an older pixie woman, about one grapefruit and a fig tall, hovered near the totem, examining it with care. She couldn't see him; the spell offered only one-way vision. Moments later, she beckoned another fey to join her.

A male pixie with silver hair and a royal-blue cloak flew in and hovered near the totem, eyes narrowed. He was about two large pears and a plum tall.

The woman asked, "Lord Winter, what is it?"

"I don't know," he replied.

Victor's smile curled. So, this was Lord Rowan Winter. But his satisfaction vanished as Rowan gripped the totem and gave it a hard yank—he was trying to uproot the totem! If he succeeded, if the totem was dislodged, Victor's entire plan would collapse. Victor cursed. He couldn't let that happen. He had to act now.

Victor seized the Crown of Dreams and slammed it onto his head.

Void magic tore through him instantly, like lightning. His body went rigid, and he screamed in agony as icy darkness surged into his veins—electrifying and draining him at once, as if he were being pulled into a collapsing star.

The pain was so intense that Victor nearly blacked out. But he gritted his teeth and clung to consciousness, battling the flood of nothingness. Even with his training, it took everything he had to weave a protective ward, redirecting the magic through the crown rather than letting it consume him.

At last, he stabilized the pain, isolating it to a corner of his mind where he could manage it. With a sharp breath, Victor gave the Crown of Dreams its first command: *Tear the veil.*

The crown glowed as Void magic surged from the obsidian orb, through the crown, and across the boundary between realms. The very fabric separating the material plane from the fey realm stretched, strained... and ripped.

The Vorrash Totem flared, and a small crossing erupted at its crown. Normal crossings opened and closed with the natural ebb and flow of the ocean's tide. But this crossing was not normal, this was a violent puncture, a jagged tear gnawed through the fabric of the realms itself. This was a crossing that would never mend, like slicing a waterskin with a knife.

And from this new unnatural crossing, both the fey realm and the material plane began to slowly unravel, drawn, thread by thread, into the waiting Void.

I glance around the room at The Stag, checking to see if the crowd is following me.

"Folks, I need to make sure you understand what Victor just did. Crossings, the ones Escala and most fey use, are natural. They open and close in cycles, in rhythms, like sunsets and tides. Even the blood crossings, like the ones Morvena and Audrey use, while dark, are still natural.

"You see, fey blood is magical; it's part of the realm itself. When a fey bleeds, the realm reacts as if pricked by a knife. It flinches, just like you would. And in that flinch, it senses trouble. It opens, just slightly, ready to receive what it thinks is coming home: the dying fey, the fading magic. That brief opening, a blood crossing, allows the fey who bleed to slip through. Yes, it's dark, but natural."

I scan the common room, making sure they're with me. "But what Victor did?" I shake my head. "That was something else entirely. He didn't just open a crossing, he ripped a hole in the fabric between realms and forced one into being. A crossing that will never close.

"Because the Void is the emptiness between realms, a realm of silence, cold, and endless pull. Mages say it behaves like a vacuum, drawing all things inward, like a Charybdis—one of those legendary whirlpools that swallowed entire ships whole. To grasp how dangerous this is, think of leaving a window open during a bitter winter. The warmth in your home doesn't just linger, it's pulled out, replaced by freezing air. Now imagine that on a cosmic scale.

"This new crossing acts like that open window, only worse. It's not just letting the Void in; it's letting the Void pull. Because a crossing connects two worlds, this rip has created a vacuum between the fey realm and the material plane, slowly drawing things out of both.

"That's how serious this is. A crossing that can't be closed is like a hole in the universe."

I set my mug down and slowly glance around The Stag, gauging the room. I need to know if they understand, if they truly grasp what Victor's done.

From the grim expressions staring back at me, I can tell they do and that they realize that Victor has done something extremely dangerous.

"I need to pause the story here because you need to understand what Victor just did with that crown. It may have doomed us all. And if that sounds dramatic, let me explain it another way.

"Imagine we're all aboard a ship in the middle of the sea... and Victor just punched a hole below the waterline. No one's noticed yet but the water's rising in the hold. Soon, we won't be able to patch it, or bail fast enough, and we won't be able to make it back to shore before we sink. That, in fairly grim terms, is what Victor just did."

I see more heads nodding; they finally comprehend the seriousness of what Victor did. I take a sip of ale and continue.

Victor, now wearing the Crown of Dreams and having torn a small but unstable crossing into the fey realm atop the Vorrash Totem, let out a manic laugh. Through his scrying spell, he watched Rowan trying to pull the totem from the dirt.

Victor cast his first spell through the crossing.

Without warning, a grotesque shadow-hand erupted from the totem, grabbing Rowan by the throat and clamping down with cruel force.

Victor violently yanked his arm to his chest, and across realms, the shadowy hand obeyed. It tightened around Rowan's throat, dragging him downward, trying to slam him onto the jagged edge of the Vorrash Totem—to impale him like a sacrificial offering.

Rowan's wings thundered, straining against the pull. "Junel!" he choked out.

She was already there, hands locked on his arm, heels dug into the moss. Two nearby sprites dove in, seizing his other arm, struggling with all their might to stop him from being impaled.

Back in the sanctum, Victor's eyes burned as he clenched his fist tighter, channeling more Void magic through the crown.

"Jonathan!" he roared.

The zombie lumbered in.

"Grab my arm and pull—now!"

And so began a tug-of-war between realms.

Victor and his undead son, through Victor's shadow arm, yanked Rowan's throat toward the totem, while Junel and a growing line of fey fought to tear Rowan free from the shadow's crushing grip.

Cries of alarm echoed through the royal garden. Sprites, nixies, and pixies raced to Rowan's side, forming a flailing chain as they fought the pull of darkness of the zombie and a mad wizard.

Victor snarled and unleashed a massive surge of Void through the crown, but it was too much. The magic ripped through him, forcing him to throw up a ward to avoid being dragged into the Void himself. The backlash hurled him across the sanctum, and he slid, hitting a table. This broke his concentration.

The shadow-hand around Rowan's neck vanished, and with the dark force gone, the fey pulling on him all tumbled backward into the hedges. Rowan collapsed among them, coughing and clutching his throat.

Victor staggered to his feet, blood on his lip. He had no time to waste. He began the incantation again.

In the garden, Rowan rose, eyes locked on the totem. A small crossing hovered above it.

"Uproot it!" he shouted.

Fey swarmed, clawing at the soil, but the black tendrils dug deeper. The Vorrash Totem had anchored.

In his sanctum, Victor watched through the swirling scrying cloud, it was already too late.

He adjusted the crown atop his brow and raised both arms, beginning the forbidden rite: to project a sliver of his will into the Court of Dreams in the form of a shadow beast—just as he had once conjured animal totems like the wolf.

Void magic surged through him. With a cry of pain, Victor channeled the torrent and unleashed the spell.

In the royal gardens, the air rippled, and from the dark ether, a shadow beast emerged. Towering, black, and reeking of hunger, it stepped forward, silent and menacing.

Cries of panic rang out as the fey launched spells, bolts of blue and gold streaking toward the creature, but their magic vanished into its form, absorbed without effect.

The beast did not strike back. It merely planted itself over the Vorrash Totem, unmoving, a sentinel of darkness, as black roots crept outward beneath it like veins of corruption.

Victor, still in his sanctum, roared through the shadow beast's shell, his voice thundering into the garden: "You ripped her from me, Rowan. Now I will destroy everything you love."

Rowan hovered in midair, twenty yards from the shadow creature, his expression grim. "Who are you?" he called out, concern evident in his voice.

Victor's laughter crackled through the creature as Void magic surged, thrilling, intoxicating. "I am Victor Graves, the Grand Master of the Black Order."

Rowan's eyes narrowed. "I don't know you. What wrong have I done you?"

The shadow creature contorted with rage as it screamed, "Teresa!"

The color drained from Rowan's face, Marlow Village, twenty years ago, during his time on the material plane. He had disguised himself as a young human and fallen in love with Teresa, the only woman he had ever truly loved.

Teresa had a friend back then, a strange young wizard who always lingered at the edges. What was his name?

Victor. Could he have imagined some bond with her? Real or delusional, what kind of madness festers a grudge for two decades?

Was this truly the same Victor Graves Escala had named in open court, the man she trusted with the Crown of Dreams?"

Rowan tried to sound calm. "Teresa left the court twenty years ago. She's not here."

Victor's creature sneered, its voice thick with venom. "What you stole can never be returned."

"Your issue is with me, leave the court alone."

"Never!" Victor screamed. "I will destroy the Court of Dreams after I kill you!"

Rowan's eyes widened. He spun to Junel. "Go! Cross now—you must find Escala. It's the Crown of Dreams—she gave it to Victor Graves. She must stop him!"

Junel launched skyward without a word, wings beating wildly as she cut through the air, panic fueling her flight.

Rowan yelled to the remaining fey, "Retreat! Summon the War Guard! The Court of Dreams is under attack!"

Victor grinned. He knew exactly what came next. He would divide his soul, breach the veil, storm into the Court of Dreams, and kill every single fey, starting with Rowan Winter.

Chapter 85

V ictor began the arduous incantation of the Spirit Split spell. He'd split his soul twice before, both times on the material plane over short distances, but he had never attempted it across realms. To achieve this, he would need Void magic and the Crown of Dreams to bridge the gap.

Victor pulled wave after wave of Void energy through the Crown of Dreams and the obsidian orb in the dungeon as he began to cast the Spirit Split spell. The crown pulsed with each wave, crackling with black lightning, and the air hummed with strained, unstable power.

The more Void he drew, the more impossible it became to resist—it was overwhelming and intoxicating. He pulled the power through the unnatural crossing he'd torn open, funneling it from the Void into the obsidian orb, then through the crown and into the Spirit Split spell. The tear strained under the pressure, its edges fraying like overdrawn silk. But Victor didn't notice, because the Void surged through him like a storm-swollen river, drowning reason, flooding him with rapture.

Then came the split.

Agonizing pain slammed into Victor's chest like a hammer. He gasped and collapsed onto the sanctum floor, convulsing, his lungs frozen, and his soul torn in two.

As Victor staggered to his feet, a hideous Void creature began to form beside him, absorbing a fragment of his soul. Yet his own body remained standing, conscious and intact. Against every law of magic and mortality, Victor retained awareness in both his body and the Void demon.

Only the Crown of Dreams made such soul division survivable, and only Void magic could sustain it. Victor continued to draw an unbelievable amount of Void magic through the rip in the veil, which stretched the tear in the unnatural crossing.

What Victor failed to see, what his unraveling mind refused to grasp, was that the crossing was growing, and not in a controlled or natural way. The tear between realms widened, Void magic surging through it like floodwaters smashing a crumbling dam.

But even if he had seen it, Victor wouldn't have stopped—the crown's power had sunk its claws too deep. His soul was split, his thoughts scattered, his sanity fraying. Splitting a soul always came with a price.

For now, he still had control. But for the first time, he wondered if he could ever piece himself back together. Seeing Rowan again, after holding him by the throat and coming within a breath of impaling him, had reignited twenty years of pent-up rage and bloodlust. Vengeance consumed Victor. And now, fully merged with the Void demon, he commanded it to climb through the Crossing.

As the creature, now carrying half his soul, awoke, its red, malevolent eyes snapped open, and Victor saw through them as if they were his own. He could control its body because it was his body. Half his soul inside it.

Obeying his will, the Void demon thrust two colossal arms of shadow through the tear in the crossing, seizing its edges and rending them wider. Thick, muscled legs followed, then a broad, heaving chest woven from writhing black mist. Every motion streaked the air with darkness, as if reality itself recoiled from his presence.

Air ripped outward, drawn into the Void as the crossing devoured everything in its reach. Trees and hedges in the garden bent toward the widening breach, leaves tearing free. In the sanctum, loose pages swirled, drawn into the air. Victor's wild hair lashed around his face as the Void howled at the center of the room.

In the garden, the Void demon's head emerged, crimson eyes, slanted and cruel, burned like twin coals. Jagged horns curled from its brow like a war crown. Malice rolled from its form in waves, poisoning the very air of the Court of Dreams.

As it stepped fully through, the beast tore at the veil again, rending the crossing wider still before rising to its full, monstrous height—an abomination of Void and fury.

The Crown of Dreams had summoned a nightmare into the Court of Dreams, and its name was Victor Graves.

Chapter 86

A s Junel crossed over to the material plane, the crossing hummed strangely; something was wrong. The crossing was much smaller than usual, and as she slipped through, it snapped shut behind her. That wasn't normal. Crossings never closed that fast. An uneasy cold crept over her, but she had no time to dwell on it; she had a message to deliver.

Though she knew Escala was in Dunwell, Junel didn't fly there. Instead, she veered north, slicing through the afternoon sky toward a quiet village tucked beyond the hills, her wings beating with purpose.

After two hours, Junel reached a modest cottage tucked along the edge of the woods near a quiet village. She knocked twice. There was a brief pause, and the door creaked open. A few quiet words passed between her and the woman who answered, and Junel was quickly ushered inside.

An hour passed, and the door opened. An elderly elven woman emerged wearing a simple green traveling dress and black cloak. Her silver hair was pulled up in a bun.

Behind her, a middle-aged woman stepped out, dressed in plain traveling clothes—dark trousers, a white tunic, and a blue shawl drawn around her shoulders. Her walking staff tapped against the step as she descended.

Her long white hair flowed freely down her back, and her blue eyes mirrored the shawl's hue.

While no longer young, age had touched her gently, and she was still beautiful with grace and dignity. Pulling the shawl tight around her head, she stepped onto the road beside the elven woman and began the long walk south toward Dunwell, and the daughter she hadn't seen in nineteen years.

Chapter 87

A udrey seethed at the sight of Escala outside The Stag the next morning, sparring with Roedyn as if nothing had happened.

How had she survived being stabbed? Her friends were too powerful and always too close. Audrey needed to separate Escala from her friends—to isolate her, somewhere their healing spells and protection couldn't reach. But how?

She needed Morvena's counsel.

Audrey turned sharply and flew toward the crossing she'd used the night before only to find it gone. That was strange. Crossings were timed, yes, but this one should've still been open.

Irritated, she flew to another known location two hours away. It too was gone. What was happening?

She could draw blood and use a blood crossing, but she hated doing that, it was messy and painful.

No, she wasn't going to do that. Besides, how could she know if that would work if regular crossings weren't? That was too risky.

She knew that Morvena was often at Blackthorn Tower, and the tower was a few days away. She would travel there and wait for Morvena, waiting was what she had to do for her mother to arrive, and she needed answers. Still frustrated she had failed to kill Escala, she flew east.

Chapter 88

I n the Court of Dreams, Victor, his soul now fully inhabiting the Void demon, laughed as the creature stalked through the halls. Its glowing eyes swept across towers, gardens, and statues, and he vowed to destroy it all.

Fey guards rushed to stop him, but he delighted in the chaos. He hurled vases like stones, ripped pillars from their bases, and flung them like javelins. It was crude but satisfying to watch the fey scatter; it was like swatting mosquitoes. Sometimes he even hit one, and that was even more satisfying.

"Where is Rowan?" he bellowed.

Desperate defenders unleashed spells, but they vanished on impact, absorbed into the creature's body as if swallowed by the Void.

Meanwhile, in the garden, the crossing had grown into a roaring tunnel of wind. Like the Boxes of Kestrel, which once dragged dragons into the Void, this rift now siphoned the very essence of the fey realm. What once held ancient beauty was being pulled, piece by piece, into oblivion.

Victor's demon strode toward the throne and touched it with a single smoky claw. Instantly, tendrils of shadow coiled over the seat like spider-vines, spreading fast. In seconds, the throne was cocooned, then it dissolved like flesh rotting from bone, drawn into the demon's core and lost forever.

He didn't yet have the strength to do that to everything. But destroying Rowan's seat of power? That felt glorious.

Victor poured more Void magic through the crossing, widening the tear even further. The wind twisted, deepened, shifting into the first pull of an apocalyptic whirlpool. Both realms, mortal and fey, now edged toward a single truth:

The Void would take everything. But Victor didn't care, he was drunk on power and fueled by vengeance.

Now the Void demon lashed out with spells of its own. Void bolts streaked across the court like arcs of midnight flame. Fey who had thought themselves safe were struck and instantly wrapped in tendrils of unraveling magic, black, clinging webs of Void. Their faces twisted in horror. Their screams echoed for seconds before they were consumed.

Rowan heard those screams. If Junel failed to find Escala, the Court of Dreams would fall, and all fey would be lost.

Far across the palace, Morvena witnessed the devastation. This was not what had been promised. She flew to a crossing, but it was gone! She flew to another one, and it was gone as well.

"Blast you, Victor," she growled. "What have you done?"

Without hesitation, she flew to her secret chamber, the one where she performed her blood crossings. She drew her blade. She would return to Blackthorn Tower, and she would stop him.

Chapter 89

"Folks, do you remember about a year ago, when the ground shook, and the sky burned green?"

Several heads nod.

"Well, I'm getting close to that part of the story. See, Victor had been drawing too much power from the Void, that dark nothingness between realms.

"Now, I know a few of you have been hitting the dragonfire brandy tonight, and we all know what that does to a person's sense of plot continuity. So let me recap Victor's actions, because they're a lot to keep straight. And remember, I did warn you outside that if you've taken one too many knocks to the skull, you might struggle to follow along."

The room laughs. I take a long drink and press on.

"First, Victor tore open a crossing between the material plane and the fey realm, a jagged, unnatural breach, one that would never close. Using a tremendous amount of Void magic, only possible with the Crown of Dreams, he split his soul and inhabited two Void demons. Then, using one of the Void demons, he ripped that crossing even larger and crawled through into the Court of Dreams and began attacking the fey, trying to kill Rowan.

"Victor marched through the Court of Dreams, destroying it piece by piece, which took a significant amount of Void magic. And every time he channeled more Void magic through the Crown of Dreams, the tear in the crossing grew wider.

"The rip had created a hole into the Void, through which a funnel—like a great tornado—now stretched into both realms through the crossing, dragging everything into the Void and oblivion.

"At first, the tear in the veil was small, its pull into the Void no more than a gentle breeze. But as more Void magic surged through the rip, the funnel's force swelled to the strength of a summer squall, spawning dust devils that twisted through the gardens and Victor's sanctum, whipping papers and paintings into the air, toppling chairs, and forcing smaller trees to bow under the wind.

"But Victor didn't notice or care.

"And that burning green sky we all remember from a year ago? That was the Void tornado; a whirlpool of realms tearing open, dragging the material world toward oblivion.

"But that was only the beginning, and I am getting ahead of myself. We have some incredibly important parts of the story left to tell, and the next part involves that table right there."

I point to a table right in front of the stage, the one with Tully and his mangy owl.

"Tully, sir," I say, "I hope you're nice to your mother, are you?"

Tully nods and says, "Of course, my mother is a witch, and I wouldn't want to be turned into a june bug." There are laughs.

"Precisely," I say. "We should all be nice to our mothers, after all, they're usually the only ones we can count on to show up to our performances... or buy our books. But if you remember, Escala told us she hated her real mother, and what happened at that very table was... well, painful. Let me explain."

It had been about a week since Escala's appeal—that was how we measured time: before and after Escala's appeal. Not the best thing, I know, but with her, milestones were important. It had also been five days since she was nearly murdered, and we figured it was a better use of pre- and post-appeal as a milestone than pre- and post-attempted murder.

The constable had no leads as no one had seen that woman before, and we never saw her again. The woman's punch made sense—Escala could be mouthy—but a delayed knife attack? That was far too much for a bar insult, and the risk to the woman just didn't fit the insult. Roedyn, of course, stayed on high alert. He wasn't going to let that happen again.

Escala, for her part, didn't drink like that again. I think she was embarrassed. A little shaken, too. But she tried to find a rhythm. With no quest to chase, she threw herself into training with Roedyn and riding with Harper in the afternoons. She fished with Sticky. Spent evenings at The Stag with us.

She went to the market now and then, but never alone. Roedyn wouldn't allow it. And with no money, she didn't buy anything. I think she just wanted to walk and talk with him. Truthfully, I think he wanted that too.

As for me, I went back to my usual rotation, playing and performing for all of you.

That night, two women visited The Stag. One was an attractive middle-aged woman with long, white hair and blue eyes—eyes that were very much like Escala's.

She was dressed in a traveling outfit and accompanied by an elderly elven woman with silver hair pulled into a bun.

Escala didn't notice; she was laughing with Sticky, who was telling us a story about a talking raccoon named Crimson Jack Acorn III and his foolish attempts to win the heart of another raccoon named Ava Honeysuckle that lived in Silverstand Forest. Some night I will tell you of these exploits—he is quite a character.

Harper saw the two women staring at Escala and elbowed Roedyn, who looked over, his hand moving to his dagger. Escala kept laughing at Sticky's story, not noting the new arrivals.

The blue-eyed woman cautiously walked to the table, trailed by the elderly elf. Escala still hadn't noticed her when the woman said, "Escala."

Escala turned at the sound of her name. Their eyes met; uncertainty flickered between them. Escala glanced at the elderly elven woman standing behind her, a face that stirred something faint and familiar. But her gaze returned to the one who had spoken.

"How do you know me?"

The white-haired woman swallowed hard. "Escala, I'm your mother."

The warmth in Escala's face vanished. The tavern, the noise, the people—none of it existed anymore.

Escala stood, fists clenched so tightly her knuckles whitened. Roedyn gripped the edge of the table, half-rising, unsure whether to intervene. Harper slid her chair back a little just in case. Sticky blinked, silent and still.

"You've got to be kidding me," Escala said, her voice quieter than I expected—and somehow more dangerous for it.

Teresa took a tentative step toward her, arms out, a fragile smile breaking through the nerves.

Then Escala erupted. "You don't get to do this!" Her voice full of fury. "You don't get to show up after leaving me behind—leaving me alone—and expect a hug! You're not my mother!" She stumbled backward, bumping into me, knocking her chair to the floor with a clatter that echoed through the Stag.

Teresa froze, shock written across her face. She half-turned toward the elderly elf beside her, confusion and surprise on her face, and, looking for help, she turned back to Escala.

"Escala, I…" she began, her voice breaking.

"Who even are you?" Escala's voice trembled, but it was clear she'd already decided the answer.

Pain flashed across Teresa's face. "I'm your mother. Your real mother."

The two locked eyes—Escala's blazing, Teresa's pleading. Teresa searched her daughter's face for something familiar, something forgiving.

It wasn't there.

Escala gave a bitter laugh, hollow and sharp. "No, you're not. My mother is *dead*. My mother *never* existed. My mother didn't come back for me—because she wasn't real."

Teresa's lips parted as if to speak, but her voice faltered. Tears welled in her eyes. "Escala, I wanted to come back for you. I never stopped thinking about you. I never—"

"Don't." Escala's voice sliced through the air. "You don't get to stand here and tell me you wanted to come back. You had a choice, and you left."

No one moved. The only sound was the soft crackle of the fire and Escala's ragged breathing, like she'd been holding her pain for years and it was finally tearing its way out.

We all shifted awkwardly, exchanging glances.

Teresa drew a steadying breath, blinking away tears. "I came here to give you a message," she said softly. "So if you won't listen to me, please—listen to Junel." She nodded to the elderly elf beside her.

And then Escala's breath caught. She recognized the woman—it was Junel, her Junel, now in elf form. Memories spilled through her all at once—bright, vivid, and overwhelming: Junel's voice, her laughter, and the lullabies that once soothed her to sleep.

"Junel?" Escala managed, her voice breaking. She pushed her chair aside and rushed forward. "Is that really you? Tell me—if it's you, what was my favorite song as a child?"

The elderly elf smiled gently. "It was 'Sleep, My Starling,'" she said, and began to sing the opening verse:

Sleep, my starling, soft and small,
Moonlight's weaving through the hall.
Crickets hum and branches sway—
Your dreams are safe in the courts of fey.

Escala's eyes filled. She threw her arms around Junel, hugging her tight, laughing and sobbing all at once. "It's you," she whispered. "It's really you."

Roedyn stood, uncertain what any of this meant. The others watched in silence.

Junel held her just as tightly. They stayed like that for a long moment. But when Escala finally looked up, her gaze met Teresa's and joy turned to something else. The older woman stood apart, her expression a portrait of love and unbearable regret.

Escala's arms fell to her sides. "Why are you here?" she asked in an almost annoyed tone.

Teresa stepped forward, voice breaking. "I want to explain everything. But there isn't time. Junel brought me because your father—Rowan—is in terrible danger. The Court of Dreams is under attack."

"Danger?" Escala's tone hardened. "From whom?"

Junel's face grew grim. "Victor Graves. He blames your father for taking Teresa, the woman he believed was his, into the fey realm. He's consumed by vengeance, and with the Crown of Dreams in his hands, he's trying to kill Rowan Winter and tear the Court apart. He's striking now, Escala! Rowan sent me to find you both and bring you to Blackthorn Tower. It may already be too late."

Escala frowned. "How did you find me?"

Junel sighed. "Starling, you've never been good at keeping secrets. At your appeal, you told the entire court your companions' names, the city you were staying in, even the name of this inn."

Escala frowned. "Then how did you find her?" She pointed at Teresa—not her mother, not yet.

Junel hesitated, glancing at Teresa.

"When I left the court, I told Junel I was returning to Marlow. I begged Junel to bring me word of you whenever she could," Teresa said. "It was the only way I could bear to leave, knowing someone I trusted was watching over you."

"And I did bring her letters," Junel said quietly. "Whenever I could."

Escala stared between them, disbelief breaking into hurt. "Why didn't you ever tell me?" She asked, turning to Junel, her voice cracking. "You knew how often I crossed! You knew where she was! I could have found her, Junel, I could have seen her!"

"I promised your mother I wouldn't," Junel whispered.

Escala turned on Teresa, her voice shaking with pain. "You kept me from knowing you. You left me, and then you hid from me."

Escala's fists were clenched. "*I hate you*!" she screamed.

"Escala," Junel said softly. "I know you're angry, but if we're going to save the Court of Dreams, we have to move now."

What happened next shocked all of us.

Escala sank back into her chair, her anger shifting.

"I don't care," she said dismissively.

Junel's mouth fell open.

Roedyn stared, speechless.

"They *lied* to me," Escala said, her voice still tight with tension. "The Court of Dreams sent me chasing after imaginary boulders. That lie nearly killed my friends. Why should I risk my life for a court that never wanted me?" She folded her arms tightly.

Harper said nothing, though I saw her jaw tighten, maybe to hold back a sharp remark.

Roedyn leaned forward. "Escala, whatever you decide… I'll stand by you."

Sticky nodded. "Me too."

"I don't need help," she snapped. "Because I'm going."

Junel eased into the seat across from her and reached for Escala's hands. After a moment, Escala let her.

"Escala," Junel whispered, "your father may seem cold. He struggles to speak his heart, but he risked everything to keep you from the Wane. He begged the judges not to punish you for the same reason the Oath exists, because of love. Because of Teresa."

Teresa stood silently, tears in her eyes.

Junel continued, her voice urgent. "Rowan still loves her, even now. But Morvena has turned the court against him. She's convinced them that mortals disrupt the True Cycle, that love between realms can only bring ruin. He cannot lead while he clings to that love."

Teresa moved forward, her voice weaker. "Escala... you were just a baby, too young to remember, but the rumors were cruel. They said I'd bewitched Rowan. They said you were a mistake. If I'd stayed, you both would've been cast out. You would've grown up shunned, hunted. I couldn't let that happen."

Her words quivered, uneven and raw. "So I made the hardest choice a mother can make. I left. I thought that if I left, the court would stop whispering, and you'd have a chance to belong. I told myself you wouldn't remember me. But I remembered you every single day. I missed your smile, your first steps, every moment that should've been mine."

She took a shaking breath. "If I could change it, I would. Maybe I'd still make the same choice, but I'd have told Junel to let you know where I was. To let you visit. You deserved that much."

Teresa lifted her gaze, tears streaking down her cheeks. "I don't expect you to forgive me. I just need you to know, I did it because I loved you. I wanted you to have the life I couldn't give. I wanted you to be the fey princess you were destined to be, and if I stayed, you would have been exiled."

Escala's eyes welled with tears, but they were full of anger too. "Do you want to know what that life was like?" Her voice was jagged. "The fey children laughed at me. Called me a half-breed. Said I was so ugly that even my own mother abandoned me. I heard every rumor, every filthy joke about you—about me. I toughened up because I had to. I built a wall so high that nothing could reach me."

Her voice cracked again. "And when they stopped hurting me, it wasn't because I healed. It was because I stopped feeling. You made me stop feeling."

Teresa's face broke, as though the words themselves struck her.

Escala turned away, her voice quiet but filled with grief. "You don't exist. I don't have a mother."

Teresa's lips parted, but no sound came.

Escala's voice hardened. "The court lied to me. Victor Graves used that lie—used me—to recover the Crown of Dreams from a dragon that nearly killed all my friends and me." She looked over at us.

"And now he's destroying the very world that cast me out. So tell me, why should I save it?"

Looking at me, she said, "Wigfrith, you know everything. I don't know what to do. I need help."

"Well now," I said. "You're not the first to be lied to and won't be the last. I once spent six moons chasing a unicorn—turned out to be a painted goat with a stick tied to its head. I thought I was on a divine quest—I wasn't.

"You want advice? Grieve your gullibility—but don't wallow in it. Wear your mistake like a battle scar, not a noose. You can't undo what you were tricked into, but as sure as the sky's blue, you can decide what happens next.

"Now, I'm a storyteller," I said, "so my advice is going to sound like a storyteller's perspective. Every tale carries betrayal, loss, mistakes; that's what gives it weight. But the stories worth remembering, the ones told around fires for years, they all share one thing."

I leaned forward, voice dropping low. "They're the stories where someone had every reason to walk away... and didn't. Where someone stared down the ending everyone expected and said, 'No. That's not how this tale ends.'

"Your court lied to you when they sent you chasing a fake boulder. You have every reason to turn your back on all of them. But Victor Graves used that lie, used you, to get the crown and strike back at your father. So yes, you should be angry. I would be angry and feel betrayed too if I was in your place.

"But if you show up anyway to help them, after the court's lies, after they spat on your appeal, that'll roar louder than any speech or logbook ever could. It'll tell them you're harder than a boulder, that you don't crawl off to sulk or vanish when they turn their backs. It'll prove you still care about them, not because they deserve it, but because you choose to care. And that'll mark you as something greater than all of them, because you refused to break when they expect you to."

I lifted my mug, toasting the thought. "I would ask you, Escala, do you want your story to end with you sitting here in The Stag, feeling sorry for yourself or do you want to be the pixie who rewrites the ending?"

She looked at me; her words locked behind her teeth. Teresa and Junel exchanged a glance but stayed quiet.

Sticky rubbed the top of his round head and said, "The Court of Dreams is still your family, Escala. You may be angry with them and rightfully so, but remember when we talked about me protecting the wolves? Even though they bite, they are still part of my nature family, and I still protect them. Family's not about being perfect, it's about not giving up. Your court bit you, but aren't they still your family?"

What Sticky said was a lot more to the point than my rambling, and while he eats bugs, and I don't, he did make a very good argument.

477

Roedyn placed his hand on Escala's shoulder. His voice was firm. "Escala, you know how I feel about oaths. Before your appeal, you told me you couldn't speak your heart because doing so would break an oath."

He dropped to one knee beside her, meeting her gaze. "I need to ask you, what will you do with your oath when your court needs you most?"

Escala locked eyes with him for a long moment. Her eyes sparkled with something—thanks, perhaps—or was it something more?

Minutes slipped by in silence as Escala sat there, turning over every word in her mind. I watched the faint crease form between her brows, the little scrunch of her nose she always made when the world stopped making sense. Then, slowly, something in her shifted, the tension melted from her face, and a quiet calm settled over her, like the moment after a storm when the air finally remembers how to breathe.

She stood and said to Sticky, "Can you call some flying friends? I've got an oath to keep."

Junel's smile broke through, and Teresa let out a breath. They were both happy Escala had chosen to help but fear lingered, sharp and unspoken, that her decision might have come too late.

Harper cracked her knuckles. "Thank the gods. I was about to lose my mind with all this sitting around. I call dibs on sticking a dagger in Victor's eye."

Chapter 90

We grabbed our gear as Sticky, in eagle form, flew off to find us mounts. Hours later, he returned with seven giant eagles, one for each of us. What a sight we were as we took to the skies, heading straight for Blackthorn Tower.

The eagles were fast, blazing fast, and somehow Sticky had arranged relays ahead of us. Birds, squirrels, and whatever else he talked to had already spread the word. Fresh eagles were waiting at intervals along our path. Sticky explained that the birds used their songs to carry messages across miles, some calls could be heard half a mile away, allowing news to leapfrog ahead of us long before we arrived.

We swapped to fresh mounts mid-flight and covered in a single day what would've taken ten on foot or five by horse.

As we approached Blackthorn Tower, it was clear something was terribly wrong. A swirling dark green vortex had erupted from its top tower, spiraling upward like a whirlpool stretching into the heavens. You couldn't see through it—it was like a black hole carved out of Valla. Sticky shouted for us to stay clear, but the thing kept growing, swelling with fury. We had to get inside the tower and stop Victor before it expanded beyond the point where even he could contain it.

The eagles dropped us into the inner courtyard, where four men-at-arms attacked immediately. I'll spare you the details—we took them down fast, without a scratch. Weapons drawn and nerves sharp, we pressed into the tower.

Meanwhile, the dark green whirlpool above the tower continued to grow.

Chapter 91

As we neared the entrance to Blackthorn Tower's inner chambers, the twister from the main spire roared—its dark green and black funnel stretching ever higher into Valla's darkening sky. I've faced horrors before—a red dragon comes to mind—but nothing chills your spine like watching the sky twist itself into a raging storm with an infernal void yawning at its center. Druids say tornadoes are living rage, and I believe them. This one was worse, an unnatural storm, born of Void magic and madness.

Harper had to shout over the screaming wind. "We have to stop that thing!"

We all agreed and hurried inside the tower. The instant we stepped inside, the stench hit. It was very acidic and burnt the back of my throat. Sticky crouched low, nose twitching as he pressed two fingers to the floor, muttering something in words I didn't understand.

"That's Void rot," he said grimly.

Sniffing again, he added, "The vortex originates from the upper level, but its source, its power, is deep below, in the dungeons."

We discussed further and remembered that Victor's chambers were on the upper floors of the tower, but Sticky said that he could sense tremendous magic energy from the dungeon below the tower.

"We're going to have to split up!" Roedyn shouted, his voice raised to cut through the constant, powerful wind whipping through the halls. It wasn't blowing exactly, instead it was pulling, dragging air and dust upward toward the upper levels and Victor's sanctum.

Roedyn, ever the commander, split us into two teams. He, Junel, Teresa, and Escala would ascend the tower, aiming to reach Victor and stop him. Harper, Sticky, and I would descend into the tower's lower levels, hunting the Void source Sticky had detected and finding a way to shut it down; that was our only hope of halting the monstrous void tornadoes.

My group headed down a stone staircase, descending only one level. From the darkness below, orcs barreled up the stairs, their tusks bared, rusted blades raised. Behind them, hobgoblins in scorched armor barked orders.

Harper met them head-on, ducking beneath an ax swing and sliding forward in a flash. Her daggers danced—one slashed an orc's thigh, the other buried itself in its gut. She spun before it dropped, driving her heel into another's knee with a sickening crack.

Sticky bellowed, his body contorting into the monstrous shape of a seven-foot raptor, lean and powerful, with scythe-like claws and jaws bristling with needle-sharp teeth. This was perhaps one of the most vicious forms I had seen Sticky use.

Sticky pounced with terrifying speed, a blur of claws and muscle. The first orc's chest split open in a single, savage swipe, blood spraying across the stone. The second spun to flee, but Sticky lunged, his jaws crunching through vertebrae with a wet snap before flinging the limp corpse down the stairs like discarded meat. I took a step back, hopeful that Sticky could remember that I was a friend.

The third orc raised a wooden shield in desperation, but Sticky leapt, both clawed feet smashing into it with a splintering crack, pinning the orc hard against the stone wall. A heartbeat later, his talons ripped through armor and flesh, prying open the ribcage in a gush of gore.

He looked up from the carnage, his muzzle slick with blood and speckled with torn flesh. A slow, predatory grin split his crimson-stained snout as he rasped, voice low and edged with menace, "Never upset a druid."

"You'll get no argument from me," I said, relieved that he remembered who I was.

As Sticky tore into the three orcs, I dropped to one knee and struck a dissonant chord on my lute. The strings screamed, and a wave of force burst outward, knocking spears and a dagger off course just before they could find Harper's spine.

A hobgoblin lunged at me, snarling. I twisted aside, swinging my lute like a club. The crack of wood on bone was sharp and wet, teeth flying as he staggered backward—straight into Sticky's waiting claws. With a sickening rip, talons punched through his chest and burst out the other side, crimson spraying in a fine mist.

Harper, moving with cold precision, vaulted onto a fallen foe's chest. In one smooth motion, she flung a dagger across the chaos, burying it deep in a hobgoblin commander's throat mid war cry. The gurgle that followed was short-lived—the cry died with him.

The fight hadn't lasted long, but it left its mark—blood spattered across the steps, chests heaving, and the acrid stench of sweat and Void rot thick in the air. There was no time to celebrate. The pulling wind was intensifying, the funnel above swelling with a hungry roar. We kept running down the stairs, driven by desperation to find the source before it consumed everything.

Chapter 92

Back in the Court of Dreams, the Void demon, filled with Victor's fractured soul, stood where the Star Gallery had once stood, maniacally laughter. He was unmaking the court itself.

Just as the Void twister in Blackthorn Tower was building in power and would eventually pull everything into the Void, a second funnel formed in the Court of Dreams at the Vorrash Totem. It grew larger by the moment, a jagged vortex spearing skyward and staining the heavens black and sickly green as it tore the air apart. Fey trees bent until they splintered; branches and blossoms were torn into the swirling dark, pulled toward the Void funnel that originated at the crude crossing near the Vorrash Totem.

A nixie screamed, caught in its viscous pull, and clutched desperately at the curve of a carved archway. The Void demon raised a clawed hand and unleashed a bolt of pure shadow, which struck the nixie in the chest—there was a crack of blue light, a burst of energy, and the nixie was gone. He was dead.

"I will destroy everything you love!" the Void demon bellowed across the planes.

The tear in the crossing yawned wider, its shrieking roar joined by a relentless pull that threatened to devour the Court of Dreams itself—trees ripped from their roots, crystal spires cracking apart, fey dragged screaming toward the Void.

The Void demon stood amidst the chaos, arms raised high in triumph, its horrific face twisted in crazed delight, its laughter ringing out.

Back in the upper floors of Blackthorn Tower, Escala, Teresa, Roedyn, and Junel stormed up the velvet stairs toward Victor's sanctum. Halfway up, six armored men-at-arms burst from hidden alcoves. Escala snapped her shield into place—just as Roedyn had drilled her—and dropped into a defensive stance.

"No one touches the faerie!" she barked, then added, "Or my friends." Her sword flared as she met the first attacker head on.

Roedyn dropped to one knee, loosing two arrows that slammed into the throats of warriors above. One toppled over the balcony, smashing onto marble below. But more enemies poured in from above and below.

"They're trying to box us in!" he snarled, letting the bow fall and drawing twin short swords.

A soldier lunged and Roedyn spun him into the wall and drove his blades home. Another swung from above, and Roedyn ducked low, just in time, slashed his hamstring, and shoved him, screaming, into his comrades.

Behind them, Teresa dented a soldier's helmet with her staff but took a mailed fist to the chest, which knocked her into the banister.

"Teresa!" Junel cried—only to be slammed by a shield, sending her tumbling down the steps.

Three men blocked Roedyn's path.

"Get to them!" Escala shouted, hurling herself down the stairs, her shield smashing aside a spear thrust.

Roedyn vaulted toward the upper trio, wrenched a sword away, and smashed the pommel into its wielder's nose. Blood sprayed. Roedyn kicked one down the stairs and skewered another mid-leap. He fought like a man possessed. "You're not getting through me," he growled.

Escala reached Junel as three armored men closed on her. She ducked the first man's blade, slashed his knee, and rammed both swords into his ribs. The second warrior clipped her shoulder, but she rolled past and kicked his knee. As he fell, she swept her sword across his throat.

The third charged as an arrow whistled past Escala's head and buried itself in the man's chest. Roedyn landed a heartbeat later, boot smashing into his spine.

Together, they stood over the fallen foes; Escala's chest heaving and Roedyn bleeding from a gash above his brow.

A final warrior slipped past Roedyn, charging at Teresa. His blade swept down in a killing arc. Without thinking, Escala slid between them, her shield catching the strike with a clang of steel on steel. From the ground, she drove her sword up beneath his chin, the point bursting from the back of his neck in a spray of crimson. Blood drenched her armor and Teresa's white tunic as the man collapsed atop them.

Roedyn hauled the corpse aside while Escala pulled Teresa to her feet. Their eyes met—nineteen years of silence burning between them.

Roedyn steadied Junel, his face streaked with blood, but there was no time to rest; the roar above still pounded through the stairwell.

They charged upward, reaching a heavy door. The hinges were straining, and the wood bowed as if being pulled inward. From widening cracks bled a shrieking gust, whipping their cloaks and reeking of Void magic. The floor shuddered, dust sifting from the walls. Beyond the barrier, the vortex raged—wild and hungry. Roedyn pounded a fist against the warped wood.

"Victor!" he shouted. "Open up!" His voice was nearly lost in the wind's howl.

Inside, Victor turned toward the shouts. He knew that voice—that was the ranger with Escala. They had returned, and that was not good news. If they breached the sanctum now, everything would unravel—he needed more time, more Void magic.

"Jonathan," he yelled over the winds, "keep them out!"

The towering zombie turned, joints cracking, and threw his decayed bulk against the inside of the bowing door, bracing it with both arms and his rotting body.

Satisfied the zombie could hold them at bay, Victor raised his hands toward the Void and began the incantation, the Crown of Dreams pulsing darkly with power. The first Spirit Split had succeeded—this second would be even easier.

The wind howled louder, and Victor's eyes gleamed as more Void magic flooded into the crown.

Outside the door, Roedyn turned back, hair whipping in the wind.

"It's locked," he barked. "We're bashing this thing down." Together, he and Escala took turns pounding it, kicking it, slamming it with their shoulders, and hacking at it with their blades.

The door groaned and splintered, but Jonathan's brute strength held it shut.

After what felt like an eternity, Victor completed the casting of the Spirit Split. A second Void demon—identical to the nightmare already ravaging the Court of Dreams—materialized beside him in the sanctum. Its crimson eyes glowed with Victor's sentience, and its muscular frame stretched and flexed, poised to kill Roedyn if Jonathan failed to hold the door.

Now that Victor had split his soul, his human body stood motionless beside the demon, just as Tully told us all earlier this evening, Victor's mortal body stood rigid; eyes wide with something beyond madness. Though paralyzed, he was fully awake, his mind stretched like wire across two vessels: two Void demons—one here in the sanctum, the other tearing through the Court of Dreams. Both Void demons throbbed with his soul—both were him.

The tower groaned under the relentless pull of the vortex spilling from the crossing in Victor's sanctum. Cracks split the floor, and overhead, the ceiling gave a final shudder before detonating upward, as if the world itself had split open. The fully unleashed Void funnel screamed like a dying star, shooting skyward through the tower. Books, chairs, stones—entire shelves—were ripped free and swallowed by the churning maw above.

Outside, Roedyn let out a battle cry and threw himself backward for momentum. One final kick—BOOM—and the door exploded inward. Wood splinters and shadow shards burst through the chamber, slamming zombie Jonathan over a table and pinning him beneath a fallen bookcase, limbs splayed.

Escala and the others were pulled into the room, if you could even call it a room now. It was a storm: wind shrieked, gravity warped, and the vortex, sourced at the crossing in the center, whirled faster, dragging everything toward it.

Teresa screamed as her feet left the ground—sliding across the tile toward the Void.

Escala hurled herself after her, catching Teresa's wrist, her heels grinding against the floor, arms shaking while she held on.

Roedyn took a step and staggered as a tome the size of a paving stone struck his head with a thud. He growled in pain but didn't fall.

"Get back!" he roared, planting himself like a pillar as the wind tore at his cloak. Junel crouched behind him, holding tight to a solid oak table, shielding her eyes as shards of glowing glass ripped past.

Potion vials burst against walls. Alchemical fire spun in the air, lighting the storm in throbbing orange arcs. Smoke clouded the room. Shadows screamed from the walls. At the center of it all stood Victor Graves, motionless, wearing the Crown of Dreams, black lightning veining from it like living strands of darkness.

Beside him loomed a creature of nightmares—seven feet tall, forged of shadow, its torso a tangle of writhing forms. Muscles rippled like coiled cables beneath skin that wasn't skin at all, but smoke stitched with bone. Its eyes shone a deep, infernal red. Horns curled like a war crown. And its horrific smile, slow, deliberate, held the cruel patience of death itself.

The vortex shrieked louder, its pull intensifying until we had to brace against walls and cling to anything with weight to keep from being engulfed by that ravenous eye of nothingness. And yet, Victor was standing untouched, as was the Void demon beside him. Somehow, neither was being pulled toward the vortex.

The Void demon turned to us, and in Victor's voice, it bellowed, "You made it just in time to witness the end of everything!"

Chapter 93

Morvena stormed through the halls toward her secret blood crossing chamber, knife clutched tight in her white-knuckled grip. Fury burned in her chest, how dare Victor Graves double-cross her?

She had played the game, manipulated the pieces, and trusted him just enough to let her guard down. Now she felt like a fool, and no one made Morvena Winter a fool and lived to laugh about it.

She didn't know if Rowan was dead, but the vision of vanishing court buildings and fey being killed by the rampaging Void demon told her enough: the Court of Dreams was collapsing, and Victor had lied to her. He had never meant just to kill Rowan; he had used her to eliminate, no, exterminate, all faeries.

If she didn't act now, there would be nothing left for her to rule!

"I'll kill you myself, Victor!" Morvena screamed. Her ceremonial knife flashed in her hand as she tore it from her belt. She pressed the blade to her wrist, steel biting skin, when a hand clamped around her arm.

She twisted violently, hair whipping loose from its jeweled pins. "Who dares?"

Rowan stood before her, eyes wide, disbelief hollowing his voice. "What have you done? You've betrayed the court!"

Morvena's eyes flared with white fire as she ripped her arm free, the knife trembling in her grip as her aura flared. "Me? Betray the court? Don't you dare use that word with me, you sanctimonious coward."

Her voice rose, sharp and venomous. "This is on you, Rowan! All of it! Your precious half-breed daughter handed one of the most powerful relics in existence to a madman who's spent two decades dreaming of skinning you alive! And why? Because you couldn't keep your hands off mortals and stole the woman he loved away from him and brought her to the Court of Dreams!"

She stalked closer, her every word striking like a whip. "*You* meddled with the True Cycle because *you* thought *you* were special—*you* thought *you* could rewrite the True Cycle because *your* love was special. *You* were warned by the council, by me, by every soul in this stormed court! But no, Lord Rowan Winter *always* knows best. *Always* meddling, *always* moralizing, *always* playing the lovesick fool. And now? *You've* doomed us all with your pathetic need to love a human woman!"

The knife gleamed as she lifted it again. "This is *exactly* why the Oath exists to keep weak, sentimental idiots like you from poisoning the balance. Escala should've been given the Wane and forgotten, but no, *you* sent her *back* to Valla with a quest that *forced* her to tell everyone she was fey, and now it's *your* daughter that has delivered our doom straight into Victor's hands!"

Her voice rose to a shriek, shaking with rage.

She advanced on Rowan, the knife flashing in her hand, her eyes glinting like shattered glass. "Your love of a mortal woman will be the death of us, Rowan. You ruin everything you touch."

With a savage motion, she slashed her arm. Blood spilled across the mirror's surface, sizzling as it touched the glass. The reflection warped, swirling like molten silver.

"You don't deserve to rule," she spat, face inches from his. "You're a fraud in a crown, a lovesick hypocrite with delusions of nobility. When I return, and I *will* return, I'll see your name stricken from every Hall of Dreams. You'll be nothing but a stain on the history you ruined."

The mirror pulsed with unstable light, the surface bulging like liquid metal. Her magic burned the air; the scent of iron and ozone rolled through the chamber.

"Go!" she screamed, cutting deeper, blood running down her wrist. "Go face the monster *you* made, you arrogant, mortal-besotted fool. Go clean up the wreckage of your own storming heart."

The mirror erupted, the chamber shaking with its roar. The light swallowed her, devouring her words and form in a storm of crimson and silver.

And then silence.

Her words were not wrong. Escala had delivered the crown to Victor Graves, the very man still burning with rage over a wound Rowan had dealt him nearly two decades earlier. It was a wound born of defiance, daring to love the same woman Victor once adored, and later bringing about the death of Victor's son at the hands of a fey. That act alone had shattered the True Cycle, twisting fate itself. And

Morvena, for all her venom, had been right about one thing; everything that followed had begun with love.

A cold clarity slid through him: Morvena's fury might be true. If Rowan hadn't stepped in to sway the court's judgment, Escala might have faced the Wane... she wouldn't have been on the material plane and caught in Victor's schemes. Now, every fey life hung in the balance because he had meddled and put his daughter above the Court of Dreams.

Now, all the fey were going to die. And it was his fault.

Without another word, Rowan turned and launched into the air, his wings cutting through the smoke above the broken courts. He couldn't let the others fight alone.

If this was the end, he would meet it beside them.

It was the least he could do. It was all he could do.

Chapter 94

———————

Harper, Sticky, and I pushed deeper into the tower, battling strange, twisted creatures as we raced toward the source of the tremors that shook the very stone. The wind roared like a hurricane, rising with every step. We had to shout to be heard over its fury.

"In here!" Sticky called, bounding ahead.

We burst into a vast, circular chamber. At its center loomed a massive black orb, resting in an ivory base atop a two-foot pedestal. It wasn't night-black, it was void-black— an absence of everything. It devoured the light around it, warping the air with its presence.

Three thick streams of crackling energy surged upward from the orb, vanishing into the tower's heights. The hum it emitted was deafening, so intense I had to cover my ears.

"This has to be the source!" I shouted.

Harper, reckless as ever, hurled a dagger and it clanged off, useless. Snarling, she drew her rapier and lunged, but the instant her blade touched the orb, it erupted in a blinding explosion. The chamber convulsed as a shockwave of raw energy tore through the air, hurling her like a rag doll into the stone wall. The impact reverberated through the room, dust and shards raining down as her head struck with a sickening crack.

"Harper!" I ran to her side, dropping to my knees. "Are you alright?"

She was dazed but managed a shaky thumbs-up.

Thinking fast, I yanked my lute around and slammed a single, resonant chord, desperate to match the orb's unnatural frequency.

For a breathless instant, it worked, the tones fell into alignment. My lute shuddered violently in my hands, the strings vibrating with a hungry, predatory hum, as though the orb meant to wrench it from my grip. I stopped, heart hammering, terrified the next pull would take my arm with it.

Across the chamber, Sticky prowled around the pedestal, scanning the stairwell, then the walls. His form swelled in a sudden surge, fur bursting forth as his frame thickened and grew until a towering woolly mammoth stood where he'd been, larger than the one he'd unleashed against Myrrh.

The mammoth's tusks, massive, sweeping arcs of ivory, were made for this.

Sticky lowered his head, slid both tusks beneath the orb, and with one earth-shaking heave, tore it free of the pedestal.

The instant it left its cradle, the chamber detonated with a deafening blast, the beams of Void energy that had been tearing upward through the tower were violently severed. Power roared through Sticky, his massive body lit from within, every bone in his frame flashing white as the world around us plunged into perfect, suffocating darkness. For a heartbeat, I was certain we'd been dragged into the Void.

Then, just as suddenly, the darkness broke. Torchlight flared to life along the walls, and in the center of the room

497

stood the woolly mammoth, immense, steaming, and bearing the obsidian orb between his colossal tusks.

I turned to Harper. She just shook her head, wide-eyed.

"Unreal," she breathed.

But even with the power streams gone, and the Void magic no longer flowing from the orb into the tower above, we could still feel the entire structure shudder, the air tugging at us as if we were sliding down a steep slope.

We hadn't stopped the vortex!

Sticky grunted and began walking slowly, the massive orb balanced between his tusks, heading for the stairs. We followed in silence, one step behind the mammoth and whatever fate lay above.

Chapter 95

Escala and Roedyn steadied themselves as Junel and Teresa clasped heavy furniture, each struggling against the pull of the growing vortex. Victor's chamber had become pure chaos, wind and force tearing at everything not anchored down.

Shielding her eyes from the twisting debris, Escala squinted into the maelstrom. Through the storm of flying objects, she saw the Void demon standing beside Victor. Victor was motionless, his body unnaturally rigid as he stood with the Crown of Dreams still resting on his brow.

Above him, suspended in the air, a whirling scrying cloud showing a view into the Court of Dreams. Escala looked into the cloud, and her heart stopped.

The cloud twisted into horror, as another Void demon, identical to the one before her, tore the Court of Dreams apart. It rampaged through the palace, tearing down crystalline towers, uprooting aged trees, shattering fountains, and reducing archways to dust.

A black void tornado, just like the one in this chamber, roared in the distance, devouring everything in its path within the court. Trees splintered and vanished into the spinning maw, rubble swirled upward like toys in a storm, and the funnel only grew more frenzied with every heartbeat. Giant oaks leaned toward it, roots screaming in the soil as they fought to hold fast. Royal court buildings tilted, glass and stone shrieking as they strained.

Within the maelstrom, she saw familiar faces, sprites, pixies, and nixies, all hurling themselves into the fight with wild, hopeless defiance. Wings blurred, spells flared, and blades flashed, but it was like striking at smoke.

The Void demon swooped through them as though they were nothing but mist, its claws rending light and life alike. Bolts of black magic ripped from its hands, scorching the air and slamming into fey bodies. Every blow burst in a sharp flare of blue energy, shredding flesh and light alike, until nothing remained but drifting ash, spiraling away on the wind. Their screams were snatched, drowned in the roar of the Void.

And then, there was Rowan, her father, her daddy.

He stood at the front lines, shouting for the fey to fall back. His voice was tight, his eyes set with determination. The wind battered him, and she could see how hard he fought not to be pulled into the Void. Next to him, fey warriors cast spell after spell, holding their ground so the women and children could escape the palace. But Escala could see it in his face—he knew they were losing.

"No!" Junel's cry cut through the roar.

Before anyone could react, Junel let go of the rubble she held, shrank down to pixie size, and her wings appeared. She darted across the chamber in a blur, heading straight for Victor's motionless body.

The Void demon guarding Victor saw her and moved faster, and it quickly blocked her path, swinging its huge arm. The blow hit Junel in mid-air, knocking her aside like an insect. She crashed into the far wall, the sound echoing through the chamber. Stunned, her tiny pixie body began to slide helplessly toward the vortex in the center of the room.

Teresa lunged forward, grabbed Junel's wrist, and dug in her heels. Her muscles strained as the Void's wind tried to pull the older pixie away.

The Void demon turned to them and laughed. But the sound that echoed in the chamber wasn't its own. It was Victor's laugh, but colder, twisted, and inhuman. He was mocking them, speaking through the Void.

Roedyn fired an arrow, but as soon as it left the bow, the vortex grabbed it, pulling it into the roaring funnel and making it vanish.

Escala pushed forward against the howling wind, grabbing onto furniture and railings to keep her balance. "Victor!" she yelled. "We have what you want! You can stop this! We're here, Teresa is here!"

The Void demon turned away from her and moved toward Roedyn with a slow, hunting walk. Victor's body stayed still, the Crown of Dreams still on his head. In the swirling scrying cloud, Escala saw her father fighting the same huge Void demon. Rowan looked small and bright, standing up to the giant shadow. He wasn't winning, but he was giving them time.

Rowan darted through the air, waving his sword to keep the demon's focus on him so the others could escape the chaos swallowing the Court of Dreams. The whole realm was being pulled into the Void, a storm that was both hurricane and tornado, just like the disaster now ripping through Blackthorn Tower.

Bolts of light and fire shot from his hands, burning against the demon's skin before fading away as if swallowed. "You will not take my people," he shouted. "Not while I still breathe."

501

The Void demon rushed at him, its huge hands swinging, but Rowan dodged and drove his sword deep into its shoulder. "Victor, I mean you no harm. Retreat and live!" he shouted, pulling his blade free as black vapor poured from the wound. The attack barely slowed the demon, and its flesh healed in seconds.

Spells from other faeries shot past him—ice arrows and lightning bolts—but the Void demon absorbed them all. Only Rowan's sword left a mark, its silver runes glowing each time it hit.

The Void demon struck back with thunderous force. One swing shattered a marble pillar, sending shards flying across the court. Sprites fled in panic. A sprite was caught mid-air by the demon and immediately tore off its wings. The sprite cried out in pain before the monster crushed its skull, bursting it in a flash of blue energy.

"Fall back!" Rowan ordered, his voice firm. "Everyone, return to Fern Hollow. That's a royal command."

Still, Rowan moved forward, his wings glowing as he thrust his sword at the demon's heart. "You will not take this court," he said, his voice calm. "Dreamlight crafted it, and dreams endure." He sent a wave of white fire from his free hand, covering the demon's chest in bright light. For a moment, the entire court shone with moonlight. But when the light faded, the Void demon was unharmed. Was it truly unstoppable?

Victor's laughter rolled like thunder through the shattered palace. "I will destroy you and your kind!"

Rowan hovered before the Void demon, wings tattered, and proclaimed, "Then let the Court of Dreams fall with honor. I am its Lord, and you shall not pass through me unbloodied."

The Void demon swung again, its blow missing Rowan by inches but striking the faerie soldiers behind him, flinging them into the storm. Escala pressed closer to the scrying cloud, her heart hammering. Alone now, her father hovered, his scorched armor and fading magic unable to unbend his posture or lower his raised sword.

Through the clouds, she saw him glance once toward the horizon toward her, though he could not know she was watching. "If I fall," he said, talking to the other fey warriors, his voice shaky, "tell Escala that her father fell protecting the Court of Dreams. It is the duty of House Winter."

"Teresa!" the Void demon yelled at her. "Your fey lover, Rowan, took everything from me. Now, I destroy everything he loves!"

Void energy surged, and the rip in the crossing between the mortal realm and the fey tore wider, the wound stretching with a sound like rending metal. The beams of power streaming from the dragonbone gems into the Crown of Dreams suddenly faltered and vanished.

It didn't matter now; the crown had done its work. There was a gaping breach between worlds, and Void magic poured through unhindered, fueling the tornado's ravenous pull. Victor no longer needed the obsidian orb as a buffer; the Void was here, its raw power at his fingertips. Without the orb's restraint, there was nothing to keep him from drawing too much... or from being swallowed whole.

Paralyzed in body but alive in mind, Victor surrendered to the Void. The crown flared, and the Void demon answered, feeding him more power than any mortal should

503

touch. The chamber groaned like a dying beast. A fresh rupture split the veil, and the vortex doubled in size, shrieking with fury. Furniture spun through the air, walls cracked, and the floor shuddered. Everyone clung to whatever they could find or risked being dragged into the screaming maw.

Roedyn charged, hands outstretched, reaching for the fallen crown. But the Void demon moved with terrifying speed and it backhanded Roedyn across the room and lunged after him, claws poised to finish the job. Roedyn scrambled to his feet, drawing his longsword just in time to block a brutal swipe. He staggered back, slashing wildly, forced to retreat while clutching at stone pillars and heavy benches to keep from being pulled into the storm.

Victor's rigid body remained unmoving, but his voice rose above the chaos. He saw his zombie son finally free himself from the rubble and regain his feet.

"Jonathan... my son... you've waited for this. Take your revenge."

Escala turned at the sound of his voice and froze.

The zombie was wrenching itself free from the fallen bookcase that had pinned it down when she saw him. Jonathan. The boy she had once kissed was now lurching toward her, a hideous, half-rotted corpse with hollow, lifeless eyes.

She staggered back in horror, fingers clawing for the edge of a heavy desk as the wind howled and tore at her, the screaming vortex behind her roaring with a pull that promised only death. One hand clutched her shield, the other clung to the desk—leaving no chance to draw her sword without risking being ripped from the floor. And even if she freed it…could she strike him? She had already caused his first death; could she bring herself to be responsible for his death a second time?

In the Court of Dreams, the Void demon had finally grabbed Rowan, and its clawed hand closed around Rowan's throat, crushing him in its grip. Through the scrying mist, Escala could hear her father's strangled gasp, see the faint glow of his wings faltering against the darkness. Her pulse roared in her ears, and she wanted to scream, to reach through the cloud, but all she could do was watch as she clung to the desk with one arm and held her shield to ward off the attacks of the zombie.

Across the room, Roedyn saw it too. He slammed his sword against his shield, sparks bursting from the impact, trying to draw the attention of the Void demon.

The Void demon turned, its massive head pivoting toward Roedyn.

Roedyn braced his feet against the stone, the wind tearing at his cloak and hair. "You want a soul to drag into the dark?" he shouted. "Then try to take mine!"

Roedyn charged—shield raised, sword gleaming. Each step was a battle against the storm, his body leaning into the gale, his boots sliding over the fractured floor. He drove forward, teeth bared, shouting above the chaos.

Roedyn swung with everything he had, cleaving through the storm's blur to strike at the Void demon's shadowed flank. His blade met something solid and sank deep. A shriek tore from the Void demon's shoulder, and black blood sprayed from the gash, thick, tar-like, and hissing where it touched stone. The wound pulsed, seething with Void energy that crackled around its edges like burning smoke. Roedyn stumbled from the backlash but steadied himself, eyes locked on the injury.

"You can bleed," he snarled through clenched teeth.

In the scrying cloud, Escala saw her father hovering below the Void demon, his armor cracked, his crown of light flickering. He turned his gaze upward, not at the monster, but beyond it, as if looking toward her through the magic that linked them.

The zombie swung an arm at Escala, but she dove over the ruined table, catching herself with one hand as the vortex threatened to drag her in. She braced her feet, held up her shield to block the next blow, and managed to put some space between them. The zombie, undeterred, lumbered after her with slow, relentless purpose.

Across the room, Teresa clung to a stone table, still holding on to Junel as the tiny faerie had nearly been pulled into the Void. They gripped each other, trembling, their strength slipping.

"Victor, please!" Teresa cried, clutching the edge of the stone table, her knuckles bone-white. The storm outside shrieked through the shattered windows, whipping her hair into her face. "Spare him, if there's any shred of mercy left in you, take me instead. I'll come back, just don't hurt him."

Victor's laugh was jagged and cruel. "Mercy? You beg for him? For this coward who couldn't even keep you safe at the Court of Dreams?" His tone twisted into mockery. "The same Rowan who let your precious fey friends turn their backs on you, the same ones who mocked you, and drove you out of the Court of Dreams? And when you left, Teresa… did he chase after you? Did your noble king fight for your love?"

Teresa's face drained of color. "How… how could you know that?"

Victor smiled, a slow, poisonous curl of his lips. "I know everything. And the truth is you were a fool to believe in him, just as you were a fool to believe in the fey."

"Faeries are horrible creatures!" he screamed. His arm snapped out, pointing at Escala, his eyes burning. "And your daughter is one of them. She killed my son."

The words slammed into the chamber like a hammer blow.

Teresa recoiled as if struck. "No…" she whispered. "No, not Escala… not my daughter…" Tears blurred her eyes as she turned toward her. "Tell me it isn't true. Tell me you didn't—"

Escala shook her head furiously in wild denial as the zombie drew closer. "No! Mother, no! It wasn't me, I swear." The words broke against the roar of the surrounding storm. Before she could say more, the zombie lunged, its massive, club-like arms crashing down. She barely had time to raise her shield; the blow slammed into it with a bone-rattling crack, driving her back a step.

Victor's grin widened, savoring the chaos he'd unleashed. "Deny it all you want. The blood still stains the fey. Do you remember Teresa? The wolf totem I gave you long ago, the one you abandoned in the Court of Dreams? That totem was used to summon the beast that tore my boy apart."

Teresa looked shaken as she held onto to Junel and the stone table, trembling, her face ashen, tears streaking her cheeks. "Escala… my Escala… How could anyone say you… killed a child?" Her voice broke, half a sob. "My daughter… my little girl…"

Victor roared with laughter.

Escala shook her head violently, panic and desperation evident in her face as she raised her shield to block another crushing blow. "Mother, please, you have to believe me. It wasn't me!" The zombie's weight forced her backward; she stumbled, crashing against the shattered table. Splinters dug into her palms as she clung to the edge, the pull of the vortex growing stronger, dragging at her hair and cloak, threatening to pull her into the Void.

Rowan's voice cut through the chaos, strangled by the demon's grip. "Teresa, listen!" His wings beat frantically, his body twisting against the claw at his throat. "Escala speaks the truth. Our daughter is no murderer." His words were fierce. "Do not let him poison you; don't let him turn you against her." So he could hear what was happening in this sanctum through the scrying cloud!

Victor snarled, his face twisting with rage. "Pathetic. Even now, you cling to her. You're too blind to see the fey for what they are, parasites! They tricked you, Teresa. They ruined you. And now your daughter carries on their vile ways." His eyes burned as he twisted the knife deeper. "All the fey must die."

Teresa gasped, torn apart, her gaze flicking helplessly between Victor, Escala, and Rowan. Teresa's heart tore in three directions at once.

The zombie's blows came harder now, each one jarring Escala's bones and sending tremors through her weakening arms. Her shield shuddered under the relentless assault, metal screeching against rotted flesh and brute force. She couldn't keep this up much longer. One more hit, maybe two, and her arms would give out. Then the shield would fall, and so would she.

Her voice shook with panic as she shouted over the noise, "It wasn't me! It was never me! The wolf killed his son, but I didn't have the wolf totem. I've never seen it before."

As the zombie moved closer, Escala grabbed for her sword. Her shield arm struggled to hold on to the bookcase while the wind tried to pull her away. She knew she couldn't hold on much longer. If she didn't act now, she would be either ripped apart or pulled into the roaring vortex and lost to the Void.

Teresa looked at her daughter, caught between incredulity and a small hope that Escala wasn't the monster Victor claimed. "Escala…" she shouted over the noise. "Do you swear this is true?"

Escala's voice shook but stayed steady. "I swear it, Mother. On the Dream itself."

She fumbled nervously with her sword, uncertain whether to hold her shield, cling to the bookcase, or meet her mother's pleading eyes as she tried to prove her innocence. Her hesitation cost her. She barely saw the zombie's fist before it slammed into her flank.

CRACK. The blow knocked the air from her lungs in a flash of pain, and she was thrown sideways into a fallen chair. Her sword dropped from her hand and was swept away by the vortex into the darkness. Gasping and dazed, she grabbed at the broken wall, her fingers searching for a hold as the Void pulled at her. Stars flashed in her vision as she struggled to breathe, every single nerve on fire.

"Escala!" Teresa screamed, straining against the wind.

The vortex became louder, wind rushing through the room like a wild storm. Escala's vision clouded. Her sword, the one Roedyn had chosen for her, was gone. Only her shield was left.

She grimaced and pushed herself up, one shaky hand on the floor as she grabbed the battered shield near her. It was stuck under debris; otherwise, it would have been pulled into the void. Her side ached, but she made herself stand.

The zombie lurched forward again.

Teeth clenched, Escala raised the shield.

The zombie lunged at Escala, its heavy arms crashing down with enough force to break bones. She blocked the attack with her shield, bracing herself as her whole body shook under the weight. The blow was too strong, and she fell to her knees. Her sides throbbed.

The storm kept growing in strength, making the walls shake. Dust fell from the ceiling as the floor cracked under the zombie's feet. Victor's magic saturated the air, smelling of sulfur and ash.

The zombie roared, sensing Escala's weakness. It lifted both arms and slammed them down in a brutal double strike, which shook the floor. The blow tore her shield from her hands, sending it clanking across the stone. The force shot through her arm and almost knocked her onto her back.

Gasping, Escala scrambled away, moving around the heavy bookcase as splinters fell from the impact. Pain shot through her arm, but she gritted her teeth and stared up at the towering corpse.

The zombie moved toward Escala, each step heavy. She knew the next hit would knock her out and send her into the Void.

Victor looked toward the scrying cloud, where Rowan's struggle was still flickering in the dusky light. "That thing took everything from me—my son, my love, my purpose. He acts so virtuously, but his hands are as stained as any warlord's. And now I will show you my revenge."

"Victor, please!" Teresa cried, tears streaming down her face. "Spare him. If there's any humanity left in you, let him go." She took a step forward, trembling but resolute. "You once loved me. If any part of that remains, show it now. Let him live."

Victor's hand rose, fingers curling into a fist. Inside the scrying cloud, Rowan screamed, the sound muffled and distant, like a soul being crushed under the weight of a collapsing world. His wings faltered; the surrounding light dimmed.

"Father!" Escala shouted, and she quickly crawled around the zombie as she tried to retrieve the shield.

The zombie swung, its massive arm slicing through the air, and Escala barely ducked in time, but she couldn't grab the shield. The blow passed just inches above her head, close enough for her to feel the rush of air and the stink of decay.

Victor's expression twitched, just for an instant, and the mask of fury faltered. Looking at Teresa, he said, "He took you from me. And his daughter took my son. He has taken everything from me, and I am going to take everything from him!"

Teresa was crying, tears streaming down her face. "I am begging you, Victor."

His form flickered between man and shadow, grief and rage, until the two were indistinguishable. "You would beg for him?" he whispered. "You would plead for that thief of my dreams?"

Escala's tears ran freely now. "He's my father!" she cried, her voice raw and desperate. "Please, Victor, if there's any part of you that remembers love, let him go."

Escala had to duck another wild swing from the zombie.

Victor's eyes flickered, pain, memory, doubt, before the red light consumed them once more. Then his voice dropped to a whisper, full of cold finality. "Love is the lie that made me weak."

He raised his hand toward the Crown of Dreams.

"No!" Escala screamed, reaching toward it. "Please, don't!"

But Victor did not stop.

The Crown of Dreams ignited, pulsing with raw power as the vortex above erupted, expanding like a living storm. Shadows bent toward him, drawn to the surge of Void magic he summoned with a furious cry.

Victor raised one hand skyward, veins glowing with obsidian light.

The demon obeyed.

It hoisted Rowan higher, claws tightening around his throat. Black lightning danced along its fingers, searing the air with every crackle. Rowan's wings beat frantically, then faltered, fluttering, failing, his limbs trembling against the grip of pure darkness.

Victor's voice rang out, filling the sanctum with triumph. "Rowan, look. Your daughter and Teresa are watching. I want them to see you break. You stole Teresa from me, and now she will watch you die."

"No! Stop, Victor!" Teresa cried, clutching the table, her voice raw with anguish.

"Silence!" Victor bellowed.

The Void demon's claws ignited with jagged black fire. A bolt of lightning ripped across the chamber, striking Teresa in the shoulder and hurling her into the rubble. She screamed in agony, clutching the smoking wound, eyes wide with pain and terror. And in that look, frozen between agony and disbelief, Escala saw it: the dawning horror that there would be no reasoning with him.

A violent gust from the vortex tore through the chamber, shattering a display case that held a dozen magical wands. The impact sent a massive glass globe, previously perched on a stone pedestal, toppling onto its side. It struck the floor with a thunderous crack, splintering into jagged shards. But the core of the globe, a dense crystalline sphere, remained intact and rolled toward the vortex, becoming wedged in the rubble just short of the swirling maw.

Wands spun through the air like shooting stars, caught in the pull of the howling Void. Roedyn lunged, snatching one as it whipped past his head. The moment he grabbed it, the wand erupted in unstable light, sparks leaping up his arm in chaotic arcs.

The zombie loomed over Escala, raising its arms for another killing blow. Roedyn aimed the wand, and a burst of wild energy exploded from its tip, slamming into the zombie's chest and sending it staggering backward in a spray of rot and smoke.

"Get away from her!" Roedyn shouted, firing again. The next blast tore through the air, searing across the zombie's shoulder and bursting against the wall in a shower of molten stone. The recoil nearly tore the wand from his grasp.

He tried to steady it for a third shot, but the magic writhed and sparked, fighting him. Before he could release it, the Void demon lashed out, its leg snapping forward, a metal spike bursting from its foot like a blade. It drove deep into Roedyn's thigh, dropping him to one knee with a cry of pain. As the wand clattered across the floor, still crackling wildly, it slipped from his grasp. The roaring vortex instantly sucked the wand in and exploded it into a brilliant display of a dozen distinct colors.

"Roedyn!" Escala cried as the zombie swung again, and she slid beneath its blow.

Roedyn grimaced, one hand clutching his leg, but he managed a faint, breathless grin.

The Void Demon straightened to its full height, towering over him, its shadow stretching long across the shattered stone.

The zombie lashed out again and again. Escala ducked under the blow, but she was exhausted and nearly lost her grip on the bookcase, her boots skidding toward the screaming vortex. She caught the edge just in time, the pull of the wind tearing at her cloak. As she tried to steady herself, the zombie connected, its heavy fist slamming into her ribs for the second time. The impact drove the air from her lungs in a ragged gasp, and she nearly lost consciousness.

"Escala!" Roedyn shouted.

Tears blurred her vision, but she clung to the bookcase, refusing to let go. Somehow, she rolled clear of the next strike, landing hard on her side. When she looked up, her gaze caught the scrying cloud swirling above the vortex, and what she saw froze her blood.

Through the shifting mist, the Void Demon's claws closed around Rowan's throat. He struggled for breath, words rasping through crushed lungs. "Teresa… my dearest… I love you… Forgive me…"

Victor sneered, his face twisted with hate. "Pathetic."

The demon's fist slammed into Rowan's chest with a sickening crack, the sound echoing through both realms. Blood burst from his mouth, his body going limp in its grip.

Still, somehow, Rowan stirred. His eyes found the scrying cloud and found Escala. His voice was faint, wet with blood. "Escala… my starling…" He coughed, shuddered, then whispered, "Stay curious… that's what it means to be fey. I love you."

Victor's only answer was another brutal punch.

Teresa screamed. Her voice broke on the sound, raw and wordless.

Roedyn, bleeding and gasping, tried to remain conscious. "You… won't… touch them," he choked out.

Escala trembled, gasping as pain seared through her ribs. Each breath stabbed like fire, every heartbeat a hammer blow inside her chest. The zombie loomed closer, its shadow stretching across her; the next strike would end her. She could feel it. One more hit and her body would give out.

Chapter 96

E scala clung to the bookcase, the horrific zombie poised to bring his devastatingly strong arms down upon her, a blow that would likely knock her unconscious and hurl her straight into the void maelstrom, killing her.

Her mind spun through the chaos, the screaming wind, the thunder of collapsing stone, but somewhere inside that storm, a single memory cut through. The kiss. The one that had set everything in motion. Her blue eyes narrowed. Gripping the edge of the bookcase, she reached for a nearby dragonbone stand for balance and staggered to her feet.

Staring into the rotting face of the zombie, she yelled, "I am Escala Winter from the Court of Dreams. I've changed your life forever—with a kiss."

Jonathan, the zombie, staggered. Something deep inside twitched.

"You will never know a kiss like a faerie's!"

She took a step toward him, still holding on to the dragonbone stand as the vortex tried to yank her into the Void.

Roedyn still grappled with the Void demon, their forms locked in an eerie dance, blood oozing from his leg wound.

On the scrying cloud, Escala saw Rowan go limp, blood streaming from his face in the other Void demon's grasp.

Her eyes blurred with tears as she reached out a trembling hand toward the zombie.

Jonathan had stopped attacking and was staring at her, transfixed. "You'll search all of Valla, but no kiss will ever satisfy," she said, batting her eyes seductively. The zombie had taken two steps toward her; they were close enough to kiss. "You'll always think of me... and you'll want to please me when I call."

She fought the urge to recoil from his rotting body. If she didn't do this, her father would die.

Steeling her resolve, she reached up and brushed her hand against his decomposed cheek, swallowing her revulsion. "Do you remember?" she yelled as sweetly as she could.

The zombie slowly nodded.

Tears streamed down her cheeks. "Then serve me, please me... and stop him."

She pointed at Victor's rigid body standing on the left side of the chamber, wearing the Crown of Dreams, which pulsed with void magic as the roaring maelstrom grew in the center of the room.

Jonathan turned in the direction she was pointing.

Victor's eyes widened—but it was too late.

Jonathan lumbered toward Victor with surprising speed.

The Void demon broke off from Roedyn, scrambling to intercept the zombie, but it was too late.

Jonathan raised a massive arm and struck his father with a single, brutal backhand, knocking his father's rigid body to the floor.

As Victor's body fell, the Crown of Dreams flew from Victor's head and clattered across the stone, but amazingly, it was not pulled into the Void Tornado roaring in the room.

Without the crown's power, Victor's stiff, lifeless body began to slide toward the vortex, pulled by its relentless force.

The Void demon lunged, desperate, and caught hold of Victor's leg just as his arm vanished into the swirling Void. The Void demon now lay prone, holding onto Victor's prone body.

But Roedyn and Escala were already in motion. They tore into the Void demon's back with sword and steel, forcing it to stay down, even though their weapons were not harming it.

"Stop it now!" the Void demon shrieked with rage and fear.

But the creature was down, pinned to the floor, clinging desperately to Victor's body with one hand as the pull of the Void dragged at them both. His host form was rigid, unable to move, leaving the demon helpless as blow after blow rained down upon its back.

Maybe, just maybe, we had a chance.

We were wrong.

Chapter 97

Sticky, Harper, and I were slowly making our way up from the dungeon. Sticky, still in the massive form of a woolly mammoth, carried the obsidian orb carefully between his tusks. The trip up the stairs was madness. The whole tower shook like a ship in a storm, groaning under the strain. Debris and loose furniture slid across the floors below as we climbed, and everything that wasn't nailed down was being dragged upward—books, paintings, shattered armor, even the weapons of the guards and monsters we'd already killed. They whirled through the air, clattering off the walls and ricocheting down the stairwell.

We ducked and dodged as best we could. A spear flew past my head, followed by a rain of loose parchment and a broken spear that clanged off the railing. Every step upward was a fight against the pull of the wind, our boots slipping on the trembling stairs. Harper shouted something I couldn't hear over the roar, her hair whipping wildly around her face.

At the top of the stairs, a massive chandelier swung violently from the ceiling. It was an enormous thing—iron-framed, hung with glass and crystal drops, and still studded with melted stubs of candles. Each swing made the entire structure groan, scattering shards of wax and glass as it scraped the cracked stone ceiling. One bad swing, and it would come down hard enough to crush half the hall.

We grabbed the railings as the building rocked again, the vibration rattling through our bones. Dust rained from above, and a jagged crack split the wall beside us. I glanced at Harper, our eyes locking in the same silent question—what in all the hells was happening? Were Escala and Roedyn still alive? Teresa? Junel?

We didn't have time to ask. We had to move.

Harper and I raced upward, fighting the pull of the wind. Sticky was still two flights below—mammoths move slowly—and though his heavy steps shook the stairs, we were already bursting into the upper hall.

But we were no help. The moment we arrived, the air hit us like a physical blow. We both lunged for the doorway's edges, gripping the stone for dear life to keep from being torn into the roaring vortex ahead.

The Void demon in the sanctum knew it was losing. Escala and Roedyn struck with fury, raining blow after blow on the massive hand that gripped Victor's leg. The Void demon's grip was weakening, and Victor's body would soon be torn from its grasp—and dragged into the vortex.

Sensing the inevitable, the Void demon on the Court of Dreams—still clutching Rowan by the throat—threw back its head and screamed, drawing every eye toward the swirling scrying cloud.

"The vortex will take me!" it roared. "And it cannot be stopped. The rip in the veil is growing—soon it will devour the material plane and the fey realm."

It laughed, a deep, hideous rumble, as Rowan's limp body dangled from its massive arm like a child's discarded doll. In the swirling cloud behind him, the Court of Dreams lay in ruins: once-proud towers shattered, ancient trees torn from the earth, and above it all a black-and-green tornado churned, devouring the sky.

Across the realm, fey—pixies, nixies, even proud satyrs—were wrenched screaming into the black storm, clawing at trees, fences, and crumbling walls. We clung just as desperately, gripping pillars, stone tables, and jagged fragments of the tower to keep from being torn away.

The end had begun—the Void would take everything.

The Void demon threw its head back and laughed— wild, manic, triumphant.

"But before the end," it snarled, "I want you to see that I kept my promise... I've killed Rowan Winter."

In a flash, steel erupted from Rowan's chest—driven clean through by the demon's other arm, the blade bursting forward in a spray of blood.

Rowan screamed—a raw, agonizing sound as his wings shot upward, stiff with pain. His entire body arched, trembling in midair.

Then, with a deafening crack, a burst of brilliant blue energy erupted from his chest, and his small, battered pixie frame slumped lifelessly forward, still impaled on the blade.

Teresa screamed, "Rowan!"

"Daddy!" cried Escala.

In the sanctum, the Void demon laughed and released Victor's leg and the sorcerer was instantly wrenched into the vortex, his body torn apart in a savage spiral of wind and debris.

The instant he vanished, both Void demons screamed, their forms unraveling into ash that was whipped away into the same abyss. They were, after all, each one half of Victor's soul. As his body left the material plane, his soul was pulled back together, quite violently, I might add; his spirit spell over and his Void demons no more.

Without Victor's magic to bind it, the zombie crumpled into a lifeless heap, only to be seized moments later by the roaring maelstrom, dragged into the Void along with everything else.

Amazingly, the Crown of Dreams—its glow extinguished—remained where it lay on the sanctum floor. Yet the crown didn't so much as move.

All around it, hurricane-force winds tore at stone and flesh alike, dragging everything toward the crossing and up into the ravenous vortex.

Chapter 98

Escala and Teresa remained paralyzed, clinging to furniture and walls to resist the roaring vortex, their hearts broken by their recent experience.

Victor's monstrous Void demon form had struck down Rowan, her father, and Teresa's only true love, tearing him from them. For Escala, it was unthinkable; for Teresa, it was the death of the one soul she had ever loved. Shock and grief tore through their bodies like lightning.

But there was no time to mourn. The crossing ripped wider; the chamber collapsed into a maelstrom of shrieking wind and splintering stone. Teresa held onto the stone table, sobbing, her knuckles turning white as the vortex jerked at her hair and cloak.

The enormous chandelier in the hallway, already swinging in the wild wind, fell away from the ceiling with a loud screech. It shot through the doorway in a swirl of glass, candles, and chain, casting shards everywhere. The rush of air almost pulled Harper and me from the doorframes where we held on, our fingers gripping tight. The chandelier spun by, its chain whipping until a sharp hook snagged the black leather bag at Harper's waist. She cried out as the strap went tight, with the force dragging her sideways toward the roaring vortex.

"Cut the bag off!" I shouted, voice nearly overwhelmed by the storm.

Harper looked at me. She held the doorframe with one hand, pulled out her knife with the other, and cut the bag's strap. The black bag flew off and headed toward the whirling vortex in the center of the room. It caught on the remains of a broken glass globe, just as the chandelier broke apart into countless pieces that disappeared into the blackness.

Harper slumped against the doorjamb, breathing hard, with glass dust in her hair. I held on tighter next to her. The wind kept howling, and we both shook, but we were still alive.

Just moments before, Escala had been standing, but now she was thrown to the ground and dragged across the floor. She scrambled until she grabbed the leg of a large bookcase, holding on as the Void tried to pull her away.

The floor moved under us, tilting sharply as everything slid toward the growing funnel. Books, chairs, and pieces of brick flew, hitting the walls before disappearing into the black hole below. The noise was overwhelming: stone scraping on stone; air whistling through cracks.

"What's happening?!" Roedyn shouted, holding himself balanced against the rush, his voice almost drowned out by the storm.

Escala's face showed her fear and grief. "It's a crossing!" she yelled. "It's tearing open the realms and pulling everything into the Void!"

But the storm kept getting stronger.

At last, Sticky climbed the stairs and entered the room, carrying the big obsidian orb in his tusks. My heart beat fast with hope as Sticky, the huge woolly mammoth, fought against the pull and moved toward the screaming tear in the air.

The crossing had grown to five feet wide, a swirl of black and green filling the room. Our only hope was the black obsidian orb, heavy and full of power, that might be able to close the gap between the realms and end this chaos.

I believed it. Gods help me, I really did. I was sure this black obsidian orb would close the hole, just like a cork in a keg.

Sticky, fighting the wind, swung his colossal head and threw the orb into the vortex. It hit the center and disappeared with a loud WHOOMPH, then exploded. For a moment, I thought it had worked. But it wasn't like sealing a bottle with a cork. It was more like the cork blasting off a champagne bottle.

The noise sounded like the sky itself was tearing apart. A shockwave blasted through the room, knocking down walls, dropping heavy stones, and pulling the ceiling up into the roaring funnel. The mammoth was thrown backward like a rag doll, hit the doorframe, and Sticky turned back into his small, fragile frog form. Roedyn and Escala were tossed to opposite sides of the room, crashing into stone and broken wood as the wind shrieked. The Void tried to pull them away, dragging debris past their faces, but somehow, both managed to grab onto something solid before they were swept away.

Sticky, dazed, and helpless, he was caught by the pull right away. Before I could think, I jumped forward, grabbed Sticky's slippery foot at the last second, and wrapped my other arm around the doorframe. The vortex pulled at us both so hard that every muscle in my arms burned.

I prayed no one would ever know how close I came to being ripped apart, stretched between worlds like some poor soul drawn and quartered.

I clung there, holding Sticky. The truth sank in; the black obsidian orb had failed to plug the hole. Our last chance, one last desperate gamble, was gone. We had staked everything on that orb, and it had done nothing.

The maelstrom was growing. and the crossing widened, pulling harder with every inch, its hunger infinite. Around me, oak beams in the Blackthorn tower snapped, and bricks were wrenched loose like teeth. Escala clung to a towering bookcase as the wall itself buckled beneath her.

My chest went cold. This wasn't like facing Myrrh, where at least there had been a creature to face, a chance to fight, a way to bluff, or a chance to run for survival. This was worse. This was despair.

This wasn't just the end for us; this was the end of everything.

The vortex would keep expanding until it swallowed the material plane, and its twin devoured the fey. Nothing left, nothing anywhere, just the endless hunger of the Void.

We had failed, and Valla would pay for it.

This was the end.

Escala turned to us, clinging with one trembling hand, hair whipping wildly.

A silent apology passed between us.

We had done everything.

Fought until nothing was left.

And still… it hadn't been enough.

What we once dismissed as a fool's errand, Escala's quest to remove the boulders from the True Cycle, had been terrifyingly real.

The Crown of Dreams, in Victor Graves's hands, was the boulder.

And now it was tearing apart everything: the fey realm and the material plane, both on the brink of annihilation.

Escala had tried to remove it, but it was too late.

She lay on the floor, holding on to a bookcase with one hand and looking at each of us, tears streaking her face, but her bright, unbreakable blue eyes were calm.

I clung to the door, my small legs straining against the pull, while I held Sticky's foot.

The wind howled, but in that moment, there was only her.

Escala met my gaze first.

Her hair whipped around her face, her hand slipping from the splintering bookcase. She gave me the softest smile and yelled, "Thank you for knowing everything."

She turned to Harper, who was gripping the opposite frame from me, her boots dragging across the floor. Escala yelled, "Stab something in the eye for me." Harper's face twisted in confusion, and then she nodded, not really understanding.

Escala's gaze locked on Teresa, who was clinging desperately to a pillar as the Void vortex tried to pull everything through the crossing. Escala's lips curved into a trembling smile. She shouted, her voice breaking against the wind: "Mom, I know what you did for me. Thank you."

Teresa's eyes widened, mouth forming words lost to the gale.

Then Escala turned to Junel, who braced her small frame against the pull of the vortex. "Tell them," she cried, her voice cracking, "tell them I did this for the Court of Dreams!"

Finally, her eyes found Roedyn. He was across the room, clinging to a cracked pillar, his face and leg covered in blood. Their eyes locked, and so much passed between them in that glance.

She thought of their early mornings, just the two of them, training in silence broken only by his calm, patient voice correcting her stance. She remembered how he always insisted on taking first watch, even when he was clearly exhausted. The quiet nights beside the fire, where he polished her blade not because it needed it, but because it gave his hands something to do while they talked.

She remembered the day at the circus. The broken smile he wore when she first dragged him through the tents, the way he resisted her joy until she caught him laughing, really laughing, for the first time. She'd held onto that sound ever since, like it was proof that magic still worked.

And the days after, foraging for carrots and berries together, talking late into the night. His humble confidence. The way he made her feel safe.

She remembered the night under the stars after the fire had burned low. They'd danced clumsily at first, laughing, his boots too heavy, his steps unsure until she showed him how to follow the rhythm in her hands. His fingers had lingered longer on her waist than they needed to. She hadn't minded.

She remembered the battle with Myrrh, the dragon's wings beating like war drums, hurling a storm of gold and ash through the cavern. The heat had been suffocating; the chaos was overwhelming. They should have died that day. All of them.

He had faced the ancient dragon not with a sword, but with a bluff wrapped in truth, holding out a fake relic and speaking in calm riddles, never breaking his oath, never wavering in his bravery. She had watched in breathless awe, her heart pounding, not just with fear, but with something else. That was the moment she saw him fully. That was the moment she understood her feelings.

He was trustworthy, steady, and loyal. He was brave and cared deeply for her and the things she valued, putting his own interests on hold for her. And she had loved him for it.

She never said the words, and she never could. The Oath stood between them like a wall that neither courage nor love could break. It bound her to duty, and duty demanded silence.

But in her heart, she knew the truth.

This was the man she wanted beside her.

If not for the Oath, she might have told him earlier.

If not for the Oath, they might have had a forever.

But the vow that kept them apart could not keep her from loving him.

Love turned into memory, painful and vivid, the last part of him she had left.

The bookcase she held groaned; it was being ripped from the wall, and it started to slide toward the crossing, pulling her closer to her death.

Tears glistened on her cheeks as she smiled the most radiant smile I had ever seen.

"I love you, Roedyn Hammerfell," she yelled into the storm.

"Escala, no!" he roared, voice raw. "Don't you dare let go! Hold on!"

But she was already letting go.

Roedyn screamed, "Stop! No!"

The maelstrom claimed her in an instant. One moment, Escala was clinging to the floor. The next, the maelstrom ripped her upward and dragged her straight into the crossing, the raw wound between worlds where fey and flesh alike bled into the endless Void.

We screamed her name, but the storm stole our voices.

Her body hit the threshold and slammed against the jagged seam of reality itself. Her screams of pain pierced through the sound of the screaming torrent. Her limbs twisted, flailing as debris tore into her petite frame. It was merciless, as though the realms themselves had chosen to destroy her.

And then right at the heart of the crossing, she was ripped apart. In that instant, her form shattered, torn violently asunder, a blue flame burst from her, like the last spark of a dying star. For a breathless heartbeat, that quiet blue light pushed back the darkness. And then it was gone.

So was she.

The maelstrom howled louder than ever, the chamber convulsing as though the world itself was splitting apart. We clung on, desperate, certain the next pull would take us all.

And then the vortex vanished.

The chamber went still.

Chapter 99

R oedyn dropped to his knees, his sobs so raw and gut-wrenching they broke my heart.

For a man of his strength, his iron stoicism… hells, for someone as stoic and stubborn as he could be, I'd never imagined he was capable of crying. But he did, and honestly? I didn't blame him.

We had just watched our friend, a unique person we had spent months with, be ripped apart before our very eyes. It's an image I will never shake and one I almost hesitated to share with you tonight. But I swore I would tell this story truthfully when I promised you "Escala's Wish." Earlier this evening, I told you I would recount what happened at Blackthorn Tower on the day the sky burned green. And as much as it hurts me to remember, I have kept my word.

We stood in shock at what Escala had done. With the crossing and its vortex gone, I took in what remained of Victor's tower. The roof was gone, torn away by the storm. The upper floors had been sheared clean off. Below, deep rifts split the stone, plunging into the heart of Valla, jagged wounds opening into blackness, into caverns that whispered of things best left undisturbed.

Teresa sat among splintered furniture, shattered glass, torn books, her hands limp in her lap, tears tracing silent paths down her cheeks.

Junel, back in her small pixie form, lay on the cold floor, eyes wide, staring up into the sky through the gaping ruin overhead.

Sticky's grief was plain. I could see it in his shoulders, which sagged, and how his webbed hands hung limp at his sides.

And Harper, ever the tough one, turned her back to us, fumbling with her belt. But I saw the sharp swipe across her eyes.

No one spoke–there are no words for moments like that.

I look around the Stag's common room and see the shock written plain across their faces; no one expected Escala to die.

"I'm sure some of you weren't expecting that." I say, "But I promised you a true story, and when it's the truth, a good bard doesn't need to invent a thing; he reports it."

Steepling my fingers, I lean in with a grin. "Friends, don't leave yet. We haven't even got to the good part yet."

Chapter 100

L et's go back to when Escala was clinging to the bookcase in Victor's sanctum. Her father had just been killed, Sticky's attempt to cork the crossing with the obsidian orb had failed, and now this vile, unnatural rift was about to consume both the material and fey realms.

The world had dissolved into chaos as the hurricane-force winds were tearing the realms further apart and pulling both realms into the Void. Escala's gaze was fixed on the unnatural crossing Victor had made.

She could see a jagged wound in the fabric of realms, and every second it was widening. Left unchecked, it would devour both realms.

But Escala understood crossings. She had used them for most of her life. The magic of the faeries was the veil itself, the boundary that kept the planes apart, and because the boundary was pure magic, the truth began to crystallize in her mind.

She thought of what happened when a fey was forgotten during the Wane, how their magic returned to the realm. They were forgotten by the living not because they ceased to exist, but because their existence was no longer individual; they became part of the realm. The same happened in death: a fey's essence, their blue-spark fey magic, flowed back into the realm's magical fabric.

It was like water in the mortal world that had a life cycle, rain to river, river to sea, sea to sky, sky to rain. The cycle of fey magic was the same: fey were born of the realm's magic, and when they died, the realm reclaimed them.

Clinging to the bookcase, she looked at her friends who had given so much to help her. They were about to die. All of Valla was about to be pulled through a rip in the fabric between the two realms, this unnatural crossing, and all mortals would die. The fey realm itself would be destroyed in the same way, and all faeries would die.

She could see it now, the massive rip in the fabric between the two realms, this horrific, unnatural crossing. It was dreadful a raw, widening wound in the fabric of the fey realm, like a tear in fine silk that someone kept tugging, pulling, unraveling, making it worse. The rip pulsed, jagged and trembling, just feet from where she lay. She clung to a bookcase that was already tilting toward the Void.

And in that instant, the answer came into focus.

She heard the Dream Weaver's voice echoing through her mind like a song half-remembered:

"There are greater weights in the river of life, immovable stones that strain the current and alter its flow."

Then another memory, the Dream Weaver's voice softer this time, patient, kind:

"One day, little spark, you will learn that such boulders are not always what we expect."

Boulders are not always what we expect, she thought, her mind drifting to all the weight she'd carried, some chosen, some thrust upon her. She remembered what I had told her the first day we met:

"*Sometimes a boulder isn't made of stone at all—it might be a test of the soul.*"

And then my words returned to her, clear as starlight across still water:

"*A boulder can be many things. a lie we tell ourselves, a wrong we have done to someone, or worse, a refusal to move forward toward our destiny in the True Cycle.*"

The phrases overlapped, winding through her like threads, and she finally saw how they fit together.

"*It will take a lifetime to truly understand the weight of your task*," the Dream Weaver had said.

The weight of your task. It echoed in her mind.

All this time, she had been searching for a boulder as a thing to remove, an object to push aside or maybe a curse to break or a creature to banish.

She remembered what I had told her when I first met her in the Stag.

A boulder could be something that doesn't belong but won't move.

But the boulder had never been something outside her. It had been *her* all along.

She was fey. She was magic. Fey magic was the fabric of the realm itself.

And yet here she was in the material plane.

She was a fey in the True Cycle, and she was in the way. She was impacting lives. The young man who had died. Sticky, Harper, me, and, of course, Roedyn had all been impacted by her. Perhaps permanently, she had made things worse.

She was the boulder.

She didn't belong but wouldn't move.

And she had to be removed.

It was so obvious now. So painfully, heartbreakingly clear.

She was not meant to stay here on the material plane, her very presence here was interference, constant interference.

She was the boulder.

And she had to be removed from the True Cycle.

She understood what she had to do. She had to be grafted into the very fabric of the fey realm, here, in this exact place, at the heart of the wound. This tear, this unnatural crossing, could only be sealed by fey magic returned at its source. If she died here, if her essence was pulled into the fey realm through the violence of the vortex itself, her magic would stitch the realms together, patching what had been torn apart.

If she had died anywhere else, fifty feet, even five feet away from the tear in the fabric of the realms, her plan would fail. What she had in mind would only work if she was unmade right at the center of the tear; she had to die at the point where the crossing had ripped reality wide open. To mend the realms, she would have to die in the maelstrom.

And with a cold certainty, she knew now that this was the quest all along. The Dream Weaver knew she was the boulder; this was the meaning.

She was the boulder.

When she had said goodbye to Roedyn had told her that her heart was bigger than any boulder they had faced.

Hadn't the old man by the river warned her? Some boulders are written on the soul. Now she understood. The obstacle to be removed wasn't around her. It was her.

The old man by the river was right; her soul was the boulder.

And she had only seconds to decide.

If she didn't act now, everyone she loved would die.

A thousand memories of love rushed through her.

In an instant, all the conversations she'd had with Crurri, Sticky, the old man building the stone wall, even with Morvena, had helped her see that love wasn't about a kiss, nor was it weakness or something to wait for. It flooded through her mind and crystallized into one thought.

She finally knew what love was.

Love was a choice.

She heard Sticky's voice in her mind: "When you love something… you give it whatever it asks."

She saw Rihanna's laughter and the countless hours they had shared in youth, the love of a best friend. She thought of Harper's endless eye rolls, the sparring that left them both bruised and grinning, and the way Harper always stepped in to shield her when it mattered. Beneath the sarcasm, Harper had guarded her like a big sister, and Escala knew that was love.

She remembered Junel's fierce loyalty and the soft lullabies whispered when she was small, love as steady and enduring as a grandmother.

She thought of Sticky with his odd starfish halves and his reverence for the wilds, even the parts that bite, love born of responsibility, the love of a caretaker.

She saw Teresa's tears and, at last, grasped the depth of the sacrifice her mother had made for her.

And she thought of Rowan, of the crown he bore, of the loveless marriage he accepted so she might grow into her place as a pixie princess.

From both her parents, she saw it now: the hidden truth of love is sacrifice. They had given up their happiness for her because they loved her.

Each of those memories involved choices someone had made for her.

And Roedyn, she knew now that he loved her. He had said the words aloud, but long before that, his actions had spoken louder. He had put his own life on hold to train her, to walk at her side through wild forests and hostile lands, never letting her face the dangers of the world alone. He had stood beside her when monsters nearly tore them apart, teaching her to fight, refusing to give up even when she wanted to. He had stood between her and the world when others could not understand her need for distance, stepping in when careless hands reached toward her, making certain no one touched her against her will. And when she was at her most broken, cast out by the Court of Dreams, he was there, his arms wrapping her in safety and comfort. He spoke no words, but the strength of his embrace carried the promise that he would protect her.

He understood her restlessness, her hunger for discovery, the thrill of the next secret waiting to be found, the very same spirit she had shared with Rihanna. Quiet though he was, he always seemed to want to be near her, and his presence alone was enough to quicken her heart. She trusted his wisdom, valued his insight, and felt the strength of every choice he made for her sake.

When he risked everything against Myrrh, shattering his cover, revealing himself as a Ghost Warden, and daring to outwit the most powerful dragon on Valla, it was for her. Roedyn loved her, she knew, and for him, love meant staying, even when it hurt.

For her mother, love had meant leaving, walking away even when it broke her heart, so that Escala and Rowan would not be exiled from the Court of Dreams, and so Escala could still have a chance to grow up as a pixie.

As Escala clung to the bookcase, the maelstrom howling around her and her friends staring death in the face, her mind flashed back to the old man stacking stones for a wall that might never stand. He had told her that love was doing what must be done simply because you couldn't bear not to.

Crurri had challenged her to consider whether love was something you felt or something you did.

Now, after everything that she had been through, she knew that love was something you did, it was a choice.

Finally, she remembered when I'd asked her if she wanted to be the pixie who rewrote the ending of the story. And as the seconds to the end of everything ticked away, her father's last words echoed in her mind: Protecting the Court of Dreams is the duty of House Winter.

With her father now dead, she was the last of House Winter. It was her duty to protect the Court of Dreams, even the part of the court that bites, as Sticky had taught her.

The decision was no longer hard.

She was the boulder.

It was time to remove herself from the True Cycle, to save the fey realm, the material plane, and those she loved.

She turned, looking at all of us in turn, her eyes full of everything, regret, hope, joy, pain, and love.

Her gaze lifted through the storm. Teresa was clinging to a pillar, wind tearing at her hair and cloak. Junel was holding onto the frame of a shattered mirror, screaming something Escala couldn't hear. Roedyn was across the room, bloodied and broken, still fighting to reach her.

Her chest ached from love.

She shouted, her voice breaking against the wind, "Mother! I know what you did for me, thank you!"

Teresa's eyes widened, lips moving soundlessly.

Escala turned to Junel, her voice proud and fierce. "Tell them I did this for the Court of Dreams!"

And then, Roedyn.

He was clinging to a cracked pillar, armor splintered, face streaked with blood and disbelief. For a heartbeat, everything else fell away. They just looked at each other, everything they'd never said passing between them like a final confession.

In that instant, the world slowed. The storm became a whisper. She saw it all again, the ruined cabin where they first met, his teasing smirk as he told her to stay close. The training, the laughter in the markets, the long nights by the fire. The dancing. The forging. The way he had revealed his secret to trick a dragon and save her life. The circus, oh, the circus, their first day of joy, when he'd finally laughed, truly laughed, and she'd realized she loved him.

All of it, their whole story, brought her here.

Tears streamed down her face as she smiled radiantly. "I love you, Roedyn Hammerfell!" she shouted into the storm.

"Escala, no!" he screamed. "Don't you dare let go! Hold on!"

"I am the boulder," she whispered, but no one heard her.

And she let go.

The maelstrom took her in an instant. One heartbeat, she was there, glowing, alive, and the next, she was gone, ripped upward into the crossing.

The sound was beyond thunder; that was the sound of the world being torn apart. She hit the threshold hard, her body twisting, as shards of stone and wild magic slashed through the air. Her scream rose over the storm.

"ESCALA!" Roedyn roared.

Teresa reached out, voice breaking. "My daughter!"

At the heart of the crossing, Escala's form convulsed, light pouring from every wound.

The storm tore through her like a thousand blades. Rocks and shards of glass pummeled her. Every fragment of the collapsing world struck her at once. Her body twisted in agony, bones shattering, flesh dissolving in the torrent. And yet, through the pain, she felt something rising, something great and ancient unfurling inside herself.

Then she exploded into brilliance; a blue flame burst from her, like the last breath of a fading star. She was no longer flesh and bone. She was light and memory, song and spark.

What remained was magic. Pure, radiant, fey magic, alive and aware.

And then, something miraculous began.

The edges of the torn veil stirred. The very threads of the fey realm stretched toward her. From the ragged borders of the crossing, strands of silver-blue light extended, silken strands of power, delicate and desperate. One thread reached her, then another.

As a wound remembering how to heal, the realms began to knit themselves back together.

The tendrils didn't seize her; they enfolded her. They touched her being with reverence, as though Valla itself bowed before her sacrifice. Her magic beat in rhythm with the fey realm's heartbeat.

And then the weaving began.

Her light spun into threads of its own, intertwining with the fey's silken cords. She became the weaver, the needle, and the thread, her very being passing through the eye of creation. Every flicker of her light sealed a fracture. Every pulse of her magic stitched shut another wound.

As the stitching went on, the tear grew smaller, and the storm quieted.

With each stitch, the wound between the realms slowly closed.

When it was finished, the unnatural crossing disappeared. The river of the True Cycle moved freely again.

The fey realm became what it was always meant to be: a living place of balance and grace.

When the last stitch was done, Escala Winter was gone.

She was no longer apart from the Dream. Her light was everywhere: in the faint shine of moonlit water, in the breeze through the leaves, and within the quiet magic that held the worlds together.

She was simultaneously the thread and the weave, the dream and the dreamer.

Both worlds were safe.

Somewhere amid the quiet that followed, a whisper that could have been her sound traveled on the breeze.

"*Stay curious.*"

Chapter 101

I pause to rub my eyes, blaming some sudden dust that somehow managed to hit both of them at the same time and make them water. When I lower my hands, I notice that others here must have caught the same dust, judging by their damp cheeks.

I force a smile, but there's a lump in my throat I can't quite swallow. Talking about friends who have died is harder than I let on. I need to take a few deep breaths before I can trust myself to continue.

"She felt no pain," I finally said, "only release, a surrender of the very notion of weight or form." I share this in hopes it eases the horror for them, and maybe for me, that Escala's end in the maelstrom, torn before my eyes, was at least without suffering.

Escala floated, or maybe she was the floating itself, drifting in a place beyond shadow. She no longer remembered having arms, legs, or wings. No breath moved in her lungs, no heartbeat counted the seconds. Still, she existed.

Above all, she felt joy as she became light and sound, memory and magic, all entwined with the fabric of the fey realm.

The fibers of the fabric spread before her in every direction, endless and alive.

She realized, without surprise, that each thread carried a soul that had once lived, and as she came closer, fragments touched her awareness: laughter within moonlit groves, dawn rising over the Silverstand forest, and the quiet grief of love slipping past mortal time. The weave held them all, every story. It bound every memory and every dream.

The tapestry was never still. It rose and fell as if it breathed, and when one strand thinned, another curved toward it. When the light dimmed in one place, it brightened softly somewhere else, keeping the balance without effort. The tapestry was always growing, always adding more threads.

She passed through its threads, or maybe they moved through her. The difference faded as each transient strand carried feelings that merged into a harmony of memory.

This was the Dream itself, a song that had never stopped playing. Escala drifted toward where all threads converged, where she sensed unseen weavers at work, shaping the tapestry as they always had. Her own light extended outward in response, threading itself gently into the weave, and wherever it touched, broken strands mended and frayed crossings strengthened, the weave accepting her as though she had always belonged.

For the first time, she grasped what it meant to exist without boundaries or a body, to be the space between leaf and light and the echo that stays after laughter fades. Others were there too, some familiar and some ancient. Among them, she recognized a strength like Rihanna's courage, a calm that carried her father's wisdom, and a comfort that could only be her mother's love.

No words passed between them. Then, as naturally as a dream becoming clear, he appeared.

She was not afraid. She only felt harmony.

"Escala," he uttered quietly. "My curious little spark."

She headed toward him.

It was Dream Weaver Volpe. His form was like a mist. The strands of the fey realm seemed to bow toward him, rippling with gentle respect. His voice was everywhere and nowhere, as soft as a breeze through willow leaves and as deep as eternity.

"You understand now, little spark," the Dream Weaver said. "You were never apart from the weave. You were always its thread."

Escala's essence shone all the brighter. If a soul could smile, hers was smiling now.

"I figured it out," she spoke quietly. "Your quest."

"Did you now?" He asked.

"I was the boulder," she said, "But I didn't see it until I finally understood what love truly is."

She hummed with soft joy. "I found out that love is giving everything, not because you must, but because you want to, because you care. I learned it from mortals, from Sticky, Wigfrith, Harper, Crurri, and…. Roedyn. I told him I loved him. I'm quite sure that breaks the Oath, so it's a good thing I'm already dead, right?"

She laughed, or something close to it. The sound was bright and musical, blending with the realm's mild hum.

The Dream Weaver chuckled. "The Oath was never about punishment, Escala. It was created to safeguard the True Cycle, to remind the fey of who they are and who they are not. Yes, the fey can bring harm to mortals… but they can also bring hope, healing, and love. The way the Oath has been wielded has stripped the fey of that potential, forbidding any meaningful bond with mortals. That was never my intent. It was your love and your defiance of that narrow interpretation that preserved both the Cycle and the fey realm. You did not violate the Oath, not as I envisioned it."

Escala blinked or felt the memory of blinking. "Wait... you're not mad?"

He smiled, an expression made of light rather than lips. "Mad? No, my spark. I'm proud of you. You gave yourself openly to love. You reminded even me what it means to care. And for that, I am grateful."

She shone more brightly, her feelings clear. "But I broke the rules."

"The Court of Dreams," Volpe said, "was never meant to be governed by rules. It was meant to be guided by wonder, by joy, laughter, and love. It was designed for the curious. That is the first language of creation, Escala— curiosity. It is how the Dream shapes itself."

He moved closer, his shape breaking into tiny points of light that touched her gently. "But over time, the court's leaders forgot that. They became careful and proud. They were afraid of questions without easy answers, so they stopped asking. They made laws to control what should have been explored, and rituals to take the place of real feelings."

His voice grew wistful. "Without curiosity, even dreams lose their magic. The court needed a signal, a flash to show them that wondering is part of living."

"Maybe," Escala said slowly, "they need someone to lead them who still remembers that."

A smile seemed to pass through the very fabric of the fey realm. "Perhaps they do," Dream Weaver Volpe said. "And perhaps that someone already has."

Escala's light quivered. "Me?"

"You were always meant to guide them, not as a queen or ruler, but as a reminder," the Dream Weaver said. "Your story will echo through every sprite and pixie who dreams of more than the stars above them. They will speak your name, Escala Winter, and remember that curiosity is what keeps the Dream alive."

A warm, bright feeling passed between them, bringing peace to Escala's heart.

"You did not fail your purpose, little spark," the Dream Weaver said. "You fulfilled it. You've returned balance to the realms and to the minds of those who had forgotten why they were made."

Escala's essence shimmered with calm, glowing light. "Then I guess my story's done," she said quietly.

Volpe smiled. "No, Escala. It's being told."

"So… what happens now?" she asked.

"You'll listen and wait near a crossing. And one day, a soul in need of a dream will pass near your thread, and you will shine again."

She felt herself stretch, turning into light, then thread, and finally becoming the breath of the fey itself.

Her story no longer stood apart; it flowed through every leaf, every whisper of magic, woven into the vast, living tapestry of the Great Story.

And maybe, someday, far from now, a single dream would pass near her thread. She would stir and maybe fill someone's dreams.

The Dream Weaver hovered beside her, his presence gentle. "You could do that," he said. "You could watch and wait, or" a flicker of mischief entered his voice, "we could do something else entirely."

Then, softly, she heard a song and a melody sounding in the fabric of the fey realm:

> *Our friendship and trust I did betray.*
> *Now the echoes of your laughter fade—*
> *My heart lies broken, alone, afraid.*
>
> *I wish that fate would let me mend*
> *My mistake that lost you, my friend.*
> *I would trade my wings, embrace my fall—*
> *To bring you back, I'd give my all.*

Escala gasped, or would have, if she had lungs.

"I sang that in my bedroom after Rihanna died," she whispered, awestruck.

The Dream Weaver's form pulsed with soft golden light. "I listened, and I heard your wish," he said gently. "And you did give your all."

His voice deepened with warmth. "And I do grant wishes, if you're curious."

Escala's soul fluttered.

.

Chapter 102

Roedyn staggered forward, into the hollow center of the chamber where the vortex had raged only moments before. His eyes were wide, haunted, as he turned in a slow circle, searching for something, anything.

"She's gone," he said at last.

"No…" Sticky whispered. "No, she can't be; there has to be something left. We could take her body to a cleric and try to resurrect her."

"I'm going to kill her," Harper muttered suddenly.

"What?" I asked, startled.

"When I get to the afterlife, I'm going to wring her little neck." Her voice was sharp, defiant, but her hands trembled as she rubbed hard at her eyes. "That crazy, infuriating pixie, she didn't even ask permission. That's supposed to be me doing the reckless things, taking the risks." She gave a bitter laugh. "I'm the one with nothing to lose." Her fingers brushed the burn scar on her chest, lingering there. "Not her."

"There isn't an afterlife for her, Harper," Junel said softly. "Even in her elf form, she was still fey. And fey are pure magic. When our bodies die, that magic returns to the fey realm. She can't be resurrected."

Sticky's throat worked, but his voice was barely a breath. "We won't ever see her again?"

Junel lowered her head and shook it slowly.

"She told me she loved me." Roedyn's voice broke as the words escaped him. His face was pale, stricken, as though he couldn't make sense of what he'd just confessed or that she was gone before he could answer.

None of us knew what to say. We closed in around him, each of us reaching for him, for each other, trying to hold on to something solid in a world that suddenly felt broken.

We tried to console him. We tried to console ourselves. But the truth was plain—there were no words left to say. Roedyn knelt in the rumble of the destroyed room, head bowed, his blood mixing with the dust. Teresa was silent, one hand pressed against her heart, eyes empty. Junel had folded in on herself, her wings dim, her small frame trembling. None of us spoke.

And then suddenly—

BOOM!

A radiant burst of light erupted from the center of the chamber so brilliant that we threw up our hands to shield our eyes. The glow wasn't harsh like lightning; it was warm, gold, and violet, spiraling like threads of dawn weaving through shadow.

When the light finally dimmed, we saw her.

A tiny-winged figure hovered in the air, no more than four apricots and two cherries tall. Her hair was jet-black and tied high in a ponytail. Her skin glowed with the warmth of amber, and her violet dress shone faintly as if woven from twilight itself. Her wings—translucent, veined with silver— beat in slow, uncertain rhythm.

She looked around, eyes wide with confusion and wonder. "Where... where am I?" she stammered.

Junel gasped, her hand flying to her mouth.

The tiny faerie turned toward the sound, and when her gaze landed on Junel, her whole face transformed. Confusion melted into astonishment, then dawning joy.

"Junel?" she said, her voice filling with hope.

Junel stared, dumbstruck. "How?"

"Junel!" she cried, streaking toward her like a bolt of light. The pixie crashed into her, arms wrapping tight, wings fluttering with joy.

"It's really you! I thought I'd never—"

Junel's eyes went wide. "Rihanna?"

"Wait. Wait, wait, wait—that's Rihanna?" I asked.

"The Rihanna?" Sticky asked.

"The actual Rihanna?" Roedyn asked numbly.

Junel laughed through a sob. "Yeah... It's her. Somehow. Escala must've..."

"She never shut up about you," I said. "It was always 'Rihanna this,' 'Rihanna that.' And she said a wolf killed you."

"It did," Rihanna said. "But then... I heard something— a song, a sad, beautiful song—and I followed it, and I woke up here!"

Harper quipped to Roedyn, "So that's Rihanna? I assumed Escala invented her for attention."

Chapter 103

———————

We were busy talking with Rihanna when—

BOOM!

A second explosion of radiant energy cracked through the ceiling like a bolt of divine thunder. A column of blue-white light tore down from above, scorching the air with pure magic. The entire room shook; dust and bits of marble rained from the already crumbled and destroyed walls and ceiling of Victor's sanctum as the glow intensified. We staggered back, shielding our eyes from the brilliance.

A streak of sapphire light shot upward from the center of the chamber. It broke into a spiral of arcs that pulled inward, tightening until they formed something small and bright.

From within that whirling column, a figure erupted—a tiny female pixie, spinning through the air like a comet set free.

The pixie twirled once, twice, then burst into a series of flips so fast they blurred into a ribbon of light. Her laughter rang out, wild and bright, scattering motes of magic that drifted like falling stars. She folded her wings and dove, a gleaming streak cutting through the air, and then flared to a halt just above Rihanna.

"Ri!" Escala yelped, spinning backward in a blur. She flipped upside down, wings flailing, and a flash of white, her delicate fey-silk fluffies, as she called them, gleamed for all to see.

Harper nearly doubled over. "Oh gods, well, the True Cycle's definitely been impacted now. Right, Roedyn?"

Rihanna was wheezing with laughter, clutching her sides.

Roedyn, however, had turned a shade somewhere between panic and tomato. He spun on his heel, muttering, "I—I didn't see anything!" and stared intently at a crack in the floor.

Escala, now upright and crimson-faced, jabbed a finger at them all. "No one touches the faerie!"

Sticky, who'd been watching it all, added through a fit of laughter, "She's so tiny!"

"And loud," Harper said.

"But she's back," I said, unable to stop smiling as I watched them twirl.

"Both of them are," Teresa whispered, unable to take her eyes off Escala. "I… I still don't understand how."

"You don't have to," Junel said, her voice warm. "This is the Court of Dreams, and sometimes dreams come true."

For one perfect moment, surrounded by laughter, we forgot every trial we'd endured because Escala was back. For the first time in ages, Valla felt whole.

Chapter 104

—————

S o, folks. You probably think this is where I say, "The End," don't you?

Once again, you'd be wrong because a minute later, all hell broke loose. Let me tell you how that happened.

Escala and Rihanna were still flying around in delight, their laughter echoing through the chamber. We were gathering our gear, half laughing, half crying, battered, bruised, but alive. The air itself felt lighter. The nightmare was finally over.

And then—

KRA-THOOOM!

A sound like the sky breaking apart thundered through the sanctum. The floor shook under us, splitting down the middle like ice. Magic burst from the ceiling in a bright, white-blue pillar that tore the air. Every instinct told us to run, but we had nowhere to go.

The shockwave hit first and knocked us flat. Then a blinding light followed, and I couldn't see.

When my vision finally cleared, I saw in the center of the ruined chamber a huge, almost invisible sphere of magic that had appeared, stretching thirty feet wide. It covered the broken marble floor and gave off energy so strong the air seemed to shake. The edges moved like liquid glass, bending light in strange, flowing shapes. Inside, the room was wrecked: broken bookcases, overturned tables, and scattered debris.

And trapped inside were Escala and Rihanna.

They floated in the air, looking confused, with their hands pressed against the barrier between us. We could hear them, but their voices sounded muffled and desperate through the swirling magic. There were no seams or cracks, no way in or out.

But they weren't alone.

On the far side of the dome, Audrey moved forward through the mist. The pale light from the sphere shone on her blade, a short sword marked with fey runes.

And then, behind her—

Morvena appeared as the smoke faded, hovering with a quiet anger. She folded her arms and slowly spread her wings. Her dark gown drifted like mist, and the silver on her dagger's hilt caught the light.

"Mother," Audrey hissed, not taking her eyes off Escala. "She broke the Oath once and continues to do so. She should never have escaped the Wane."

Morvena's eyes gleamed, a cruel smile ghosting her lips. "Yes," she growled. "Let's show her what fey justice looks like under my rule."

Teresa hurled herself at the barrier, but hit an invisible wall of force. Blue sparks snapped and crackled across it, then faded. She hit it again, her desperation breaking through. "No! Let me through!"

Harper slammed her shoulder into the barrier, trying to break through. The magic flared and threw her back. She landed hard on her side, winded.

"What is that?" Harper shouted as she regained her feet.

Roedyn drew his sword and struck the dome in anger, but the blade hit the barrier. Purple energy shot out, jolting through his arms and throwing him back. He lost his grip, and the sword slid across the stone floor, trailing blue sparks.

Junel drew closer, wings moving softly as she studied the barrier. She extended one quivering hand, slowly, carefully, and touched the surface. A ripple of light fluttered where she touched. There was no resistance, and she felt no pain as her hand passed through, as if the magic itself recognized her.

Junel pulled her hand back, eyes wide in amazement. "That's no ordinary barrier," she said, amazed. "Morvena must be much more powerful than I thought to create something like this. A spell this strong shouldn't even be possible."

But she was wrong, not that we knew it then.

The sphere hadn't come from Morvena or Audrey; It was Victor's.

It was his last resort, a spell-construct made to be a personal stronghold—a shield dome where nothing could enter or escape.

This magical totem was the one Morvena had taken the last time she saw Victor. It was supposed to be thrown in a crisis, creating a shield dome to protect the tower from any magic on the material plane. But instead of keeping Morvena safe, it ended up trapping Escala and Rihanna along with Morvena and Audrey.

The totem was made to block mortal magic, designed for the elemental forces of the material plane. But Victor never adjusted it for fey magic. So, while it kept out mortals and their magic, it did nothing to stop the fey.

Morvena had stolen Victor's shield-totem from his sanctum during one of her many visits. She turned his defenses into a prison. What was once his safe place became her own arena of torment.

"Junel!" Teresa called out, her voice faltering. "Help her!" as she watched Junel's hand slip through the dome.

Junel stopped, her hand halfway through the barrier. "I can't," she said, "I took the Oath. I can't act against another fey, not even to save her."

"Then break it! Just this once, break it!" Teresa cried.

Junel shook her head, tears running down her cheeks. "If I break it, I lose everything: my grace, my wings, my soul. I swore it before the Dream Weaver himself."

"Then forget your Oath!" Teresa shouted, hitting her hand against the barrier. "She's your child too, Junel. Maybe not by blood, but by love. You raised her!"

Inside the dome, chaos broke out as Morvena came down, her wings moving in a slow, predatory rhythm.

"Well," she said, her voice sharp-edged. "You must have missed the latest decree. With your father gone and your exile still in place, I am now Queen of the Court of Dreams. As Queen, I am changing your sentence. You won't spend your days on some pointless quest to move boulders from the True Cycle anymore. Your new sentence is death."

Escala's wings flared wide. "You have no authority over me. You can crown yourself queen, Morvena," she said, her voice steady but fierce, "but no throne forged from betrayal will ever hold."

Morvena's laugh was low and terrible. "Oh, spare me your courage, half-breed. You've always confused defiance for strength. Do you think you've saved this realm? You nearly destroyed it by bringing that evil artifact to a madman who hated your father. You'll pay for that crime!"

Escala curled her hands into fists. "You talk about destruction as if you didn't cause it! You poisoned the court, twisted the Oath, and turned love into a curse. You didn't earn the crown, you stole it."

Morvena's smile turned razor thin. "Careful, half-breed. Keep talking, and I'll let Audrey kill your friends before I finish you."

Audrey turned to Escala, her blade flashing as it caught the last rays of sun through the shattered roof.

"I'm not some rat-faced nobody," Audrey hissed, eyes blazing with hate. She spun the dagger between her fingers, the blade catching the light like a shard of moonlit ice. "I should've shoved this straight through your gut instead of your back, you worthless wretch."

Audrey pulled the wolf totem from her pelt pouch, holding it so Rihanna and Escala could see as they hovered. "Remember your little friend?" she sneered.

Escala went still. The color drained from her face as her expression hardened, every muscle pulling taut. Her wings trembled with a suppressed urge to lunge, and the heavy thrum of her pulse in her ears began to drown out the rest of the world.

And in that silence, it all clicked.

Audrey had been in the woods that night—the night Escala kissed the mortal boy. She'd been watching, waiting. The ambush at the crossing wasn't chance; it had been bait. Audrey had followed them through and had summoned the wolf that ripped through the clearing, leaving Rihanna and the boy dead. The same wolf that nearly tore Escala apart.

And the trial, oh, the trial, Escala saw it now for what it was: not justice, but theater. Every word, every accusation, every tear was part of their design. Morvena and Audrey had hoped the court would sentence Escala to the Wane.

And when that didn't kill her, Audrey had come after again, wearing another face. Waltzing into the Stag with a dagger. And when Escala's back was turned, when she dared to believe she could get away with it, when Escala was drunk and unable to defend herself, Audrey had struck.

Escala's fury was rising so fast it burned through her veins like wildfire. Her fists clenched until her nails drew blood. "You," she growled, her voice shaking with rage. "You killed Rihanna! You killed that boy, and you tried to kill me. Twice! And because of you, I was banished from my home! My father and mother are dead because of you!"

Audrey smirked, tilting her head. "And yet here you are, still making everything about yourself."

"Tsk, tsk," Morvena cooed, her tone dripping mock sympathy. "Don't act so wounded, child. You brought it all on yourself. We're just carrying out the sentence your father's laws demanded."

Escala's eyes burned with rage. "You can kill me," she said through gritted teeth, "but you'll never unmake what

I've done. I know what love is now, and that's something you'll never understand."

Morvena's voice turned bitter. "Love?" she said, laughing softly. "You're still clinging to that illusion? Love is a leash mortals wear to feel important and to control each other. Power endures, love only destroys, just look at your parents."

Escala's wings flared wide, and her voice trembled with both grief and fury. "My father is dead because of you. You'll never understand what he had with my mother," she said, more boldly. "They gave up everything for me. That isn't a weakness; that's love."

Morvena's lips curved into a predator's grin. From beneath her cloak, she drew two totems: one carved into the shape of an obsidian serpent, the other a sleek black panther. She raised them high, her eyes burning with hate.

"Well then," Morvena said, her voice rising into a chilling crescendo, "if love can save you, Escala, let it save you from me."

She hurled both totems to the ground. They struck with a thunderous crack, and violet flame raced across the floor in a ring. The obsidian serpent shuddered, its stone scales splitting as living muscle pushed through. A hiss like escaping steam filled the dome as its jeweled eyes flared to life.

Beside it, the panther's stony form rippled, melting to sinew and fur, claws gleaming as it crouched low, ready to spring. The air vibrated with their growls.

Audrey drifted forward, eyes locked on Rihanna. Holding the wolf totem aloft, she hissed, "Care to play with the wolf again?"

Audrey raised her hand and flung the wolf totem to the floor. It landed with a flash of blue fire, splitting open as the spectral beast emerged, its eyes burning with cold hunger. But unlike the others, it didn't strike. The wolf slunk backward into the wreckage of shattered columns, its spectral body phasing in and out of sight as it disappeared among the rubble.

The final battle for the Court of Dreams had begun.

Chapter 105

With a primal scream, Escala launched herself at Audrey like, slamming into her with enough force to rattle the dome. They crashed into the curved barrier with a loud *THOOM* as Audrey's spine whipped back against the dome wall, and her breath left her in a brutal, choking gasp.

Escala didn't stop. She grabbed Audrey by the collar and slammed her against the wall again, once, then twice, the back of her head hitting hard. "You killed her!" she shrieked, "You killed my best friend!"

"You stupid wretch!" Escala screamed, slamming Audrey's head against the inside of the dome again while they hovered in midair.

Audrey thrashed, twisting in her grasp, trying to escape, but Escala's fury had made her wild. She struck again, hard, until blood splattered the crystal wall behind them.

The last blow left Audrey reeling, and Escala strengthened her grip around her throat. With her free hand, Escala hit her again and again, every blow harder than the last, motivated by years of betrayal and grief. Then she drove her knee into Audrey's gut, forcing a ragged gasp from her lips.

"Why?!" Escala shouted, striking again, tears running down her cheeks. "Why did you kill them? Why?" The words burst from her like splinters of pain.

Audrey spat blood and laughed. "Because you were too stupid to die properly!"

"Get off her!" Morvena's command. Her hand ignited with cold violet fire, and five bolts of arcane light raced across the chamber. They tore into Escala's wings, blistering the delicate membranes.

Escala's wings faltered and then gave out completely. She fell, twirling down through smoke and sparks, and hit the marble floor below with a dull, nauseating thud. She lay there, breathing in hollow gasps, her vision swimming in and out of focus as she struggled to her knees.

Audrey didn't hesitate, even after the beating she had taken. She rushed toward Escala in a blur, landing a vicious backhand that snapped Escala's head to the side. Escala hit the stone again, stunned and reeling, the pungent taste of scorched magic bitter in her mouth.

Across the fractured floor, the summoned beasts moved. The serpent slithered low while the black panther circled the edge, its tail quivering and eyes fixed on Escala.

"Get up, Escala!" Roedyn yelled.

Rihanna moved forward just as Audrey's hand struck Escala, grabbing Audrey by the throat before she could react. With a snarl, Rihanna slammed her into the dome wall again. Audrey let out a stifled gasp as the sphere shook around them. Rihanna leaned in close, her breath cold as ice against Audrey's cheek. "We never liked you. Not before, not after, and definitely not now."

She clenched her grip, her voice laden with fury.

"So go ahead, see if the dead are as weak as you remember."

Audrey gagged, raking at Rihanna's hands around her neck, then drove a knee into Rihanna's stomach to break free. "You should've stayed dead!" she screamed.

Behind them, a low hiss sounded, and the huge serpentine shadow slid across the marble, coiling through the dust.

"Escala, move!" Roedyn shouted beyond the barrier.

The serpent struck, its fanged mouth snapping through the air where she had just been. Escala rolled aside at the last moment, the fangs smashing stone and sending sparks flying. She kicked upward, her shredded wings still managing a rough, uneven climb.

Morvena's laughter sounded through the dome, smooth and venomous. "How touching," she said. "Your boyfriend is going to watch you die."

Morvena's gaze slid to Roedyn. "Tell me, mortal, did she kiss you, too? She cannot help herself, always meddling in the True Cycle." Her voice hardened as she turned her attention back to Escala, who was flying up towards her. "You twist everything you touch—love, fate, even him. Gods, tell me you didn't make him fall in love with you. You probably had to charm him, didn't you?"

Roedyn's eyes darted to Escala, searching her face, desperate to see her reaction.

Escala's wings trembled with rage, not shame. "You oondie jackal!" she shouted, voice ringing. "He's none of your business! Just like my parents were none of your business."

"Oh, but they were my business." Morvena sneered. "Your mother"—she pointed at Teresa—"was a blight on the Court of Dreams, and she had to be removed."

Escala screamed, "You drove her out because you were jealous of what they had. You made her leave him—leave me. Wasn't destroying one life enough for you?"

Outside, I leaned toward Sticky. "What's an oondie jackal?"

He grimaced. "A filthy grave-jackal that eats dead bodies. They're like the catfish of the graveyards."

Harper, sweat streaming down her face as she pounded away at the dome, didn't even glance back. "Sticky," she grunted between strikes, "when in the nine hells would you ever use that form?"

"Probably never... well, maybe if the Ogland kobolds ever start a press."

I shrugged and glanced at Roedyn, who shot me a blank look before turning back to shout instructions to Escala and Rihanna. I had no idea what Sticky was talking about and from the puzzled crease on Roedyn's face, neither did he.

Chapter 106

B ack in the dome, Morvena slowly smiled, almost tenderly, and it was more terrifying than rage. "Your mother was a mistake," she said. "A frail human who thought love could make her equal to us."

But then her eyes filled with malice. "But I corrected her delusion before it spread. And you... you're proof I was right. Your infatuation with mortals is the infection she left behind. I'm saving the court by purging you."

Heat rose in Escala's chest and her wings flared.

"You broke her." Escala said, voice trembling with barely restrained fury. "You took everything—her home, her love, her dignity—and laughed while she suffered. She cried because of you. You made her believe she was less than you, when she was more."

Morvena's smile deepened. "Then consider her pain the lesson she needed. Love is weakness. I only showed her the truth."

Teresa's eyes burned. Her trembling hand lowered from her chest, curling into a fist. "You're a miserable coward," she spat through the dome glass. "You hid behind your magic and throne while others lived life. You didn't correct my 'delusion'—you envied it."

Morvena's laughed. "Oh, Teresa... you were always so easy to unravel. Humans always are. So desperate to love something—anything—that you trust the hand holding the knife. You proved me right the moment you brought that *thing* into the world." Her gaze flicked to Escala.

"Love isn't noble, it's a leash. A weapon. It makes fools destroy themselves." Morvena snapped.

That broke something in Escala. Her scream shattered the air—grief and fury woven into a single, raw sound. Her hand snapped forward, and a blast of freezing wind howled through the dome, sending shards of ice outward and coating the marble in rime.

With a casual flick of her hand, Morvena conjured a violet shield, and Escala's ice storm parted harmlessly around her like water around a stone.

"Such weakness," Morvena said softly, as if the words themselves bored her.

Escala's veins brightened until she seemed carved from starlight. "You'll never hurt her again!" she cried. "You'll never hurt anyone again!"

Escala dove, a streak of blue and silver, slamming into Morvena and hurling her backward.

"I *hate* you!" Escala screamed, driving Morvena upward in a burst of beating wings. They spun in a violent corkscrew, locked in a deadly spiral of claws and fury. Shards of frost and violet fire trailed through the air, spinning like comets in their wake.

Morvena shrieked and tried to wrench free, wings thrashing to gain altitude, but Escala seized a fistful of her hair and dragged her down. They tumbled together as gravity claimed them both.

They hit the ground in a tangle of wings and rage—screaming, clawing, scratching, biting and striking.

Morvena reeled, blood streaking down her cheek, and clamped her nails around Escala's throat. They rolled across the floor, slamming against the shattered glass globe. Escala's elbow nearly caught its jagged rim. The black leather bag still dangled nearby.

The obsidian serpent crept closer, jeweled eyes gleaming. But the true storm raged between the fey— punching, biting, tearing at hair and skin, wings tangling and snapping in the chaos.

Escala drove her knee toward Morvena's ribs, but the dark pixie snarled, caught it, and slammed her forehead into Escala's face. Blood burst into the air as sparks of pain flared behind her eyes.

They continued to grapple on the ground, and then suddenly they shot into the air again—wings carving wild currents, spells flashing like heatless lightning, their screams of fury echoing through the dome.

"Stab her in the eyes!" Harper shouted from beyond the barrier. "Go for the eyes!"

"High guard!" Roedyn yelled, bow useless in his hands.

"Careful, the serpent's circling back!" Sticky cried.

Morvena dragged Escala higher, and higher—to the apex of the dome, then slammed her head against the invisible barrier. *THUD*—like stone on iron.

Leaning close, breath hot with venom and blood on her lips, Morvena whispered, "I took such joy destroying your parents' relationship."

Morvena released her and Escala plummeted.

Rihanna tore free from Audrey and dove after the falling Escala, catching her midair. They spun together, barely righting before Morvena loosed fresh magic filling the dome with smoke and fog.

Within the haze, shapes began to move. Serpent scales glinted like wet glass, and a panther's silhouette glided low, its golden eyes visible in the dark. From farther back came the rhythmic sound of paws as a wolf emerged quietly from the smoke.

With a snarl, the panther vaulted a toppled slab and launched at Rihanna just as she steadied Escala. The panther landed on both faeries, slamming them into the ground amid splintered furniture and stone.

From outside, Roedyn's yelled, "Escala! Rihanna! Move—now!"

"Behind you!" Sticky shouted. "The snake's coming back around!"

Morvena laughed, blood running where Escala's claws had torn her. She descended slowly, regal through ruin. "How does it feel, half-breed?" she called to Escala. "Your mother's weeping, your father's dead, and soon, you'll join him."

Audrey dropped beside the panther who held Escala pinned, her face streaked with blood but wearing a smile. She drove her boot into Escala's side, pinning her harder beneath the beast's claws. "Guess what, sister," she sneered. "I'm the princess now."

The panther continued to pin Escala, its claws sinking deep into her sides. Escala cried out, wings flaring weakly as she fought to shove the beast off, but it was too strong. Above her, Audrey laughed, eyes bright with madness.

571

"Face it, sis," she hissed, striking again. "You were never meant to rule."

Rihanna had regained her feet and raised her hands to cast a spell. "Get off her!" She hurled burning violet flame ball into the panther's shoulder. The creature roared, recoiling just enough for Escala free herself.

Audrey lifted her foot for another kick, but this time, Escala was ready. Her hand shot up, catching Audrey's ankle mid-swing. Her eyes burned. "My turn," she rasped and yanked.

Audrey toppled atop the panther just as the serpent struck from the fog. The pixie sisters rolled aside, Audrey shrieking, as fangs sank deep into the panther's shoulder.

The great beast convulsed, a ragged roar ripping through the dome. Black ichor bled beneath its fur, pulsing with a dim, eerie glow where venom clashed with lingering magic. The panther staggered, claws skidding across the marble, tail lashing in final defiance. The serpent hissed in triumph. The panther gave one last shudder, then crumpled to the floor and lay still. The snake turned to find its next foe.

Overhead, Morvena began to cast again, orbs of fire and violet lightning bright and cruel. Escala twisted, rolled, dove, every motion desperate, but the barrage didn't stop.

One dive sent her too low—

—and then the wolf attacked.

It burst from the smoke, fangs flashing with that same gnashing fury that had devoured Rihanna months earlier. Escala raised her arms to protect her face, but the jaws clenched on her forearm. The bite was freezing and burning all at once, and Escala screamed, wings flaring in panic as her tiny frame thrashed against the sheer weight of the beast.

For one paralyzing heartbeat, she wasn't in the dome. Escala was back in the forest on the night Rihanna died. She had almost died like this before, pinned and helpless with her blood on its tongue. Now it was happening again.

The wolf advanced closer, muscles quivering as it exhaled loudly. She felt its claws bite into her side, each one carving fire into her side. Her sight blurred, white around the edges, as its jaws crushed harder. The skin on her forearm split, and blood flowed in thin, trembling ribbons down her arm.

She planted one hand against its snout, pushing back with every trembling ounce of strength. Its teeth hovered inches from her face, snapping and snarling, hungry for her throat. Her other hand clawed blindly at the shattered floor until she felt something rough and solid–a brick.

With a ragged cry, she swung the brick at the wolf's head, landing a solid blow as she could hear the sickening crack of brick against bone. The wolf yelped and recoiled, its form flickering as smoke and blood scattered into the mist. Escala dropped the brick and gasped for breath, her arm shaking violently as crimson dripped from the mangled flesh.

Silence followed. Then the wolf growled. Her heart raced with fear. She could hear his padding feet, but in the mist, she could not see him. Her pulse throbbed against the wound, warm blood seeping down her hand.

Then it lunged.

The wolf came from the blind side, a blur of shadow and teeth. It slammed into her, driving her hard against the marble floor. The impact ripped the air from her lungs. She screamed as claws tore through her tunic and into her shoulders, pinning her like prey once more.

Her desperation flared. She thrashed, and her gaze darted to a broken chair beside her. She snatched it up and shoved it between them, the splintered seat serving as a shield for her small pixie frame. Wood groaned as the wolf crashed against the chair and splinters bit into her cheek. The wolf's rancid breath was all around her, and its jaws were snapping inches from her face. She could feel its fury in every movement, the same monstrous hunger that had taken Rihanna months ago.

And this time, Escala swore through gritted teeth that it would not take her too.

Rihanna knifed toward them, but the panther's corpse tripped her landing. Audrey's spell burst against her ribs and slammed her into the dome. "I can't reach her!" Rihanna cried, dragging herself up as Audrey closed in with her blade flashing.

Morvena dropped through the smoke like a hawk. Steel flashed as she slashed across Escala's forearm with her dagger, carving muscle. The next drove into her thigh, ripping sideways as she rolled to block another. The third opened her calf from knee to ankle. None were killing blows, but together they were a red fog.

Teresa sobbed, helpless, as Escala screamed beneath the wolf. Her daughter, bleeding and thrashing with a wolf, was being torn apart before her eyes.

"Help her!" Harper shouted, voice hoarse with panic. "Junel, please!"

"I… I cannot attack a fey," Junel said, voice trembling. "The Oath binds me."

Teresa turned on her, wild with grief. "Then give me something!" she cried, clutching Junel's arm with both hands. "A weapon, a spell, anything—please—I won't just stand here and watch her die!"

Tears streaked her face. "She's my daughter."

Junel's trembling fingers went to her cloak and drew out a small silver ring. "Teresa," she whispered, pressing the ring into her hand. "Rowan told me to give you this if you ever wanted to return to the Court of Dreams."

Teresa's eyes widened. "What is it?"

"A ring of polymorph," Junel rasped. "It'll make you what you need to be." She gripped Teresa's wrist. "You didn't swear the Oath. Rowan would want you to save her. But the magic of the dome won't let you leave once you go in, you can't get out until the totem is disabled."

Teresa nodded.

Inside the circle of mist and chaos, the wolf continued to maul Escala, its jaws tearing and shaking as she struggled beneath it. Blood slicked her skin, her cries growing weaker. Then low and silent through the swirling fog the serpent slithered forward. It coiled just inches from the ground, invisible until the last moment.

With a snap, it struck.

Fangs punched deep into Escala's thigh. She screamed as white fire exploded through her nerves and venom scorched her veins like molten glass. The serpent recoiled, hissing in agony as steam rose from its scorched scales its own venom reacting with her fey-touched blood.

But the strike had landed true.

It would be the creature's final act because Rihanna had separated from Audrey and dove from above, her hands clutching one of Audrey's daggers. With a furious cry, Rihanna slashed through the serpent's neck nearly to the spine. The snake's body convulsed, then flopped to the ground, lifeless.

Morvena whirled on Rihanna, both hands rising as black lightning erupted from her fingers in a wide, crackling cone. It slammed into Rihanna's tiny body, flooding through her in a torrent of shadowed energy; it was horrifying to watch.

"You killed my pet!" Morvena shrieked as Rihanna arched in agony, the lightning crawling up and down her small frame. "You will die!"

Rihanna screamed, her wings faltering. Then they stopped entirely. She dropped from the air and hit the rubble below with a sickening thud.

"Rihanna!" Escala cried.

Morvena only laughed, turning back toward Escala who was still lying on the ground. Rihanna had managed to kill the serpent—very likely saving Escala's life—but the damage was already done. Escala had been bitten, and the venom was spreading fast, clouding her thoughts, slowing her every movement.

"Transform to your elf form!" Sticky yelled, "It will help dilute the venom."

"Escala!" Roedyn shouted, "Change!"

Escala struggled to her knees. She was dizzy.

"Wolf, off," Morvena commanded, as she swooped down, hovering inches from Escala's face. "I should have spanked you far more when you were little, maybe then you'd have learned to obey." And with that, she slapped Escala. Hard.

Teresa headed towards the edge of the dome, ring in hand. Harper caught her at the edge of the sphere, shoving a dagger into her hands. "You know how to use this?"

Teresa nodded once, slipping the dagger into her belt. In her human hands, it was small—a desperate weapon at best—but once she put on the ring and turned into a pixie, a dagger would become a sword.

Morvena had now drawn her own dagger and stabbed her in the shoulder.

Escala screamed in pain as the wolf stood ready, waiting for the command to kill.

"Beg," Morvena said.

"No-never!" Escala yelled out through her cries of pain as Morvena stabbed her in her other shoulder, and she grabbed Escala by the throat.

Her gaze locked on the dome where her daughter lay dying. There was no time left.

As Teresa put the ring on, she was enveloped in light, her form dissolving and compacting into a luminous point roughly the size of two apples and a prune. She hovered there, glowing softly, her hair lifting in an unseen breeze. A mother, remade by grief and grace, weightless in the moment her world was breaking.

Venom coursed through Escala's small pixie body as blood seeped from both shoulders. With multiple gashes and deep cuts layering her arms and legs, she was in desperate trouble. Morvena stopped stabbing her long enough to backhand her with her dagger hand and hiss, "You are a disgrace to House Winter."

Morvena tightened her grip around Escala's throat. Escala was kneeling, barely. The venom had nearly dragged her into unconsciousness, and the only thing keeping her upright was Morvena's hand clamped around her neck. In her heart, she wanted to fight, to resist, to scream—but her body would not obey.

"I'll kill you," Morvena said as she raised the dagger.

Escala heard Roedyn, Harper, Sticky, and me shouting. She heard Junel's cries, but where was her mother?

Then, Escala saw a silver-white haired, middle-aged, beautiful pixie cross into the dome. As Teresa entered, she moved quickly to her daughter's aid, quietly but quickly flying up behind Morvena. Her eyes locked on the source of her daughter's peril. She struck from behind, her fist connecting with the back of Morvena's head in a blinding flash.

"No one touches the faerie!" Teresa yelled.

The impact cracked like thunder, snapping Morvena's head to the side and staggering her. The dagger in her hand skittered harmlessly across Escala's ribs as her grip broke.

Teresa spread her wings, planting herself between Escala and the fallen blade. Her eyes blazed gold as she raised a trembling hand toward the shadow-wolf.

"That totem was carved for me—out of love," she said, ringing with command. Looking at the wolf, Teresa said. "You answer to me now."

The wolf froze beside the fallen pixie, its glowing eyes flickering from cold blue to a wavering gold. A low, uncertain whine rose in its throat.

"Off," Teresa commanded, her voice iron. "Release her".

The wolf staggered back from Escala's side, its claws screeching against the marble. Escala rolled weakly onto her side, coughing blood, her limbs trembling with exhaustion as venom continued to race through her small frame. Crimson soaked her tunic, pouring from deep gashes along her arms and ribs.

Roedyn, seeing that she was about to lose consciousness, screamed, "Escala, CHANGE NOW!".

Her mind was so clouded, but she thought she heard Roedyn yelling 'down' like he did when they were attacked by the direwolves.

Down.

Down? What did he mean, she tried to clear her mind, but it was too hard.

She heard him again, "Change down...change now...change NOW!"

Then she understood. With a groan, Escala shifted, her body swelling with light as she shed her pixie form and returned to her elven shape. It brought no relief to the cuts; but her thoughts cleared a little as the poison was indeed diluted in her now larger body. And she wasn't dead, at least not yet.

Morvena staggered upright rising into the air, blood trickling from her lip, and smiled darkly. "So, the mortal returns. Tell me, Teresa, what does it feel like to crawl back into the nightmare you begged to leave?"

Teresa's chest rose and fell, trembling as she hovered feet from Morvena, the two women staring at each other for the first time in almost twenty years.

"You'll never understand," Teresa rasped. "I didn't leave—I escaped you."

"Escaped?" Morvena cooed, circling closer to her. "I forced you to leave— you had to go."

"You talk like you were owed something," Teresa said, her voice defiant. "Like Valla had wronged you. All you ever wanted was power, and you used love like a ladder to reach it."

Morvena's laugh was soft and venomous. "Love? Is that what you call what you did to Rowan? You seduced a prince and gave birth to a curse."

"Don't," Teresa shook with rage. "Don't you dare speak his name."

Morvena's smile curved into a cold smirk. "Why not?"

As she spoke, she stooped quickly, retrieving the dagger from where it had fallen near her boots. Rising slowly, she hid it behind her thigh, blade turned inward. Her tone softened, almost pitying. "Do you think he loved you? He pitied you, mortal. You were the accident that ruined the line of House Winter."

Teresa didn't notice the dagger—she saw only her daughter bleeding in the corner and the hatred burning in Morvena's eyes.

Morvena stepped close, their foreheads almost touching. "Look at your child," she whispered, voice low and silken. "Bleeding and broken. A reminder of everything you ruined. And you still call that love?"

She leaned in close to Teresa, her breath ghosting across her ear. "For me… this is closure."

Harper saw it first and shouted, "She has a knife!"

But it was too late.

Morvena's dagger flashed, and she drove it into Teresa's stomach.

Once.

Twice.

Three times.

The sound of the stabs was sickening—the wet thud of metal meeting flesh, followed by the patter of blood dripping onto the stone below. Teresa gasped, a sound caught somewhere between a sob and a choke, as the blade sank deep. Blood poured through her fingers as she clutched the wound, staining her hands crimson. Her wings spasmed, struggling to keep her aloft.

"Mom!" Escala screamed as she struggled to her knees.

Harper cursed. Sticky covered his mouth, eyes wide. Roedyn's roar in fury.

Morvena's voice dropped to a mock whisper, eyes bright with cruel satisfaction. "Goodbye, Teresa. You should've stayed out of Court affairs." She twisted the blade one last time before yanking it free.

Teresa staggered backward in the air, unsteady, her wings faltering, and her world spinning. Blood cascaded down her front of her white tunic in dark sheets, each drop hitting the marble like rain. Her mouth parted; a thin ribbon of red slid down her chin. Her wings faltered, then folded against her back as she landed on the stone.

She gasped, voice broken. "Escala…"

Her body convulsed once, but she forced herself to stay upright, trembling on her feet. She flickered between pixie and human, a transformation that seemed compelled by her very nature to confront death as she had lived, before she hit the floor with a heavy sound.

Morvena still hovering above her laughed.

Teresa rose to her knees and her eyes found the wolf, half-crouched near Escala, still bound to the totem's command.

"Wolf…" she choked out, blood bubbling in her throat. "Kill… Audrey."

Across the haze, Audrey, who had been watching this, hovering with her dagger drawn, a mocking smile curling on her lips as she fixed her gaze on Escala. "I'm about to become the princess," she said.

Audrey eyes widening as Teresa commanded the wolf.

"No—wait—"

The wolf launched itself and hit Audrey like an avalanche, jaws locking around her waist as she hovered near Escala. Audrey screamed, and the sound of the wolf's jaws crunching her ribs echoed through the dome.

Blue sparks burst from her body as the beast shook her once, then twice and tore her apart. Audrey's upper half vanishing into its jaws; her lower falling away in a crimson arc of fey blood that hissed on marble floor.

Rihanna lifted her head from the rubble where she lay, barely. "The wolf… it listened…" she gasped.

Morvena let loose a blood-curdling scream, "You killed my daughter!" And black lightning burst from her hands, slamming into Teresa's chest.

Suddenly, Teresa screamed in pain and fell onto her back, blood oozing from stabs in her abdomen. In her agony, she lost command of the wolf, which turned its focus toward Audrey.

"Mother!" Escala clawed to her knees, one hand pressed to her slashed thigh, black veins already spidering from the serpent's bite. The venom still burned like molten fire in her veins, but her elf size had diluted its effects.

Morvena descended on her, eyes wild with murder. Seeing the wolf frozen, Morvena commanded it, "Wolf, kill Escala Winter." Instantly, the wolf lunged toward Escala for the third time as Morvena raised her dagger to attack Escala.

Escala had no weapon or shield. Then she spotted the remains of a shattered wooden chair from earlier in the fight. She snatched up a chair leg, holding it like a makeshift club just in time to block Morvena's stabbing jabs. Splintered wood met steel with a jarring crack. Morvena snarled, forcing the blade downward as Escala kicked wildly. Her heel connected with Morvena's shin—enough to throw the strike off but not stop it. The dagger slashed across Escala's arm, drawing fresh blood.

Escala clenched her teeth, anger fueling her as she swung the chair leg with all her strength. It hit Morvena's ribs with a hollow crack, knocking her back toward Teresa, who was still on the ground.

Outside the dome, Roedyn shouted. "Flow, Escala! Ride her angle, don't meet it!"

"High guard! Left flank!" Harper yelled, hitting the barrier with her fists.

Teresa moved, barely alive and fully human again, blood seeping beneath her. She pulled herself forward, gasping, her eyes focused on her daughter, but she was unarmed.

Then she observed the small black bag hanging from the broken glass globe, just close enough to reach near Morvena's boots.

"Use the bag!" Harper called out.

Teresa pushed herself up to one knee, pressing one hand tightly to her stomach wound. Blood covered her fingers, and her breath turned shorter and wetter. With a rough cry, she grabbed the bag, stood, turned, and threw it with all the force she had left at Morvena's head.

Crack.

The satchel hit Morvena right in the temple. Her eyes rolled back, her mouth opened in shock, and she collapsed into the rubble, unconscious. Her bloodied dagger dropped to the floor with a clank.

The wolf crouched, its hackles up, growling softly.

Teresa, bleeding and shaking, her white tunic soaked with blood, raised a quivering hand toward the wolf. Her voice sounded like a rough whisper, "Rest... wolf..."

The creature stopped. Its eyes twitched, then faded. With a moan that sounded almost human, it folded upon itself and vanished into the wooden totem.

Teresa wobbled, then her legs gave way. She dropped to the marble floor with a quiet, final sound. Blood pooled beneath her.

Outside the dome, Sticky hit the glass in desperation. "No, no, no!" He shouted spells and prayers, but the magic only sparked against the barrier and slid away like rain on steel.

Roedyn pressed his forehead to the dome, his fists bleeding from hitting it. "Break, storm you!" he shouted. "Break!"

Harper stood still next to him, her sword hanging at her side, "She's dying… we're watching her die."

Inside, Escala, covered in blood, crawled to her mother's side, her sobs breaking up her breathing. Rihanna crawled to Teresa too, then stood just behind Escala.

Teresa lay on her back, her chest barely moving with each gasping breath. Blood leaked from her wounds in steady pulses, staining the marble in red circles. Her lips were pale and her face was gray.

Escala held her, trembling. "Mom, please, stay with me," she said, her voice faint and breaking. "You can't go. I just found you. You can't…"

Teresa lifted her shaking hand and touched her daughter's cheek. A delicate smile appeared upon her lips. "Escala…" she spoke quietly. "My beautiful girl…"

Her hand trembled while blood gathered at the corners of her mouth. "I love you… so much."

Escala's tears fell onto her mother's hand. "No… no, please don't go. Please don't leave me." She turned to us beyond the glass, her eyes begging. "Help her! Please!"

We couldn't help. The dome stood between us, cold and solid, and all we could do was watch.

Escala laid her forehead to Teresa's, her shoulders shaking with quiet sobs. "I don't want to lose you," she whispered, her voice cracking. "I never even got to know you."

Teresa's eyes opened again. She looked at Junel, who stood near the edge of the dome, shaking, tears twinkling in her eyes. Teresa grinned gently, as if seeing something from long ago. Then she looked back at Escala and said, "Your father…" she uttered softly. "He used to… dance at dusk…I want you to hear it…. to remember us."

Escala grasped her mother's hand more tightly, whispering anything she could—prayers, promises—just to keep her there. She sobbed openly, rocking her mother's body as the tune faded away.

Teresa tried to sit up, struggling against her weakness as blood leaked from her stomach and the wounds on her side. She only managed to rise a little before Escala gently lowered her, whispering, "Mom… no. Rest."

Teresa lifted her hand to Escala's face and began to sing. Her voice was soft and beautiful.

Your laughter is the song I chase
Through moonlit woods and endless space.
No dream nor dawn could shine so true—
My heart was made to simply love you.

Escala's tears slid unchecked down her face, falling onto her mother's trembling hand.

"I loved your father with all my heart…" Teresa whispered, blood bright against her teeth. Her breath came shallow, trembling. "I still do…"

A savage cough wracked Teresa, doubling her over in pain. Blood spattered her lips. Her words broke into pieces between ragged breaths. She was slipping away.

"I still sing that song... every night..." she whispered, her voice barely more than a breath. "Hoping he can hear me..."

"Mom—please—Mother!" Escala cried. She pressed Teresa's hand against her chest, as if the rhythm of her own heartbeat could keep her mother tethered to life. "Don't go. Please don't go."

Rihanna bowed her head beside them, silent, wings folded tight, tears sliding down her cheeks.

Teresa's gaze softened, drifting somewhere far away. Then her eyes locked on Escala's, and for a heartbeat, nothing else existed. Only a mother seeing her daughter's face for the last time.

Her lips trembled, shaping the faintest smile. She squeezed Escala's hand one last time, weak but full of everything she could not say.

Her chest stilled. The light faded from her eyes.

The song was over.

Chapter 107

——————————

I look around the room and can tell that no one expected the story to end this way. Some stare into their mugs; others shift in their chairs, trying to make sense of it.

I lift my own mug, not entirely sure what to say next— not sure there *is* anything to say. Still, I find myself speaking.

"If you've ever lost a parent, then perhaps you understand the hole it leaves behind. But try to imagine losing both parents—not years apart, not even months—but on the same day."

I would have expected Escala to be overcome with emotion, completely broken. Oh, don't get me wrong, she was emotional, as tears often came easily to her, but she wasn't crying in the same way she had earlier when her father had died.

These tears were different.

I pause, still unsure how to explain it.

"What she did was extraordinary. And to this day, I don't fully understand it."

Escala rose slowly from her mother's side. Blood pooled beneath Teresa's still form like spilled starlight, fading as her warmth left the world. Escala's hands trembled, stained red, her fingers tightening as if she could somehow press life back into the stillness.

For a long time, she didn't move. The air hung heavy with the smell of iron and magic, the remnants of battle echoing faintly beyond the dome. When she finally looked up, her face was calm, but her eyes told another story. They burned with grief so raw it hollowed her.

Her gaze drifted toward the swirling remnants of the scrying cloud. The image was gone now, but she could still see him there—her father, gasping his last words, whispering her name through blood and light. The memory struck like a blade to the heart.

He was gone.

But so was her mother.

Her chest tightened until breathing felt impossible. The wish throbbed inside her, alive in a way that made her uneasy—her last chance to undo what fate had already done. It would cost more than she wanted to give, and she knew it.

Her father was the dream that shaped her. The one who taught her wonder, curiosity, and song. The one who made her fey.

Or her mother, the mortal who had loved fiercely and sacrificially given everything for her, who had fought her way through pain and time and death itself to protect her. It was she who made her *feel* as mortals do.

She closed her eyes.

In the silence, both called to her—one in memory, one in blood.

Tears spilled freely now, falling to her mother's cheek. Her lips parted, trembling, but no sound came. She pressed her palms to her eyes, choking back a sob that tore her throat raw.

"I can't—" she whispered to no one. "I can't lose them both."

Rihanna stepped forward, eyes glistening, but she didn't speak. She knew words couldn't touch the place Escala stood now—the place between love and surrender.

Escala wiped her tears, though they wouldn't stop. She took a long, shaking breath, her shoulders trembling under the weight of her choice. Then, at last, she reached for Rihanna's hands, taking both in hers.

"I only have one more—"

Rihanna nodded, understanding something we didn't.

Across the room, Junel had been watching in silence. Her eyes narrowed as she clearly tried to make sense of what was unfolding. She wasn't alone—none of us understood what Escala meant.

Escala nodded and said to Rihanna, "I'll take care of it, but not here."

Rihanna nodded back.

I looked over at Sticky, who gave me a confused look.

Escala took her mother's hand. Carefully, she slipped the polymorph ring from Teresa's finger, her own trembling so hard the silver nearly slipped from her grasp.

"Goodbye, Mom," she whispered, voice barely audible. She leaned down, pressed a kiss to Teresa's forehead, and gently closed her mother's eyes. "You did it. You saved me. Again."

And then, at last, the walls of the sphere flickered— once, twice—then dissolved like mist burned away by sunlight.

We rushed in.

The sight that met us froze us in place.

Escala was a ruin of herself, her face streaked with soot and blood. Her arms and legs were crisscrossed with gashes and cuts, her shoulder punctured where the wolf's claws had raked deep, and poison pulsed through her veins. Blood seeped through the rags of her clothing. She shivered uncontrollably, her eyes unfocused, and her breath came in wheezing gasps teeth.

Rihanna was little better. Her wings were charred and frayed at the edges, her neck dark with bruises from the serpent's coils. Her armor hung in scorched ribbons; one arm was twisted awkwardly, her face slick with blood and ash. Both of them looked half dead, held upright only by willpower and the sheer refusal to fall.

Roedyn reached Escala first. "Easy, hey, I've got you," he whispered, trying to hug her.

She flinched hard, pain flooding her body. "Don't—" she gasped, reeling back, clutching her midsection.

He froze. For an instant, something raw flickered in his eyes, hurt, confusion, but then comprehension settled there. He nodded once, jaw rigid. "All right," he said in a low voice. "No touching. I get it." He didn't, not fully—but the gray between them said enough.

Harper was already on her knees beside Rihanna; panic carved across her face. "Come on, Ri—don't you dare check out now!" she barked. "I've had enough ghosts for one day."

Sticky darted to Teresa. He laid a hand against her chest. The magic flared once… then fizzled, fading into the air.

Sticky bowed his head. "She's gone," he spoke quietly. "I can't reach her. She's already—" His voice broke.

Escala caught his wrist weakly. "Stop," she said, voice frayed. "Please. You'll hurt yourself."

He met her eyes, tears welling. "She saved you," he said. "She saved all of us."

Sticky gave a sharp nod and darted to Escala and Rihanna, his little body moving so fast he was almost a streak. His hands flamed with green and gold, and the air snapped with the keen tang of magic. "Hold still!" he snapped, voice shaking. "You're not dying. Not today."

Magic crawled over their battered bodies, dim at first, then swelling bright and fierce. Escala jerked, a raw cry tearing from her throat as the healing light forced the venom out. "It burns," she gasped.

"I know," Sticky said. "That means it's working. Breathe, Escala."

He moved to Rihanna, pressing both hands to her wounds. "Come on, open your eyes." The glow from his hands flared, bruises fading a little, her breathing becoming steadier, but lines of exhaustion were evident on her face.

Roedyn's fists balled tight. He stood and stalked over to Morvena's motionless form, jaw set with hate. "Then we make sure she never hurts anyone again." He grabbed a length of rope and bound her wrists, knotting it with the same stubborn strength he used to cinch his pack straps on the road. I'd seen him do it a hundred times—nobody was getting loose from that.

"If she tries to escape," he muttered, "she'll wish she hadn't."

Harper exhaled shakily as she knelt beside Teresa's body, gently brushing blood from her hair. "Burn my luck," she whispered. "She didn't deserve this. If that blasted dome hadn't been up, I could've done something."

"She was more than brave," Rihanna croaked, leaning heavily on her good arm. "She was love itself."

Roedyn turned back, his face softening when he saw Escala still trembling on her knees. "You should sit," he said quietly. "You must be exhausted."

Escala shook her head. Her eyes were red and swollen, her lips pale. "Not yet," she rasped as she reached down and picked up the Crown of Dreams where it had fallen, its jewels dimly pulsing like a heartbeat.

"You're Ghost Wardens—can you and Harper keep that safe?" Escala asked, standing up and handing Roedyn the crown. Her eyes searched his face.

He nodded once. "With my life."

I bent down and picked up the wolf totem from the rubble. It pulsed faintly, still warm. "What do we do with this?" I asked.

Escala turned toward me, bloody but resolute. "It should never return to the Court of Dreams," she said. Then, bolder, "In fact, I order it."

Harper blinked. "You *what*?"

I tilted my head in confusion and said, "Did she just... give an order?"

Junel's lips trembled, but she smiled faintly. "It will be as you say, Your Majesty."

"W-wait," I stammered, still holding the wolf totem.

"Harper," Escala called, her voice steadier now. "Can you keep watch over the totem?"

Harper smirked. "Sure. I've always wanted a magical wolf that eats royalty. Adds a little spice to my arsenal."

Sticky hopped over, clutching a small black bag. "Uh, Harper, what was in this thing anyway?"

He untied the drawstring, reached in, and pulled out a gleaming golden chamber pot.

"You've got to be joking," I said flatly.

"I never joke about chamber pots," Harper said solemnly.

We all laughed.

Escala laughed too and added, "Rihanna, did you see how my mother ordered the wolf to bite my stepsister in half?"

Rihanna smiled. "I loved it—it was the perfect payback."

Escala smiled faintly, thinking of how Audrey had once unleashed the wolf to kill Rihanna and how now, by her mother's command, that same beast had brought justice in kind. The symmetry of it felt right... righteous, even.

As she shifted into her pixie form, her wings trembled but still caught the air. "The Court of Dreams is in chaos," she stated. "I have to go back."

I stepped forward. "Escala, forgive me. Are they going to let you back in? Your appeal was denied just a few days ago."

Escala smirked faintly, flicking her wings in that way only she could. "Oh, they'll let me in."

Roedyn crossed his arms. "And how can you be so sure?"

She looked up at him, blood-streaked but smiling. "Because, silly—I'm in charge now."

We exchanged uncertain glances.

"I am the queen," Escala said. Her voice carried quiet authority. "And my first act as ruler is to ensure she"—she pointed to Morvena—"is brought before the Wane."

Roedyn bowed his head. "Then justice will finally have its day."

Junel wiped a tear from her cheek. "That's... that's wonderful, Escala."

I adjusted my lute strap, still catching my breath. "Your Majesty, forgive the curiosity—but last we heard, you were dead. Now you're crowned, breathing, and giving orders. How exactly can that be? I thought you were banished and out of the succession line?"

Escala turned to Rīhanna, then back to me. "Wigfrith," she said, a weary smile touching her lips, "when my father died, the title passed to me. By blood, I became queen."

Roedyn frowned, brow furrowed. "But at your trial, you said your title was stripped—you were banished from House Winter. When your father died, the line of succession wouldn't have gone through you..." He hesitated, the thought turning heavy. "You're not in the line of succession."

Escala's smile didn't fade. "Oh, but I am," she said quietly.

We exchanged uncertain looks, each of us trying to piece it together.

And then, of course, Harper broke the silence. "Okay, wait—how do you go from banished to dead to back in the line of succession? And also—how do you go from I'm the queen to flashing your unmentionables ten minutes ago?"

We all laughed, even Escala, and she said, "What I said then was true," she began quietly. "I was stripped of my title... and denied appeal. But then I died."

"I died when I entered the vortex," Escala said. "It was the only way to seal the rift Victor tore between our world and the mortal one. That rip... it wasn't just a portal. It was a hungry wound in the realms. It was feeding on everything—light, magic, time itself. It pulled the fabric of both realms into the void."

Her hand trembled as she touched her chest. "If I hadn't entered the vortex when I did... it would've grown faster, and in just a few minutes more, both realms would have been swallowed by the void. Not just Blackthorn Tower, but cities and kingdoms—all of it. Everything, gone."

"Wow," Harper said.

"So how did you stop it?" I asked.

"You see, fey aren't made of flesh and bone like mortals," Escala explained. "We're made of magic—pure, living magic. The fey realm is that same magic, a great current that flows through all creation. Every fey is born from that current, and when we die, we return to it. It is the beginning and the end of what we are."

She lifted her hand, and faint sparks drifted from her fingertips like dust caught in sunlight. "When I crossed into the vortex, my body unraveled back into that fabric of the fey realm. My essence was drawn into the tear itself, pulled right into the wound between worlds. My magic spread across the edges of the rift, binding them together, stitching the torn fabric between the fey and mortal planes. My death became the patch that mended the wound. I wasn't gone... I had become part of the fey realm itself."

"But that doesn't explain how you are here," Sticky said. Trust Sticky to blurt out the question everyone else was thinking.

"You're right, Sticky. There is more that happened. At first, I didn't understand. When I was alive, I thought the 'boulder in the True Cycle' was something outside myself; a curse or an obstacle I had to destroy. But when I became one with the Dream, I saw the truth. I was the boulder. I was the piece of the Cycle that didn't belong. My fear, my pride, my refusal to let go... all of that was blocking what was meant to flow. The True Cycle couldn't move forward until I chose to remove myself from it."

She looked around at us Rihanna, Harper, Roedyn, Sticky, and me. Her eyes lingered on each of us, as if she was carving our faces into her memory. There was warmth in her gaze, but I saw the weariness there too, and the heavy ache of what she'd given up.

"It was all of you who taught me how," she said, her voice soft but unwavering. "Traveling with you, fighting beside you, I finally learned what it meant to live. Not just to exist, but to care. To belong and to love something outside of myself."

A shiver ran through her, but she stood her ground. "That's what gave me the strength when the moment came. I didn't hesitate. I knew what I had to do. I had to step out of the True Cycle to save everything I loved, and everyone I was meant to protect. When I became part of the fey realm, the tear closed. The vortex we all felt? Gone. And you all lived."

Escala said, "I became part of something bigger, the endless river of light and memory that is the Dream. That's where the Dream Weaver found me."

A hush fell over the room.

"He told me I had done what no mortal and no fey had ever done," she continued. "My sacrifice had healed both realms—the waking world and the Dream. He said that it could not go unanswered. So he gave me three wishes."

Her wings fluttered faintly as she spoke,

"And beyond the wishes…by removing myself from the Cycle, I completed the quest. I restored balance between the realms. And when the Cycle realigned, I was drawn back to finish what remained, recognizing, at last, the true heir of House Winter once more."

Roedyn frowned, confused. "Then when Morvena claimed she was queen—?"

Escala met his eyes. Her voice no longer trembled. It rang with quiet, undeniable truth. "She was wrong," she said. "The Dream itself corrected what had been broken. The bloodline of House Winter was restored. The crown did not belong to her. It never did."

She straightened then as if claiming her space in the world once more. Her wounds remained, but her presence filled the room.

"I didn't just come back from death," she said. "I returned to my birthright."

Rihanna's expression softened, pride glowing faintly through her fatigue. "Then it's true," she said. "You're Queen of Court of Dreams."

Escala nodded slowly. "I am. Not because I demanded it… but because the Dream Weaver decided it."

She drew a breath, steady but weary. "The Dream Weaver told me that every choice has a cost—and that every wish would tug on the weave of the world. So I chose carefully. My first wish was for Rihanna—to bring her back to life. My second was for myself—to return and finish what had begun."

"When the Dream Weaver came," she continued, "he told me I had completed the quest. And because of that… he granted me my wishes."

Rihanna blinked. "You asked for me back?"

"I did. You're my best friend, and I am so sorry for what happened back in the meadow." Escala smiled.

Rihanna flew over and the two embraced.

When they let go, Escala added, "And I asked to return, too."

I tilted my head, "Escala… did you have one more wish?"

She nodded.

"And you just used it to bring your mother back, didn't you?"

Another nod.

Junel smiled faintly. Harper raised an eyebrow. "I thought you hated her."

Escala turned, tears glistening in her eyes. "I did," she whispered. "Until I didn't."

She knelt beside Teresa's body again. Firelight flickered across her face as soft wind stirred, and motes of gold lifted from Teresa's skin like fireflies rising toward the heavens. Her color faded; her form softened, and then she was gone.

When the last trace of light vanished, Escala whispered, "She's not gone. My final wish was to send her back home to Marlow. She'll awaken there... alive, safe... and free of all this."

She added with more confidence, "She won't remember the battle or even meeting me at The Stag. She won't remember seeing Rowan die." She paused. "She won't remember me telling her I hated her. The next time I see her, it will be for the first time. I'll have a second chance... to start over."

Her wings flickered faintly as she looked down. "It'll take time. I'll have to learn who she is and let her learn me. But I want to, more than anything."

Junel smiled through her tears. "That," she said softly, "is a very wise wish."

I plucked a quiet chord on my lute, my throat thick. "A queen's wish," I said. "And a daughter's."

Rihanna rested her hand on Escala's shoulder. "You did right," she whispered.

Silence rippled through the chamber. Even the lingering hum of magic seemed to quiet.

Roedyn's voice was low, reverent. "You gave everything... and still found a way to give more."

Escala smiled. "No," she said, "I only followed what you all taught me. That love is the one magic worth dying for—and the only one strong enough to bring us back."

Silence came over us.

Harper was the first to break it. "All right," she said, clearing her throat. "That was the most inspiring and everything... but someone please tell me this doesn't mean we have to bow to her now."

Escala gave a faint, exhausted laugh. "No, you're not fey."

Roedyn managed a quiet smile, but he stayed silent. His gaze rested on Escala, full of understanding and something else, distance, maybe. He reached out to steady her, but she pulled away, wincing as she forced herself upright. Hurt flashed in his eyes, but he said nothing.

We stood shoulder to shoulder in the wreckage of Blackthorn Tower. Shattered walls surrounded us, and the bodies of monsters and minions sprawled at our feet. Blood—ours and theirs—still shone wet on the broken stones.

Here, the worlds of mortals and fey had almost come apart. But as we stood in the calm after the storm, for the first time in months, it felt like we could breathe again. Maybe, just maybe, we could rest.

We walked with them through the battered woods, searching all day for a crossing that would hold.

We held no funeral for Teresa. There was no need. Escala had told us her mother was safe in Marlow, alive and totally unaware of the war that had virtually torn two worlds apart. That helped us deal with the shock of losing Teresa in the battle.

When we found the crossing at last, Junel stepped through first, then came back with a line of fey guards. They bound Morvena's wrists in silverlight chains and ushered her away, to face whatever justice the broken Court of Dreams could offer. Rihanna and Junel left with them, their wings melting into the mist while they vanished across the threshold.

Escala waited at the edge of the crossing, deciding whether to follow the guards, but then she said she could give us one more night. The court needed her, but she wasn't ready to let us go.

Tomorrow, she promised, we would say our last goodbyes.

Chapter 108

We spent our last night together at The Stag, merriment and warmth circling around us, the sort of stories spinning out that always grow taller with every telling. Escala kept to her elf shape, moving through the crowd unnoticed. No need for the whole tavern to realize they were sharing drinks with the queen of the Court of Dreams.

We raised our mugs, traded jests, and drank deep, but not too deep, and this time, we kept Escala well away from the dragonfire brandy. Sticky swore it was for her own good. Harper insisted it was for ours.

We recited tales of our travels, every blunder, every narrow escape, and the laughter itself rolled on as the hours went by. Midnight came and went, last call faded, and still we lingered. The fire shrank to a glow, and even the barkeep surrendered, leaving us alone with the embers.

Once dawn arrived, one by one, we excused ourselves and headed upstairs, claiming whatever beds we could. Only Escala and Roedyn lingered below, sitting close across the table, their tankards forgotten and cold.

They just watched each other, caught in that silent look that holds every word you dare not speak and every truth you wish you could forget.

Escala's hair tumbled loose over her shoulders, her eyes tired but shining in the fire's glow. Roedyn leaned in, elbows planted on the table, watching her like he feared she might disappear back into the dream that had called her here.

Neither spoke for a long while. Then Roedyn said quietly, "You don't have to go back. You could stay."

Escala's expression relaxed, but her voice stayed steady. "You know I can't. The Oath would break me. And now that I wear the crown, there's no escaping what it binds."

He gave a small, humorless laugh. "So you'll save their world and lose your own."

She said nothing at first, only gazed at him, her eyes shining in things she could not say.

He bent closer, his voice faint and raw. "Then permit me to say it once, just once. I love you."

Escala went still, and I caught the quiver in her hands as she folded them tight in her lap. For a second, I thought she might reach for him, but she didn't. She only closed her eyes, gathering herself like a queen who couldn't afford to be human, and said quietly, "Don't."

Roedyn flinched as if struck. "Why not?"

"Because if you say it," she whispered, "I'll want to believe it. And if I believe it, I'll never leave."

Her voice was barely audible. "And I have to leave."

The silence that followed was unbearable. He turned his face away, his hands clenching into fists, and for the first time since I'd known him, Roedyn looked utterly defeated.

I watched from the stairwell, my heart twisting. It was love, pure and unspoken, bound in tragedy. I'd seen passion, I'd sung of longing, but never this: two souls chained by duty and undone by silence.

They stayed there until the first light crept through the windows, washing the table in pale gold. When Escala finally rose, her chair scraped softly against the wood. She looked down at him—hesitated—then reached out and rested a trembling hand on his shoulder.

"Thank you," she said.

For what, she didn't say. Maybe for following her through hell. Maybe for loving her when he shouldn't. Maybe just for surviving beside her long enough to understand why she couldn't stay.

Roedyn nodded.

By the time I stepped forward, she was gathering her cloak, her movements quiet and deliberate. When she turned to us, the firelight caught the edge of her profile, and for a moment, I thought I saw tears glinting there, but maybe it was just the light.

The sun had begun to climb over the hills when she finally said, softly, "It's time."

Together, we walked the familiar path to the old crossing. This time, she was going back on her own terms. Escala Winter of the Court of Dreams was returning as its queen.

And this was goodbye.

She stood for a moment at the crossing entrance and transformed into her proper pixie form. The morning sun illuminated her wings, making them sparkle like delicate frost, and she hovered a short distance above the earth, evidently happy to be in her own form.

This was going to be the hardest part. We had said goodbye to her before; this wasn't the first time. But we all knew—and she knew it too—that this was the last.

Escala turned to each of us, starting with Harper.

Harper crossed her arms, giving Escala a once-over. "You've gotten a lot better in a fight," she said. "But you still take too many hits. You need to stay and train."

Escala smiled softly. "I can't, Harper, you know that. But I'm so grateful for everything you did for me."

Harper gave a playful, dismissive wave. "Yeah, yeah. I'm still looking out for you. I told every barkeep from Dunwell to Marlow never to sell you dragonfire brandy again."

Escala, now in her pixie form, flew up close and hovered at Harper's eye level. "That's a little harsh, don't you think?"

"Harsh?" Harper arched a brow. "You got drunk, insulted some woman's dress, and didn't realize she was your stepsister until she stabbed you."

Escala winced, then managed a crooked smile. "In my defense, it was an awful dress."

Harper chuckled. "And yet, she wore it better than you wore that knife in your back."

Escala groaned, half laughing, half in pain. "You're never going to let that go, are you?"

"Not a chance," Harper said, grinning.

Next, Escala fluttered toward Sticky. The little frog looked up, eyes glistening.

"You live in a swamp, you smell like a swamp, and you eat bugs. And yet… you're one of the truest friends I've ever had. What does that say about me?"

Sticky croaked, "It means that the healing potion I gave you back at the lily pad worked. Turns out it really was a love-a-frog-forever potion."

Escala laughed. "Sticky, you're a ridiculous toad," she said, "but I am so grateful you joined me on my quest." She swooped down and tried to hug him, and her wings brushed his shoulders. "Next time I see you, I want to see a new animal form."

Sticky rubbed the back of his neck. "Oh, I still have some animal forms that will surprise you, like drama llama."

"Drama llama? When would you ever possibly need that form?" Harper asked.

"Anytime someone breaks up with their boyfriend during a dungeon crawl," said Sticky.

Harper looked over at Roedyn. "Well, we could've used that form at least twice on our adventures."

Roedyn just shook his head.

Escala laughed and squeezed Sticky's arm. "You saved my life, Sticky. And more than that, you reminded me how to laugh when I'd forgotten how."

He gave a bashful croak, and his tongue flashed out to snag a passing fly.

Then Escala turned to me.

"Wiggie," she said, fluttering close and circling once before hovering at eye level. "Your songs made me feel like I never left home. When I was at my lowest, you helped lift me back up. You saved my soul more than once—especially with your healing songs."

Cutting straight to the chase, I said. "You know I'm charging people to tell this story, right?"

She gave a sly look. "Of course you are. But I am trying to thank you for your help. You know everything, and without you, I would never have succeeded. Thank you."

I placed a hand over my heart, feigning offense. "Observation is an art. I simply apply my many talents."

"Talents?" She laughed. "You gave me a fey test the first time we met!"

"That was poetic critique," I said with mock dignity. "A rare gift, really. You should be thanking me."

Harper snorted. "Oh, it was poetic all right, especially the part where you ranked her behind a chamber pot."

Escala chuckled softly. "If anyone can make even that sound noble, it's Wiggie."

Sticky folded his arms. "As long as I get a verse too, and preferably one that rhymes with handsome amphibian."

"Done," I said. "Though I may have to invent a few syllables."

"Wouldn't be the first time," Harper muttered with a grin.

The laughter that followed was real. We were just friends again, together in the quiet after the storm.

Finally, Escala flew to Roedyn, and he lifted a hand so she could perch lightly on it. He was smiling, but a touch of sadness lingered in his eyes. This was going to be hard for him.

"You're still not as good with a bow as you think you are," she teased. "You shot me multiple times."

Roedyn arched a brow. "Maybe I just got tired of hearing you say, 'No one touches the faerie,' and an arrow to the shoulder made you say something new, like 'ouch.'"

She feigned outrage. "You were using me for target practice?"

"Worked, didn't it?"

Escala glared, then launched into the air and flung herself at his face, hugging him hard. Her wings tickled his cheeks.

"I'm going to miss you most of all, Roedyn Hammerfell," she whispered. "And I promise, I will no longer say 'no one touches the faerie.'"

He looked away, then muttered to Harper, "I give her eight minutes."

We laughed.

Together, Escala, Rihanna, and Junel stepped toward the crossing.

Escala paused, turned back, and blew Roedyn a kiss.

We watched them disappear, and Sticky, Harper, and I turned toward the horses, but Roedyn didn't follow.

He stood alone, staring at the crossing. He wasn't ready to let go, and I wasn't sure he ever could be.

We waited. A minute passed. Then five. Then fifteen.

Harper cleared her throat, but Roedyn didn't move toward his horse.

With a sigh, Harper stomped back toward him.

"She's gone, Roedyn, we have to go."

He didn't respond.

Harper grabbed his arm.

"I don't think I'll ever get over her." He sighed, then turned and started walking toward us.

As he passed, he muttered, "Let's find some dragonfire brandy strong enough to burn the memories clean. Maybe if I'm lucky, I'll get stabbed in the back too and forget the rest."

We chuckled as we began to pack.

"You'll be fine," Harper said, nodding toward Dunwell. "Plenty of other girls in Valla, and now you've got experience."

Roedyn's voice snapped. "Other girls? I fell for *her*— there won't ever be another girl that compares."

He was heated.

"I actually told her I was falling in love with her."

Harper crossed her arms.

"Yeah, and she told you she loved you."

"In the middle of a world-ending black hole! Right before she sacrificed herself—that doesn't count!"

Roedyn's voice echoed across the glade, raw and frayed. He was pacing in tight circles, boots grinding grass into mushed dirt, his hands flexing as though they needed something—anything—to hold on to.

"And she left in pixie form! No real hug—nothing!" He stopped abruptly, looking back toward the faint magical glow that still hung in the air where the crossing had been. His voice broke. "Not even a kiss."

Harper stood with her arms crossed, trying—and failing—to hide the ache in her expression. "Poor Roedyn," she said quietly.

But I couldn't resist adding, "Roedyn, don't even think about kissing her. Remember what happened to the zombie—you'd be charmed into oblivion."

"Maybe I already am," he muttered.

I honestly did feel bad for him. He was going to miss her most of all.

Then—

A sound, soft and playful, drifted from the crossing. A hum, like strings being plucked on an unseen harp. Gold dust began to swirl above the grass, rising in delicate spirals, and from within came a faint whistle.

"Wheee-ooop!"

We turned in disbelief.

The crossing flared open—an explosion of sapphire light streaked with silver, petals of pure energy unfurling like a dawn blooming after endless night. The glow resolved into the shape of a female elf stepping through.

Escala.

She was breathtaking. Her long, golden curls cascaded in soft spirals down her back, catching the light with a faint, iridescent sheen. Her eyes—clear, brilliant blue—sparkled with life and laughter. She wore a form-fitting tunic of midnight blue trimmed in silver, a soft belt at her waist, and leggings the color of twilight, sleek and elegant.

She stood at the edge of the crossing like it was the step of a waiting stagecoach. One hand gripped the swirling frame of the magic gate. The other held the same polymorph ring—the one Junel had given Teresa. She was grinning like pure trouble.

"Roedyn Hammerfell Dor'lean," she called, voice rich with joy, "I'm the queen of the Court of Dreams. That means I can kiss any boy I want. What are you waiting for? Come with me—I have so much to show you in the fey realm. And besides… we need to find a better hiding place for your little Box of Kestrel—I know about the cave."

Roedyn turned to Harper. "You told her about the cave?"

"Forget about the cave, you idiot!" Harper groaned. "Go!"

Roedyn took off—walking, then jogging, then running. As he passed Sticky and me, he shouted, "I'm in love with the queen of the Court of Dreams!"

Escala laughed.

When he reached her, she flung an arm around his neck and kissed him full on the mouth, one foot kicking up like every storybook kiss.

Her other hand held tight to the edge of the crossing.

In one fluid motion, Roedyn swept her into his arms, and together they vanished into the crossing, falling into the Dreaming Court as Sticky would say.

Harper crossed her arms and squinted after them.

"Well," she said, "looks like I need a new roommate. Hey, Sticky—what's swamp life like?"

Chapter 109

A few weeks later, we had a wonderful surprise. The front door of The Stag opened, and they walked in. Roedyn was grinning, and beside him stood Escala, in her elf form—radiant as ever, as if the nightmare they'd endured a few weeks earlier had been nothing more than a bad dream.

Escala told us that we were all needed at the Court of Dreams for Morvena's trial.

I jumped for joy, as did Sticky—we were going to the Court of Dreams!

We peppered Roedyn with questions while we packed. Harper was relentless. "Please tell me you have wings!"

Roedyn, of course, was evasive and kept his answers short, giving us wonderfully helpful answers such as, "It's hard to explain."

Harper just shook her head.

Escala, on the other hand, couldn't stop talking. She was electric, just like when she used to tell stories about Rihanna. It was wonderful to see her so happy, so full of energy and excitement.

Harper checked with Roedyn to confirm he had indeed moved the Box of Kestrel to the Court of Dreams. It was good news, and with luck, it would stay sealed forever. That single act might well secure Roedyn's place as the greatest Ghost Warden in Valla's history.

Harper, ever the curious one, asked Roedyn, "So... where exactly in the Court of Dreams did you hide it?"

When Roedyn refused to answer, she narrowed her eyes. "Please tell me you didn't shove it under the queen's bed."

Escala's cheeks flushed crimson.

"Unbelievable." Harper groaned.

I gave Roedyn the raised-brow-and-wink combo, and he blushed.

Sticky stood by, snatching flies from the air with a flick of his tongue, completely oblivious to what we were talking about.

With Harper's interrogation finally over and our packs crammed full, we set out once more for the now-familiar crossing near Dunwell, this time under far brighter circumstances than our last journey there.

Yet nothing, absolutely nothing, could have prepared me for what awaited on the other side. Even as a bard, one who makes a living in words and wonder, I found my tongue faltering. How could I possibly capture the fey realm... or the Court of Dreams itself?

I could call it beautiful, but that wouldn't do it justice. Angelic and celestial aren't the right words, either.

Ah, that's it—resplendent!

It means it was glowing in pure brilliance and splendor. Yup, that is the right word; there is no other way to describe the Court of Dreams.

It had been only weeks since Victor Graves had dragged the Court of Dreams to the brink of ruin, yet somehow, it had endured.

More than endured—it still shone with defiant splendor. Many buildings lay shattered, some reduced to nothing, but in the great garden where the court now gathered, beauty had returned.

Blossoms bloomed wildly, their bright colors standing out against the damaged land. Fey birds, as bright as jewels, circled above, filling the air with songs that brought joy and wonder.

Even the air seemed magical, filled with the scent of renewal. The fragrance was strong enough to recall the ruins' former beauty.

Standing in that garden, I could feel my soul leap for joy, and I finally understood why Escala was so homesick and why she talked so much about the Court of Dreams.

Once we had gathered in the gardens, the Court Recorder's voice rang clear:

"The Court of Dreams is now called to order in the palace gardens, as the Star Gallery is presently unavailable."

We rose to our feet as hundreds of fey streamed into the gardens. Rihanna flitted nearby, while Morvena stood rigid in the center, still bound tightly.

At her feet lay the Vorrash Totem, nothing more than a withered, ashen stick. Once the Crown of Dreams stopped feeding it Void magic, the fey had torn it from the earth. Its sickly glow was gone, leaving only the hollow shell of what had once threatened the court.

The five judges entered the gardens and took their places on hastily assembled thrones, and truth be told, they looked more like park benches than seats of power. One remained conspicuously empty: Lord Winter's.

A moment of silence was held as a solemn tribute to the pixie lord who had died defending the Court of Dreams.

Then Queen Escala Winter appeared above us, hovering on a second-story balcony that overlooked the gardens. She was magnificent in her complete pixie form; her blonde hair draped over one shoulder and spilling down her back. A royal-blue silk gown clung elegantly to her frame, cut to the knee, with silver slippers on her feet and a delicate silver crown on her brow. She looked every inch the queen.

Beside her stood Roedyn. He wore a high-collared black coat with silver buttons, black trousers, and gleaming knee-high boots—formal enough, yet his mortal height still towered over her. Escala gestured for him to join her in the air.

He shook his head.

She gestured again, more firmly. Still, he refused.

She fixed him with a stern gaze. "Roedyn, we talked about this."

With a resigned sigh, he drew the polished silver polymorph ring from his pocket, its gem glinting like captured starlight. He slid it onto his finger, and with a burst of magic, his form collapsed inward, then blossomed outward again, this time into a majestic pixie.

His gossamer wings unfurled and were even larger and more iridescent than Escala's. Yet his face and sharp, knowing eyes were unmistakably his own. I'd peg him at two apples and three grapes tall, give or take, and he was now dressed in the finery of a royal prince: embroidered tunic, jeweled belt, and a cape so fine it seemed woven from moonlight.

Harper burst out laughing, Sticky applauded, and I couldn't help but grin.

Roedyn looped once in the air before hovering beside Escala, arms flung wide like Crurri after sticking a flawless flip. Harper doubled over in fresh hysterics.

Beaming, Escala slipped her arm through his and addressed the crowd. "Fey of the Court of Dreams, I am glad to see you alive after Victor's attack. But today is not a happy occasion. One of our own—our consort, my stepmother—is accused of attempting to murder both me and Rihanna, and of conspiring with Victor Graves to kill her husband, Lord Winter—and perhaps all of you—when she planted this"— she gestured toward the totem lying at her feet—"in the heart of these very gardens."

Escala introduced the witnesses: Junel, Rihanna, other fey, and even the wolf totem, whom Sticky was able to get to speak through a "speak with wood" spell.

I'll spare you every detail, but Junel testified to Morvena planting and activating the totem. We all spoke of Morvena's attacks against Rihanna and Escala at the destroyed Blackthorn Tower.

Morvena said nothing, staring at Escala with hatred.

The judges didn't even deliberate—the verdict was immediate: guilty on all charges.

"Give me the Wane," Morvena spat.

Escala shook her head. "The Wane is too merciful. It is too good for you."

Escala looked out at her court and thought of all she had been through. Then she said, "Morvena shall be banished— just as I once was—to seek and remove boulders."

A collective gasp swept through the fey. Banishing her to Valla? To the material plane? It was unthinkable—reckless, perhaps even dangerous. I was shocked; what was Escala thinking?

But Escala was not finished. "Harper, did you bring the item?"

Harper stepped forward and laid the Crown of Dreams down in front of Morvena.

"If you would," Escala asked.

Harper nodded, and with a flick of her wrist and a single arcane word, the Crown of Dreams began to glow. From its apex, a gateway bloomed, a crossing to the Void. This was how the crown was meant to work, untainted by Victor's manipulations, his obscene obsidian orb, and the grotesque flood of Void magic he'd forced through it. Gone was the roaring, chaotic vortex we had once endured. In its place iridesced a controlled portal, its edges rippling with dark, opalescent light, steady and deliberate, opening like the petals of some alien flower before Morvena.

Morvena's eyes widened, whether in awe, fear, or recognition, I couldn't say.

Escala smiled grimly. "Unlike my sentence to remove boulders from the True Cycle in Valla, you are sentenced to remove boulders in the Void!"

"No!" Morvena hissed. "I want the Wane!"

"Harper," Escala said.

"With pleasure," Harper replied, and she pulled out the golden chamber pot from her pack and held it high for all to see.

Morvena shrieked, "Don't touch the—"

But she never finished as Harper swung the golden chamber pot with both hands, slamming it square into her face. The impact sounded like a hammer hitting a bell, and Morvena was launched backward, tumbling into the swirling emptiness of the Void.

Morvena screamed as she ripped up and into the Void, "I will get—" And then she was gone.

Harper lowered the chamber pot reverently. "That makes five."

"Five?" Sticky asked.

Roedyn, in his pixie voice, said, "Don't ask."

Escala lifted the ceremonial hammer high and brought it down hard against the banister of her bedroom balcony. "It is ordered," she declared. The words echoed, and the fey below erupted into jubilant cheers.

The rest of the day was spent in joy as I danced, feasted, and laughed, joining the fey in one of the most wondrous celebrations I have been a part of.

Roedyn and Escala shone like twin constellations. Roedyn even danced—graceful in his pixie form—and, I must admit, he wasn't bad. They moved together with an ease and joy that left no doubt they were deeply in love.

"Are you staying?" Harper asked.

Roedyn gave a half-smile. "She asked me to map the entire realm—that could take a while."

Escala curled her arm through his and kissed his cheek. "Might take forever."

"We'll be back, though," she promised. "We love you all so much."

When the feasts and dancing were over, Escala and Roedyn escorted us back to the crossing.

And I had my notebook out, already composing everything I've shared tonight.

I cross the stage slowly, setting my lute against the table with care. A long breath escapes me—it was a long tale, but at least I nailed the details. I scan the room, trying to read the faces to see if they are merely entertained or if my story has struck a deeper chord. The light is too dim; I can't quite tell. Well then, on to my concluding remarks.

Dear friends, I promised you a fantastical story of love, betrayal, revenge, and redemption, all caused by a crazy little pixie named Escala.

And what you remember of my tale is important to me.

If all you remember is that chasing boulders is a fool's errand, or that dragons are deadly, or that stepmothers can be mean then I've failed you.

Because this tale was never about boulders, dragons, or stepmothers.

This was a love story.

And not the kind of love they croon about at the Golden Goose. No, the love in this tale is far messier and far more beautiful.

This story teaches us that love can be reckless when it should tread lightly, that it can wound when it ought to heal, and hide when it most needs to speak.

Escala once believed love was nothing more than a thrill—a kiss, a chase, a fleeting spark. But how could she truly know it? Her parents loved her, yet never said the words. In that silence, she went searching... and in searching, she broke everything.

But still it was love that redeemed her.

Love is a choice of sacrifice—the giving of yourself so the other person is protected, cared for, and maybe even made content and happy. Not the giddy kind, but the kind that whispers: *I see you at your worst, and I choose you anyway.* She had seen so many shades of love—between parent and child, friends, lovers, even comrades bound by battle—and each revealed another truth. Love can be fierce, tender, stubborn, or quiet, but it always demands something of you. It asks for patience when anger is easier, forgiveness when bitterness feels justified, and loyalty when walking away seems safer.

And through it all, she came to understand that love is not an accident or a passing spell. It is a choice, remade each day, in every moment, no matter the form or the relationship.

Roedyn showed Escala love through actions.

Harper offered the sharp-tongued kind of love you only get from a loyal friend—the kind she once shared with Rihanna.

Sticky taught her the hardest lesson of all: how to love her enemies, even when they were part of her family.

Crurri offered wisdom and challenged her thinking on love.

The old man helped her understand that love is when you can't *not* help those you care about.

And in the end, Escala finally saw the truth in her parents' love—both for each other and for her. It had always been there, though hidden from her eyes. They had loved each other deeply, yet each had sacrificed their own happiness so she might have a chance at an everyday fey life, because they loved her.

That was when she learned that love is not found in a kiss from an attractive boy. While delightful, that is just a fleeting moment of joy and is nothing at all like what she learned about love on her journey.

And so, friends, as with all my tales, I hope you'll do something with what you've heard.

I hope that you take something that you learned from "Escala's Wish" and weave it into your own life.

Find ways—small or grand—to make the lives of those you love better.

I know Escala talked a great deal, but we could all take a lesson from her: speak often—and I'm not kidding—talk to those you love and talk to them a lot.

Be present in their lives, like Roedyn.

Be playfully sarcastic, like Harper—it makes life funny.

Be creatively helpful in solving their problems, like Sticky.

Be like Crurri and think deeply about life, challenging others to do the same.

Tell their stories, as I've tried to do.

Like Escala, be curious about life and seek deep friendships, such as the one she shared with Rihanna.

Above all, love as sacrificially as Teresa and Rowan.

Until next time, dear listeners—remember: the greatest magic of all is the magic that changes you.

Goodnight, and may your dreams be worthy of song.

I take a deep bow.

The Stag's common room erupts—cheers, whistles, stomps, catcalls. I bow again.

And again.

And yet again.

As the noise ebbs and folks return to their seats, two chairs scrape at the back.

A male voice scoffs, "There's no way a faerie-turned-elf did all that."

I strain to see who spoke, and I see two figures standing at the bar. The firelight flickers across the golden hair of a female elf, and for a moment, I think I catch the glint of sharp blue eyes. Beside her stands a lean half-elf man with black hair tied in a tight bun.

"Come on, Roe," the female elf says. "Let's go hear the bawdy songs at the Golden Goose."

She tips back the last of her dragonfire brandy and sets the mug down with a proud little thud. The room sways, and so does she—until his hand finds her elbow, steady and sure.

"No one touches…" she starts, then stops herself with a soft laugh as she presses closer, letting the words trail off into the comfort of his side. He only smiles, kisses the top of her head, and draws her closer still. She giggles, cheeks warm, and leans into him, her arm slipping around his waist.

Arm in arm, they make for the door, her steps playful and uneven, his steady and protective, the two of them stumbling and laughing together as though the night belongs only to them.

Epilogue

————————

Three months later

Teresa sat on the front steps of her small cottage as the sun dipped behind the hills. She held a cup of tea in both hands, its warmth and aroma soothing her.

She had sat in her gardens every evening since returning from the Court of Dreams nearly twenty years ago.

The stone bench pressed against her legs, smoothed by years of use. Ivy curled thick along the trellises, wild and tangled where she and Rowan once worked side by side. She remembered the first time she saw him striding beneath the rose arches, the way his laughter resounded under lantern-lit trees, the instant her heart tumbled headlong into love. As the sun lowered and the air cooled, petals folding for the night, she felt him everywhere, in the fragrance of the blossoms, in the calm of the garden paths. Old memories pressed close, heavy and sweet, and she wished, just for a moment, that the night might bring a dream where they walked here together again.

She tried to move on, but her mind always wandered back to Rowan. Even when she shoved the memories aside, they slipped into her dreams. No one else had ever loved her like Rowan did.

Then there was Escala. Teresa smiled, unfolding Junel's latest letter with trembling fingers. Smudged ink stained the page, Junel's hand always shook, but the words comforted her heart: stories of Escala darting above the court, chasing adventure with Rihanna, clever remarks that sounded just like Rowan.

Escala had friends and respect, not simply as House Winter's daughter, but as a bold, curious pixie, so much like Rowan at that age. She was the princess Teresa had always hoped for.

Teresa pressed the letter to her chest and smiled. Escala was thriving. She was happy. That was all any mother could wish.

Still, it stung, not seeing Escala, not sharing the small things: late-night worries, quiet victories, laughter that arose for no reason at all. Teresa often pictured herself brushing Escala's hair or watching her dart barefoot after fireflies among the grass.

But Teresa had made her choice. Escala belonged in the court. She had given up everything for that, not for duty, but for love.

Her heart pained by missing, but pride filled every throb. Her daughter had become something wondrous.

She rose and went into the garden, ready for her twilight stroll. Dusk had always been her favorite, the hush, the night sounds, the fading golden light. This time of the day always made her think of Rowan. She would never know love like that again... but she cherished what they'd shared.

Then she heard a voice—a man's—singing by the creek, hidden somewhere behind the thick tangle of bushes. She followed the sound, the melody drawing her closer until the words became clear. She knew them. The moment they reached her ears, a lump rose in her throat. The male voice sang:

Your laughter is the song I chase
Through moonlit woods and endless space.
No dream nor dawn could shine so true—
My heart was made to simply love you.

She stepped off the path and rounded the bushes.

There, by the water's edge, stood an older man with hazel eyes and graying hair.

When he saw her, he smiled and said, "You're my dream."

"Rowan?" she whispered in surprise.

They ran to each other, and he swept her into his arms, spinning her in a joyful whirl as she cupped his face, kissing him through a blur of tears.

"How?" she whispered.

He laughed. "Our daughter has a very powerful friend."

She pulled back. "Rowan, I love you—but I can't go back. The court… it's not my home."

He set her down gently. "It isn't mine either."

"But… you're lord of the court."

"Not anymore, Escala is queen now."

Her eyes went wide. "I still don't understand."

He kissed her forehead and pulled back just enough to wrap her in a fierce bear hug, his hands resting at her waist. "If you haven't already heard," he said, "you will from Junel.

I died when Victor Graves attacked the court. I know Junel writes to you," he said.

Before she could deny it, he added, "I know, I helped her write them. I wanted you to know that your sacrifice gave Escala her chance."

Teresa smiled.

He added, "Junel will also tell you that Escala died, too."

Teresa gasped.

"For fey, death is the end. Our magic returns to the realm so she returned to the fey realm." Rowan explained.

Teresa's eyes brimmed with tears, but Rowan kissed her tears away. "But our daughter," he said, "searched for love as we once did, and in that search, she saved everything."

Teresa looked up at him, confused.

"She was rewarded," he said softly. "With three wishes. The first brought back her best friend. The second... herself."

Teresa asked. "And the third was you?"

Rowan shook his head gently. "No. She used the third wish to bring back someone else. Someone she is hoping to get to know very well."

Teresa looked confused. "Then how are you here?"

Rowan smiled. "All I can say is our daughter is now the queen of the Court of Dreams, and she has a powerful friend. And that friend dreamwove me here as a man."

She stared at him, tears forming. "But you're fey."

"No, I am a man. I am no longer fey. I am just like you." He smiled and squeezed her hand.

Still holding her hand, he went down on one knee. With the other hand, he drew a ring from his pocket, an exquisitely crafted band of intertwined silver and gold, set with a gem that glowed with a soft, swirling blue light, its patterns moving gently within the stone.

"Teresa Whitmore, I love you. I am just a man now, and I can't offer wealth or palaces, but I offer you my heart, my soul, and whatever years I have left. Will you marry me?"

She didn't answer with words; she was already in his arms, hugging him so tightly he could barely breathe.

Twenty yards away, two pairs of small hands held the branches of a hedge steady so they could watch.

Escala was barely able to contain her glee. "She said yes!"

"Shhh… you want to get caught again for messing with the True Cycle?" the male pixie chided.

"Oh, Roedyn," she said, nuzzling close to him. "I asked permission from the Dream Weaver."

He looked down at her, and she glowed. "I told him that since I was a boulder removed from the True Cycle, we needed to put a boulder back in, you know, to balance it out. Plus, the Cycle was missing something."

"What was it missing?" Roedyn asked, surprised.

"It was missing a Winter," she said, giggling.

Rowan groaned.

Escala continued whispering, "I asked the Dream Weaver to unstitch Rowan from the fabric of the fey realm and reweave him into the material plane—a dream-woven creation, something spoken of only in legend, never actually attempted."

She clapped her hands. "But it worked—Volpe finished it this morning! And look." She pointed. "My parents are together again, and now I can visit them... and finally get to know my mother."

Roedyn smiled. "Let them have a proper honeymoon first."

"Oh, a wedding!" Escala squealed. "Ri and I are going to plan the best wedding ever!"

Together they continued to peek through the bushes, watching Rowan and Teresa dance beneath the stars, their laughter mingling with the song.

After a while, they let the branches slip back into place. Escala looked up at him, eyes sparkling with delight. "I moved the last boulder," she whispered. "I've finished my quest."

Then, standing on her toes atop a swaying branch, she wrapped her arms around his neck, batted her eyelashes, and in a silky voice said, "I am Escala Winter of the Court of Dreams."

Roedyn leaned his head down to hers, so their foreheads were touching. Escala playfully rubbed her nose against his and whispered, "I've just changed your life forever. You'll never know another kiss as good as a faerie's."

Nibbling on his ear, she whispered, "You could search all of Valla, but no kiss will ever satisfy you again. You'll always think of me and want to please me whenever I call."

Roedyn pulled her close. "That's my wish," he whispered back.

"That's my wish, too," she purred.

Escala pulled back from his hug just enough to kiss him, softly saying, "I love you, Roedyn Hammerfell."

Roedyn looked up, as if talking to the sky, and said, "Harper, she finally said it."

Escala playfully punched him on the arm. He laughed, and then, hand in hand, they flew back to the crossing.

They had a lot to do. They had two weddings to plan, after all.

—The End—

About the Author

David James (DJ) lives in Northborough, Massachusetts, with his wife, Tonya, who has somehow endured thirty years of his endless parade of ridiculous character voices echoing through the house. Together they've raised three wonderful children, now off conquering the world through college, law school, and Boston courtrooms.

When he's not writing fantasy novels, designing campaigns, or crafting multi-page backstories, DJ records and publishes Christian hip-hop under the stage name "DJ the Not So Ordinary." His music can be found on all major streaming platforms.

DJ is the creator and Dungeon Master of his homebrew fantasy world Valla™ (www.vallaworld.com).

He is already hard at work on his second novel set in Valla, because, apparently, sleep is optional when your imagination won't shut up.

You can learn more about DJ's next project at www.davejames.com.

Acknowledgements

_____

<u>To my parents</u>: Thank you for letting me dive into the world of roleplaying games back when it wasn't cool, accepted, or understood. Your trust gave me a lifetime of imagination, joy, friendships, and stories.

<u>To my wife:</u> Thank you for everything—and for always letting me be me. You've made my life richer, fuller, and better in every way. I'm endlessly grateful that we've walked this road together. I love you!

<u>To my children</u>: I love you all beyond words. My greatest hope is that you embrace all that God has prepared for you. I will never stop loving you, cheering for you, and being your biggest supporter.

This book is shaped by emotions born of my own failures, regrets, and missteps. If, as you read, you recognize pieces of your dad in these characters, I ask for your grace—and your forgiveness.

<u>To my sister</u>: I remember every stick sword, every muddy adventure, and every backyard battle we had with imaginary monsters—thank you for playing along and dreaming big with me.

<u>To the late Gary Gygax</u>: Thank you for creating the greatest roleplaying game the world has ever known. For what it's worth, I am boycotting Hasbro and Wizards of the Coast for the OGL debacle in 2023 and what they have done to your great game.

To Kogarashi Team:

Thank you for your support when I asked to include your characters. Your enthusiasm meant everything. I am also grateful that you gave me creative license to modify your characters to fit my story (sorry, Roedyn, for the role he played), so special thanks to:

- Emmi, for sharing "Sticky"
- Ethan, for sharing "Harper"
- Will, for sharing "Roedyn"
- Jim, for sharing "Volpe"
- John, for sharing "Wigfrith"
- Paul, for sharing "Crurri"
- Victor (our Dungeon Master), for inspiring me to write for all the villains

I also want to thank my other close roleplaying friends—DJ, Cindy, Chris, Daniel, Dominic, Jim, and Nico—for tolerating my crazy characters over the years.

To Oondie Jackals: You are not the "catfish of graveyards." You are beautiful creatures that are cunning, patient, and very agile. Let the Ogland Kobolds start their press; it changes nothing.

To My WorkCentral Friends (Jensen, Tori, Lisa, and Scott): Thank you for cheering me on and all the emotional support on my journey to publish this book.

Note from the Author

_____

Thank you for reading my first novel.

Honestly, I always thought my debut would be a legal thriller, and I do have a half-finished one saved on my hard drive, but this story pushed its way to the front of the line.

I've been rolling dice and roleplaying since 1980, when my parents—bless them for ignoring all those rumors about Dungeons & Dragons being the "devil's game"—gave me the Red Box Basic Rules Set for my tenth birthday. Not just any Red Box, either, but the cooler one with the green dragon on the cover. From that day on, roleplaying became a part of my life. For more than forty years, I've been building worlds, writing character backstories that got way too detailed, and creating stories with friends around a table. Escala Winter came out of that tradition, and she quickly became my favorite character I've ever played.

I first made her during the COVID lockdowns in 2020, for a D&D campaign on Roll20. When that game ended, I wasn't ready to let her go, so I brought her into a Pathfinder 2E campaign that's still running as I write this. At the time of the first printing of this book in December of 2025, every Monday night, I still play Escala in new adventures with my group, and she continues to grow in those games.

But let me be absolutely clear: *Escala's Wish* is not a record of those sessions. This novel is a wholly separate story. None of what you've just read is a campaign recap or a transcript of dice rolls. It was never played at a table. Instead, the hours I spent roleplaying Escala gave me her voice, her spirit, and the foundation of the Court of Dreams. From there, the novel took shape in my imagination, her journey, her heartbreaks, her triumphs, until it became a story of its own that demanded to be told.

Part of the reason Escala feels so alive on these pages is because pieces of her are pieces of me. Her curiosity about love, her naivety, her stubborn hope, those come from the hopeless romantic in me. Writing from that perspective came naturally, maybe too naturally at times. And because I've spent years playing her week after week, slipping into her voice and her mindset, I've come to know her as deeply as I know myself. I guess this is as close to method acting as I'll ever get.

This story is shaped by so many influences that I could never list them all. But I know in my heart that the authors who first made me fall in love with fantasy—J.R.R. Tolkien, Stephen R. Donaldson, Terry Brooks, Terry Goodkind, and Robert Jordan—left their mark on me. Their worlds and characters have stayed with me for years, and I'm certain they've found their way into my own writing, sometimes without me even realizing it. More specifically, for this story, I drew inspiration from those 1980s comedies I grew up on: *Can't Buy Me Love, Pretty in Pink, Better Off Dead*— those messy, awkward, beautiful coming-of-age stories of young love. The movie *Mean Girls* inspired me as well, because every good story thrives on drama, rivalries, and just a touch of cruelty, and that spirit fit perfectly into the cutthroat world of faerie court politics. I also drew from the intrigue, brutality, and layered political storylines of *Game of Thrones*, and I daresay Morvena Winter could give Cersei Lannister a run for her money.

LL Cool J's love song "Two Different Worlds" from his third album *Walking with a Panther* (maybe the panther in the final battle?) sums up the forbidden love between Escala and Roedyn nicely. This song meant a lot to me back in 1989, and deep inside, I think it helped me write their love story arc.

When I first pitched Escala to my dungeon master back in 2020, I asked if I could play a pixie. His answer wasn't just "no," it was more like, *"Come on, pick something normal from the Player's Handbook."* So, I got sneaky. I created a pixie exiled from the fey realm but trapped in an elf's body. Technically, she counted as an elf, which satisfied his rule, but her heart and backstory were pure pixie, and I roleplayed the heck out of it. Ironically, about a year later, both D&D and Pathfinder introduced pixies as playable options. If I'd only waited, I could have played Escala as the pixie I wanted from the start, but then I never would have invented her tortured backstory, the very chapters that became the seeds of this book (chapters 3 and 17 were the original backstory I wrote for Escala).

When the campaign began, I played Escala as an elf, but I insisted to everyone that she was really a pixie trapped in an elf's body. That single idea sparked endless role-playing fun. Both the players, through their characters and the dungeon master, through NPCs, constantly prodded Escala about her outrageous claim, and with every exchange, her backstory deepened. Bit by bit, I built out mischievous faeries, fey courts with all the drama of high-school cliques, tricksters, betrayals, and impossible quests. I even gave Escala a vague, mysterious mission to "remove boulders from the True Cycle" so that the dungeon masters could weave her story into their worlds however they wished. Week after week, as the adventures unfolded and the party pressed her with questions about her past, her banishment, the courts, and the boulders, the world of the Court of Dreams grew clearer.

As the roleplaying unfolded, the world of the fey began to take root in my mind. Escala's parents, their conflicts, her stepmother and stepsister, her best friend, all of them started as fleeting ideas at the table, but over time they grew into living, breathing characters. That's the magic of roleplaying: it plants seeds. Some fade, some blossom, but every now and then, one grows into something far larger than you expect.

For me, that seed became *Escala's Wish*: a story woven from laughter, heartbreak, cruelty, and courage, shaped not only by the game but by the countless stories that inspired me. What began as improvisation around a table has grown into the story you now hold in your hands.

Why is Escala Female?

I could have written the story with the main character as a male fey, but I wanted to explore, from a roleplaying perspective, the female experience of betrayal and rejection, something that, heartbreakingly, happens all too often to women.

When I play a character, I go deep into that role (just ask my tablemates). I knew that by embodying a female protagonist, I could better understand the emotional weight carried by the women in my life. This wasn't just a narrative choice. It was a personal challenge to grow my empathy, to listen better, and to tell a story rooted in emotional truth.

Additionally, as I thought about my role models, I realized that many of my greatest role models have been women, starting with my mother, whose sacrifices gave me opportunities she never had. Her belief in me shaped the man I have become.

My wife Tonya, brilliant and fiercely independent, has supported me through every chapter of life, including late-night roleplaying sessions and the absurd voices echoing from my office. Just trying to keep pace with her has made me a better person.

Professionally, I've been guided by mentors like Julie Tedesco and Mary Zeven, both accomplished and respected attorneys who encouraged me to chase my dream of writing a novel.

And then there's my daughter, Tessa—bold, bright, and already forging her own path. Her energy and determination inspired much of Escala's "never-quit" spirit!

Escala is, in many ways, a tribute to these women: their strength, independence, professionalism, and quiet, relational heroism rooted in sacrifice and love for those around them.

Final Thoughts

There are scenes in this book that bring me to tears, and others that make me laugh out loud. Not because the story is sad or funny in the usual sense, but because those moments echo something raw and deeply personal, choices I've made, regrets I carry, or dreams I'm still chasing.

When I laugh, it's because the sarcasm and quips in this story remind me of the players I've adventured with over the years, their quick wit, sharp banter, and unforgettable one-liners. I've tried to honor that spirit here.

Every laugh is a tribute to those memories, those friendships, and the joy we created together around the table.

When I cry, it's because the characters' struggles feel like my own, their pain echoes something in me, something real and familiar. I feel the release because, in writing those words, I'm not just uncovering the character's truth, I'm uncovering my own.

As an author, I've done my best to open that door and welcome you inside to share Escala's emotional journey in the hope that, somewhere along the way, you feel something too.

Whether you laugh, cry, or just enjoy the ride, I hope Escala's Wish touches you in some small way because creating it has meant the world to me.

—DJ

Tales of Valla ™

Mad as a Hornet

Double-crossed and Mad as a Hornet — Ms. Cassidy Vance wants Crimson Jack Acorn III dead. But to save the world, she'll have to keep him alive. Can she resist pulling the trigger long enough?

Discover the firestorm in *Mad as a Hornet*

Coming December 2026

Trash Panda Publishing
www.trashpandapublishing.com

We publish novels written by raccoons

Explore the World of
Escala's Wish

If you'd like to carry a bit of the adventure with you, visit

<u>**www.trashpandapublishing.com/store**</u>

For exclusive *Escala's Wish* merchandise—featuring
Escala, Sticky, and other beloved characters.

Discover limited-edition items including:			
T-shirts	Sweatshirts	Hats	Coffee Mugs
Car Magnets	Keychains	Slides	Socks

New designs and collectibles are released regularly,
so check back often.

Your support helps bring more Valla stories to life.